RENEWALS 458-
D0712852

Friedrich Dürrenmatt

Friedrich Dürrenmatt

Selected Writings

Volume 2 · Fictions

Translated by Joel Agee

Edited and with an Introduction by Theodore Ziolkowski

THE UNIVERSITY OF CHICAGO PRESS *Chicago & London*

FRIEDRICH DÜRRENMATT was born in 1921 in Konolfingen (near Bern), Switzerland. An essayist and fiction writer, he was also a playwright and received a *New York Times* Drama Critics Award in 1958 for the American premiere of his play *The Visit*. He died in 1990. JOEL AGEE has translated numerous German authors into English, including Rainer Maria Rilke and Elias Canetti. His translations of Heinrich von Kleist's *Penthesilea* and Hans Erich Nossack's *The End: Hamburg 1943* won, respectively, the 1999 Helen and Kurt Wolff Prize and the 2005 Lois Roth Prize of the Modern Language Association. He is also the author of two memoirs, *Twelve Years: An American Boyhood in East Germany* and *In the House of My Fear*. THEODORE ZIOLKOWSKI is the Class of 1900 Professor of Modern Languages emeritus of Princeton University and the author of more than twenty books, the most recent of which are *The Mirror of Justice*, which won the 1997 Christian Gauss Prize of the Phi Beta Kappa Society, and *Ovid and the Moderns*, which won the 2005 Robert Motherwell Book Award.

Complete publication history appears on page 363.

The University of Chicago Press, Chicago 60637
The University of Chicago Press, Ltd., London

Printed in the United States of America

15 14 13 12 11 10 09 08 07 06 1 2 3 4 5

ISBN-13: 978-0-226-17429-7 (cloth)
ISBN-10: 0-226-17429-8 (cloth)

Library of Congress Cataloging-in-Publication Data

Dürrenmatt, Friedrich.
[Selections. English 2006]
Friedrich Dürrenmatt : selected writings / translated by Joel Agee.
v. cm.
Contents: v. 1. Plays / edited and with an introduction by Kenneth J. Northcott—v. 2. Fictions / edited and with an introduction by Theodore Ziolkowski—v. 3. Essays / edited by Kenneth J. Northcott ; with an introduction by Brian Evenson.
ISBN 0-226-17426-3 (v. 1 : cloth : alk. paper)—ISBN 0-226-17429-8 (v. 2 : cloth : alk. paper)—ISBN 0-226-17432-8 (v. 3 : cloth : alk. paper)
1. Dürrenmatt, Friedrich—Translations into English. I. Agee, Joel. II. Northcott, Kenneth J. III. Ziolkowski, Theodore. IV. Evenson, Brian, 1966– V. Title.
PT2607.U493A6 2006
832′.914—dc22

2006013388

♾ The paper used in this publication meets the minimum requirements of the American National Standard for Information Sciences—Permanence of Paper for Printed Library Materials, ANSI Z39.48-1992.

Contents

Introduction

Theodore Ziolkowski

Audiences of the 1960s, following the worldwide successes of *The Visit* (1956) and *The Physicists* (1962), viewed Friedrich Dürrenmatt (1921–1990) primarily as a dramatist—as, along with Max Frisch, one of the brilliant Dioscuri who put Switzerland on the map of the theatrical world. His fictional efforts, the alleged "dead end" of his early stories and even the sensationally popular detective novels of the 1950s, were regarded as chips from the workbench of the playwright, hackwork turned out by the young apprentice seeking to support his family as he established himself as a journeyman in his true métier. The prizes later awarded to the master institutionalized that view.

From our perspective today, surveying the completed life of this major European writer, we place the emphases differently. We see that Dürrenmatt's career from start to finish embraced prose works, both fictional and essayistic, whose quality and significance within his oeuvre have become increasingly apparent. Following a series of theatrical failures that culminated in 1973 with the spectacular flop of the comedy *The Collaborator* (*Der Mitmacher*), Dürrenmatt made an almost complete break with the theater. Disillusioned with the public that now looked to the stage for something other than the tragicomedies of the absurd with which he had captivated the world for more than twenty years, he turned to other modes of expression. During the last two decades of his life, in fact, he wrote only three more plays but published some twenty volumes of prose amounting to roughly three thousand pages.

Unlike the cosmopolitan Max Frisch, who lived much of his life abroad and whose novels and plays recorded that outside world, Dürrenmatt was the archetypical Swiss—engaged in a paradigmatic love-hate relationship with the mountain country that provided the locales for almost all of his plays and fictions. Yet even within his native land Dürrenmatt maintained the sense of alienation and distance familiar to him since his boyhood as the parson's son in a small town in the canton of Bern. Symptomatically, this German-speaking writer spent the last forty years of his life in the linguistic isolation of his house high above French-speaking Neuchâtel, with its view across the lake toward the alpine massif of Eiger, Mönch, and Jungfrau.

It was here in the early 1970s that he undertook the project that occupied the final two decades of his life and that he called simply *Stoffe*, which means something like "materials" or "subject matter" or "themes." The two volumes of *Stoffe* (1981 and 1990) amount to one of the most remarkable autobiographical initiatives in the history of literature. Dürrenmatt acknowledges the common temptation, as mortality makes itself felt, to write an account of one's life even though, through the act of shaping that life, one inevitably falsifies it. If he nonetheless proposes to write about himself, he continues, it will be to recount the story not of his life but of his themes. "For it is in my themes, since I am a writer, that my thought expresses itself, even though of course I do not think exclusively in themes."

The nine parts of *Stoffe* constitute a strange mélange of autobiography and essay, often culminating in a piece of prose fiction exemplifying the "theme" of each section. Dürrenmatt is attempting nothing less than to recapitulate the process of literary creation. "It is not my thoughts that compel my images," he insists; "my images compel my thoughts." The first section, for instance, seeks to present an archaeology of the labyrinth that is so conspicuous in his work—and that provided the subtitle of the first volume of *Stoffe*. It begins with the reminiscences about his childhood in the village of Konolfingen, located on a high plateau of the Emmental valley at the crossing of the roads from Bern to Lucerne and from Burgdorf to Thun, where his father served as the Protestant clergyman. When he accompanied his father on visits to the isolated peasant dwellings high above the village, the learned cleric, who regularly read the Bible in Hebrew, Greek, and Latin, would while away the time by recounting to his eager son the classical myths. Dürrenmatt tells us he was especially drawn to the tale of the labyrinth built by Daedalus for King Minos to contain the Minotaur later slaughtered by Theseus—an image and a set of characters that became associated with a recurrent nightmare the boy suffered whenever he slept in the attic guestroom of the parsonage and imagined himself in the role of the Minotaur threatened by murderers lurking outside. When the family moved to Bern in 1935, Dürrenmatt—feeling because of his rural background and his physical ungainliness a Minotaur-like alienation from the city-folk surrounding him—began to associate the landmark-arcades of that city with sinister labyrinths. "The labyrinth is a metaphor and as such polyvalent like every metaphor."

But it became one of the most pervasive metaphors in Dürrenmatt's literary imagination, supplying the appropriate vehicle for his conviction that the world itself is a labyrinth, a moral mire from which man cannot extricate himself by any ancient principles of justice. While the image received its final and finest treatment in the "ballad" *The Minotaur* (1985), it manifested itself early in the fragmentary story "The Winter War in Tibet," which Dürrenmatt conceived in 1942 during his brief tour of military training and which, never previously published, appears in the first section of *Stoffe* along with autobiographical reminiscences and essayistic ruminations on the labyrinth as an early example of his attempt to deal with this central theme.

According to many accounts, Dürrenmatt was a captivating storyteller, capable of extemporizing almost on demand. We know that several of his major works—for example, the early detective fictions as well as the plot for *Greek Man Seeks Greek Wife*—originated in precisely this kind of spontaneous narration for potential publishers and filmmakers. Yet it is the singularity of this febrile literary art that it revolves around a relatively limited set of images or *Stoffe* that he reworked endlessly and filtered through various genres until he found the most suitable one—at least for the moment. His best-known work, the "tragic comedy" *The Visit*, was first conceived as a prose narrative entitled "The Lunar Eclipse," in which the principal roles were reversed. Rather than a rich and vengeful old lady who descends from the express train that unexpectedly stops in her former hometown and offers the citizens a fortune if they will murder the man who seduced and betrayed her in her youth, the original story introduces a man who, having made his fortune in Canada, returns in his Cadillac to the mountain village and bribes the villagers to kill the husband of the woman who rejected him in his youth. As Dürrenmatt explains, he would never have reworked this "material," which was suggested by experiences on holiday just before he began his university studies, had he not years later wondered why the express train from Neuchâtel to Bern made the unexplained stop at an insignificant little village along the route, and to explain the incident, resurrected the old material of the homecoming vengeance seeker.

Similarly, the "material" of the novella *Traps* was first written as a radio play, subsequently produced for television, and then, years later, recast as a stage play. The detective novel *The Pledge* began as a film scenario; but Dürrenmatt was so unhappy with what he regarded as its trivializing conclusion that he rewrote the story as a novel, giving it this time a more ambiguous ending that reflects the labyrinthine reality of the moral universe. The prose comedy *Greek Man Seeks Greek Wife* even comes equipped with two different endings: a cynically realistic one and second happy one "for lending libraries." From these and many other similar examples—the revisions, the shifts in form, the explanatory afterwords—we begin to understand that for Dürrenmatt his works are in a very literal sense always works in progress. "I don't start out with a thesis but with a story," he observed in the "Twenty-one Notes" appended to *The Physicists*. But he attaches a corollary: "A story has been thought to its conclusion when it has taken the worst possible turn."

The Dürrenmatt who emerges from a literary career embracing some forty-five years and especially from the essayistic autobiographies of *Stoffe*, then, is not a conscious craftsman who sits down to create plays or novels according to a carefully constructed plan. He is more like a chaotic child playing with a kaleidoscope, which exposes at each turn of the lens a vividly new configuration of the same few bits of colored glass. From the very beginning, thanks to *Stoffe*, we recognize the themes or images that recur even in the latest works—labyrinth, Minotaur, tower, menacing dogs. And we recognize the forces—notably the powerful narratives of the Bible and classical mythology—that shape his moral imagination, causing it ceaselessly to experiment with new possibilities.

Dürrenmatt shifted easily from genre to genre, excelling not only in the dramatic forms of radio play, film, and theater but also in forms of prose ranging from anecdote, story, novella, and novel to the essay, philosophical or political treatise, and autobiographical narrative. (He has also published a volume of his poems.) Yet his first career choice was not between such literary modes as fiction and drama but between literature and painting. Dürrenmatt belongs to that not insignificant number of twentieth-century writers—including in German literature alone Hermann Hesse, Oskar Kokoschka, Ernst Barlach, and Günter Grass—in whom literary genius is combined with a significant talent in the visual arts. In Dürrenmatt's case the attraction to art showed up much sooner than any tendency toward writing: the six-year-old was fond of illustrating the apocalyptic scenes he knew from the Bible and from Swiss history, especially the Flood and great battles. And until the end of his life these drawings in ink and gouache, usually featuring apocalyptic or catastrophic themes, played an increasingly important role. From boyhood on Dürrenmatt populated his rooms, apartments, and houses with wall paintings of scurrilous figures; he filled the margins of his dramatic texts with drawings indicating his vision of the scenes and figures; he provided the designs for the covers and dust jackets of his works; and he produced scores of watercolors. Following his turn away from the theater in the late 1970s his works were exhibited with increasing frequency (first in 1976 and later in 1994 in Zürich and Bern) and reproduced in catalogs—including prominently a 1968 drawing of a fat-faced critic gorging himself on a plate full of shrimplike authors.

There is no need to discuss Dürrenmatt's often noted "double gift"; Dürrenmatt himself readily conceded that he drew technically "like a child." But precisely the same cluster of images that recur obsessively in his literary works also constitutes the basis of his art. The earliest extant drawing is a grotesque crucifixion by the eighteen-year-old, which depicts four weird figures dancing around a cross exposed on a barren hilltop against a sky featuring—what else?—a lunar eclipse. And variations on the crucifixion—showing, for instance, rats devouring the body on the cross or a dog skulking away bearing in its teeth a body part—occur over and over for the next forty years, a grotesque image exemplifying that intermingling of the tragic and macabre that characterizes Dürrenmatt's writing. Another recurrent image among the drawings is the Tower of Babel, a symbol of human hubris, which occurs with such frequency in his work that it provided the title of the second collection of *Stoffe.* (In 1949 Dürrenmatt tried unsuccessfully to dramatize the building of the tower but finally burnt his manuscript in despair; some of the material was eventually reworked in the play *An Angel Comes to Babylon.*) Another, which is refined over and over until it reaches its culmination in the illustrations for *The Minotaur,* is the labyrinth. In sum, Dürrenmatt is not so much a dramatist or writer as, rather, an irrepressible creative energy whirling around a core of a few basic images or *Stoffe* and precipitating itself in the course of fifty years in varied forms and modes. Whether it expresses itself in drama, prose, or ink drawing, however, one immediately recognizes the unique stamp of his energy.

Although the young man, when he spent a semester in 1942–43 at the university in Zürich, promptly put a sign on his door announcing the presence of "Friedrich Dürrenmatt, Nihilist Poet," he had not yet actually written a word. Dismayed by the teaching of literature both at Bern and at Zürich, he thought of himself primarily as an aspiring artist with philosophical leanings. (He had turned to painting partly in compensation for his marginal academic performance, and he ultimately failed to take a degree even after ten semesters of enrollment.) It was from a circle of friends, principally those surrounding the expressionist painter Walter Jonas, that he received his literary education and first heard the names of such darlings of the intellectual avant-garde as Franz Kafka, the poet Georg Trakl, and the dramatist Georg Büchner.

Büchner played a key role in Dürrenmatt's baptism as a writer. One of the bleakest moments in literature occurs in Büchner's drama *Woyzeck,* when the old grandmother relates a nihilistic fairy tale in which an orphaned child in a dead world vainly explores the universe in search of companionship and, finding none, sits down and cries. In his *Stoffe* Dürrenmatt tells us that he wrote his first story, "Christmas," on Christmas Eve in 1942 when, following a night of drinking with friends, he happened upon the memorial stone to Büchner, who died in Zürich in 1837. Sitting down in a nearby café with a glass of gin and vermouth, Dürrenmatt wrote down the following story in his notebook:

> It was Christmas. I was walking across the vast plain. The snow was like glass. It was cold. The air was lifeless. No movement, not a sound. The horizon was round. The sky black. The stars dead. The moon carried to its grave yesterday. The sun not risen. I screamed. I could not hear myself. I screamed again. I saw a body lying on the snow. It was the Christ child. Its limbs white and rigid. Its halo a yellow frozen disc. I took the child in my hands. I moved its arms up and down. I opened its lids. It had no eyes. I was hungry. I ate the halo. It tasted like old bread. I bit his head off. Old marzipan. I continued on my way.

This story, Dürrenmatt's earliest literary work (though not published until 1952), is revealing. Clearly imitative of the grandmother's tale in *Woyzeck*, it expresses the sense of alienation of the young man who has not yet found his way or his calling. Like Dürrenmatt's earliest crucifixion scenes, it combines the sacred and the macabre in an effort to shock the reader—not just a complacent Switzerland but also the domineering pastor-father against whom the young student was rebelling and whom he was later to caricature in various figures of clergymen in his plays. However, the sequence of simple declarative statements to which the young writer resorts to depict a universe from which all life and meaning have vanished is more than a stylistic device. Brought up speaking a country dialect from Bernese Oberland, Dürrenmatt still had an insecure command of literary "high German." The simple syntax is not merely an effort to expose meaninglessness through the contrast with stylistic banality. German was for him in fact an acquired language, one that the aspiring author still wrote only with difficulty. From this difficulty, strikingly evident in the early works, we can draw several conclusions. First, the constant evasion into image and into the visual arts amounts to a gesture of frustration with a language regarded as a hurdle. Second, Dürrenmatt's reliance, as a playwright, upon the actors and their gestures, along with his rejection of the modern "director's theater," is a symptom of his continuing distrust of the written language as a mode of expression. Finally, the fact that his works, plays and prose alike, have become perennial favorites of classroom instruction is a token of the stylistic simplicity that Dürrenmatt preserved in his written German long after he had become a master of prose.

Another early prose piece, "The Sausage" (written in that same winter of 1942–43), displays the same qualities: each sentence consists of a declarative statement of usually no more than five or six words. Again the simplicity is invoked in the service of the grotesque. But here a new element has been added that becomes central to Dürrenmatt's work: the question of justice and its perversion. Dürrenmatt's favorite teacher at the University of Bern was a professor of philosophy named Richard Herbertz. Herbertz taught a course in criminal psychology for law students in which he recounted the case of a mass murderer who had killed apprentices and turned them into sausages. (Herbertz had drafted the expert opinion for the court.) Seizing upon that case, grotesque in itself, Dürrenmatt gave it a further twist: the person murdered and sausaged by the accused is his own wife; and in the course of the trial the judge absentmindedly consumes the *corpus delicti.* As he will do so often in his later works, Dürrenmatt calls into question the whole notion and system of justice. "The world becomes an enormous question mark" is the conclusion of the story.

While other pieces were written earlier, Dürrenmatt's first publication was the story "The Old Man," which appeared in the Bern newspaper *Bund* in March 1945 (shortly before Germany's final collapse in World War II). In this political allegory the sentences, like the narrative itself, have grown longer and more secure; the author is feeling more comfortable in his acquired literary language. While familiar images appear—notably the large black dog that provides a menacing presence in many later works—the story goes beyond the simple grotesqueries of the early prose to attempt something more complicated. As a student in neutral Switzerland Dürrenmatt had remained largely apolitical; even a brief teenage flirtation with Nazism signaled youthful rebellion rather than political conviction. Although he was not concerned with politics per se, he was not unaffected by the pervasive fear of German invasion that the Swiss felt during World War II. In his political parable, which probably owes something to Ernst Jünger's *On the Marble Cliffs*, he shows how a generalized political anxiety tends to concentrate itself in the hatred of a single symbolic individual—the Old Man, who as an image resembles no one so much as Hitler in his Berlin bunker. But the Old Man is more than Hitler: he embodies a sense of power that has become so absolute that it no longer thinks in human terms, but in mathematics and logic. It is this inhuman contempt for the individual that enables the young woman, initially disarmed by the sheer power of his presence, to seize her revolver and shoot him, feeling "the hatred human beings sometimes feel toward God."

From 1942 to 1947 Dürrenmatt wrote some ten stories, many of which were collected in 1952, following his first theatrical successes, in a volume entitled *The City*, on which he—a "born villager," as he was fond of calling himself—focused all his suspicions of modern society. As he explained in the afterword to that edition, he was seeking through his prose, and through the study of philosophy, to overcome art's enormous power of attraction by establishing a kind of spiritual distance from his work as a painter. "This prose is not to be understood as an attempt to tell stories but as a necessary attempt to fight something out within myself or, as I can perhaps state it better retrospectively, to conduct a battle that can have a meaning only if it is lost." The central image governing the stories in *The City*, he continues, is Plato's image of the cave, which struck the young student of philosophy as the most appropriate metaphor for a neutral Switzerland that experienced the horrors of the war only as reflected indirectly in the radio and newspaper reports.

The sense of shadowy community that defines the city in "The Old Man" is ominously present in "The Theater Director," also written in 1945. Again Dürrenmatt is concerned with the conflict between freedom and repression, but in the expressionistically surreal city of this story we witness the triumph of evil in the person of the director, who first mesmerizes the citizens by his virtuoso exploitation of theatrical devices and finally enslaves them politically by stirring up in his theater a revolution that spills over into the streets of the city. Again it is a young woman who alone resists the director's blandishments; but rather than triumphing, she finally perishes in a terrifying stage spectacle featuring a killing machine straight out of Kafka's "In the Penal Colony."

The early stories collected in *The City*, played out against the labyrinthine background of what has been aptly designated a "mythicized Bern," display already the themes and images that persist through his works for the next forty years. The corruption of a community by power and violence, for instance, becomes the central theme of *The Visit*. But, stylistically unsure and dependent as they are upon such models as Büchner, Kafka, and Ernst Jünger, they are fledgling works of a talent still seeking its appropriate form. Following the outpouring of prose from 1942 to 1947, Dürrenmatt produced almost feverishly a series of plays, including *Romulus the Great* and *The Marriage of Mr. Mississippi*. When he returned to prose fiction again in the early 1950s, the two works that he wrote, though first published in *The City*, demonstrated a new mastery of tone and form. "The Dog" (1951) revolves around the familiar image of the terrifying black dog that appeared repeatedly in Dürrenmatt's works (and drawings) ever since as a boy in Bern he was attacked by such a beast. The story takes place in the same mythical city, with its underlying mood of anxiety, as "The Theater Director"; indeed, the narrator alludes in passing to the events going on in the theater. Here, however, it is not the sinister director who represents the triumph of evil, but the huge mastiff that accompanies the itinerant preacher and holds at bay anyone who seeks to approach his voice of truth. Finally, when the narrator—the same alienated figure we know from Dürrenmatt's other works—succeeds in making contact, the dog tears his master to pieces and terrifies the city. At the end of the story the beast has attached itself to the minister's beautiful daughter, who has deserted the narrator after several months of love. Through his powerful parable Dürrenmatt seems to suggest that the force of evil destroys not just the truth but also beauty and innocence.

"The Tunnel" (1952) is the unquestionable masterpiece included in *The City* and has been justifiably often anthologized. In its central figure Dürrenmatt provides us with an accurate and amusing self-portrait—a fat, bespectacled twenty-four-year-old student smoking Ormond 10 cigars and commuting back to the university in Zürich by the Sunday evening train after a weekend at home in Bern. But here the youthful *Weltschmerz* and lugubrious nihilism still evident in "The Dog" have given way to a fully developed sense of the absurd, narrated with the utmost restraint, that characterizes Dürrenmatt's most mature works. It is no accident that, unlike the first-person narrator who relates most of the other early stories, this one is written from the standpoint of an ironic third person. The story is quite simple. On a routine run the intercity express train enters, blatantly contrary to schedule, a tunnel that seemingly never ends. At the conclusion of the story, the young man and the conductor have made their way to the front of the train and see that they are hurtling downward into the abyss. "What shall we do?" asks the conductor. And the student, with a ghostly serenity, responds: "Nothing." In its first published version the student's reply continued: "God caused us to fall and so we are hurtling toward him"—a conclusion that invited theological interpretations by Christian readers. But Dürrenmatt, when asked about the influence of his father's orthodox Christianity upon his own thought, was fond of answering: "I am a Protestant. So I protest." In the 1978 revision of the story he revised the last paragraph and, in particular, cut the last sentence so that the story now ends with the word "nothing."

Is this ending a suggestion of serious nihilism or simply a gesture by "Friedrich Dürrenmatt, Nihilist Poet" to preclude any easy Christian reading of his work? Does it suggest a passive acceptance of destiny, whether Christian or not? Certainly it is possible to read the work in a nontheological fashion. Indeed, until the last paragraph there was nothing in the first version to suggest the Christian conclusion. Then, as now, it was easier to view the action as an intrusion of the fantastic into the placidity of a Swiss society that irritated Dürrenmatt. The solid citizens, who sit unperturbed as their train plunges into the abyss, may also be seen as an image of neutral Switzerland going about its business while wartime Europe was being consumed by Hitler's conflagrations. Or, finally, the train that leaves the clear sky of an Alpine evening to enter the darkness of the never-ending tunnel may be post-Enlightenment Europe forsaking the rationalities of the eighteenth century for the postmodern uncertainties of the late twentieth century, industrial technology giving way to cyberspace. The multiplicity of plausible interpretations indicates that Dürrenmatt has succeeded with this story—which he has also rendered visually in his drawings—in creating an unforgettable image of our time and thereby entering the period of his own maturity as an artist.

Even before writing "The Dog" and "The Tunnel," Dürrenmatt had enjoyed with his prose a success that matched that of his plays. In 1950, under the pressure of extreme financial need, the now well-known but still impecunious young writer approached several publishers with a proposal for a detective story and, in fact, came home with an advance of five hundred francs that his wife felt sure he must have stolen. The initial result was the novel *The Judge and His Hangman*, which was first serialized in 1950–51 in the newspaper *Der Schweizerische Beobachter* and subsequently exceeded a million copies in book form. This novel introduced the figure of Inspector Barlach, a sick and aging detective with a primitive sense of justice and little patience with the modern methods favored by his junior colleagues. This Swiss Maigret senses quickly that the murder of a detective with which the action begins was carried out by a jealous fellow officer. But rather than convicting him, the cunning old man manipulates the younger detective, Tschanz, to kill an old nemesis, a figure of evil clever enough to have avoided for many years Barlach's efforts to bring him to justice. At the end Barlach, rather than employing his power of judgment a second time, lets Tschanz go free, no doubt knowing full well that the young executioner will carry out his own sentence by hurling himself beneath the wheels of a train.

Barlach was such a popular success, and the royalties so gratifying, that Dürrenmatt immediately undertook a sequel, *Suspicion*, which again ran in *Der Schweizerische Beobachter* in 1951–52. Here too Barlach is seeking to bring to justice a figure of evil—this time a suspected Nazi war criminal who has found refuge as head physician in a Zürich private clinic. Using his illness as a disguise—at the end of the first novel he had only a year left to live—Barlach has himself admitted to the clinic, where he succeeds in exposing the concentration camp torturer and, by implausible means, narrowly escapes the clutches of the sadistic doctor who proposes to operate on him without anesthesia. Again Barlach manages to exact vengeance from a master criminal who has escaped the sword of official justice.

Despite—or more likely precisely because of—their enormous popularity, critics have long been perplexed by Dürrenmatt's detective stories. Are they simply entertainments (*Trivialliteratur*) or do they have the weight of "philosophical thrillers"? Dürrenmatt provided his own response to this question in a talk on "Theater Problems" (1954). Hostile since his student days to both the academic and the critical establishment, Dürrenmatt often railed against an age that has trained the public to regard art as something sacral, sacred, and filled with pathos—and to look down on anything comic as trivial, dubious, inept. "How does the artist survive in an educated world, the world of the literate?" he asks at the end of his talk. "Perhaps by writing mystery novels, by making art where no one expects it. Literature must become so light that it will weigh nothing on the scale of today's literary criticism: that is the only way it will regain its true weight." This is precisely what he sought to achieve with his next detective novel, *The Pledge* (1958). It is not simply another sequel to the Barlach stories. Barlach is by now presumably dead from his cancer. Moreover, this novel is specifically designated in the subtitle as a "requiem to the detective novel" because it goes beyond the expectation prevailing in the traditional detective story by such masters as George Simenon, Dashiell Hammett, and Agatha Christie—the notion, namely, that justice will ultimately prevail and that the detective, by the sheer force of intellect and moral commitment, will inevitably catch the criminal. Dürrenmatt's "requiem" shows, in contrast, how the very reasonable calculations of an experienced detective can be upset by sheer bad luck.

In 1957 Dürrenmatt wrote the scenario for a film entitled *It Happened in Broad Daylight*, which was intended as a warning for parents about the dangers of sex crimes against minors. In the film, the monomaniacally persistent detective, who makes a promise to the murdered child's parents, sets a trap and ultimately captures the murderer. But Dürrenmatt was uneasy with this neat conclusion. Accordingly he rewrote the story with a different ending: the murderer is never caught and brought to justice but is killed in an automobile accident; Matthäi, the brilliant detective who has given up his career and tried for years to entrap him, thinks he has failed and drinks himself into oblivion. To intensify the irony Dürrenmatt encloses the story in a first-person framework in which he reports on a trip to the town of Chur, where he gave a talk on the art of writing detective stories. (He includes on the first page a dig at his onetime Zürich professor, the literary scholar Emil Staiger: Dürrenmatt tells us that his own talk was only sparsely attended because Staiger had drawn the crowd to hear his lecture on the elderly Goethe.) At the hotel bar he meets Dr. H., the former chief of police of the canton of Zürich, who invites him to drive back with him the next day. On the way Dr. H. tells Dürrenmatt that he has never thought highly of detective stories. He can understand why, given the present state of the world, people long for fairy tales in which crime is punished and justice prevails. But what he cannot tolerate is the fraudulent implication that reality can be apprehended by reason alone. In fact, he argues, results in life depend to a great extent upon sheer chance. Following a stop at a roadside bar and filling station where they see the bedraggled Matthäi, the chief of police tells his story to illustrate the point.

The theme of justice perverted obsessed Dürrenmatt from his earliest stories—for example, "The Sausage"—to his late novel *The Execution of Justice* (1985), in which a young attorney works to prove the innocence of a Zürich councilman, who years earlier had murdered a university professor before a crowd of witnesses. Having succeeded, however, he realizes that he has blundered into a dilemma in which justice can be restored only through another crime. This theme, which Dürrenmatt called "the most fixed of *idées fixes*"—namely, the belief in a justice in whose name people slaughter one another—was at no time more pervasive than in the mid-1950s, when Dürrenmatt wrote *The Visit*, *The Pledge*, the first draft of *The Execution of Justice*—and *Traps*. The saying is attributed to Dürrenmatt's countryman, C. G. Jung: "Show me a sane man, and I will cure him for you." Dürrenmatt appears to be saying: "Show me a man who claims to be innocent, and I will demonstrate his guilt." Nowhere do we see more clearly than in *Traps* Dürrenmatt's resemblance—not indebtedness!—to Kafka. For here, as in *The Trial*, we witness the "trial" of an ordinary businessman who, at the beginning, considers himself completely "innocent," only to be persuaded in the course of a "trial" by a wholly irregular agency that he is indeed guilty.

Here again Dürrenmatt was troubled by the ironies of justice, for he wrote virtually simultaneously in 1955 two versions of the same story. In the original radio play the salesman Alfredo Traps, who enters into the postprandial trial game of the four retired court officials who take him in for the night when his car breaks down, is found guilty, at least indirectly, of the murder of his boss. But on the following morning Traps climbs into his car and drives happily away, at peace with his own conscience. In the prose version, in contrast, Traps is so profoundly moved by the events of the evening that he goes upstairs and hangs himself—to the dismay of his elderly dinner companions, who exclaim that he has ruined their lovely game by taking it seriously. Again the author has prefixed his tale with an interpretation in which he points out, like the chief of police in *The Pledge*, that we live in a world in which we are no longer threatened by God, by Justice, by Fate. Instead, it is only accident or chance that produces "a still possible story" (the subtitle of this work)—chance that inserts Traps, this representative of a modern, conscienceless, technological world, into the company of these four old men with their almost primitive sense of justice and their telling names. (The name of the prosecutor, Zorn, means "wrath" in German, and the defense attorney's name, Kummer, means "worry" or "concern." Traps's own name, according to Dürrenmatt, designates in Swiss dialect someone who has blundered into an unfortunate situation.) In *either* version we recognize in Traps a moral breakdown of society exemplified by the mechanical breakdown of his Studebaker. (The title in German is *Die Panne*—"The Breakdown.") But through the ambiguity of possible endings Dürrenmatt leaves it unclear whether the power of ancient Justice can actually still make itself felt in our world or whether it has been reduced to no more than a lovely entertainment for a party of bachelors. He once remarked that he loves to tell stories without feeling constrained to solve the problems of the world.

Critics have often been perplexed by Dürrenmatt's sudden shifts—from stage to prose and back, from comedy to tragedy and vice versa, from writing to drawing. During the very years when he was composing the grim tragicomedy *The Visit* and the judicial fables of *Traps* and *The Pledge* he also produced—again under pressure for money, this time to finance a major operation for his wife—the delightful "prose comedy" *Greek Man Seeks Greek Wife* (1955). Dürrenmatt has identified the German *Kunstmärchen* (fairy tales) of the romantic poet Clemens Brentano as the literary model for this work, but *Candide* offers a closer analogy for its social satire, which exposes the corruption of almost every major institution—government, church, business—in the vaguely Franco-German-Swiss metropolis in which the action takes place. Like Voltaire's hero, Arnolph Archilochos is introduced to us as a mild-mannered innocent sustained in his lowly position as bookkeeper in a labyrinthine factory by his absolute belief in the moral and rational order of his world—a belief whose naïveté is emphasized by the hero's name, which when pronounced as in German sounds remarkably close to the vulgarism *Arschloch* ("asshole"). He emerges from his improbable adventures, however, bloodied by experience and clear-eyed about the nature of reality. (Note that he has lost his glasses.) Even the alternate ending "for the lending libraries," which brings the lovers together again, does nothing to mitigate the sobering view of bourgeois civilization advanced by Dürrenmatt. Regarded with a certain reserve by German critics, who (as Dürrenmatt frequently reminds us) are not accustomed to dealing with the seriousness of comedy, this novel has gradually come to be appreciated by many readers as one of his most perfect prose works.

During the 1960s Dürrenmatt was occupied principally with the theater. Following several notable successes—*The Physicists* (1962) and *The Meteor* (1966)—he engaged himself actively in the adaptation and production of works by Shakespeare, Goethe, Büchner, and Strindberg. But the failures of his own works toward the end of the decade plus conflict with the theater direction in Basel and Zürich precipitated his turn away from the theater and a return to prose. Dürrenmatt had made two trips to the Soviet Union: in 1964 to commemorate the Ukrainian national poet Shevchenko and again in 1967 to attend the Fourth Soviet Writers' Congress in Moscow. Sitting with two thousand Soviet writers in the vast hall, Dürrenmatt studied the "power collective" of the Kremlin, who had appeared for the occasion. Riding back to the hotel afterward, he listened to an excited conversation among the writers concerning the seating order of the politburo members and its implications for the future of an organization in which power stems not from conviction but from one's relative position in a numerical hierarchy. By the time they reached the hotel, Dürrenmatt reports, the plot for his political parable "The Coup" ("Der Sturz," 1971), was already clear in his mind. Dürrenmatt had long been interested, as he said in a piece on "Kafka and the News" for the *New York Times* (July 11, 1971), in "the power struggles [that take place] in a secretive body, in a politburo." Using a closed form reminiscent of the film classic *Twelve Angry Men* and generalizing the fifteen characters to such an extent that they are identified only by initials and by the seating arrangement at the conference table, Dürrenmatt has created an utterly plausible model of group dynamics that, while fascinating in itself, is easily transferable from totalitarian politics to other situations. Dürrenmatt suggested that the action could just as well take place among Mafia dons or Pentagon officials; but the possibilities are endless, ranging from governing boards of corporations to university faculty committees. The outcome of the power struggles, which here again is brought about by chance, is illustrated visually by the altered positions in the table positions diagrammed at the beginning and end of the narrative.

Other stories of the 1970s were also stimulated by Dürrenmatt's travels. His thoughts on the perennial conflict between Judaism and Islam, catalyzed by a lecture tour of Israel in 1974, produced "Abu Chanifa and Ana ben David" (1975), a fable that begins in the year 760 when a rabbi and a Koran scholar are imprisoned together for theological offenses in a labyrinthine subterranean cell somewhere in the Middle East. In the course of the years they begin a conversation that extends for centuries. The rabbi is eventually released from prison, only to become a kind of Wandering Jew who survives the Holocaust and then makes his way back to the Middle Eastern prison, where he celebrates a moment of recognition and reconciliation with his Muslim counterpart. Another story from these years is "Smithy" (1976), which was conceived as early as 1959 during Dürrenmatt's sojourn in New York City. In this gangster tale, Smithy works with a surgeon whose business it is to dispose of the corpses of the victims of gangland slayings. He enjoys his moment of heroic rebellion when he refuses to accept money for doing away with a mobster's wife—a woman with whom Smithy himself had been briefly infatuated. But his contemptuous rejection of the gangland boss leads inevitably to his own death.

"Smithy" belonged to the complex of materials and troubled ruminations that Dürrenmatt published following the failure of his play *The Collaborator*. His meditations on the theater also generated what he considered "one of the stories most important to me," "The Dying of the Pythia." It is the premise of the tale that the familiar legend of Oedipus is triggered when the Delphic priestess, in a foul mood because it is already time to close up the temple for the day, concocts an outlandish prophecy for the blasé prince from Corinth who comes limping up to the sanctuary: she tells him, improbably, that he will kill his father and sleep with his mother. In the remaining pages Dürrenmatt not only shows us, in a grotesquely original way, how the casually uttered prophecy gets fulfilled; he also provides a cynical interpretation of Greek credulity and readiness to believe the nonsense of its oracles. The modernizing re-vision of the myth is pure madcap: we know that from childhood on Dürrenmatt enjoyed his father's tellings of the Greek myths and that one of his favorite books was Gustav Schwab's popular collection of *The Loveliest Tales of Classical Antiquity*. Later he consulted such sources as Robert Graves's *The Greek Myths* and Herbert Hunger's standard German lexicon of classical myths. But the conversation between the priestess Pannychis and the seer Tiresias—the tale consists largely of their dialogue—shows why this story is so important to Dürrenmatt: it amounts, as he confided in an interview (1980), to an intellectual dispute with Bertolt Brecht on the nature of drama. "I am not a disciple of Brecht's," Dürrenmatt insists. "His mistakes were never mine: I err in my own way." When the priestess and the seer are discussing the case of Oedipus, their wholly different approaches to reality become apparent. Both hope, like the two dramatists, to bring through their oracles a tentative semblance of order, a gentle hint of conformity, into the clouded and bloody tide of human events. But whereas the prophetess has always "oracled" in a spirit of fantasy with a degree of whim and disrespectful boldness and even blasphemous wit, the seer has operated with cool reflection, uncompromising logic, and reason. Looking back over their careers, Tiresias acknowledges that the Pythia's oracles, though statistically improbable, were inevitably accurate; his own, for all their rationality, usually disintegrated into nothing. Their dispute, he realizes, is perennial. Just as some people will always claim that the world operates according to certain laws, others will always say that the laws exist only in human imagination according to ideological convictions. So the witty retelling of the most famous Greek myth constitutes at the same time a profound meditation on destiny and chance, on pessimism and utopianism, on logic and imagination. (*Stoffe* contains another example of the same genre: a cynical re-vision of "The Death of Socrates.")

In addition to the re-visions and unfinished stories published as part of the project *Stoffe*, Dürrenmatt published four major prose works in the last decade of his life. The novel *The Execution of Justice* (1985) belongs in conception and first draft to the fables of justice that Dürrenmatt wrote in the 1950s. The late novel *Valley of Confusion* (1989) is a medley of not wholly integrated plots related to the gangster materials of "Smithy." But two works from these years can stand on their own along with Dürrenmatt's finest and most representative prose fiction.

We have already noted Dürrenmatt's childhood obsession with the myth of the Minotaur. Later, as a young man from the country, he regarded the city of Bern as labyrinthine: "By imagining a labyrinth, I was unconsciously identifying myself with the Minotaur, the inhabitant of the labyrinth, I was making the primal protest, I was protesting against my birth; for the world into which I had been born was my labyrinth, the expression of a puzzling mythic world that I did not understand." The labyrinth provided the setting for such early works as *The City*, and the image haunted his drawings. A watercolor from 1958, for instance, shows Theseus squatting atop the wall of the labyrinth and gleefully urinating on the Minotaur below—a none too subtle indication of Dürrenmatt's own feelings of alienation. In his *Stoffe*, finally, he published a so-called dramaturgy of the labyrinth, which developed a theory to explain his understanding of the image and its occurrence in his writing and drawing. "By representing as a labyrinth the world into which I see myself abandoned, I am seeking to gain distance from it, to step back from it, to look it in the eye like an animal-tamer vis-à-vis the wild animal."

In the "dramaturgy" Dürrenmatt's interest has clearly shifted from the labyrinth to the figure of the Minotaur itself. In handbooks of classical mythology the Minotaur always appears as a minor character in someone else's story—his mother Pasiphaë, his half-sister Ariadne, his murderer Theseus. But Dürrenmatt's interest focuses on the Minotaur himself. Given his anatomy, for instance, the birth must have been unusually difficult. Since he has the head of a steer, he is no intellectual, but lives in his instincts. Moreover, since as half-steer he is presumably a vegetarian, why does he kill the Athenian youths and maidens sacrificed to him in his labyrinth? Above all, since he has been punished by being put into the labyrinth for no fault of his own, he symbolizes—and here we arrive at Dürrenmatt's theme of themes—"innocent guilt" or "guilty innocence."

The culmination of Dürrenmatt's lifelong preoccupation with these matters is evident in his "ballad" *The Minotaur* (1985), a handsomely printed prose poem accompanied by ink drawings from the author's hand. The immediate instigation came from a young Greek composer who, having seen in an exhibition several of Dürrenmatt's drawings of the Minotaur and his labyrinth, approached the author to write a scenario for a ballet on the subject. The ballet was never composed, but Dürrenmatt was inspired by the conversation to write his "ballad," which is anything but simply another cynical re-vision of a classical myth: it amounts to a poignantly serious, almost painfully revealing portrait of the alienated individual seeking companionship in a hostile world. The scene differs from the labyrinth that Dürrenmatt so often painted: here the Minotaur is enclosed in a hall of mirrors in which he sees reflected nothing but himself and where he dances with a joyous abandon until his solipsistic innocence is shattered by intruders: first the girl whom he unwittingly destroys through his lovemaking and then the youth who, matador-like, taunts him with sword and cape. Perplexed and enraged by these incidents, the Minotaur kills the youths and maidens who approach him. But out of this confusion arises consciousness, the awareness that an Other exists in his world beside himself. When that Other again appears looking like his counterpart, the Minotaur greets him joyously, only to be killed by the Other, who turns out to be Theseus in disguise. The ballad is Dürrenmatt's perhaps most sobering comment on the inevitability of conflict and guilt stemming from the human encounter of the Self with the Other.

In 1983 Dürrenmatt's first wife, the actress Lotti Geissler, died. Shattered by the loss of his companion of almost forty years, Dürrenmatt plunged into his work—principally preparations for the premiere of his late play *Achterloo*. The reception of the play was problematic, and Dürrenmatt spent the next five years working on various revisions of the monstrous work that he finally acknowledged to be "unperformable." At the Munich opening, however, he met the actress and documentary filmmaker Charlotte Kerr, whom he married the following year. (Her 1984 documentary on Dürrenmatt, *Portrait of a Planet*, provides one of the most illuminating insights into her husband's life and work.) In November of 1985 the couple made a vacation trip to Egypt, where Charlotte Kerr was contemplating another documentary film. Although the film was not made, the trip produced a literary result: Dürrenmatt's political thriller *The Assignment; or, On the Observing of the Observer of the Observers* (1986). The story, which bears on its title page the designation "Novella in Twenty-four Sentences," constitutes a formal experiment that attains an extreme diametrically opposed to Dürrenmatt's first prose work, "Christmas." That grim story consisted of twenty-eight extremely short sentences. Here the narrative comprises twenty-four chapters, each of which consists in turn of a single sentence—some as long as ten or twelve pages in the German original. The central figures in the story, indicated as in "The Coup" only by initials, clearly represent Kerr and Dürrenmatt: the television journalist F., who entertains the "vague idea of creating a total portrait, namely a portrait of our planet," and her friend and adviser the logician D., who like Dürrenmatt lives in a house in the mountains featuring a telescope through which he observes the people who scrutinize his house with their binoculars.

The thriller plot bears a family resemblance to Dürrenmatt's earlier fables of justice. The wife of a psychiatrist has been raped and killed near a desert ruin in North Africa, and her husband hires F. to reconstruct the unsolved crime in a documentary film. But the plot is rapidly expanded to embrace the world of international politics and espionage with its arms dealers, desert testing grounds, and spy satellites. The story is dedicated to Charlotte, but it is much more than an unusual holiday memento. It amounts to a brilliant fictionalization of concerns that Dürrenmatt frequently addressed in his essays and autobiographical writings: the dangers of a technological society that threatens to turn the entire world into a labyrinth in which we are constantly scrutinized like the Minotaur—the menace of a political society in which arms manufacturers and purchasers through their wealth can transform the entire world into a slaughterhouse with the same ease with which Claire Zachanassian corrupts her village in *The Visit*. The threats are the same, but the stakes have become higher, as is suggested by the motto from Kierkegaard. As a student Dürrenmatt had contemplated a dissertation on "Kierkegaard and the Tragic." Although that project was never undertaken, Dürrenmatt later stated that "As a writer I cannot be understood without

Kierkegaard." He was referring in particular to Kierkegaard's conviction that man is condemned to guilt and tragedy by his very existence and that the harmony of the world can be reestablished only through his death—a view ultimately underlying Dürrenmatt's works from *The Visit* and *Traps* to *The Minotaur* and *The Assignment*.

Despite the urgency of his concern, Dürrenmatt has here shaped his political views with the same care with which he rendered his existential state in *The Minotaur.* "A scream is not a poem," he once remarked. "Every work of art needs distance from its context." The intense aesthetic effort required to control the enormous sentences of his narrative also serves to distance and control the immensity of his apocalyptic political vision, which appears even more timely twenty years after its writing. These two late prose works, *The Minotaur* and *The Assignment*, display yet again the consistency of Dürrenmatt's "themes" and "materials" over a period of almost fifty years. But they also demonstrate the mastery of language and form attained through constant experimentation in fiction and drama in the course of one of the most remarkable careers in postwar European literature.

The Sausage

A man killed his wife and turned her into sausages. The deed gave rise to rumors. The man was arrested. One remaining sausage was found. There was great public outrage. The supreme judge of the land took over the case.

The courtroom is bright. Sunlight pours through the windows. The walls are bright mirrors. The people are a seething mass. They fill the courtroom. They sit on the window sills. They hang from the chandeliers. On the right burns the prosecutor's bald head. It is red. The defense attorney is on the left. His glasses are blind discs. The accused sits in the middle between two policemen. His hands are large. His fingers have blue edges. The supreme judge sits enthroned above everyone. His robe is black. His beard is a white flag. His eyes, grave. His forehead, clarity. His eyebrows, wrath. His face, humanity. Before him the sausage. It lies on a plate. Enthroned above the supreme judge sits Justice. Her eyes are bandaged. In her right hand she holds a sword. In her left, scales. She is made of stone. The supreme judge raises a hand. The people fall silent. Their movement freezes. The court room rests. Time lurks. The prosecutor stands up. His stomach is a globe. His lips are a guillotine. His tongue is a falling blade. The words hammer the courtroom. The accused flinches. The judge listens. Between his eyebrows stands a steep furrow. His eyes are like suns. Their rays strike the accused. He sinks into himself. His knees quake. His hands pray. His tongue hangs. His ears protrude. The sausage in front of the supreme judge is red. It is still. It swells. Its ends are round. The string at the tip is yellow. It rests. The supreme judge gazes down at the lowest human being. He is a small man. His skin is like leather. His mouth is a beak. His lips, dried blood. His eyes, pin heads. His forehead, flat. His fingers, thick. The sausage has a pleasant smell. It moves closer. The skin is rough. The sausage is soft. It is hard. The nail leaves a mark in the shape of a half moon. The sausage is warm. Its shape is plump. The prosecutor is silent.

The accused raises his head. His gaze is a martyred child. The supreme judge raises a hand. The defense attorney leaps to his feet. His glasses dance. Words leap into the courtroom. The sausage steams. The steam is warm. A little knife snaps open. The sausage squirts. The defense attorney falls silent. The supreme judge sees the accused. He is far below. He is a flea. The supreme judge shakes his head. His gaze is contempt. The supreme judge starts talking. His words are swords of justice. They fall like mountains on top of the accused. His sentences are ropes. They scourge. They choke. They kill. The meat is tender. It is sweet. It melts like butter. The skin is a little tougher. The walls resound. The ceiling clenches its fists. The windows grind. The doors shake in their hinges. The walls stamp their feet. The city grows pale. The forests wilt. The waters evaporate. The earth quakes. The sun dies. The sky collapses. The accused is damned. Death opens his mouth. The little knife lies down on the table. The fingers are sticky. They stroke the black robe. The supreme judge is silent. The courtroom is dead. The air is heavy. The lungs are full of lead. The people are trembling. The accused sticks to his chair. He is condemned. He may make a last request. He cowers. The request creeps from his brain. It is small. It grows. It becomes a giant. It forms into a compact mass. It takes shape. It forces the lips apart. It plunges into the courtroom. It sounds. The pervert wants to eat the remains of his poor wife: the sausage. Revulsion cries out. The supreme judge raises his hand. The people fall silent. The supreme judge is like God. His voice is the last trumpet. He grants the request. The condemned man may eat the sausage. The supreme judge looks at the plate. The sausage is gone. He falls silent. The silence is hollow. The people stare at the supreme judge. The eyes of the condemned man are large. There is a question in them. The question is terrible. It streams into the courtroom. It descends to the floor. Clings to the walls. Squats on the ceiling above. Takes possession of every person. The courtroom widens. The world becomes an enormous question mark.

The Old Man

The swarms of tanks came rolling across the hills with such might that all resistance became futile. Still the men fought, perhaps believing in a miracle. Split up into separate groups, they dug themselves in. Some surrendered, the majority were killed, and only a few escaped into the woods. Then the fighting stopped as abruptly as storms sometimes cease. Those who were still alive threw their weapons away and ran toward the enemy with their hands raised over their heads. The people were paralyzed by horror. The foreign soldiers spread across the land like locusts. They moved into the old cities. They walked with heavy steps through the streets and drove the people into their houses when evening came. Heavy armored cars rolled through the villages, often right through the huts, which collapsed on top of them, for resistance had not yet died out in the villages. It was a resistance that smoldered secretly, in the corners of the boys' eyes, in the careful movements of the old men, in the strides of the women. It was a resistance that polluted the air, causing the strangers to breathe as one does in countries where a plague has broken out. Men emerged from the woods, some alone, some in groups, and vanished again in the impassable forests where no stranger dared to follow them. As yet there were no collisions with the enemy, but people who had collaborated with him were found dead. Then came the uprising. Using old guns, the youths and aged men threw themselves upon the enemy, who struck back as if released from a nightmare; women were seen fighting with pitchforks and sickles. The struggle lasted a night and a day, then the uprising broke down. The villages were surrounded, the inhabitants driven together and mowed down with machine guns. The burning forests lit up the nights for weeks.

Then it got quiet, the way it gets quiet in the grave when earth covers the coffin. The people walked about as if nothing had happened. They buried their dead. The peasant returned to his plow, the artisan to his workshop. But deep inside them something they had never known before had grown powerful: it was hatred. It took complete possession of them, filled them with burning strength and controlled their life. It was not a wild impatient hate that has to act precipitously in order to stay alive, it was a hate that could wait, for years, that rested calmly within them, not on the surface, but deep down, at one with their being, a hate that, not needing to find a way out, dug into the soul like a sword, not to kill it but to harden it with its fire. But as the light of those stars that move through enormous distances finds its way to us, that hatred found its way to a figure who was completely in the background, somewhere in those realms where no light can penetrate, invisible like many figures of the abyss, about whom they knew nothing definite except that all the horrors of their hell emanated from him, and so utterly was the hatred of the oppressed focused on this figure, whom they called the old man, that they ceased to care about the foreign soldiers and often even found them ridiculous. With the instinct of hate, they sensed that these men who all looked the same in their uniforms and steel helmets and their short heavy boots did not torment them out of cruelty but because they were completely in the power of the old man. These soldiers acted as instruments without a will of their own, without freedom, without hope, without meaning, and without passion, lost in a foreign land, among people who despised the stranger who had forced his way into their land, much as instruments of torture are despised, or the way the hangman is regarded as a man without honor. An enormous compulsion was placed upon everyone, chaining oppressors and oppressed to each other like galley slaves, and the law that drove them was the power of the old man. The people were at each other's throats, all vestiges of humanity had fallen away among them, and the more the people hated, the crueler the foreign soldiers became. They tortured the women and children in order not to feel the torments they themselves had to endure. Everything was necessary, the way everything is necessary in mathematical books. The enemy army was a monstrous, complicated machine that weighed on the land and crushed it, but somewhere there had to be the brain that steered it for its own purposes, a man of flesh and blood whom you could hate with all your senses, and that was the old man, of whom they dared to speak only in whispers when they were quite sure of being among themselves. No one had ever seen him, they never heard his voice, they did not even know his name, the cruel measures they were forced to endure bore the signatures of indifferent generals who obeyed the old man without ever having heard of him, and who perhaps imagined that they were acting at their own discretion.

That they knew of the old man, and that they hated him—this was the secret strength of the oppressed that made them superior to their enemies. The foreign soldiers did not hate the old man, they knew nothing about him, just as machine parts know nothing about the man they are made to serve, nor did they hate the people they were oppressing, but they sensed that these people were becoming more and more powerful in their hatred, which was directed at something the soldiers did not know, but with which they must be mysteriously connected. They saw themselves being treated more and more contemptuously by the people, and they became more and more cruel and helpless. They did not know what they were doing and why they were among these foreigners who hated with such deadly persistence. There was something above them that treated them the way one treats animals trained to perform some action or other. And so they lived from day to day like ghosts who wander about in the long winter nights.

But above everyone, above the foreign soldiers, the peasants, and the inhabitants of the old cities, there circled by day and by night huge silver birds which—the people were certain of this—were under the old man's direct control. The birds circled very high, so that one could only rarely hear the roar of their motors. Once in a while they would plunge down like vultures to drop their deadly loads on the villages, which would flare up in a red blaze below them, or on their own units when they had not carried out their orders swiftly enough.

But then the hatred of the oppressed rose to those high degrees where even weak people become capable of supreme achievements, and thus a young woman was destined to find the person she hated more than anything in the world. We do not know how she managed to reach him. We can only surmise that extreme hatred lends human beings the power of clairvoyance and makes them unassailable. She came to him without anyone's trying to stop her. She found him alone in a small antique room, its walls lined with books and the busts of thinkers, sunlight and birdsong streaming in through its wide-open windows. There was nothing unusual, nothing to indicate that he must be in this room, and yet she recognized him. He was sitting bent over a large map, huge and motionless. He looked at her calmly as she approached, one hand resting on a large dog that was sitting at his feet. His eyes held no threat, but neither did they ask where she came from. She stopped and realized that her game was up. Nevertheless she took the revolver from the folds of her garment and pointed it at the old man. He didn't even smile. He looked at the woman with indifference, and finally, when he understood, he stretched out his hand a little, the sort of gesture we make to a child when it wants to give us a present. She approached him and put the gun in his open hand, which enclosed it quietly and slowly laid it on the table. All these movements had something soundless about them, and there was a childlike quality about the entire transaction, but at the same time it was all terrifyingly meaningless and irrelevant. Then he lowered his eyes and looked at the map as though he had forgotten the whole event. She wanted to escape, but then the old man began to talk.

"You came to kill me," he said. "It's completely useless, what you wanted to do. There is nothing more insignificant than death." He spoke slowly and his voice was melodious, but he did not seem to attach any importance to his words. "Where are you from?" he asked then, without raising his eyes from the map, and when she named the city, he remarked after a long pause, during which he eagerly searched the map, that this city must have been destroyed, because it was marked with a red cross. Then he fell silent and began to draw large, crisscrossing lines on the map. They were heavy, fantastical lines he drew, strangely symmetrical curves of the kind that force the eye to follow them in pursuit of a meaning that is invariably thrown into confusion. She stood just a few feet away from him, looking at him as he stood bent over the map like a huge dark mass. She stood there in the evening sun, which was casting soft gold on the old man. He paid no attention to the sun or to the woman who wanted to kill him and had failed. He was in the void, in that place where there are no more relationships and no responsibility toward others. He did not hate people, he did not despise them, he did not notice them, and the woman sensed that this was the secret source of his power. So she stood before him like one who has been judged, incapable of hating him, and waited for the death that would be her lot at his hands. But then the woman realized that he had forgotten her and her deed and that she could go where she wanted, but also that this was his vengeance, an annihilation more terrible than death. She slowly went to the door.

At that moment the black dog at his feet let out a sharp bark. She turned back to the old man, and he looked up. His hand took the revolver with which she had wanted to kill him. Then she saw the weapon lying in his open palm, which he was holding out to her. Thus, with an inhuman gesture that was infinitely humiliating, he bridged the abyss that separated them and revealed the inmost nature of his power, which would have to destroy itself in the end, like all things whose nature resides in the absurd. She looked into his eyes, which regarded her without derision and without hatred, but also without kindness, and which did not so much as surmise that he had given her back everything he had taken from her, her hatred and the strength to kill him.

Calmly she took the weapon from his hand, and when she shot, she felt the hatred human beings sometimes feel toward God. He proceeded carefully to put on the table the pencil with which he had streaked the map, but then he slowly keeled over, felled like an ancient sacred oak, and the dog calmly licked the dead man's face and hands without paying the slightest attention to the woman.

The Theater Director

The man to whom the city would eventually succumb already lived among us before we paid him any heed. We didn't notice him until he began to attract attention by his behavior, which seemed ludicrous to us and gave rise to a good deal of mockery at the time: but he was already in charge of the theater when we became aware of him. We didn't laugh at him the way we laugh at people who entertain us by their simplicity or their wit; it was more the sort of amusement we sometimes find in things that are indecent. But it is difficult to indicate what it was that provoked our laughter when he first began to perform, especially since later he was met not only with slavish deference—this we could still understand as a sign of fear—but also with sincere admiration. His appearance above all was peculiar. He was short. His body seemed to have no bones, so that he emanated a kind of sliminess. He had no hair, no eyebrows either. He moved like a tightrope walker who is afraid of losing his balance, with soundless steps whose speed varied unpredictably. His voice was soft and halting. When he came into physical contact with a person, he always directed his gaze at inanimate objects. But it is not clear when we first sensed the possibility of evil in him. Perhaps it occurred when certain changes attributable to him became noticeable on the stage. Perhaps, but we must consider that changes in the aesthetic realm are not generally associated with evil when they excite our attention for the first time: What we really thought then was more that this was in bad taste; or we would poke fun at his presumed stupidity. No doubt these first performances he directed at the City Theater did not have the importance of those later ones that became so famous, but there were indications of what he was planning. For example, his productions evinced a peculiar tendency early on to use masklike effects, and that quality of abstraction in the sets that became so pronounced later on was already present then. These characteristics were not particularly obtrusive, but there were more and more signs that he had a definite purpose in mind, which we sensed but were unable to assess. He might have resembled a spider about to weave a gigantic web, but he seemed to be operating without a plan, and perhaps it was precisely this planless approach that tempted us to laugh at him. Of course, after a while I could not fail to notice that he was imperceptibly striving to get into the forefront, which was something everyone noticed once he was elected into parliament. By misusing the theater, he was preparing to seduce the masses in a place where no one suspected any danger. But I did not become aware of the danger until the changes on the stage had reached a degree that uncovered the secret aim of his actions: as in a chess game, we perceived the move that would destroy us only after it had been made, too late. We often asked ourselves then what it was that drove the masses to go to his theater. We had to admit that this question was almost impossible to answer. We thought of an evil instinct that forces people to search out their murderers and deliver themselves to them, for those changes revealed that he was intent on subverting freedom by proving its impossibility, so that his art was an audacious attack on the very meaning of humanity. This intention led him to eliminate everything accidental and to establish the most intricate reasons for everything, so that the events on the stage became subject to a monstrous coercion. It was also remarkable how he dealt with language, suppressing those elements by which one author differs from another, distorting the natural rhythm of speech to produce the steady, unnerving beat of hammering pistons. The actors moved like marionettes, but the power that controlled their actions did not stay in the background, on the contrary, it was that power above all that revealed itself as a meaningless violence, so that we had the impression of gazing at an engine room where a substance was being produced that would have to annihilate the world. Here I should also mention the way he used shadow and light, which did not serve to suggest infinite spaces and thus establish a connection with the world of faith, but to reveal the finiteness of the stage, using peculiar cubic shapes to block and limit the light, for he was altogether a master of abstract form; also, by the use of secret contraptions, he saw to it that there were no half shades, so that the action appeared to be taking place in the narrow rooms of a dungeon. He employed only red and yellow in a fire that injured the eye. But the most devilish thing of all was that, imperceptibly, every occurrence took on a different meaning and the various genres began to get mixed up, a tragedy being turned into a comedy, a farce misconstrued as a tragedy. At the time we also often heard of revolts on the part of those unfortunates who were eager to improve their lot by means of violence, but there were only a few who lent credence to the rumor that the driving force behind these incidents was to be found in him. But actually his only use for the theater, from the beginning, was as a means to acquire the power that would eventually unmask itself as the brutal dominion of terror and violence. What prevented us at the time from recognizing these developments for what they were was the fact that, to a discerning observer, the actress's situation was beginning to look more and more precarious. Her fate was peculiarly linked to that of the city, and he was trying to destroy her. But by the time his intentions toward her became apparent, his position in our city was so firmly established that this woman's cruel fate could come to pass, a fate that would prove calamitous for all, and which not even those who could see the nature of his seduction had the power to avert. She succumbed to him because she despised the power that he embodied. It cannot be said that she was famous before he took over the direction of the theater, but she did hold a position in the theater that was uncontested, if minor, and thanks to the general esteem in which she was held, she was also able to practice her art without any of those concessions that others, who aspired to more or whose position was more important, had to make to the public; and it was characteristic of him that he would use this circumstance to destroy her, for he knew how to bring about a person's downfall by exploiting his or her virtues.

The actress had not subordinated herself to his regulations. She paid no attention to the changes that were taking place in the theater, thus distinguishing herself more and more clearly from the others. But it was precisely this observation that worried me so, for it was quite obvious that he was taking no steps to force her to acquiesce in his regulations. Her setting herself apart was his plan. He was said to have once made a comment about her acting, shortly after he had taken over the theater; however, I have never been able to confirm that this altercation really took place. But since then, he left her alone and did not undertake anything to remove her from the theater. Instead, he placed her more and more clearly in the foreground, so that eventually she was the star of the theater, even though she was not equal to this task. So it was this procedure that made us suspicious, for after all, her art and his conception were opposed to such a degree that a conflict appeared inevitable, and the later it occurred, the more dangerous it would have to be. There were also signs that her position was beginning to alter in a decisive way. Where at first the crowd praised her acting with enthusiasm and a unanimity that was quite thoughtless (she was considered his great discovery), there was now a first stirring of voices determined to find fault with her, reproaching her for not measuring up to his directorial genius, and praising his rare patience (and humanity) in allowing her to remain in her leading position. But since she was being attacked especially for abiding by the laws of classical acting, her defenders were precisely those people who had recognized the real limitations of her art, a lamentable struggle that unfortunately confirmed her in not voluntarily leaving the theater—a recourse that might still have saved her, even though our city at that point had almost no chance of escaping him. But the decisive turn did not come about until it started to become clear that her art was producing a peculiar effect on the masses that had to be painful for her, and that consisted in people beginning to laugh at her, first in secret and then during her performances as well; an effect that he of course had precisely calculated and was intent on developing more and more. We were dismayed and helpless. The cruel weapon of inadvertent comedy was something we had not reckoned with. Even though she continued to perform, there could be no doubt that she noticed this, just as I suspect that she knew before we did that her downfall was inevitable. Around this time, a project was being completed about which there had been a great deal of talk in our city, and to which we had looked forward with great expectation. Now while it is true that many have expounded their views about this building, I must, before giving my own opinion, mention that to this day I would find it impossible to understand how he managed to acquire the means for this new theater, were it not for the arising of a suspicion that, in my view, cannot be dismissed out of hand. But at the time, we were not able to lend credence to the rumor that linked this building to those unconscionable circles of our city that have always been solely intent on increasing their riches beyond all limits and against whom the uprisings were directed, which he also influenced. Whatever the case may be, this building, which is said to have been destroyed since then, was tantamount to an act of sacrilege. But it is difficult to speak about this building, which presented itself outwardly as a monstrous mixture of all styles and forms, not without an undeniable grandeur. This building was not a revelation of the living spirit, which can be brought to expression in rigid matter by the transformative action of art; instead, it consciously set out to emphasize deadness, which is without time and is nothing but motionless gravity. But all this presented itself to us without mitigation, naked and shameless, without any beauty, with iron doors that were often huge beyond measure and then again squat like the gates of a prison. The building seemed to have been heaped up by the ponderous hands of a Cyclops, meaningless blocks of marble with heavy columns pointlessly leaning against them, but this was only apparently so, for everything about this building was calculated to produce specific effects that were intended to violate human nature and bring it under the spell of an arbitrary and despotic will. Thus, in contrast to these crude, massive volumes and brutal proportions, there were individual objects crafted with a precision that was said to be calibrated to the ten thousandth part of a millimeter. Even more frightening was the interior with the auditorium. It was modeled on the Greek theater, but its form became meaningless, because a strangely vaulted ceiling extended above it, so that as we walked into this hall, we did not seem to be going to a play but to a festival in the bowels of the earth. And so the catastrophe happened. We were awaiting the play in soundless expectation. We sat pressed together in ever-widening circles, our faces pale, staring at the curtain, on which a crucifixion was depicted as a mocking farce: this, too, was taken for art, not sacrilege. Then the play began. There was talk later on about how this revolution had been brought about by unruly elements from the street, but sitting in the auditorium at that time where those people of our city who had most prided themselves on their brilliance and education, who celebrated the theater director as a great artist and revolutionary of the stage and regarded his cynicism as wit, never realizing how soon this fellow would start breaking out of the aesthetic stance they so admired in him, to advance into realms that were no longer aesthetic; which was why, on the opening night of the new house, even before the play began, our nation's president awarded him the Shakespeare Prize amid thundering cheers from the festive assembly. I no longer remember which classical work was played for the occasion, perhaps it was *Faust* or *Hamlet*, but as the curtain with the crucifixion rose, the director's inventions were such that this question became irrelevant before it was possible to pose it: what was taking place before our eyes, frequently interrupted by the enthusiastic applause of the government and the social and academic elite, no longer had anything to do with a classic or with the work of another author. A terrifying force took possession of the actors the way a tornado whirls houses and trees about and leaves them lying in a heap. The voices did not sound human but more the way shadows might speak, but then suddenly and without transition their tone would resemble the mad drumming of savage tribes. We sat in his theater not as human beings but as gods, taking delight in a tragedy that was actually our own. But then she appeared, and I had never seen her as awkward as she was in those moments preceding her death, but also never as pure. If the crowd's first response when she stepped onto the stage was to burst out laughing—so precisely was her entry calculated that it had the effect of an obscene punch line—that laughter soon turned into rage. She appeared as a heretic who had the temerity to oppose a force that not only crushes everything but also absolves every sin and cancels all responsibility, and I understood that this was the real means by which the masses were seduced to relinquish freedom and surrender to evil, for guilt and atonement only exist in freedom. She began to speak and her voice was to them a sacrilege against those cruel laws that men will embrace when they want to raise themselves to the level of gods by nullifying good and evil. I recognized his intention and knew now that he had planned all along to bring about her destruction in front of everyone and with the approval of all. His plan was perfect. He had opened an abyss, and the masses plunged into it, avid for blood, demanding new murders again and again, because only in this way could they find that insensate delirium that alone enables one not to freeze in infinite despair. She stood in the midst of the crowd as a criminal, and the people turned into beasts. I saw that there are horrible moments when a deadly upheaval takes place and the innocent must appear to the others as guilty. Thus our city was prepared to witness an act that was tantamount to a savage triumph of evil. It began with a peculiar contraption that descended from the ceiling of the stage. It may have been light metal rods and wires to which clamps and knives were attached, as well as steel bars with strange joints that were connected in such a way that the device seemed to resemble a monstrous supraterrestrial insect, and we did not take notice of it until it had seized the woman and lifted her up. No sooner had this happened than the crowd broke into boundless applause and shouts of "bravo!" Then, as more and more clamps descended on the actress and held her athwart, the audience was virtually rolling in the aisles with amusement. When the knives began to slice off her clothes, so that she hung naked, there arose from the mass of tightly wedged bodies a shouting that must have originated somewhere, that was picked up and passed on again and again, spreading with the speed of thought, until it rose to infinity and became a single scream: Kill her! and her body was severed by the knives, in such a way that her head fell into the midst the spectators, who had risen to their feet, seized it, soiled themselves with its blood, whereupon it was tossed like a ball from one person to another. And as the stream of people poured out of the theater, forming dense, thickening clots, trampling each other down, kicking the head before them as they moved through the winding streets in long undulating chains, I left the city, in which the garish flags of the revolution were already flaming and the people were attacking each other like animals, surrounded by *his* rabble and, as the new day dawned, forced into submission by *his* order.

The Dog

Already during the first days after I had arrived in the city I found several people gathered around a man in rags who was reading from the Bible in a loud voice on the little square in front of the town hall. I did not take note of the dog lying at his feet until later; I was amazed that such a huge and dreadful animal had not caught my attention right away. It was of a deep black color, its smooth fur drenched in sweat. Its eyes were a sulfurous yellow, and when it opened its enormous mouth, I noticed with a shudder that its teeth were of the same color. Its appearance was such that I could not compare it with any living creature. I could no longer bear the sight of this colossal animal and turned my eyes back to the preacher, who was stocky, and whose clothes hung from his body in shreds: but his skin, shining through the rags, was clean, and his torn garments, too, were spotless: the Bible, however, with gold and diamonds glittering on its cover, looked precious. The man's voice was calm and firm. His words were distinguished by an extraordinary clarity that made his message sound simple and sure; I also noticed that he never used metaphors. It was a calm and unfanatical interpretation of the Bible he was giving, and if his words were nonetheless unconvincing, it was only due to the appearance of the dog, which lay motionless at the man's feet, watching the audience with its yellow eyes. At first, then, it was the strange connection between the preacher and his animal that captivated me and drew me to seek out the man again and again. He preached every day on the public squares of the city and in the streets, but it was not easy to find him, even though he went about his business until late at night, for the city was a bewildering place, despite its clear and simple layout. Also, he must have left his house at various times of the day, without any discernible plan or pattern, for I was never able to establish any regularity in his movements. Sometimes he would spend an entire day preaching without interruption in the same place, but at other times he would change his location every fifteen minutes. He was always accompanied by his dog, which was always striding next to him, black and enormous, as he walked through the streets, and would settle down heavily on the ground as soon as he began to preach. He never had many listeners, and usually he stood by himself, but I noticed that this did not unsettle him or prompt him to leave the square: he would continue speaking. I often saw him standing motionless in a narrow lane, praying in a loud voice, while quite nearby people were walking on a wider street without giving him any heed. Since I was unable to devise a sure method of seeking him out and always had to rely on chance, I now tried to find out where he lived, but no one was able to give me directions. I therefore decided to follow him for an entire day. I had to repeat this several times, for by the evening I would always lose sight of him, since I was trying to keep myself hidden so that he would not discover my intentions. But then, finally, late one night, I saw him entering a house on a street that I knew was inhabited only by the richest people in the city. Naturally I was surprised. From now on I changed my behavior by no longer hiding from him and standing very close to him instead, so that he would have to see me, but I never disturbed him. Only the dog growled every time I came near them. Many weeks passed in this manner, and it was late summer when he approached me after finishing his exegesis of the Gospel according to John and asked me to accompany him to his house; however, he did not say another word as we walked through the streets, and by the time we entered the house, it was already so dark that in the large room into which he led me, the lamp was already turned on. We had to descend several steps to enter the room, which was below street level, and I couldn't see the walls, because they were covered with books. Beneath the lamp stood a girl, reading, next to a large, plain pinewood table. She was wearing a dark blue dress. She did not turn around when we entered. Beneath one of the curtained basement windows was a mattress and by the opposite wall a bed; also, two chairs stood by the table. There was a stove near the door. But as we approached the girl, she turned, so that I saw her face. She gave me her hand and with a gesture offered me a chair, whereupon I noticed that the man was already lying on the mattress; the dog, however, lay down at his feet.

"This is my father," the girl said, "who is already asleep and cannot hear us talking, and the big black dog has no name, it just came to us one evening as my father was beginning to preach. We hadn't locked the door, and so it was able to press down the latch with its paw and jump in." I stood before the girl as if stunned and quietly asked what her father had been. "He was a rich man with many factories," she said, lowering her eyes. "He left my mother and my brothers to proclaim the truth to the people." "Do you believe it is the truth your father is proclaiming?" I asked. "It is the truth," said the girl. "I have always known it is the truth, and that is why I came to live with him in this cellar. But what I didn't know was that when the truth is proclaimed, the dog would come too." The girl was silent and looked at me as if to ask me for something she did not dare to say in words. "Then send the dog away," I replied, but the girl shook her head. "He has no name, so he wouldn't leave," she said softly. She saw that I was uncertain, and sat down on one of the two chairs by the table. So I sat down too. "Are you afraid of this animal?" I asked. "I have always been afraid of him," she replied, "and a year ago when my mother came with a lawyer and my brothers to bring my father back home, they too were afraid of our dog without name, and all the while he was standing in front of my father, growling. When I'm in bed, too, I'm afraid of him, in fact especially then, but now it's all different. Now you have come and now I can laugh about the animal. I always knew you would come. Of course I didn't know what you would look like, but one day, I knew, you would come with my father, on an evening when the lamp is already lit and it's getting quieter on the street, to celebrate the wedding night with me in this room that's half underground, in my bed next to the many books. So we will lie side by side, a man and a woman, and my father will be on the mattress over there, in the dark like a child, and the big black dog will guard our pitiful love."

How could I forget our love! The outlines of the windows hovered as narrow rectangles above our nakedness somewhere in space. We lay with our bodies pressed close together, sinking into each other again and again, clutching each other more and more avidly, and the sounds on the street mingled with the lost cry of our pleasure. Sometimes it was the sound of staggering drunks, sometimes the pattering steps of whores, once the long, monotonous stamping of a column of soldiers passing by, followed by the bright clinking of hooves, the dark rumble of wheels. —We lay together under the earth, wrapped in its warm darkness, no longer afraid, and from the corner, where the man lay asleep on his mattress, silent as a corpse, the dog's yellow eyes glared at us, round discs of two sulfurous moons, spying on our love.

Thus a glowing autumn rose out of the summer, yellow and red, and was followed by a winter that came late that year, mild, without any of the extreme cold of previous years. But I was never able to entice the girl to leave her cellar room and meet my friends, to go to the theater (where important changes were under way) or to walk together through the dusky woods spread over the hills that surround the city in gentle waves: She would always sit there by the pinewood table until her father came home with the big dog, until she would draw me into her bed by the yellow light of the windows above us. But as spring approached, while there was still snow in the streets, dirty and wet, several feet high in the shadows, the girl came to my room. Slanting sunlight was falling through the window. It was late afternoon and I had put wood in the stove, and now she appeared, pale and shivering, probably cold as well, for she had come without a coat, as always, wearing her dark blue dress. Only her shoes were unfamiliar, they were red and lined with fur. "You must kill the dog," the girl said, still on the threshold of my door, with wide open eyes, and her appearance was so ghostly that I did not dare to touch her. I went to the closet and took out my gun. "I knew you would ask me for this some day," I said, "so I bought myself a weapon. When shall it be?" "Now," the girl softly replied. "My father is afraid of the animal too, he has always been afraid, now I know it." I examined the weapon and put on my coat. "They're in the cellar," the girl said, lowering her eyes. "My father lies on the mattress all day long without moving, that's how frightened he is, he can't even pray, and the dog is lying in front of the door."

We went down to the river and then across the stone bridge. The sky was a deep, menacing red, as if lit up by a conflagration. The sun had just set. The city was livelier than usual, full of people and cars that moved as if under a sea of blood, for the houses mirrored the evening light with their windows and walls. We walked through the crowd. We hurried through traffic that was getting more and more dense, through rows of stopping and starting cars and buses that swayed like monsters, their eyes shining with a dull, evil gleam, past gray-helmeted policemen urging the traffic on with flailing arms. I forged ahead with such determination that I left the girl behind; finally I ran up the street, breathing heavily, with my coat open, toward a dusk that was darkening more and more powerfully into violet: but I arrived too late. When I leaped down into the basement room with the gun in my hand and kicked open the door, I saw the terrible beast escaping through the window, shattering its glass, while on the ground, a white mass in a black puddle, torn to shreds by the dog, lay the man, so mangled that he was no longer recognizable.

As I leaned against the wall, trembling, half collapsed into the books, the sirens came wailing toward the house. A stretcher was brought in. As if through a fog I saw a doctor in front of the dead man and heavily armed policemen with pale faces. There were people standing everywhere. I shouted the girl's name. I hurried through the city and across the bridge to my room, but I did not find her. I searched desperately, restlessly, without eating. The police were sent out on a search, and also, since people were afraid of the enormous animal, the soldiers from the barracks combed through the woods, forming long chains. Boats pushed out into the dirty yellow river, its depths were probed with long poles. As spring was now bursting in with warm showers and boundless floods, the search teams went into the caverns of the stone quarries, calling and raising their torches high. They climbed down into the sewers and searched the attic of the cathedral. But the girl was never found and the dog did not reappear.

After three days I returned to my room late at night. Exhausted and hopeless as I was, I threw myself onto my bed in my clothes, when I heard steps in the street below me. I ran to the window, opened it, and leaned out into the night. The street lay beneath me, a black ribbon, still wet from the rain, which had fallen until midnight, so that the lamps were reflected as blurred golden spots, and across the way, walking alongside the trees, was the girl in her blue dress with the red shoes, her hair flowing around her with a bluish sheen, and by her side, a dark shadow, gentle and soundless as a lamb, walked the dog with yellow, round, sparkling eyes.

The Tunnel

A twenty-four-year-old man, fat, who in order to prevent the horror he saw behind the scenes from coming too close (that was his ability, perhaps his only ability) liked to stop up the holes in his flesh, since it was through them that the monstrousness could stream in, and did so by smoking cigars, Ormond Brasil 10, and by wearing a pair of sunglasses over his regular glasses, and wads of cotton in his ears; this young man, still dependent on his parents, and enrolled in some nebulous course of study at a university that could be reached by railroad in two hours, boarded his usual train one Sunday afternoon, time of departure 5:50 p.m., time of arrival 7:27 p.m., in order on the following day to attend a seminar that he had already decided to cut. The sun was shining in a cloudless sky when he left his place of residence. It was summer. The train ran between the Alps and the Jura mountains, past rich villages and small towns, then alongside a river, and after a little less than twenty minutes, shortly after Burgdorf, it dipped into a small tunnel. The train was overcrowded. Having entered in the front of the train, the twenty-four-year-old man laboriously worked his way through the crowds to the back, sweating and making a somewhat befuddled impression. The travelers were crowded together; many of them sat on suitcases. The second-class compartments were filled up as well; only the first-class cars were sparsely booked. When the young man had finally struggled through the tangle of families, recruits, students, and lovers, constantly tossed back and forth by the train, thrown against one body and then another, lurching against stomachs and breasts, he found some room in the last car, indeed so much room that in this third-class section—where cars with compartments are rarely found—he had a whole bench to himself. Directly opposite him in the closed chamber sat a man who was even fatter than he, playing chess by himself, and in the corner of the same bench, near the aisle, sat a red-haired girl who was reading a novel. Thus he was already sitting by the window and had just lit an Ormond Brasil 10 when the tunnel came, which seemed to last longer than usual. He had traveled this line many times before, almost every Saturday and Sunday for the past year, and had sensed the tunnel's presence but never really taken note of it. A few times he had intended to give it his full attention, but each time it came, he would be thinking of something else and not catch the brief dip into darkness, and when he would remember to look, determined to notice this time, the tunnel had already passed; that's how short the tunnel was and how quickly the train passed through it. It was no different now: once again he had not taken off his sunglasses when they entered, since he wasn't thinking of the tunnel. Just a moment before, the sun had been shining with full intensity, and the landscape through which they were traveling (the hills and forests, the distant Jura mountains, and the houses of the small town) had looked like gold, so brightly had everything shone in the evening light, so brightly that now he became conscious of the abrupt change to darkness. Probably that was the reason why the passage through the tunnel seemed longer to him. It was completely dark in the compartment, since, due to the tunnel's shortness, the lights had not been turned on; for, any second, the first glimmer of day would surely appear in the window, and widen with lightning swiftness, and burst in mightily with a full, golden radiance; but when the darkness continued, he took off his sunglasses. At the same moment, the girl lit a cigarette, evidently annoyed that she couldn't go on reading her novel, or so it appeared to him in the reddish flare of the match; his wristwatch with the phosphorescent dial showed ten after six. He leaned back into the corner between the wall of the compartment and the window and busied himself with his confused studies, which no one quite believed in, with the seminar he had to attend the next day and which he would stay away from (everything he did was just a pretext for achieving order behind the facade of his activities, not the order itself, just the sense of a possible order, in view of the horror against which he padded himself with fat, stuck cigars in his mouth, stuffed wads of cotton in his ears), and when he looked back at his watch, it was six fifteen and they were still in the tunnel. This confused him. Although the lights went on in the compartment and the red-haired girl was able to continue reading and the fat man resumed his chess match against himself, outside, beyond the windowpane, in which the whole compartment was now mirrored, the tunnel was still there. He stepped into the aisle, where a tall man in a light-colored raincoat was walking to and fro, a black scarf wrapped around his neck. Why would he do that in this weather, he thought and looked into the other compartments of the car, where people were reading newspapers and chatting. He went back to his corner and sat down. The tunnel had to end at any moment, any second; his wristwatch indicated almost six twenty; he was annoyed at himself for not having ever noticed the tunnel, which had been going on for fifteen minutes already and was evidently a very significant tunnel, considering the speed at which the train was running—probably one of the longest tunnels in Switzerland. It seemed rather likely, therefore, that he had taken the wrong train, even though for the moment he couldn't remember a tunnel of this length and importance just twenty minutes away from his home town by rail. So he asked the fat chess player whether this was the train to Zürich, which he confirmed. The young man replied that he'd had no idea there was such a sizable tunnel on this route, but the chess player retorted, somewhat angrily, since this was the second time he had been interrupted in the middle of a difficult calculation, that there were lots of tunnels in Switzerland, a very large number of them indeed, and that even though this was his first visit to this country, it was something one noticed right away; and besides, he had read in a statistical yearbook that there were more tunnels in Switzerland than in any other country. But now, he said, he was awfully sorry, but he had to give all his attention to an important problem in the Nimzovich defense, so he must ask to be left undisturbed. The chess player's reply was polite but unequivocal; the young man realized he could not expect an answer from him. He was convinced that his ticket would not be accepted; and when the conductor, a pale, gaunt man, remarked, rather nervously it seemed, to the girl, whose ticket he had taken before anyone else's, that she had to change trains in Olten, the twenty-four-year-old man still did not abandon hope, so firmly convinced was he that he had boarded the wrong train. "I'm sure I owe something, I'm supposed to be going to Zürich," he said without taking the Ormond Brasil 10 out of his mouth, and handed the conductor his ticket. "You're in the right train, sir," the conductor replied after examining the ticket. "But we're driving through a tunnel!" the young man exclaimed with annoyance and quite forcefully, for now he was determined to clear up this bewildering situation. The conductor said that they had just passed Herzogenbuchsee and were approaching Langenthal. "It's true, sir, it's twenty past six now." "But we have been driving through a tunnel for the past twenty minutes," the young man insisted. The conductor seemed not to understand. "This is the train to Zürich," he said, glancing at the window himself now. "Twenty after six," he said again, somewhat uneasily this time, it seemed; "Olten's coming up soon, time of arrival six thirty-seven p.m. There must have been bad weather all of a sudden, that would account for the night, maybe a storm, yes, that must be it."

"Nonsense." The remark came from the man occupied with the problem of the Nimzovich defense, who was annoyed because he was still holding out his ticket without the conductor's taking any notice. "Nonsense, we are driving through a tunnel. You can see the rock wall clearly. Looks like granite. There are more tunnels in Switzerland than anywhere in the world. I read it in a statistical yearbook." The conductor, finally taking the chess player's ticket, assured the passengers again, almost pleadingly, that the train was heading for Zürich, whereupon the twenty-four-year-old demanded to speak to the chief conductor. He was at the front of the train, the conductor said, and besides the train was heading for Zürich, it was six twenty-five now, and in twelve minutes they'd be stopping in Olten, according to the summer schedule; he traveled on this train three times a week, he said. The young man set out toward the front of the train. He found it even harder to walk in the overcrowded train than he had earlier going in the opposite direction. The train must have been running at great speed, for it was making a fearsome thundering noise. He had removed the cotton wads from his ears when he entered the train; now he replaced them. The people he passed behaved calmly. The train was in no way different from other trains he had taken on Sunday afternoons, and he could see no signs of alarm anywhere. In a second-class car, an Englishman stood in the aisle by the window with a radiant smile, tapping his pipe against the glass. "Simplon," he said. In the dining car, too, everything was normal, even though all the seats were taken and any one of the travelers or the waiters serving cutlets and rice could have noticed the tunnel. The young man found the chief conductor, whom he recognized by his red pouch, at the exit of the dining car. "May I help you?" asked the chief conductor, a tall, calm man with a carefully tended black moustache and rimless eyeglasses. "We have been in a tunnel for the past twenty-five minutes," said the young man. The chief conductor did not look at the window, as the twenty-four-year-old had expected; he turned to the waiter instead. "Give me a box of Ormond 10," he said, "I smoke the same brand as this gentleman here." But that brand of cigars was not available, so the young man, happy to have found a point of contact, offered the chief conductor a Brasil. "Thanks," said the chief conductor. "I'll hardly have any time to buy one in Olten, so you're doing me a big favor. Smoking is important. May I ask you to follow me?" He led the twenty-four-year-old into the baggage car, which was in front of the dining car. "After this comes the engine," the chief conductor said as they entered the room. "We're at the head of the train." A feeble yellow light was shining in the baggage car. The greater part of the car was only vaguely discernible. The side doors were locked, and the darkness outside only penetrated through a small barred window. There were suitcases standing about, many of them with hotel stickers pasted on them, and some bicycles and a baby carriage. The chief conductor hung his red pouch on a hook. "May I help you?" he asked again, without looking at the young man; he began instead to fill out forms in a booklet he had taken from his pouch. "We've been in a tunnel since Burgdorf," replied the twenty-four-year-old with determination. "There is no such tunnel on this line, I know the route, I take it both ways every week." The chief conductor kept writing. "Sir," he finally said, stepping up close to the young man, so close that their bodies nearly touched, "sir, there is not much I can tell you. I don't know how we got into this tunnel, I have no explanation for it. But I ask you to consider that we are moving on tracks. The tunnel therefore must lead somewhere. There is no evidence of there being anything wrong with the tunnel, except of course that it doesn't end." The chief conductor, still holding the Ormond Brasil 10 between his lips without smoking, had spoken extremely softly, but with such dignity and so clearly and emphatically that his words were audible despite the wads of cotton and even though the roaring sound of the train was many times louder here than in the dining car. "In that case I must ask you to please stop the train," said the young man impatiently. "I don't understand a word you're saying. If something's not right about this tunnel, the existence of which you yourself can't explain, then it's your duty to stop the train." "Stop the train?" the chief conductor slowly replied. This, he said, had certainly crossed his mind too. Whereupon he closed his booklet and put it back into the red pouch, which was swinging back and forth on its hook. Then he carefully lit his Ormond. "Should I pull the emergency brake?" the young man asked and was about to reach for the brake handle above his head when he lurched forward and banged into the wall. A baby carriage rolled toward him, valises came sliding along, and the chief conductor, too, staggered oddly through the baggage car with his arms stretched out before him. "We're going downhill," the chief conductor said, leaning against the front wall of the car next to the twenty-four-year-old man, but the anticipated crash of the hurtling train against a rock wall, the telescoping of jammed, crumpled cars, did not happen. Instead the tunnel appeared to resume a level course. The door at the other end of the car opened. In the glaring light of the dining car they could see people raising glasses to each other; then the door closed again. "Come into the engine room," the chief conductor said, looking into the twenty-four-year-old man's face with a pensive and, it suddenly seemed, threatening expression. Then he unlocked the door next to which they were leaning against the wall. A stormlike, hot blast of air struck them with such force that they staggered against the wall. At the same time a terrifying tumult filled the baggage car. "We have to climb over to the engine," the chief conductor screamed almost inaudibly into the young man's ear, and disappeared in the rectangle of the open door, through which one could see the brightly lit windowpanes of the locomotive swinging back and forth. The twenty-four-year-old followed with determination, even though he couldn't see what the sense of this climbing was. He clung to one of the iron railings that were attached to either side of the platform he had stepped on, but the terrifying thing was not the horrendous wind, which abated as the young man approached the engine, but the close proximity of the walls of the tunnel, which he couldn't see, since he had to fully concentrate on the engine, but which he could sense as he stood there, shaken to his bones by the pounding of the wheels and the whistling of the air. He felt as if he were rocketing with the speed of stars into a world of stone. A narrow ledge ran along the side of the locomotive, and above it an iron railing curved around the length of the engine: This must be the way, he concluded; he would have to risk a leap of about three feet. And so he succeeded in grasping hold of the railing, and inched his way along the ledge, with his body pressed against the locomotive; but this gradual advance did not become truly terrifying until he had reached the side of the engine, where he was now fully exposed to the impact of the roaring hurricane and the menacing walls of stone, which came sweeping in, brightly lit by the engine. It was the chief conductor who saved him by pulling him through a little door into the engine room. Exhausted, the young man leaned against a wall, when all of a sudden it became quiet, for as soon as the chief conductor shut the door, the steel plates of the giant locomotive muted the racket so that it could hardly be heard. "We lost the Ormond Brasil as well," said the chief conductor. "It wasn't smart to light one before all that climbing, but they break easily if you don't have a box with you, on account of their length." After the perilous proximity of the stone walls, the young man was glad to be distracted by something that reminded him of his ordinary life less than half an hour ago, of those changeless days and years (changeless because he had only been living toward the moment at which he had now arrived, this moment of caving in, of the earth's surface suddenly giving way, of plunging precipitously to the bowels of the earth). He pulled one of the brown cartons from his right coat pocket and offered the chief conductor another cigar, put one in his own mouth as well, the chief conductor offered a light, and carefully they both drew on the flame. "I think very highly of this Ormond," the chief conductor said, "but you have to draw hard, otherwise they go out," words that made the twenty-four-year-old suspicious, because he sensed that the chief conductor didn't like to think about the tunnel either, which was still continuing outside (it was still conceivable that it would suddenly end, as a dream can suddenly end). "Six forty p.m.," said the young man after looking at the luminous dial of his watch. "We're supposed to be in Olten by now." And he thought of the hills and forests that had still been there recently, showered with gold by the setting sun. Thus they stood, smoking, leaning against the wall of the engine room. "Keller's my name," the chief conductor said, drawing on his Brasil. The young man did not relent. "All that climbing around the engine was pretty dangerous," he remarked, "at least for someone like me who isn't used to it. So I'd like to know why you brought me here." The chief conductor replied that he didn't know, that he had only wanted to give himself time to think. "Time to think," repeated the twenty-four-year-old. "Yes," said the chief conductor, "that's it," and continued smoking. The engine seemed to tilt forward again. "We could go into the engineer's cabin," Keller suggested; however, he remained standing irresolutely by the engine wall. Thereupon the young man walked down the aisle. When he opened the door to the engineer's cabin, he stood still. "Empty," he said to the chief conductor, who joined him at the door, "the engineer's cabin is empty." They entered the room, lurching due to the enormous speed with which the engine dashed further and further into the tunnel, tearing the train along with it. "See for yourself," said the chief conductor, pressing down several levers. He also pulled the emergency brake, but the engine did not obey. They had done everything to stop it as soon as they had noticed the change in the train's route, Keller assured him, but the machine had just raced on and on. "It'll keep on racing," said the twenty-four-year-old, pointing to the speedometer. "Ninety. Has this engine ever done ninety?" "No more than sixty-five," replied the chief conductor. "Precisely," said the young man. "Precisely. The speed is increasing. It's pointing to a hundred and twelve now. We're falling." He stepped up to the window, but was unable to hold himself upright. His face was pressed against the glass, due to the fantastic speed of their descent. "The engineer?" he shouted, staring at the masses of rock that soared upward in the glaring arc lights, zooming toward him and vanishing above and beneath him and on both sides of the engineer's cabin. "Jumped off," Keller shouted back. He was sitting on the floor now, leaning against the switchboard. "When?" asked the twenty-four-year-old stubbornly. The chief conductor hesitated a little and had to light another Ormond, his legs level with his head, since the train was tilting more and more steeply. "Five minutes after it started," he said then. "A rescue was out of the question by then. The man in the baggage room jumped off too." "And you?" asked the twenty-four-year-old. "I'm the chief conductor. Besides, I have always lived without hope." "Without hope," repeated the young man, who now lay snug against the glass pane of the engineer's cabin, his face pressed over the abyss. "We were still sitting in our compartments and had no idea it was all over," he thought. "It seemed as if nothing had changed yet, but actually the shaft leading down had already swallowed us up." "I have to go back," the chief conductor shouted now, "they're probably panicking in the cars, trying to climb back as far as possible." "I'm sure," replied the twenty-four-year-old man, thinking of the fat chess player and the girl with the novel and the red hair. He offered the chief conductor his remaining cartons of Ormond Brasil 10. "Take them," he said, "you'll just lose your Brasil again while climbing back." "Aren't you coming along?" the chief conductor asked. He had raised himself up and with a great effort began to crawl up the funnel of the aisle. The young man looked at the meaningless instruments, at the ridiculous levers and switches surrounding him in the glaring light of the cabin. "A hundred and thirty," he said. "I don't think you'll be able to reach the cars above us at this speed." "It's my duty," the chief conductor shouted. "Certainly," the twenty-four-year-old man replied, without looking back to witness the chief conductor's senseless undertaking. "I must at least try," shouted the chief conductor, who had climbed to the far end of the car by now, pressing his thighs and elbows against the metal walls for support, but as the locomotive tilted down further, plunging straight toward the earth's core with terrifying speed, so that the chief conductor found himself dangling directly over the twenty-four-year-old, who was lying face down at the bottom of the engine on the silver window of the engineer's cabin, his strength gave way. The chief conductor dropped and fell onto the switchboard. There he lay, bleeding profusely, next to the young man, gripping his shoulders. "What shall we do?" the chief conductor shouted once more into the young man's ear through the echoing roar of the walls hurtling toward them, while the young man, his fat body useless and no longer a protection, lay glued to the window of the engineer's cabin, sucking in the abyss with his eyes, which he had opened wide for the first time. "What shall we do?" screamed the chief conductor again; to which, without turning his face from the spectacle as the two wads of cotton were blown upward with arrowlike swiftness by the monstrous draught that burst in of a sudden, the twenty-four-year-old replied with spectral serenity: "Nothing."

The Pledge

Requiem for the Detective Novel

1

Last March I had to give a lecture in Chur on the art of writing detective stories. My train pulled in just before nightfall, under low clouds, in a dreary blizzard. As if that wasn't enough, the roads were paved with ice. The lecture was being held in the hall of the Chamber of Commerce. There wasn't much of an audience, since Emil Staiger was lecturing in the school auditorium about Goethe's late period.* I couldn't summon up the right mood, and neither could anyone else; several local residents left the room before I had ended my talk. After a brief chat with some members of the board of directors, with two or three high school teachers who also would have preferred the late Goethe, and a philanthropic lady whose honorific function it was to govern the League of Domestic Employees of Eastern Switzerland, I received my fee and traveling expenses and withdrew to the room I had been given at the Hotel Steinbock, near the train station—another dismal place. Except for a German financial newspaper and an old illustrated magazine, I couldn't find anything to read. The silence of the hotel was inhuman. Impossible to even think of falling asleep, because that would give rise to the fear of not waking again. A timeless, spectral night. It had stopped snowing outside, no movement anywhere, the streetlamps were no longer swaying, not a puff of wind, no denizen of Chur, no animal, nothing at all, except for a single heaven-rending blast from the train station. I went to the bar to have another whiskey. There, in addition to the elderly barmaid, I found a man who introduced himself the moment I sat down. He was Dr. H., the former chief of police in the canton of Zürich,† a large and heavy man, old-fashioned, with

*Emil Staiger (1908–1987), noted literary theorist, critic, and scholar; author of a three-volume study of Goethe.

†*Canton*: One of the states of the Swiss confederation.

a gold watch chain running across his vest. Despite his age, his bristly hair was still black, his moustache bushy. He was sitting on one of the high chairs by the bar, drinking red wine, smoking a Bahianos and addressing the barmaid by her first name. His voice was loud and his gestures were lively, a blunt and unfastidious sort of person who simultaneously attracted and repelled me. When it was nearly three o'clock and our first Johnnie Walker had been followed by four more, he offered to drive me to Zürich the next morning in his Opel Kapitän. Since I did not know the surroundings of Chur or that whole part of Switzerland, I accepted the invitation. Dr. H. had come to Graubünden as a member of a federal commission, and since the weather had prevented his departure, he, too, had attended my lecture, about which he had nothing to say beyond remarking that I had "a rather awkward delivery."

We set out early the next morning. At dawn, I had taken two Medomins to catch a little sleep, and now I felt virtually paralyzed. The day seemed still dark, though the sun had risen a while ago. There was a patch of metallic sky gleaming somewhere through a covering of dense, sluggishly lumbering, snow-filled clouds. Winter seemed unwilling to leave this part of the country. The city was surrounded by mountains, but there was nothing majestic about them; they rather resembled heaps of earth, as though someone had dug an immense grave. Chur itself was quite evidently made of stone, gray, with large government buildings. It seemed incredible to me that this was a wine-growing region. We tried to penetrate into the old inner city, but the heavy car strayed into a network of narrow lanes and one-way streets, and only a complex maneuver in reverse gear got us out of the tangle of houses. Moreover, the streets were icy, so we were glad to have the city behind us at last, although I had seen almost nothing of this old episcopal residence. It was like a flight. I dozed, feeling leaden and weary; vaguely, through the low scuttling clouds, I saw a snow-covered valley gliding past us, rigid with cold. I don't know for how long. Then we were driving toward a large village, perhaps a small town, carefully, and suddenly everything was illuminated by sunlight so powerful and blinding that the snowy planes began to melt. A white ground mist rose, spreading imperceptibly over the snowfields until, once again, the valley was hidden from my sight. It was like a bad dream, like an evil spell, as if I was not supposed to experience these mountains. My weariness came back. The gravel with which the road had been strewn clattered unpleasantly; driving over a bridge, we went into a slight skid; then we passed a military transport; the windshield became so dirty that the wipers could no longer clean it. H. sat sullenly next to me at the wheel, absorbed in his own thoughts, concentrating on the difficult road. I regretted having accepted his invitation, cursed the whiskey and my sleeping pills. But gradually, things improved. The valley became visible again, and more human too. There were farms everywhere, and occasionally a small factory, everything spare and clean, the road free of snow and ice now, glistening with wetness, but safe enough for us to accelerate to a decent speed. The mountains no longer hemmed us in from all sides but had opened out, and then we stopped next to a gas station.

The house immediately struck me as peculiar, perhaps because it stood out from its neat and proper surroundings. It was a wretched-looking thing with streams of water flowing down its sides. Half of it was made of stone, the other half was a wooden shed whose front wall was covered with posters. Evidently this had been its use for a long time, for there were whole layers of posters pasted one over the other: Burrus Tobacco for Modern Pipes, Drink Canada Dry, Sport Mints, Vitamins, Lindt's Milk Chocolate, and so on. On the side wall, in giant letters: Pirelli Tires. The two gas pumps stood on an uneven, badly paved square in front of the house; everything made a rundown impression, despite the sun, which was now exuding a stinging heat that seemed almost vicious.

"Let's get out," said the former chief of police, and I obeyed without understanding what he had in mind, but glad to step into the fresh air.

Next to the open door sat an old man on a stone bench. He was unshaven and unwashed, wore a pale smock that was smeared and stained, and dark, grease-spotted trousers that had once been part of a tuxedo. Old slippers on his feet. His eyes were staring, stupefied, and I could smell the liquor from afar. Absinthe. The pavement around the stone bench was littered with cigarette butts that were floating in puddles of melted snow.

"Hello," said the police chief, and he suddenly sounded embarrassed. "Fill-up, please. Super. And clean the windshields." Then he turned to me. "Let's go in."

Only now did I notice a tavern sign over the only visible window, a red metal disc. And over the door was the name of the place: Zur Rose. We stepped into a dirty corridor. The stench of beer and schnapps. The chief walked ahead of me. He opened a wooden door; evidently he'd been here before. The barroom was dark and dingy, a couple of rough-hewn tables and benches, the walls papered with cutout pictures of movie stars; the Austrian radio was giving a market report for the Tyrol, and behind the counter, barely discernible, stood a haggard woman in a dressing gown, smoking a cigarette and washing glasses.

"Two coffees with cream," said the chief.

The woman went about preparing the coffee. From the adjoining room came a sloppy-looking waitress who looked about thirty years old to me.

"She's sixteen," the chief muttered.

The girl served us our coffees. She was wearing a black skirt and a white, half-open blouse, with nothing underneath; her skin was unwashed. She was blond, as the woman behind the counter must once have been, and her hair was uncombed.

"Thank you, Annemarie," the chief said, and laid the money on the table. The girl, too, did not reply, did not even thank him. We drank in silence. The coffee was awful. The chief lit himself a Bahianos. The Austrian radio was now discussing the water level, and the girl shuffled off to the room next door, where we saw something whitish shimmering, probably an unmade bed.

"Let's go," said the chief.

Outside, after a glance at the pump, he paid the old man for filling the tank and cleaning the windshields.

"Next time," the chief said by way of farewell, and again I noticed his helpless air; but the old man still didn't reply; he was back on his bench, staring into space, stupefied, obliterated. When we had reached the Opel and turned around again, the old man was clenching his fists, shaking them, and whispering, pressing the words out in brief, forceful gasps, his face transfigured by an immense faith: "I'll wait, I'll wait, he'll come, he'll come."

2

"To be honest," Dr. H. began later, as we were approaching the Kerenz Pass—the road was icy again, and beneath us lay Lake Walen, glittering, cold, forbidding; also, the leaden weariness from the Medomin had come back, the memory of the smoky taste of the whiskey, the feeling of gliding along in an endless, meaningless dream—"to be honest, I have never thought highly of crime novels, and I rather regret that you, too, write them. It's a waste of time. Though what you said in your lecture yesterday was worth hearing; since the politicians have shown themselves to be so criminally inept—and it takes one to know one, I'm a member of Parliament, as I'm sure you're aware . . ." (I had no idea, I was listening to his voice as if from a great distance, barricaded behind my tiredness, but attentive, like an animal in its lair) ". . . People hope the police at least will know how to put the world in order, which strikes me as the most miserable thing you could possibly hope for. But unfortunately, these mystery stories perpetrate a whole different sort of deception. I don't even mean the fact that your criminals are always brought to justice. It's a nice fairy tale and is probably morally necessary. It's one of those lies that preserve the State, like that pious homily 'crime doesn't pay'—when all that's required to test this particular piece of wisdom is to have a good look at human society; no, I'd let all that pass, on principles of commerce if nothing else, because every reader and every taxpayer has a right to his heroes and his happy ending, and it's our job to deliver that—I mean ours as policemen, just as much as it's your job as writers. No, what really bothers me about your novels is the story line, the plot. There the lying just takes over, it's shameless. You set up your stories logically, like a chess game: here's the criminal, there's the victim, here's an accomplice, there's a beneficiary; and all the detective needs to know is the rules, he replays the moves of the game, and checkmate, the criminal is caught and justice has triumphed. This fantasy drives me crazy. You can't come to grips with reality by logic alone. Granted, we of the police are forced to proceed logically, scientifically; but there is so much interference, so many factors mess up our clear schemes, that success in our business very often amounts to no more than professional luck and pure chance working in our favor. Or against us. But in your novels, chance plays no part, and if something looks like chance, it's made out to be some kind of fate or providence; the truth gets thrown to the wolves, which in your case are the dramatic rules. Get rid of them, for God's sake. Real events can't be resolved like a mathematical formula, for the simple reason that we never know all the necessary factors, just a few, and usually a rather insignificant few. And chance—the incalculable, the incommensurable—plays too great a part. Our rules are based only on probability, on statistics, not on causality; they apply to the general rule, not the particular case. The individual can't be grasped by calculation. Our criminological methods are inadequate, and the more we refine them, the more inadequate they get. But you fellows in the writing business don't care about that. You don't try to grapple with a reality that keeps eluding us, you just set up a world that can be managed. That world may be perfect, but it's a lie. Forget about perfection if you want to do a man's job, which is to get at the way things actually are, at reality; otherwise you'll be left behind fooling around with useless stylistic experiments. But let me get to the point.

"I'm sure you were surprised by a few things this morning. First of all, by my own talk; a former chief of the Zürich cantonal police should express more moderate views. But I am old and I no longer lie to myself. I know very well what a dubious bunch we all are, how little we can accomplish, how easily we make mistakes; but I also know that we have to act anyway, even if we run the danger of acting wrongly.

"Then you must also have wondered why I stopped at that miserable gas station, and I'll confess it to you right away: that pathetic drunken wreck who filled up our tank used to be my most capable man. God knows I knew something about my profession, but Matthäi was a genius, and this to a degree that puts all your paper detectives to shame.

"The story happened almost nine years ago," H. continued after passing a Shell oil truck. "Matthäi was one of my inspectors, or rather, one of my first lieutenants—we use military ranks in the cantonal police. He was a lawyer, like me, a Baseler who had taken his doctorate in Basel, and among certain groups that made his acquaintance 'professionally' his nickname was 'Nobody Home.' After a while we called him that too. He was a lonely man, always neatly dressed, impersonal, formal, aloof; he didn't smoke, didn't drink, but on the job he was tough as nails, downright ruthless, and as hated as he was successful. I was never able to figure him out. I think I was the only person he liked—because I have a soft spot for clearheaded people, even though his lack of humor often got on my nerves. He was extremely bright, but the all too solid structures in our country had made him emotionless. He was what you'd call an organization man, and he used the police apparatus like a slide rule. He wasn't married, he never spoke of his private life—probably he didn't have one. The only thing he thought about was his job. He was a top-notch detective, but he worked without passion. He was stubborn, tireless, but when you watched him in action, he appeared to be bored; until one day he got embroiled in a case that suddenly stirred him to passion.

"He was at the pinnacle of his career at the time. There had been some difficulties with him in the department. I was going to be retired, and my most likely successor was Matthäi. But there were obstacles in the way of his appointment that couldn't be ignored. Not only that he didn't belong to any party, but the rank and file would have objected. The cantonal government, on the other hand, was hesitant to pass over such a capable man. So when the government of Jordan asked the federal government to send an expert to Amman to reorganize their police, it was like a godsend: Matthäi was recommended by Zürich and accepted by Bern and Amman. Everyone heaved a sigh of relief. He, too, was pleased, and not just for professional reasons. He was about fifty then—a little desert sun would do him good, he figured; he looked forward to the trip, to the flight across the Alps and the Mediterranean; probably he imagined this would be his final farewell from us, for he hinted that afterward he would move to Denmark to live with a widowed sister there—and he was just clearing out his desk in the cantonal police headquarters on Kasernenstrasse when the call came."

3

"Matthäi had a hard time making sense of that jumbled report," the chief continued. "It was one of his old 'clients' calling from Mägendorf, a little hole in the wall near Zürich. The man was a peddler named von Gunten. Matthäi wasn't really in the mood to take up this case on his last afternoon on the job. He had already bought his plane ticket, he'd be leaving in three days. But I was away at a conference of police chiefs and wasn't expected back from Bern until evening. This case called for competent handling; inexperience could spoil everything. Matthäi called the police station in Mägendorf. It was near the end of April, buckets of rain splashing down outside, the föhn-storm had reached the city,* but the unpleasant, nasty heat persisted, and people could hardly breathe.

"Officer Riesen picked up the phone.

"'Is it raining in Mägendorf too?' Matthäi asked, ill-humored, even though he could guess the answer, and when he heard it, his face looked even gloomier. Then he gave the man instructions to keep an inconspicuous watch on the peddler at the Stag in Mägendorf.

"Matthäi hung up.

"'Something happen?' Feller asked curiously. He was helping his boss pack his belongings—mainly books, which Matthäi had accumulated over the years, a whole library.

"'It's raining in Mägendorf too,' the inspector replied. 'Get the emergency squad ready.'

"'Murder?'

"'Damned rain,' Matthäi muttered in place of an answer, indifferent to Feller's hurt feelings.

"But before he joined the district attorney and Lieutenant Henzi, who were waiting impatiently in their car, he leafed through von Gunten's dossier. The man had a record. Sexual molestation of a fourteen-year-old girl."

4

"That very first order to have the peddler watched turned out to be a mistake that could not have been foreseen. Mägendorf was a small community. Mostly farmers, though some men worked in the factories down in the valley or in the brickyard nearby. There were a few city people living out there,

*_Föhn:_ A notoriously dry, warm wind, especially from the northern slopes of the Alps.

two or three architects, a neoclassical sculptor, but they played no part in the village. Everyone knew everyone else, and most people were related. The village was in conflict with the city, not officially, but secretly; for the woods surrounding Mägendorf belonged to the city, a fact that no real Mägendorfer had ever taken into account, to the great annoyance of the Forestry Department, who finally insisted that a police station be set up in Mägendorf. And there was another problem: on Sundays, people came from the city and took over the village; and many others came flocking to the Stag at night. With all these factors to consider, the man stationed there had to be a capable policeman, but he also had to be on good terms with the village. Officer Wegmüller, who was assigned there, understood this fairly quickly. He came from a peasant family, drank a lot, and kept his Mägendorfers well in hand, though with so many concessions, I really should have intervened; but to me—in part because of our shortage of manpower—he was the lesser evil. I had my peace of mind and I let Wegmüller have his. It was his substitutes—when he was on leave—who were put through the mill. As far as the Mägendorfers were concerned, they couldn't do anything right. Those were boom times, no one went poaching or stealing wood in the forests, and there hadn't been a brawl in the village for ages, but you could still feel the traditional defiance of state power smoldering among the people. Riesen, in particular, had a rough time. He was a simpleminded fellow, humorless, easily offended, no match for the villagers' constant mocking, and really too sensitive even for a more normal district. He was so intimidated by the people that he would make himself scarce as soon as he was done with his daily rounds. Under such conditions it proved impossible to keep an 'inconspicuous watch' on the peddler. Riesen usually stayed far away from the Stag, so his sudden appearance there had all the weight of a federal inquest. And when the policeman demonstratively took a seat facing the peddler, the farmers fell silent, tense with curiosity.

"'Coffee?' the innkeeper asked.

"'Nothing,' Riesen replied. 'I'm here on duty.'

"The farmers stared at the peddler.

"'What did he do?' an old man asked.

"'None of your business.'

"The tavern was low and filled with smoke, a wooden cave, oppressively hot and dark, but the innkeeper didn't turn on the light. The farmers sat at a long table, perhaps over white wine, perhaps over beer, invisible except as shadows against the silvery windowpanes with their trickles and streams of rainwater. From somewhere came the clatter of a game of table soccer; from somewhere else, the ringing and rumbling sounds of an American pinball machine.

“Von Gunten was drinking a cherry liqueur. He was afraid. He sat hunched in a corner, his right arm propped on the handle of his basket, waiting. It seemed to him that he had been sitting here for hours. Everything was densely quiet, but menacing. The windowpanes started lightening, the rain lessened, and suddenly the sun was out again. Only the wind was still howling and shaking the walls. Von Gunten was glad when the cars finally pulled up outside.

“‘Come,’ said Riesen, getting up. The two men stepped outside. In front of the tavern stood a dark limousine and the emergency squad’s big van. The ambulance was on its way. The village square lay in the glaring sun. Two five- or six-year-old children stood by the well, a girl and a boy. The girl had a doll tucked under one arm, and the boy was holding a little whip.

“‘Get in next to the driver, von Gunten!’ Matthäi called from the window of the limousine, and then, when the peddler had taken his seat with a sigh of relief (as if he were safe now), and Riesen had climbed into the other car: ‘All right, now show us what you found in the woods.’”

5

“After a short walk through wet grass—the path to the woods was a single muddy puddle—they found the small body in the leaves among the bushes not far from the edge of the forest. The men were silent. The storm was still lashing the treetops and shaking loose large silver drops that glittered like diamonds. The district attorney tossed away his cigar and stepped on it, embarrassed. Henzi didn’t dare to look. Matthäi said: ‘A police officer never looks away, Henzi.’

“The men set up their cameras.

“‘It’ll be hard to find tracks after this rain,’ Matthäi said.

“Suddenly the boy and the girl were standing in their midst, staring at the body, the girl still with her doll under her arm, the boy still with his whip.

“‘Take the children away.’

“A policeman took them by the hand and led them back to the road, and there they stayed.

“The first people from the village approached. The owner of the Stag was recognizable from afar by his white apron.

“‘Cordon her off,’ the inspector ordered. Several men posted themselves as guards. Others searched the immediate vicinity. Then the first flashbulbs went off.

“‘Do you know the girl, Riesen?’

"'No, sir, I don't.'

"'Did you ever see her in the village?'

"'I believe I have, sir.'

"'Has the girl been photographed?'

"'Two more shots from above.'

"Matthäi waited.

"'Tracks?'

"'Nothing. Everything's mud.'

"'Check the buttons? Fingerprints?'

"'Hopeless after this cloudburst.'

"Then Matthäi carefully bent over. 'With a straight razor,' he noted, picked up the pieces of bread strewn about and carefully put them back in the little basket.

"'Pretzels.'

"News came that someone from the village wanted to talk to them. Matthäi stood up. The district attorney looked over toward the edge of the woods. There stood a white-haired man with an umbrella hanging from his left forearm. Henzi was leaning against a beech tree. He was pale. The peddler sat on his basket, quietly repeating, over and over, with a soft voice: 'I came by here by chance, just by chance!'

"'Bring the man here.'

"The white-haired man came through the bushes and froze.

"'My God,' he murmured, 'my God.'

"'May I ask for your name?' Matthäi asked.

"'I am the teacher Luginbühl,' the white-haired man replied, and looked away.

"'Do you know this girl?'

"'It's Gritli Moser.'

"'Where do her parents live?'

"'Down in the Moosbach.'

"'Far from the village?'

"'Fifteen minutes.'

"Matthäi looked at the body. He was the only one who didn't flinch. No one said a word.

"'How did this happen?' the teacher asked.

"'A sex crime,' Matthäi replied. 'Did the child go to your school?'

"'To Fräulein Krumm's class. Third grade.'

"'Do the Mosers have any other children?'

"'Gritli was the only one.'

"'Someone has to tell the parents.'

"The men fell silent again.

"'Will you, sir?' Matthäi asked the teacher.

"There was a long pause before Luginbühl replied. 'Please don't consider me a coward,' he finally said, hesitantly, 'but I would rather not. I can't,' he quietly added.

"'I understand,' Matthäi said. 'How about the pastor?'

"'He's in the city.'

"'All right,' Matthäi calmly said. 'You may leave, Herr Luginbühl.'

"The teacher went back to the road. More and more people from Mägendorf had assembled there.

"Matthäi looked over at Henzi, who was still leaning against the beech tree. 'Please, no, sir,' Henzi said softly. The district attorney also shook his head. Matthäi looked at the body once more, and then glanced at the little red skirt lying torn in the bushes, soaked through with blood and rain.

"'Then I'll go,' he said, and picked up the basket of pretzels."

6

"The Moosbach was a small marshy dale near Mägendorf. Matthäi had left the police car in the village and walked. He wanted to gain time. He could see the house from far away. He stopped and turned around. He had heard footsteps. The little boy and the girl were there again, with flushed faces. They must have taken short cuts; there was no other way to explain their reappearance.

"Matthäi walked on. The house was low, with white walls, dark beams, and a slate roof. Fig trees behind it, black soil in the garden. A man was chopping wood in front of the house. He looked up and saw the inspector approaching.

"'What can I do for you?' the man said.

"Matthäi hesitated, unsure how to proceed. Then he introduced himself, just to gain time. 'Herr Moser?'

"'That's me, what do you want?' the man said again. He came closer and stood in front of Matthäi with his ax in his hand. He must have been about forty. He was lean, with a furrowed face, and his gray eyes scrutinized the inspector. A woman appeared in the doorway; she too was wearing a red skirt. Matthäi searched for words. All along on his walk he had been searching for the right formulation, but he still didn't know what to say. Then Moser came to his aid. He had noticed the basket in Matthäi's hand.

"'Did something happen to Gritli?' he asked, his eyes probing the stranger's face again.

"'Did you send Gritli somewhere?' the inspector asked.

"'To her grandmother in Fehren,' the farmer replied.

"Matthäi reflected; Fehren was the neighboring village. 'Did Gritli go that way often?' he asked.

"'Every Wednesday and Saturday afternoon,' the farmer said. Then, in a sudden rush of fear, he asked: 'Why do you want to know? Why are you bringing her basket?'

"Matthäi put the basket on the stump on which Moser had been chopping wood.

"'Gritli has been found dead in the woods near Mägendorf,' he said.

"Moser did not move. Nor did the woman, who was still standing in the doorway in her red skirt. Matthäi saw beads of perspiration form on the man's forehead; a moment later, sweat was streaming down his white face. Matthäi would have liked to look away, but he was spellbound by this face, by this sweat, and so they stood staring at each other.

"'Gritli was murdered,' Matthäi heard himself say, with a voice that seemed devoid of compassion. This annoyed him.

"'It can't be,' Moser whispered, 'there can't be such devils.' The fist holding the ax was quivering.

"'There are such devils, Herr Moser,' Matthäi said.

"The man stared at him.

"'I want to see my child,' he said almost inaudibly.

"The inspector shook his head. 'I wouldn't do that, Herr Moser. I know it's a cruel thing to say, but it's better if you don't go to your Gritli now.'

"Moser stepped up very close to the inspector, so close that the two men stood eye to eye.

"'Why is it better?' he shouted.

"The inspector said nothing.

"For a moment Moser weighed the ax in his hand as though he wanted to strike out with it, but then he turned away and went to his wife, who was still standing in the doorway. Still motionless, still mute. Matthäi waited. Nothing escaped him, and he suddenly knew he would never forget this scene. Moser gripped his wife in his arms. He was suddenly shaken by a silent sob. He hid his face against her shoulder, while she stared into space.

"'Tomorrow evening you may see your Gritli,' the inspector promised. He felt feeble, helpless. 'By then the child will look as if she's asleep.'

"Then the woman suddenly spoke.

"'Who is the murderer?' she asked in a voice so calm and sober that Matthäi was frightened.

"'I intend to find that out, Frau Moser.'

"The woman just looked at him. Her gaze was threatening, imperious. 'Is that a promise?'

"'It's a promise, Frau Moser,' the inspector said, solely impelled by the desire to leave this place.

"'On your eternal salvation?'

"The inspector hesitated. 'On my eternal salvation,' he finally said. What else could he do.

"'Then go,' the woman commanded. 'You have sworn by your eternal salvation.'

"Matthäi wanted to add a consoling word, but he could think of no consolation.

"'I'm sorry,' he said softly, and turned around. Slowly he walked back the way he had come. Before him lay Mägendorf with the forest behind it. Above, the sky, which was cloudless now. He saw the two children again, crouching by the side of the road. He walked past them wearily, and they followed with quick, tripping steps. Then suddenly he heard from the house behind him a scream like the bellow of an animal. He hurried his steps, and did not know whether it was the man or the woman who was crying so."

7

"Back in Mägendorf, Matthäi met with his first difficulty. The emergency squad's large van had driven into the village and was waiting for the inspector. The location of the crime and its immediate vicinity had been carefully searched and then cordoned off. Three plainclothes policemen were hiding in the woods. Their assignment was to observe passersby. The rest of the squad was to be taken back to the city. The sky was swept clean, but the rain hadn't relaxed the atmosphere. The föhn still lay heavily upon the forests and villages, still came wafting along in great soft gusts. The unnatural heavy warmth made people angry, irritable, impatient. The streetlamps were already lit, even though it was still day. The farmers had been massing together. They had discovered von Gunten. They considered him to be the murderer; peddlers are always suspect. They assumed he was under arrest and surrounded the van. The peddler inside kept quiet. Trembling, he cowered among the stiffly upright policemen. The Mägendorfers moved more and more closely against the van, pressing their faces against the windows. The policemen didn't know what to do. The district attorney's limousine was also being blocked by the crowd. So was the coroner's car, which had come in from Zürich. So was the white ambulance containing the little corpse. The men stood there, threatening but silent; the women stood pressed against the walls of the houses. They too were silent. The children had climbed onto the rim of the village fountain. A dark rage without plan or direction had bonded the farmers into a mob. They wanted revenge, justice. Matthäi tried to fight his way through to the emergency squad, but this was not possible. The best thing would be to find the mayor. He asked for him. No one answered. All he could hear were a few quiet threats. The inspector reflected and went into the tavern. He wasn't mistaken, the mayor was sitting in the Stag. He was a small, heavy man with an unhealthy appearance. He was drinking one glass of Veltliner after another and peering through the low windows.*

"'What can I do, inspector?' he asked. 'The people are stubborn. They feel that the police aren't good enough, and that they have to take care of justice.' Then he sighed: 'Gritli was a good child. We loved her.'

"The mayor had tears in his eyes.

"'The peddler is innocent,' Matthäi said.

"'If he was, you wouldn't have arrested him.'

"'We haven't arrested him. We need him as a witness.'

"The mayor fixed a baleful look on Matthäi. 'You're just trying to talk your way out of it,' he said. 'We know what's going on.'

"'As mayor, your first obligation is to ensure our free passage.'

"The mayor emptied his glass of red wine. He drank without saying a word.

"'Well?' Matthäi asked impatiently.

"The mayor remained stubborn.

"'The peddler's going to get it,' he mumbled.

"The inspector made himself clear. 'There would be a fight before that happened, Mayor of Mägendorf.'

"'You want to fight for a sex fiend?'

"'Guilty or not, we'll have law and order here.'

"The mayor angrily walked back and forth in the low-ceilinged tavern room. Since no one was there to serve him, he poured wine for himself at the bar. He drank it so hastily that large dark stripes ran over his shirt. The crowd was still quiet outside. But when the driver tried to set the police car in motion, the ranks closed more tightly.

"Now the district attorney entered the room. He had squeezed through the tightly packed crowd with difficulty. His clothes were rumpled. The mayor

Veltliner: Wine from the region of Valtellina, which extends from northern Italy into southwestern Switzerland.

was alarmed. The arrival of a district attorney put him on edge; like any normal person, this profession filled him with queasy discomfort.

"'Mayor,' the district attorney said, 'the Mägendorfers seem to want to resort to a lynching. I don't see any other way out than to call for reinforcements. That should bring them back to reason.'

"'Let's try and talk to them once more,' Matthäi suggested.

"The district attorney tapped the mayor with his right index finger.

"'If you don't get these people to listen to us, and I mean on the spot, you'll be sorry.'

"Outside, the church bells started to ring up a storm. More and more men came from all directions to join the crowd. Even the fire squad marched in and took up fighting positions in support of their townsmen. The first shrill, isolated shouts rang out, imprecations against the police.

"The policemen readied themselves. They expected the crowd to attack any minute, but they were as helpless as the Mägendorfers. Their usual activities were a combination of routine patrols and individual assignments; here they were confronting something unknown. But the agitated farmers became suddenly quieter. The district attorney had stepped out of the Stag with the mayor and Matthäi. Using a stair in front of the tavern door as platform, holding on to an iron banister, the mayor addressed the mob: 'Citizens of Mägendorf! I ask you to listen to District Attorney Burkhard.'

"There was no visible reaction in the crowd. The farmers and workers stood again as before, silent, menacing, motionless under the sky, which was putting on the first shining lights of the evening; streetlamps swayed over the square like pale moons. The Mägendorfers were determined to seize the man they took to be the murderer. The police cars stood like large dark beasts, at bay in this human tide. Again and again they attempted to break loose, revved their motors to a howling pitch, then subsided with a discouraged grumble. No use. The whole village—the dark gables, the square, the crowd in its uncertainty and rage—staggered under the burden of the day's event, as if the child's murder had poisoned the world.

"'People,' the district attorney began, in a low, anxious voice, but every word was audible, 'Mägendorfers, we are shocked by this horrible crime. Gritli Moser has been murdered. We don't know who committed the crime . . .'

"The district attorney got no further than that.

"'Hand him over!'

"Fists were raised, whistles rang out.

"Matthäi watched the mob, fascinated.

"'Quick, Matthäi!' the district attorney commanded. 'Call for reinforcements!'

"'Von Gunten is the killer!' shouted a long, gaunt farmer with a sunburned face that hadn't been shaved in days. 'I saw him! There was nobody else in the dale!'

"He was the farmer who had been working in the field.

"Matthäi stepped forward.

"'People,' he said, 'I am Inspector Matthäi. We are prepared to hand over the peddler to you!'

"Immediately, a profound silence descended on the square.

"'Are you out of your mind?' the district attorney hissed at Matthäi.

"'It is an ancient custom in our country to put criminals on trial and to judge them if they are guilty, and set them free if they are innocent,' Matthäi continued. 'You have decided to make yourselves the court that will pass this judgment. Whether you have the right to do so is something we won't examine here. You have taken that right.'

"Matthäi spoke clearly and distinctly, and the farmers and workers listened attentively. Every word mattered to them. Because Matthäi took them seriously, they took him seriously too.

"'But there is something I must ask of you,' Matthäi continued, 'that I would ask of any other court: justice. For obviously we can only deliver the peddler to you if we are convinced that you want justice.'

"'That's what we want!' one man shouted.

"'Your court has to meet one condition if it is to be a just court. That condition is: there must be no injustice. You have to submit to this condition.'

"'Agreed!' cried a foreman from the brickyard.

"'Therefore you have to examine whether the charge of murder against von Gunten is just or unjust. How did the suspicion arise?'

"'The bastard has a record already,' a farmer screamed.

"'That makes von Gunten more suspect,' Matthäi explained, 'but it doesn't prove that he committed the murder.'

"'I saw him in the dale,' the farmer with the tanned, bristly face called out again.

"'Come up here,' the inspector said.

"The farmer hesitated.

"'Go, Heiri,' another man called, 'don't be a coward.'

"The farmer walked up the steps. He looked uncertain. The mayor and the district attorney had stepped back into the doorway of the Stag, so that Matthäi stood alone on the step with the farmer.

"'What do you want from me?' the farmer asked. 'My name's Heiri Benz.'

"The crowd stared intently at the two men. The policemen had hung their night sticks back on their belts. They, too, were watching the proceedings breathlessly. The boys of the village had climbed up the half-raised ladder of the fire truck.

"'You watched the peddler von Gunten in the dale, Herr Benz,' the inspector began. 'Was he alone in the dale?'

"'Alone.'

"'What kind of work were you doing, Herr Benz?'

"'I was planting potatoes with my family.'

"'How long had you been doing that?'

"'Since ten o'clock. I also had lunch with my family in the field,' the peasant said.

"'And you saw no one except the peddler?'

"'No one, I swear,' the peasant insisted.

"'Come on, Benz!' a worker called out. 'I passed your field at two!'

"Two other workers spoke up. They, too, had crossed the dale on bicycles.

"'And I drove my cart through the dale, you nitwit,' a peasant shouted. 'But you're always working like a dog, you miser, and you work your family so hard their backs are all crooked. A hundred naked women could pass you and you wouldn't look up.'

"Laughter.

"'So the peddler wasn't the only one in the dale,' Matthäi continued. 'But let's keep searching. There's a road to the city running parallel to the woods. Did anyone take that road?'

"'Fritz Gerber did,' someone called out.

"'I took the road,' a heavyset farmer admitted from his seat on the fire engine. 'With my cart.'

"'When?'

"'At two.'

"'There's a path leading from that road to the scene of the crime,' the inspector noted. 'Did you see anyone there, Gerber?'

"'No.'

"'How about a parked car?'

"The farmer hesitated. 'I think so,' he said uncertainly.

"'Are you sure?'

"'There was something there.'

"'Maybe a red Mercedes sports car?'

"'Could be.'

"'Or a gray Volkswagen?'

"'That's possible too.'

"'Your answers are pretty vague,' Matthäi said.

"'Well, I was half asleep on that cart,' the farmer admitted. 'It happens to everyone in this heat.'

"'In that case I'd like to point out to you that people shouldn't sleep while driving on a public road,' Matthäi reprimanded him.

"'The horses stay awake,' the farmer said.

"Everyone laughed.

"'Now you can see the difficulties you face as judges,' Matthäi said. 'The crime was by no means committed in solitude. It happened just fifty meters away from the family working in the field. If they had watched out, this awful thing could not have happened. But they were unconcerned, because they hadn't the slightest idea that such a crime was likely to happen. They didn't see the little girl or the others coming down the road. They noticed the peddler, that's all. Herr Gerber, too, was dozing on his cart. He can't give any significant testimony with the necessary exactness. That's where things stand. Does that prove the peddler guilty? You have to ask yourselves that question. One thing that speaks in his favor is that he alerted the police. I don't know how you intend to proceed as judges, but I want to tell you how we of the police would like to proceed.'

"The inspector paused. Once again he stood alone in front of the Mägendorfers. The embarrassed Benz had returned to the crowd.

"'Every suspect, without regard for his position, would be investigated with the greatest precision. Every conceivable clue would be followed up. Not only that, the police of other countries would be put on the case if that should prove necessary. You see, your court does not have many resources for finding out the truth. We have a huge apparatus at our disposal. Now decide what should be done.'

"Silence. The Mägendorfers had grown thoughtful.

"'Will you really hand him over to us?' the foreman asked.

"'Word of honor,' Matthäi replied. 'If you insist on it.'

"The Mägendorfers were undecided. The inspector's words had made an impression. The district attorney was nervous. The situation looked dangerous to him. But then he sighed with relief.

"'Take him with you,' a farmer had yelled.

"Silently, the Mägendorfers cleared a lane for the cars. The district attorney lit himself a Brissago.

"'That was risky, Matthäi,' he said. 'What if you'd been forced to keep your word?'

"'I knew that wouldn't happen,' the inspector calmly replied.

"'Let's hope you never make a promise you can't keep,' the district attorney said. He relit his cigar, said good-bye to the mayor, and went back to his car, which was now free to leave."

8

"Matthäi did not drive back with the district attorney. He climbed into the van with the peddler. The policemen made room for him. It was hot inside the big car. They didn't dare open the windows yet. Although the Mägendorfers had cleared a space, the farmers were still there. Von Gunten cowered behind the driver. Matthäi sat down next to him.

"'I am innocent,' von Gunten said softly.

"'Of course,' Matthäi said.

"'No one believes me,' von Gunten whispered. 'The police don't either.'

"The inspector shook his head. 'You're just imagining that.'

"The peddler was not reassured. 'You don't believe me either, sir.'

"The car started. The policemen sat in silence. Darkness had fallen outside. The streetlamps cast golden lights on the stony faces. Matthäi felt the distrust with which everyone regarded the peddler, the suspicion that had risen up against him. He felt sorry for him.

"'I believe you, von Gunten,' he said, and noticed that he wasn't quite convinced of that. 'I know you are innocent.'

"The first houses of the city were drawing near.

"'We're going to introduce you to the chief, von Gunten,' the inspector said. 'You're our most important witness.'

"'I understand,' the peddler murmured, and then he whispered again: 'You don't believe me either.'

"'Nonsense.'

"The peddler insisted. 'I know it,' he said very softly, almost inaudibly, and he stared into the red and green neon-lit advertisements that flashed through the windows of the steadily advancing car like eerie constellations."

9

"Those were the events that were reported to me at headquarters after I had come back from Bern on the seven-thirty express. It was the third infanticide of this kind. Two years earlier, a girl had been killed with a razor in Schwyz canton, and three years before that, another girl in St. Gallen canton. No trace of the perpetrator in either case. I sent for the peddler. The man was forty-eight, short, fleshy, unhealthy, probably a big talker and rather brazen, but now he was intimidated. His testimony was clear at first. He had lain down by the edge of the woods, taken off his shoes, put his peddler's basket beside him on the grass. He had intended to go to Mägendorf, where he hoped to sell his brushes, suspenders, razor blades, shoe laces, and so on, but on the way he had learned from the mail carrier that Wegmüller was on vacation and that Riesen was substituting for him. So he hesitated and lay down in the grass; he said young policemen are usually prone to fits of efficiency—'I know those guys,' he said. He started to doze off. He described the place: a little valley in the shadow of the woods, with a road running through it. Not far away, a family of farmers on their field, with their dog circling around them. Lunch at the Bear in Fehren had been hefty, he said, a 'Berner platter' and red wine. He liked rich food, he said, and he had the means to pay for it. 'I may look ragged, unshaved, and disheveled,' he said, 'but I'm not the way I look, I'm the sort of peddler who earns his living and has some money on the side.' He'd had lots of beer, too, he said, and later, in the grass, two bars of Lindt chocolate. Eventually the advancing storm with its gusts of warm wind had put him to sleep. But a little later he had the impression that a scream had awakened him, the high scream of a little girl, and staring out into the dale, dazed and still half asleep, he thought he saw the peasant family on the field lift their heads in surprise for a moment and then return to their stooped positions, while their dog continued to circle around them. It must have been some bird, he thought, maybe an owl, how would he know? That explanation reassured him. He dozed on, but then he noticed how deadly quiet the landscape had suddenly become and how the sky had darkened. Thereupon he slipped into his shoes and slung his basket over his back, feeling uneasy and apprehensive as he thought back on that mysterious bird cry. On account of this mood, he decided not to risk a run-in with Riesen and to forget about Mägendorf, which had always been an unprofitable hole anyway. He decided to go back to the city and took the forest path as a short cut to the train station, whereupon he bumped into the body of the murdered girl. Then he ran to the Stag in Mägendorf and informed Matthäi; he said nothing to the farmers, for fear of being suspected.

"That was his testimony. I had the man taken away, but not released. Not quite correct, I suppose, since the district attorney hadn't given orders for his arraignment, but we didn't have time to be dainty. His story sounded true to me, but it had to checked, and after all, von Gunten had a record. I was in a foul mood. This case gave me a bad feeling; everything had somehow gone wrong; I didn't know exactly how, but I felt it. I withdrew to my 'boutique,' as I called it, a smoke-filled little room next to my office. I ordered a bottle of Châteauneuf du Pape from a restaurant near the Sihl bridge, drank a few glasses. There was always an awful mess in that room, I won't deny it, a jumble of books and files. I did that on principle, because in my opinion it's everyone's duty in this well-ordered land to maintain little islands of chaos, even if only in secret. Then I asked to see the photographs. They were horrible. Then I studied the map. You couldn't have come up with a more perfidious choice of a location. It was theoretically impossible to determine whether the murderer came from Mägendorf, from one of the surrounding villages, or from the city, or whether he had come by foot or by train. Everything was possible.

"Matthäi came.

"'I'm sorry you had such a sad case to deal with on your last day,' I said to him.

"'It's our job, Chief.'

"'When I look at the pictures of this murder, I feel like tossing my job out the window,' I said, and put the pictures back in the envelope.

"I was annoyed and perhaps not fully in control of my feelings. Matthäi was my best inspector—you can see how I call him Inspector instead of Lieutenant, it's less correct, but friendlier, somehow. What am I saying? His departure went very much against my grain.

"He seemed to guess my thoughts.

"'I think you had best turn over the case to Henzi,' he said.

"I hesitated. I would have accepted his proposal immediately if we had been faced with something other than a sex murder. Any other crime is easier to deal with. All you have to do is consider the motives—lack of money, jealousy—and already you've got a circle of suspects and can start closing in from there. But in the case of a sex crime, this method leads nowhere. A guy could be on a business trip, he sees a girl or a boy, he gets out of his car—no witnesses, no observations, and in the evening he's back home, perhaps in Lausanne, perhaps in Basel, somewhere, and there we are, standing around without any clues. I didn't underestimate Henzi, he was a capable public servant, but he didn't have enough experience, in my opinion.

"Matthäi did not share my reservations.

"'He's been working under me for three years,' he said. 'I taught him everything he knows, and I can't imagine a better successor. He will do the job the way I would. And besides, I'll still be here tomorrow,' he added.

"I sent for Henzi and ordered him to take over the murder department with Officer Treuler. He was delighted; this was his first 'independent case.'

"'Thank Matthäi,' I muttered, and asked him what the mood in the rank and file was like. We were floundering, had nothing to go on, no results, and it was important that the men didn't sense our uncertainty.

"'They're convinced we already have the killer,' Henzi remarked.

"'The peddler?'

"'It's not a far-fetched suspicion. Von Gunten was already convicted of molesting a minor.'

"'A fourteen-year-old,' Matthäi interjected. 'That's a little different.'

"'We should cross-examine him,' Henzi suggested.

"'That can wait,' I decided. 'I don't believe the man had anything to do with the murder. He's just not very appealing, and that brings out a certain distrust in others. But that's a subjective response, gentlemen, not criminological evidence. It's not the sort of clue we want to rely on.'

"With that I dismissed the two men. My mood did not improve."

10

"We sent out all our available men. That night already and on the following day, we called garages to ask whether traces of blood had been observed in a car, and later we called the laundries. Then we checked all the alibis of everyone who had had a brush with certain paragraphs in the civil code. Near Mägendorf our people scoured the woods with dogs and even with a mine detector, hoping to find tracks and especially the murder weapon. They systematically searched every square meter, climbed into the gorge, searched the brook, collected everything they found there, combed through the woods all the way up to Fehren.

"I, too, took part in the search in Mägendorf, which wasn't my usual way. Matthäi, too, seemed on edge. It was a perfectly pleasant spring day, the air was light, no föhn, but our mood was dark. Henzi interrogated the farmers and factory workers in the Stag, and we set out to visit the school. We took a short cut and walked straight through a meadow with fruit trees. Some of them were already in full bloom. We could hear the sound of children singing in the schoolhouse: 'Then take my hands and lead me.' The school yard was empty. I knocked on the door of the room where the hymn was being sung, and we stepped in.

"The singers were girls and boys, six to eight years old. The three lowest grades. The teacher who was conducting dropped her hands and looked at us suspiciously. The children stopped singing.

"'Fräulein Krumm?'

"'Yes?'

"'Gritli Mosler's teacher?'

"'What do you want?'

"Fräulein Krumm was about forty, thin, with large unhappy eyes.

"I introduced myself and addressed the children.

"'Good morning, children!'

"They looked at me full of curiosity.

"'Good morning!'

"'That's a lovely song you were singing.'

"'We're practicing a hymn for Gritli's funeral,' the teacher explained.

"In the sandbox was a model of Robinson Crusoe's island. Children's drawings hung on the walls.

"'What sort of child was Gritli?' I asked hesitantly.

"'We all loved her,' the teacher said.

"'What about her intelligence?'

"'She was an extremely imaginative child.'

"Again I was hesitant.

"'I should ask the children a few questions.'

"'Go ahead.'

"I stepped in front of the class. Most of the girls still had braids and brightly colored aprons.

"'I'm sure you have heard what happened to Gritli Moser,' I said. 'I'm the police chief, which is like a captain in the army. It's my job to find the man who killed Gritli. I want to talk to you now as if you were grownups, not children. The man we are looking for is sick. All men who do such things are sick. And because they are sick, they try to lure children to a hiding place where they can hurt them, a forest or a cellar, all sorts of hidden places, and it happens very often. In our canton, we have more than two hundred cases a year. And sometimes it happens that such a man hurts a child so badly that it has to die, like Gritli. That's why we have to lock these men up. They're too dangerous to be allowed to walk around freely. Now, you may ask, why don't we lock them up before something bad happens to a child like Gritli? Because there is no way to recognize these sick people. Their sickness is inside, not outside.'

"The children listened breathlessly.

"'You must help me,' I continued. 'We must find the man who killed Gritli Moser, otherwise he will kill another little girl.'

"I was now standing in the midst of the children.

"'Did Gritli tell any of you that a stranger talked to her?'

"The children were silent.

"'Did you notice anything unusual about Gritli recently?'

"The children knew nothing.

"'Did Gritli have anything new recently that she didn't use to have?'

"The children didn't answer.

"'Who was Gritli's best friend?'

"'Me,' a girl whispered.

"She was a tiny little thing with brown hair and brown eyes.

"'What's your name?' I asked.

"'Ursula Fehlmann.'

"'So you were Gritli's friend, Ursula.'

"'We sat together.'

"The girl spoke so softly I had to bend down to hear her.

"'And you didn't notice anything either?'

"'No.'

"'Gritli didn't meet anyone?'

"'Someone, yes,' the girl replied.

"'Whom did she meet?'

"'Not a person,' the girl said.

"That answer startled me.

"'What do you mean by that, Ursula?'

"'She met a giant,' the girl said softly.

"'A giant?'

"'Yes,' the girl said.

"'You mean she met a big man?'

"'No, my father is a big man, but he's not a giant.'

"'How big was he?' I asked.

"'Like a mountain,' the girl replied, 'and black all over.'

"'And did this—giant—give Gritli a present?' I asked.

"'Yes,' said the girl.

"'What was it?'

"'Little hedgehogs.'

"'Hedgehogs? What do you mean by that, Ursula?' I asked, completely nonplussed.

"'The whole giant was full of little hedgehogs,' the girl said.

"'But that's nonsense, Ursula,' I objected. 'A giant doesn't have hedgehogs!'

"'He was a hedgehog giant.'

"The girl insisted on her story. I went back to the teacher's desk.

"'You are right,' I said. 'Gritli does seem to have had a lot of imagination, Fräulein Krumm.'

"'She was a poetic child,' the teacher replied, turning her sad eyes away from me. 'I should go back to practicing the hymn now. For the burial tomorrow. They're not singing well enough yet.'

"She gave the pitch.

"'Then take my hands and lead me,' the children sang out again."

11

"We went to the Stag, where we relieved Henzi and continued with the questioning of the Mägendorf population. Nothing came of that either, and in the evening we drove back to Zürich no better informed than we had been in the morning. Silently. I had smoked too much and had drunk the local red wine. You know those slightly dubious wines. Matthäi, too, sitting next to me in the back of the car, was in a dark, brooding mood. He didn't start talking until we were almost in Römerhof.

"'I don't believe the killer was a Mägendorfer,' he said. 'It must be the same perpetrator as the one in St. Gallen and Schwyz; those murders were all alike. I consider it probable that the man is operating from Zürich.'

"'Possibly,' I replied.

"'Most likely it's a man with a car, maybe a traveling salesman. That farmer, Gerber, saw a car parked in the woods.'

"'I personally questioned Gerber today,' I said. 'He admitted he was too sound asleep to notice anything.'

"We fell silent again.

"'I'm sorry I have to leave you in the middle of an unresolved case,' he began then, in a somewhat tentative tone of voice, 'but I have to honor my contract with the Jordanian government.'

"'You're flying tomorrow?' I asked.

"'At three p.m.,' he replied. 'Via Athens.'

"'I envy you, Matthäi,' I said, and I meant it. 'I, too, would rather be police chief for the Arabs than here in Zürich.'

"Then I dropped him off at the Hotel Urban, where he had been living for years, and went to the Kronenhalle, where I ate under the painting by Miró.* That's my regular table. I always sit there and eat 'from the trolley.'"

**Kronenhalle:* A well-known Zürich restaurant.

12

"But when I went back to headquarters around ten and passed by Matthäi's former office, I ran into Henzi in the hallway. He had already left Mägendorf at noon. I found that rather surprising, but since I had put him in charge of the case, it wasn't for me to criticize him. At least, that was my principle. Henzi was a native of Bern, ambitious, but popular among the men. He had married a girl from one of the most respectable families in Zürich, had switched from the Socialist party to the Liberals, and was well on his way to making a career for himself. I'm just mentioning this on the side; he's with the Independents now.

"'The bastard still won't confess,' he said.

"'Who?' I asked, very surprised, and stopped in my tracks. 'Who won't confess?'

"'Von Gunten.'

"I didn't know what to think. 'Are you drilling him nonstop?' I asked.

"'All afternoon,' Henzi said, 'and we'll go on through the night if we have to. Treuler's handling him now. I just stepped out for a breather.'

"'I want to see that,' I said—I was curious—and stepped into Matthäi's former office."

13

"The peddler had taken a seat on a backless office chair. Treuler had moved his chair over to Matthäi's old desk, which served him as a support for his left arm. His legs were crossed and his head was propped on his left hand. He was smoking a cigarette. Feller was taking down the testimony. Henzi and I stood in the doorway, invisible to the peddler, whose back was turned to us.

"'I didn't do it, Officer,' the peddler mumbled.

"'I didn't say you did. I only said you could have done it,' Treuler replied. 'We'll see whether I'm right or not. Let's start from the beginning. So you settled down comfortably by the edge of the woods?'

"'Yes, Officer, that's what I did.'

"'And you slept?'

"'That's right, Officer.'

"'Why, when you were on your way to Mägendorf?'

"'I was tired, Officer.'

"'Then why did you ask the mail carrier about the policeman in Mägendorf?'

"'To find out, Officer.'

"'To find out what?'

"'My permit hadn't been renewed. So I wanted to know how things stood policewise in Mägendorf.'

"'And how did things stand policewise?'

"'I found out that there was a substitute in Mägendorf. That scared me, Officer.'

"'I'm a substitute too,' the policeman dryly declared. 'Are you scared of me too?'

"'Yes, I am, Officer.'

"'And that's the reason why you didn't want to go to the village?'

"'Yes, Officer.'

"'That's not a bad version of the story,' Treuler said with, it seemed, genuine appreciation. 'But perhaps there is another version that would have the merit of being true.'

"'I have told the truth, Officer.'

"'Weren't you really trying to find out from the mailman whether there was a policeman nearby or not?'

"The peddler looked at Treuler suspiciously. 'What do you mean by that, Officer?'

"'Well,' Treuler replied in a leisurely, unhurried tone, 'you wanted assurance from the mailman that there were no police in that little valley, because you were waiting for the girl, I believe.'

"Horrified, the peddler stared at Treuler. 'Officer, I didn't know the girl,' he cried desperately, 'and even if I had, I couldn't have done it. I wasn't alone there. Those farmers were working on their field. I'm not a murderer. Please believe me!'

"'I do believe you,' Treuler placated him, 'but I have to check your story, you have to understand that. You said that after your nap you went into the woods in order to return to Zürich?'

"'There was a storm coming,' the peddler explained, 'so I wanted to take the short cut, Officer.'

"'And that's when you came across the body?'

"'Yes.'

"'And you never touched the body?'

"'That's right, Officer.'

"Treuler was silent. Even though I couldn't see the peddler's face, I could feel his fear. I felt sorry for him. And yet I was more and more convinced of his guilt, though perhaps only because I wanted badly to find the murderer.

"'We took away your clothes, von Gunten, and gave you other clothes. Can you guess why?'

"'I don't know, Officer.'

"'To make a benzidine test. Do you know what that is, a benzidine test?'

"'No, Officer, I don't,' the peddler weakly replied.

"'A chemical test to find traces of blood,' Treuler declared in an eerily good-natured manner. 'We found blood on your jacket, von Gunten. It's the girl's blood.'

"'Because . . . because I stumbled over the body, Officer,' von Gunten groaned. 'It was horrible.'

"He covered his face with his hands.

"'And of course you concealed this fact from us because you were afraid?'

"'Yes, sir, that's right.'

"'And now we're supposed to believe you again?'

"'I am not the murderer, Officer,' the peddler pleaded desperately, 'please believe me. Send for Herr Matthäi, he knows I'm telling the truth. Please.'

"'Lieutenant Matthäi has nothing to do with this case any longer,' Treuler replied. 'He's flying to Jordan tomorrow.'

"'To Jordan,' von Gunten whispered. 'I didn't know that.'

"He stared at the floor and fell silent. The room was profoundly still. The only sound was the ticking of the clock. Now and then, a car passed by on the street.

"Now Henzi took over. First he closed the window; then he sat down behind Matthäi's desk with a friendly, considerate air, except that he set the table lamp in such a way that its glare shone into the peddler's face.

"'Don't get upset, Herr von Gunten,' the lieutenant said very politely. 'We don't wish to hurt you in any way, we're just trying to find out the truth. That's why we're turning to you. You are the most important witness. You must help us.'

"'Yes, sir,' the peddler replied. He seemed to regain some courage.

"Henzi stuffed his pipe. 'What do you smoke, von Gunten?'

"'Cigarettes, sir.'

"'Give him one, Treuler.'

"The peddler shook his head. He stared at the floor. The light was glaring in his eyes.

"'Is the lamp bothering you?' Henzi asked amiably.

"'It's shining right in my eyes.'

"Henzi changed the position of the shade. 'Is that better?'

"'Better,' von Gunten quietly replied. His voice sounded grateful.

"'Tell me, von Gunten, what sort of objects do you sell? Dishrags?' Henzi began.

"'Yes, dishrags too,' the peddler said hesitantly. He didn't know what the question was leading to.

"'And what else?'

"'Shoelaces, sir. Toothbrushes. Toothpaste. Soap. Shaving cream.'

"'Razor blades?'

"'That too, sir.'

"'What brand?'

"'Gilette.'

"'Is that all, von Gunten?'

"'I think so, sir.'

"'Fine. But I think you forgot a few things,' Henzi said, and started fussing with his pipe. 'It won't draw,' he said, and then casually continued: 'Go ahead, von Gunten, just list the rest of your little things. We've examined your basket carefully.'

"The peddler was silent.

"'Well?'

"'Kitchen knives, sir,' the peddler said softly and sadly. Beads of sweat gleamed on the back of his neck. Henzi puffed out one cloud of smoke after the other, looking perfectly calm and relaxed, a friendly young gentleman, full of goodwill.

"'Go on, von Gunten, what else, besides kitchen knives?'

"'Straight razors.'

"'Why did you hesitate to admit that?'

"The peddler was silent. Henzi casually stretched out his hand as if to readjust the lamp shade. But he removed his hand when von Gunten flinched. The policeman stared fixedly at the peddler, who was smoking one cigarette after another. Henzi's pipe, too, was filling the room with smoke. The air was suffocating. I wanted to open the windows, but keeping them shut was part of the method.

"'The girl was killed with a straight razor,' Henzi said discreetly. It almost sounded like an incidental remark. Silence. The peddler sat slumped, lifeless, in his chair.

"'My dear Herr von Gunten,' Henzi continued, leaning back, 'let's talk man to man. We don't have to pretend to each other. I know that you committed the murder. But I also know that you are just as shocked by the deed as I am, as we all are. It just came over you. You suddenly became like an animal, you attacked the girl and killed her without wanting to, and you couldn't do otherwise. Something was stronger than you. And when you came back to your senses, von Gunten, you were horrified. You ran to Mägendorf because you wanted to turn yourself in, but then you lost courage. The courage to confess. You must find that courage again, von Gunten. And we want to help you find it.'

"Henzi fell silent. The peddler swayed slightly on his office chair. He seemed about to collapse.

"'I am your friend, von Gunten,' Henzi asserted. 'Take advantage of this opportunity.'

"'I'm tired,' the peddler moaned.

"'So are we all,' Henzi replied. 'Sergeant Treuler, bring us coffee and later some beer. For our guest, too. We play fair here, at the cantonal police.'

"'I am innocent, inspector,' the peddler whispered hoarsely. 'I am innocent.'

"The telephone rang; Henzi answered, listened attentively, hung up, smiled.

"'Tell me, von Gunten, what was it you had for lunch yesterday?' he asked, as if idly.

"'Berner platter.'

"'Very nice, and what else?'

"'Cheese for dessert.'

"'Emmentaler, Gruyère?'

"'Tilsiter and Gorgonzola,' von Gunten replied, wiping the sweat from his eyes.

"'Peddlers eat well,' Henzi replied. 'And that's all you ate?'

"'That's all.'

"'I would think that over carefully,' Henzi admonished him.

"'Chocolate,' Gunten remembered.

"'You see, there was something else,' Henzi said, giving him an encouraging nod. 'Where did you eat it?'

"'By the edge of the woods,' the peddler said, with a tired, mistrustful look at Henzi.

"The lieutenant switched off the desk lamp. Only the ceiling lamp was still weakly shining through the smoke-filled room.

"'I just received the coroner's report, von Gunten,' he declared in a regretful tone. 'They've done the autopsy on the girl. There was chocolate in her stomach.'

"Now I too was convinced of the peddler's guilt. His confession was only a question of time. I nodded at Henzi and left the room."

14

“I was not mistaken. The next morning, on a Saturday, Henzi called me at seven. The peddler had confessed. I was in the office at eight. Henzi was still in Matthäi’s former office. He was looking out of the open window and turned tiredly to greet me. Beer bottles on the floor, ashtrays overflowing. No one else was in the room.

“ ‘A detailed confession?’ I asked.

“ ‘He’ll give one,’ Henzi replied. ‘The main thing is, he confessed the murder.’

“ ‘I just hope you stayed within bounds,’ I grumbled. The interrogation had lasted over twenty hours. Of course that wasn’t legal; but in the police force, you can’t always play by the rules.

“ ‘We didn’t use any irregular methods, Chief,’ Henzi declared.

“I went into my ‘boutique’ and had the peddler brought in. He could hardly stand on his feet and had to be supported by the policeman who escorted him; but he didn’t sit down when I invited him to.

“ ‘Von Gunten,’ I said, with an inadvertently friendly note in my voice, ‘I hear you have confessed to the murder of little Gritli Moser.’

“ ‘I killed the girl,’ the peddler replied so softly that I could hardly hear him, staring at the floor. ‘Now leave me in peace.’

“ ‘Get some sleep, von Gunten,’ I said. ‘We’ll talk later.’

“He was led away. In the doorway he encountered Matthäi. The peddler stopped. He was breathing heavily. His mouth opened as though he wanted to say something, but no words came out. He just looked at Matthäi, who seemed faintly discomfited as he stepped aside to make room for the peddler.

“ ‘Go ahead,’ the policeman said, and led von Gunten away.

“Matthäi stepped into the ‘boutique,’ closed the door behind him. I lit myself a Bahianos.

“ ‘Well, Matthäi, what do you think?’

“ ‘The poor guy was questioned for over twenty hours?’

“ ‘That’s a method Henzi learned from you. You were always a tenacious interrogator,’ I replied. ‘But he handled his first independent case nicely, don’t you think?’

“Matthäi didn’t reply.

“I ordered two coffees and croissants.

“We both had a bad conscience. The hot coffee didn’t improve our mood.

“ ‘I have a feeling,’ Matthäi finally said, ‘that von Gunten will retract his confession.’

"'Possibly,' I replied morosely. 'Then we'll just have to work him over again.'

"'You think he's guilty?' he asked.

"'You don't?' I asked in return.

"Matthäi hesitated. 'Well, I suppose I do,' he replied without conviction.

"The morning flooded in through the window. A dull silver. From the Sihl quay came the noises of the street, and the slap of boots as soldiers marched out of their nearby barracks.

"Then Henzi appeared. He stepped in without knocking.

"'Von Gunten has hanged himself,' he reported."

15

"The cell was at the end of the long corridor. We ran over there. Two men were already busy with the peddler. He was lying on the floor. They had torn open his shirt. His hairy chest was completely immobile. His suspenders still dangled from the window.

"'It's no use,' one of the policemen said. 'The man is dead.'

"I relit my Bahianos, and Henzi lit himself a cigarette.

"'That settles the case of Gritli Moser,' I said as we wearily walked down the endless corridor back to my office. 'As for you, Matthäi—I wish you a pleasant flight to Jordan.'"

16

"But at two o'clock, when Feller drove to the Hotel Urban for the last time in order to take Matthäi to the airport—the luggage was already in the trunk of the car—the inspector said: 'We've still got some time, let's go by way of Mägendorf.' Feller obeyed and drove through the woods. They reached the village square as the funeral procession drew near, a long line of silent people. A large crowd from the surrounding villages, and from the city as well, had streamed in to attend the funeral. The newspapers had already reported von Gunten's death. There was a general sense of relief. Justice had won. Matthäi and Feller had left the car and were now standing among children opposite the church. The coffin lay on a bier on top of a cart drawn by two horses, and was surrounded by white roses. Behind the coffin followed the children of the village, two by two, each pair with a wreath, led by

Fräulein Krumm, the principal, and the pastor, the girls dressed in white. Then two black figures, the parents of Gritli Moser. The woman stopped and looked at the inspector. Her face was expressionless, her eyes were empty.

"'You kept your promise,' she said very quietly, but with such precision that the inspector heard it. 'I thank you.' Then she walked on. Unbowed, proud beside a broken husband who had suddenly become an old man.

"The inspector waited until the whole procession had passed by—the mayor, government officials, farmers, workers, housewives, daughters, all in their finest, most solemn dress. No one spoke a word. Nor was there any stirring among the spectators. All you could hear in the glow of the afternoon sun was the pealing of church bells, the rumbling sound of the cart wheels, and the countless footsteps on the hard pavement of the village street.

"'To the airport,' Matthäi said, and they got back into the car."

17

"After he had taken leave of Feller and walked through the passport control, he bought a *Neue Zürcher Zeitung* in the waiting room. There was a picture of von Gunten in it, with a caption describing him as the murderer of Gritli Moser, but there was also a picture of the inspector with an article about his appointment to serve the kingdom of Jordan—'a man at the pinnacle of his career.' But when he stepped onto the runway, his raincoat over his arm, he noticed that the terrace of the building was full of children. Several school classes had come to visit the airport—girls and boys in colorful summer clothes. There was much waving of little flags and handkerchiefs, whoops of amazement as the giant silver machines descended and took off. The inspector halted, then walked on toward the waiting Swissair plane. When he reached it, the other passengers were already aboard. The stewardess who had led the travelers to the plane held out her hand to receive Matthäi's ticket, but the inspector turned around once more. He looked at the crowd of children who were waving, happily and enviously, at the plane that was about to start.

"'Miss,' he said, 'I'm not flying,' and returned to the airport building, and walked under the terrace with its vast crowds of children, through the building and on toward the exit."

18

"I didn't receive Matthäi until Sunday morning—not in the 'boutique,' but in my official office with its quasi-official view of the Sihl quay. Pictures by Gubler, Morgenthaler, Hunziker on the walls, all reputable Zürich painters. I was in a bad mood on account of a disagreeable call from a man from the political department who insisted on speaking French and French only; the Jordanian embassy had lodged a protest, and the Federal Council had requested information that I was in no position to give, since I did not understand my former subordinate's action.

"'Sit down, Herr Matthäi,' I said. The formality of my manner must have saddened him. We sat down. I did not smoke, and gave no indication that I intended to. That unsettled him. 'The federal government,' I said, 'concluded a treaty with Jordan concerning the transfer of a police expert to their department. And you, Herr Matthäi, signed a contract with Jordan. Due to your failure to depart, these contractual agreements have been violated. Speaking as one lawyer to another, I don't need to make myself plainer.'

"'That's not necessary,' Matthäi said.

"'I therefore ask you to go to Jordan as quickly as possible,' I suggested.

"'I'm not going,' Matthäi retorted.

"'Why not?'

"'Gritli Moser's murderer hasn't been found yet.'

"'You think the peddler was innocent?'

"'Yes, I do.'

"'We have his confession.'

"'He must have lost his nerve. The long interrogation, the despair, the feeling of being abandoned. And I'm not without blame in this matter,' he quietly continued. 'The peddler turned to me and I didn't help him. I wanted to go to Jordan.'

"The situation was peculiar. Just the day before, we had conversed in a relaxed, collegial manner, and now we were sitting face to face, stiff and formal, both of us in our Sunday clothes.

"'I request that you put me back in charge of the case, Chief,' Matthäi said.

"'I can't do that,' I replied. 'Not under any circumstances; you are no longer with us, Herr Matthäi.'

"The inspector stared at me in surprise.

"'I'm dismissed?'

"'You left the cantonal police service when you agreed to accept a position in Jordan,' I quietly replied. 'That you have broken your contract is your affair. But if we employ you again it would mean that we condone your action. I'm sure you'll understand that this is impossible.'

"'I see,' Matthäi said. 'I understand.'

"'Unfortunately, there's nothing to be done about it,' I decided.

"For a while, we were both silent.

"'Driving through Mägendorf,' Matthäi said softly, 'on my way to the airport, there were children there.'

"'What do you mean by that?'

"'In the funeral procession, lots of children.'

"'That's not surprising,' I said.

"'And at the airport there were children too, whole classes from various schools.'

"'So?' I was mildly bewildered.

"'Assuming I'm right, assuming the murderer of Gritli Moser is still alive and free, wouldn't other children be in danger?' Matthäi asked.

"'Certainly,' I calmly replied.

"'If the possibility of such a danger exists,' Matthäi continued with urgent emphasis, 'it is the duty of the police to protect the children and prevent another crime.'

"'So that's why you didn't take that flight,' I asked slowly, 'to protect the children?'

"'That's why,' Matthäi replied.

"I said nothing for a while. I saw the whole thing more clearly now and was beginning to understand Matthäi.

"'The possibility that children are in danger has to be accepted,' I said then. 'If you are right, we can only hope that the real killer will reveal himself at some point or, at worst, leave some clues after his next crime. It may sound cynical, what I'm saying, but it isn't. It is just terrible. The power of the police has limits and has to have limits. Everything is possible, even the most improbable things are possible, but we have to go by what's probable. We can't say with certainty that von Gunten was guilty; guilt is never established with certainty; but we can say, even now, that von Gunten was probably guilty. If we don't want to invent an unknown perpetrator, the peddler is the only serious candidate. He had a previous conviction for sexual molestation, he carried around straight razors and chocolate, he had blood on his clothes, and besides, he plied his trade in Schwyz and St. Gallen, where the two other two murders happened. And in addition, he gave a confession and committed suicide. To doubt his guilt at this point is pure dilettantism. Common sense tells us that von Gunten was the murderer. Yes, common sense can be wrong, we're only human—but that's a risk we have to take.

And unfortunately, the killing of Gritli Moser is not the only crime we have to deal with. We just sent the emergency squad out to Schlieren. We've had four major burglaries just last night. From a purely technical point of view, we can't afford the luxury of reopening that case. We can only do what is possible, and we have done that. Children are always endangered. There are about two hundred cases of sexual assault on children each year. In our canton alone. We can educate the parents, warn the children, and we've done all that. But we can't weave the nets of police surveillance so tightly that no crimes ever happen. Crimes always happen, not because there aren't enough policemen, but because there are policemen at all. If *we* weren't needed, there wouldn't be any crimes. Let's keep that in mind. We have to do our duty, you're right about that, but our first duty is to stay within our limits, otherwise we'll end up with a police state.'

"I fell silent.

"Outside, the church bells started to ring.

"'I can understand that your personal—situation—has become difficult. You've fallen between two chairs,' I said politely by way of conclusion.

"'I thank you, sir,' Matthäi said. 'For the time being, I'll be looking into the case of Gritli Moser. Privately.'

"'I suggest you give up on this matter,' I said.

"'I have no intention of doing that,' he replied.

"I did not show my irritation.

"'May I request, in that case, that you not bother us with this any more,' I said, standing up.

"'As you wish,' Matthäi said. Whereupon we said good-bye without shaking hands."

19

"It was hard for Matthäi to walk past his former office and leave the empty police headquarters. The name plate on his door had already been changed, and when he ran into Feller, who sometimes hung around the office on Sundays, the man was embarrassed, and barely murmured a greeting. Matthäi felt like a ghost, but what bothered him more was that he no longer had an official car at his disposal. He was determined to return to Mägendorf as quickly as possible, but this resolve was not so easy to carry out. The village was nearby, but the trip by public transportation was complicated. He had to take the number eight streetcar and transfer to the bus. In the streetcar he met Treuler, who was on his way with his wife to visit her parents. Treuler stared at the inspector, obviously surprised, but asked no questions. And then other acquaintances crossed Matthäi's path, among them a professor of the technical college and an artist. He evaded their questions about his reasons for not leaving. It was an embarrassing situation each time, because his 'promotion' and departure had already been celebrated. He felt like a specter, like a man resurrected from the dead.

"The church bells had stopped ringing in Mägendorf. The farmers were standing on the village square in their Sunday clothes or going into the Stag in small groups. The air had become cooler. Mighty cloud banks were wandering in from the west. In the Moosbach dale, the boys were already playing soccer; there was nothing to suggest that a crime had been committed near the village. Everyone was cheerful. Somewhere people were singing 'Am Brunnen vor dem Tore.' In front of a large farmhouse with half-timbered walls and a mighty roof, children were playing hide-and-seek; a boy counted up to ten with a loud voice, and the others hurried away. Matthäi watched them.

"'Man,' a soft voice next to him said. He looked around.

"Between a pile of logs and a garden wall stood a little girl in a blue skirt. Brown eyes, brown hair. Ursula Fehlmann.

"'What do you want?' asked the inspector.

"'Stand in front of me,' the girl whispered, 'so they won't find me.'

"The inspector stood in front of the girl.

"'Ursula,' he said.

"'You mustn't talk so loud,' the girl whispered. 'They'll hear that you're talking to someone.'

"'Ursula,' the inspector whispered. 'I don't believe what you said about the giant.'

"'What don't you believe?'

"'That Gritli Moser met a giant who was as big as a mountain.'

"'But there is a giant.'

"'Have you seen one?'

"'No, but Gritli did. Be quiet now.'

"A red-haired boy with freckles came slinking around the corner of the house. He was the seeker. He stopped in front of the inspector, then tiptoed around the other side of the farmhouse. The girl giggled quietly.

"'He didn't notice me.'

"'Gritli told you a fairy tale,' the inspector whispered.

"'No,' said the girl, 'every week the giant waited for Gritli and gave her hedgehogs.'

"'Where?'

"'In the Rotkehler Dale,' Ursula answered. 'And she made a picture of him. So he has to exist. And the little hedgehogs too.'

"Matthäi was startled.

"'She drew the giant?'

"'The drawing's on the wall in the classroom,' the girl said. 'Step aside.' And already she had squeezed through the pile of logs and Matthäi, leapt toward the farmhouse and with a cry of triumph touched the doorjamb before the boy who came hurrying out from behind the house could tag her."

20

"The news I received on Monday morning was strange and disturbing. First the mayor of Mägendorf called to complain that Matthäi had broken into the schoolhouse and stolen a drawing by the murdered Gritli Moser; he said he wouldn't stand for any more prying by the cantonal police in his village, that the people needed to calm down after the horrors they'd been through; and he concluded with a not very politely phrased promise to personally chase Matthäi out of town with a dog if he ever showed up again. Then Henzi complained about an extremely awkward run-in with Matthäi, right in the middle of the Kronenhalle, where his former boss, already noticeably drunk, had guzzled a whole bottle of Réserve du Patron, followed that up with a cognac, and accused Henzi of 'judicial murder.' Henzi's wife, the former Fräulein Hottinger, had been revolted by the display. But that wasn't all. After the morning briefing, Feller told me that some character from the city police—of all the embarrassing witnesses—had reported to him that Matthäi had been sighted in various bars and was now staying at the Hotel Rex. I also learned that Matthäi had started smoking. Parisiennes. It was as if the man was transformed, metamorphosed, as if he had changed his character overnight. It all sounded like an impending nervous breakdown. I called a psychiatrist whose expert opinion we often consulted.

"To my surprise, the doctor said that Matthäi had made an appointment with him for the afternoon, whereupon I informed him of what had happened.

"Then I wrote a letter to the Jordanian embassy. I told them Matthäi was ill and asked them to grant him a two-month leave, after which, I said, the inspector would come to Amman."

21

"The private clinic was far out of town, near the village of Röthen. Matthäi had taken the train and had to walk a considerable stretch. He had been too impatient to wait for the bus. Now it passed him, and he gazed after it with irritation. He walked through several small hamlets. Children were playing by the roadside, and the farmers were working in the fields. The sky was overcast, silvery. The weather had turned cold again; the temperature was sliding toward the freezing point, fortunately without quite reaching it. Matthäi wandered along the edge of the hills and after passing Röthen turned into the path that led across the plain to the clinic. The first thing that met his eye was a yellow building with a tall chimney, some gloomy old factory, perhaps. But soon the scene became more appealing. The main building was still hidden by beeches and poplars, but he also noticed cedars and a huge sequoia. He entered the grounds of the clinic. The path forked. Matthäi followed a sign: *Office.* He saw a pond gleaming through the trees and shrubs, but perhaps it was only fog. Dead silence. Matthäi heard nothing but his steps crunching on the gravel. Later he heard a rasping sound. A young man was raking the path with slow and regular movements. Matthäi halted irresolutely. He looked about for a new sign; he didn't know where to turn.

"'Can you tell me where the office is?' he asked the young man. He received no answer. The fellow kept raking, in a steady, regular motion, like a machine, as if no one had spoken to him, as if he were alone. His face was expressionless, and since he appeared to be very strong—an impression that was accentuated by the lightness of his labor—the inspector felt vaguely threatened. As though the man might suddenly strike out at him with his rake. He walked on hesitantly and entered a courtyard. This led to a second, larger yard with colonnades on both sides, rather like a cloister; but the third side was bounded by a building that appeared to be a country house. Again there was no one in sight, though he could hear a plaintive voice, high and pleading, repeating a single word again and again, without cease. Again Matthäi stopped in his tracks. An unaccountable sadness befell him. Never had he felt so discouraged. He pressed down the latch of an old portal full of deep cracks and carved graffiti; but the door did not yield. The voice kept lamenting, over and over. Like a somnambulist he walked down the colonnade. There were red tulips in some of the stone vases, yellow ones in others. But now he heard steps; a tall, elderly, dignified gentleman crossed the yard, looking displeased and faintly surprised. A nurse was leading him.

"'Hello,' the inspector said. 'I'm looking for Dr. Locher.'

"'Do you have an appointment?' the nurse asked.

"'I'm expected.'

"'Just go to the salon,' the nurse said, pointing to a double door. 'Someone will come for you.' Then she walked on, arm in arm with the old man, who appeared to be in a daze, opened a door, and disappeared with him. The voice was still crying out its litany. Matthäi entered the salon. It was a large room with antique furniture, large easy chairs, and an enormous sofa. Above it hung the portrait of a man in a heavy golden frame, probably the founder of the hospital. There were other pictures on the walls, tropical landscapes. Matthäi thought he recognized the outskirts of Rio de Janeiro. He went to another double door. It opened out onto a terrace. Large cacti stood on the stone parapet. But he could no longer oversee the grounds; the fog had thickened. Vaguely, Matthäi could make out a wide expanse of land with some tomb or monument on it, and the menacing, shadowy form of a silver poplar. The inspector was getting impatient. He lit himself a cigarette; his new passion calmed him. He went back to the room, to the sofa. In front of it stood an old round table with old books: Gustav Bonnier, *Flore complète de France, Suisse, et Belgie*. He turned its pages; meticulous drawings of flowers, grasses—beautiful, no doubt, and calming, but they meant nothing to him. He smoked another cigarette. Finally a nurse came, a small energetic person with rimless glasses.

"'Herr Matthäi?' she asked.

"'Certainly.'

"The nurse looked around. 'Don't you have any luggage?'

"Matthäi shook his head. The question surprised him for a moment.

"'I just want to ask the doctor a few questions,' he replied.

"'Follow me, please,' the nurse said, and led him through a low door."

22

"He entered a small and, to his surprise, rather humbly furnished room. Nothing about it suggested a doctor's office. On the walls were pictures similar to the ones in the salon, as well as photographs of serious men with rimless glasses and beards, monstrous faces. Predecessors, no doubt. The desk and the chairs were loaded with books; only an old leather armchair remained unoccupied. The doctor, in a white coat, sat behind his files. He was small, lean, birdlike, and wore rimless glasses, like the nurse and the bearded men on the wall. Rimless glasses, it seemed, were obligatory here, and maybe, Matthäi thought, they were the insignia of some secret order, like the tonsure of monks.

"The nurse withdrew. Locher rose and greeted Matthäi.

" 'Welcome,' he said, looking faintly embarrassed, 'make yourself comfortable. It's a little shabby in here. We're a charitable institution, so we're always short of money.'

"Matthäi sat down in the leather armchair. It was so dark in the room that the doctor had to switch on the desk lamp.

" 'May I smoke?' Matthäi asked.

"Locher seemed taken aback. 'Certainly,' he said, observing Matthäi attentively over the top of his dusty glasses. 'But you didn't use to smoke, did you?'

" 'Never.'

"The doctor took out a sheet of paper and started to scribble on it—some kind of note, apparently. Matthäi waited.

" 'You were born on November 11, 1903, am I right?' the doctor asked, writing as he spoke.

" 'That's right.'

" 'Still in the Hotel Urban?'

" 'It's the Rex now.'

" 'Oh, it's the Rex now. In the Weinbergstrasse. So you're still living in hotel rooms, my dear Matthäi?'

" 'That seems to surprise you.'

"The doctor looked up from his papers.

" 'Look, man,' he said, 'you've been living in Zürich for thirty years now. Other people establish families, produce offspring, keep the future rolling. Do you have any private life at all? Excuse my asking so directly.'

" 'I understand,' Matthäi replied. He suddenly understood everything, including the nurse's question about his luggage. 'The chief gave you a report.'

"The doctor carefully put aside his fountain pen. 'What do you mean by that, sir?'

" 'You were given an assignment to examine me,' Matthäi said, crushing out his cigarette. 'Because in the eyes of the cantonal police I am not quite—normal.'

"The two men fell silent. Outside the fog hovered in front of the window, a dull, faceless twilight that crept into the little room full of books and files. The air was chilly and stale, mixed with the smell of some sort of medicine.

"Matthäi rose, went to the door and opened it. Outside stood two men in white smocks, their arms folded. Matthäi closed the door again.

" 'Two attendants. In case I cause problems.'

"Locher remained unperturbed.

" 'Listen, Matthäi,' he said. 'I want to talk to you as a doctor.'

" 'As you wish,' Matthäi replied and sat down.

"'I have been informed,' Locher said, picking up his fountain pen, 'that you have recently committed acts that can no longer be called normal. So a few frank words are in order. You have a tough job, Inspector, and I'm sure you have to be tough with the people who come into your sphere. You'll have to forgive me for speaking straight off the cuff: my profession has made a tough man of me, also, and a suspicious one, too. When I consider your behavior, I find it peculiar that you should all of a sudden drop a once-in-a-lifetime chance like this Jordanian assignment. Then this fixed idea of having to search for a murderer who has already been found. Next, this sudden decision to smoke, and this equally sudden compulsion to drink. Four double cognacs after a bottle of Réserve! I'm sorry, my friend, that looks an awful lot like an abrupt personality change, like the symptoms of an incipient illness. It would be only to your advantage to have yourself thoroughly examined so we can clarify the picture, clinically as well as psychologically. Which is why I suggest that you spend a few days in Röthen.'

"The doctor fell silent and returned to scribbling on his sheet of paper.

"'Do you have occasional fevers?'

"'No.'

"'Speech problems?'

"'No.'

"'Voices?'

"'Nonsense.'

"'Sudden perspiration?'

"Matthäi shook his head. The deepening dusk and the doctor's talk were making him impatient. He groped for his cigarettes, found them at last, and as he took the burning match the doctor handed him, he noticed his fingers were trembling. With anger. The situation was too silly, he should have foreseen this and chosen another psychiatrist. But he had a special affection for this doctor, who was consulted at headquarters more as an act of patronage than for his expertise; he trusted him because other doctors spoke disparagingly of his abilities, because he was considered a fantast and an eccentric.

"'Agitated,' the doctor noted, almost with pleasure. 'Shall I call the nurse? If you'd like your room...'

"'Absolutely not,' Matthäi replied. 'Do you have any cognac?'

"'I'll give you a sedative,' the doctor suggested, standing up.

"'I don't need a sedative, I need cognac,' the inspector roughly replied.

"The doctor must have pushed a hidden button, for an attendant appeared in the doorway.

"'Bring a bottle of cognac and two glasses from my apartment,' the doctor ordered, rubbing his hands, presumably because they were cold. 'And hop to it.'

"The attendant left.

"'Really, Matthäi,' the doctor said, 'it's urgent that you sign yourself in. Unless you want a major physical and mental breakdown. We do want to avoid that, don't we? And I think we can, with a little finesse.'

"Matthäi did not reply. The doctor, too, remained silent. The telephone rang. Locher took the receiver and said: 'I can't talk now.' The darkness outside was almost black now. Evening had fallen with extraordinary suddenness.

"'Shall I switch on the ceiling light?' the doctor asked, merely for the sake of saying something.

"'No.'

"Matthäi had regained his composure. When the attendant came with the cognac, he poured himself a glass, drank it, filled it again.

"'Locher,' he said, 'why don't you drop this idiotic man-to-man and hop-to-it talk. Look: you are a doctor. Have you in your profession ever been confronted with a case you couldn't solve?'

"The doctor looked at Matthäi with astonishment. The question unsettled him. He couldn't imagine why it was being asked.

"'Most of my cases can't be solved,' he finally honestly replied, although at the same time he sensed that he should never have given this reply to a patient.

"'That doesn't surprise me, given the nature of your profession,' Matthäi replied with an irony that saddened the doctor.

"'Did you come here only to ask me this question?'

"'Among other things.'

"'For God's sake, what is your problem?' the doctor asked, feeling acutely uneasy. 'You used to be reason personified.'

"'I don't know,' Matthäi replied uncertainly—'the murdered girl.'

"'Gritli Moser?'

"'I can't stop thinking about that little girl.'

"'You can't get her off your mind?'

"'Do you have children?' Matthäi asked.

"'I'm not married either,' the doctor replied softly, feeling again ill at ease.

"'So you're not either.' Matthäi brooded silently. 'You see, Locher,' he explained then, 'I looked and took in what I saw, I didn't turn my eyes away like my successor, Henzi, Mr. Normal. There was a mutilated corpse lying on the leaves. Only the face was untouched, a child's face. I stared at her red skirt in the bushes, at the pieces of pretzel strewn around. But that wasn't the terrible thing.'

"Matthäi fell silent again. As if frightened. He was a man who never spoke of himself and was now forced to do so, because only this little birdlike doctor with the ridiculous eyeglasses could help him, and in exchange for that help, he had to confide in him.

"'You rightly wondered,' he finally continued, 'that I'm still living in a hotel. I didn't want to confront the world. I wanted to deal with it skillfully, I'd almost say mechanically, but I didn't want to suffer with it. I wanted to be superior to it, not lose my head, control it all like a technician. I looked at the murdered girl, and that was bearable; but when I stood in front of her parents, I suddenly couldn't bear it any longer, I had to get away from that godforsaken house, and so I promised by my eternal soul that I would find the murderer—just to turn my back on those suffering people, and I never gave a moment's thought to the fact that I couldn't keep this promise because I was going to Jordan. And then I allowed the old indifference to rise up in me, Locher. That was so horrible. I didn't fight for the peddler. I allowed everything to happen. I became my old impersonal self, "Nobody Home," as some people call me. I slipped back into the calm, the superiority, the formality, the inhumanity, until I saw the children at the airport.'

"The doctor shoved away his notes.

"'I turned back,' Matthäi said. 'You know the rest.'

"'And now?' the doctor asked.

"'And now I am here. Because I don't believe the peddler was guilty, and now I have to keep my promise.'

"The doctor rose and went to the window.

"The attendant came in, followed by his colleague.

"'Go to the ward,' said the doctor. 'I don't need you any more.'

"Matthäi poured himself another cognac, laughed.

"'Good, this Rémy Martin.'

"The doctor still stood by the window, staring out.

"'How can I assist you?' he asked dejectedly. 'I'm not a criminologist.' Then he turned to face Matthäi. 'Why do you believe the peddler was innocent?' he asked.

"'Here.'

"Matthäi put a piece of paper on the table and carefully unfolded it. It was a child's drawing. At the lower right, in clumsy script, was the name 'Gritli Moser.' It was a crayon drawing of a man. He was big, bigger than the pines that surrounded him like strange stalks of grass. The face was drawn in a child's manner—two dots, a comma, a dash, and a circle. He was wearing a black hat and black clothes, and from his right hand, which was a round disk with five lines, several small disks with many little hair lines, like stars, fell onto a tiny little girl who was even smaller than the pines. On the very top of the page—in the sky, actually—stood a black automobile, and next to it a peculiar animal with strange horns.

"'This drawing was made by Gritli Moser,' Matthäi explained. 'I got it from the schoolroom.'

"'What is it supposed to represent?' the doctor asked, staring at the drawing in bewilderment.

"'The hedgehog giant.'

"'What's that supposed to mean?'

"'Gritli said a giant had given her little hedgehogs in the woods. The drawing is about that encounter,' Matthäi explained, pointing to the little disks.

"'And now you believe . . .'

"'It's not unreasonable to suppose that Gritli Moser's hedgehog giant was her murderer, and that this is a picture of him.'

"'Nonsense, Matthäi,' the doctor retorted with irritation. 'This drawing is a pure product of the imagination. I'm sorry to disappoint you.'

"'Probably it is,' Matthäi replied. 'But the car is too well observed for that. I'd even say it's an old American model. And the giant has a lifelike quality, too.'

"'But there's no such thing as a giant,' the doctor said impatiently. 'Don't tell me any fairy tales.'

"'A tall, massively built man could look like a giant to a little girl.'

"The doctor looked at Matthäi with surprise.

"'You think the murderer was a big man?'

"'That's just a vague assumption,' the inspector said evasively. 'If I'm right, the murderer is driving around in an old black American car.'

"Locher pushed his glasses up to his forehead. He took the drawing into his hand and examined it closely.

"'So what am I supposed to do?' he asked uncertainly.

"'Assuming that all I knew about the murderer was that this drawing represented him,' Matthäi said, 'then this would be my only clue. But in that case I would be in the position of a layman confronted with an X-ray. I wouldn't know how to interpret the drawing.'

"The doctor shook his head.

"'There is nothing we can infer about the murderer from this drawing,' he replied, putting the sheet of paper back on the table. 'At best, it's possible to make a judgment about the girl who drew it. She must have been intelligent, bright, and cheerful. You see, children don't just draw what they see, they also draw what they feel about what they see. Fantasy and reality are mixed together. So some things on this drawing are real—the big man, the car, the girl; other elements seem to be in some kind of code—the hedgehogs, the animal with the large horns. These are all riddles. And the solution to these riddles—well, I'm afraid Gritli took the answer with her to the grave. I am a doctor, not a spiritualist medium. Pack up your drawing. It makes no sense to go on thinking about it.'

"'You're afraid.'

"'I hate to waste my time.'

"'What you call a waste of time may just be an old method,' Matthäi declared. 'You're a scientist, you know what a working hypothesis is. My assumption that this is a picture of the murderer is a working hypothesis. I am asking you to make believe with me. Let's see what comes of it.'

"Locher looked at the inspector thoughtfully for a moment and then examined the drawing once more.

"'What did the peddler look like?' he asked.

"'Unimpressive.'

"'Intelligent?'

"'Not stupid, but lazy.'

"'Wasn't he convicted of a sex crime once?'

"'He got involved with a fourteen-year-old.'

"'Relations with other females?'

"'Well, as a peddler, yes. He was something of a wolf, chased skirts all over the region,' Matthäi replied.

"Now Locher was interested. Something didn't sound right.

"'Too bad this Don Juan confessed and hanged himself,' he grumbled, 'because he doesn't sound like a sex maniac at all. But let's adopt your hypothesis. The hedgehog giant on the drawing—I could imagine him being a sex fiend. He's big and massive. People who commit these kinds of crimes against children are usually primitive, more or less feebleminded, imbeciles, mental defectives, as we say in the profession, robust, tending toward violence, and hampered by impotence or inferiority complexes toward women.'

"He stopped and peered more closely at the drawing.

"'Strange,' he said.

"'What?'

"'The date underneath the drawing.'

"'Well?'

"'More than a week before the murder. Gritli Moser must have met her murderer before, presuming your hypothesis is correct, Matthäi. It seems peculiar, though, that she would tell the story of her encounter in the form of a fairy tale.'

"'It's a child's way.'

"Locher shook his head. 'People don't do things without any reason, and that goes for children as well,' he said. 'Probably the big black man forbade Gritli to tell anyone about their mysterious meeting. And the poor girl obeyed him and told a fairy tale instead of the truth. Otherwise someone would have become suspicious and she might have been saved. I have to say that in this case the story becomes downright fiendish. Was the girl raped?' he suddenly asked.

"'No,' Matthäi replied.

"'And the same thing happened to the girls who were killed years ago in St. Gallen and Schwyz?'

"'Exactly.'

"'Also with a straight razor?'

"'The same.'

"Now the doctor also poured himself a cognac.

"'This is not a sex crime,' he said. 'It's an act of revenge. These murders were supposed to wreak some kind of revenge against women—regardless now of who did it, the peddler or poor Gritli's hedgehog giant.'

"'But a little girl is not a woman.'

"Locher continued undeterred. 'No, but to a sick man, she could replace a woman,' he said. 'Since the murderer is afraid of approaching women, he plucks up his courage when he sees a little girl. He kills her in place of the woman. That's why he will always approach the same sort of girl. Look at your records, you'll find that the victims are all alike. Don't forget that this is a primitive person. It doesn't matter whether the feeblemindedness is inborn or due to an illness—such people have no control over their instinctual drives. Their ability to resist their impulses is abnormally weak. It takes very little—an altered metabolism, a few degenerated cells—and such a person becomes a beast.'

"'And the reason for his revenge?'

"The doctor considered the question. 'Maybe sexual conflicts,' he explained. 'Perhaps the man was oppressed or exploited by a woman. Maybe his wife was rich and he was poor. Maybe she occupied a higher social position than he did.'

"'None of that applies to the peddler,' Matthäi said.

"The doctor shrugged.

"'Then something else will apply to him. Every kind of absurdity is possible between a man and a woman.'

"'Is there a continuing danger of new murders?' Matthäi asked. 'Assuming the murderer isn't the peddler.'

"'When did the murder in St. Gallen happen?'

"'Five years ago.'

"'And the one in Schwyz?'

"'Two years ago.'

"'The intervals are getting smaller,' the doctor noted. 'That could indicate an accelerated psychological deterioration. Apparently the sick man's resistance to affects is weakening, and he would probably commit another murder in a few months, perhaps even weeks, if an opportunity presents itself.'

"'And how would he behave in the meantime?'

"'At first he would feel something like relief,' the doctor said a little hesitantly, 'but soon new feelings of hatred would start building up, and a new need for revenge would make itself felt. He would start loitering in places where there are children—in front of schools, for instance, or in public squares. Then he would gradually move on to driving about in his car in search of a new victim. And once he found the girl, he would befriend her, until eventually it would happen again.'

"Locher fell silent.

"Matthäi took the drawing, folded it, and put it in his breast pocket. Then he stared at the window. It was night outside.

"'Wish me luck in finding the hedgehog giant, Locher,' he said.

"Startled, the doctor looked at him. Suddenly he understood: 'This hedgehog giant is more than just a working hypothesis for you, isn't it, Matthäi?'

"Matthäi admitted it. 'For me, he is real. I don't doubt for a moment that he is the murderer.'

"'But everything I told you was mere speculation,' the doctor explained. 'I was just toying around with ideas, there's no scientific value in that!' The doctor was irritated. How could he have allowed himself to be tricked like that? He had realized too late what Matthäi's intentions were.

"'I was just pointing out one of a thousand other possibilities,' he continued. 'With this method, you could prove anyone guilty of killing that child. Why not? Any absurdity can be imagined and somehow logically supported, and you know that very well. I went along with your hypothesis just to be friendly and helpful, but please, be man enough now to look at reality without hypothetical ifs and maybes, and have the courage to accept the factors that plainly prove the peddler's guilt. That drawing is just a product of a child's imagination, or else it corresponds to her meeting with some person other than the murderer, someone who couldn't possibly be the murderer.'

"'You can safely leave it to me,' Matthäi replied as he finished his glass of cognac, 'to determine the degree of probability that can be assigned to your deductions.'

"The doctor did not reply immediately. He was sitting behind his old desk again, surrounded by his books and files, worn out by the daily effort to keep afloat the antiquated and poorly equipped hospital whose director he was. 'Matthäi,' he said finally, by way of conclusion, and his voice sounded weary and bitter, 'you are trying to do the impossible. I don't want to get carried away, but this is what I feel: you have your will, your ambition, your pride, you don't like to give up. I understand that, I'm the same way. But when you set out to find a murderer who in all probability doesn't exist, and whom you would not find even if he did exist, because there are too many of his kind who just by chance haven't killed anyone—then things start getting ticklish. You're choosing madness as a method, and it takes courage to do that, no question; extreme positions impress people generally these days; but if this method does not lead to its goal, I'm afraid that in the end, all you'll be left with is the madness.'

"'Farewell, Doctor Locher,' Matthäi said."

23

"This conversation was reported to me by Locher. As usual, his Gothic script, minute and precise as if engraved, was almost illegible. I sent for Henzi. He, too, had a hard time reading the document. His comment was that the doctor himself was calling Matthäi's hypotheses untenable. I wasn't so sure; it seemed to me that the doctor just lacked the courage to stand by his own convictions. It seemed I had doubts after all. The peddler had left us no detailed confession, just a general statement concerning his guilt in the crime. Nor had the murder weapon been found. None of the razors found in the basket showed traces of blood. Naturally, this did not clear von Gunten; our original grounds for suspecting him still weighed heavily against him. But I felt uneasy. And Matthäi's actions made more sense to me than I cared to admit. To the district attorney's annoyance I went so far as to have the woods near Mägendorf searched again. Nothing came of that either. The murder weapon was not to be found. Apparently it still lay at the bottom of the gorge, as Henzi believed.

"'Well,' he said, pulling one of his awful perfumed cigarettes from the box, 'that's all we can do about this case for the moment. Either Matthäi is crazy or we are. We have to make up our minds.'

"I pointed to the photographs I had ordered. The three murdered girls resembled each other.

"'That does seem to point to the hedgehog giant,' I said.

"'Why?' Henzi replied cold-bloodedly. 'All it means is that the girls were the peddler's type.' Then he laughed. 'I just wonder what Matthäi's up to. I wouldn't like to be inside his skin.'

"'Don't underestimate him,' I muttered. 'He's capable of anything.'

"'Is he capable of finding a murderer who doesn't exist, Chief?'

"'Perhaps,' I replied, putting the three photographs back among my files. 'All I know is that Matthäi doesn't give up.'

"As it turned out, I was right. The first report came from the chief of the municipal police. After a meeting. We had just managed to settle one of those frequent cases of conflicting jurisdiction, when, in the middle of saying good-bye, this bumbler brings up Matthäi. I guess to annoy me. He said Matthäi had been seen at the zoo a number of times, and that he had bought himself an old Nash at a garage on Escher-Wyss square. Shortly after that, I received another report. This one completely confused me. It was in the Kronenhalle, on a Saturday evening, I remember it exactly. The place was full—everyone who was anybody in Zürich and up for a meal was there. Waitresses scurrying around, the food on the trolley steaming, and the rumble of traffic sounding in from the street. I was sitting under the Miró, all unsuspecting, eating my liver dumpling soup, when the sales representative of one of the big fuel companies came up to me, said hello, and sat down at my table, just like that. He was slightly drunk and in high spirits, ordered a marc and told me, laughing, that my former first lieutenant had changed his profession; that he had taken over a gas station in Graubünden, near Chur—a business the company had been intending to close down, because it had never brought in any profits.

"At first I refused to believe him. The story seemed incongruous, silly, absurd.

"The salesman insisted that what he was saying was true. He praised Matthäi for the way he was handling the job. The gas station was flourishing. Matthäi had many customers. Almost exclusively people he had had dealings with in the past, although in a different capacity. The news must have spread that 'Nobody Home' had been promoted to gas station attendant, so all the 'old-timers' were pulling up and zooming in on whatever wheels they had, from the most antediluvian jalopies to brand-new Mercedes. Matthäi's gas station, he said, had become a mecca for the underworld of all eastern Switzerland. Sales were soaring. The company had just installed a second pump for premium gasoline. They had also offered to build him a modern house instead of the shack he was living in. He turned down the offer with thanks, refused to hire an assistant, too. Often there'd be long lines of cars and motorcycles, but everyone was patient. Apparently the honor of having a former first lieutenant of the cantonal police fill your tank was worth a lot.

"I didn't know what to say. The salesman said good-bye, and when the trolley came steaming along I had lost my appetite, just nibbled a little, ordered beer. Later Henzi came, as usual, together with his former Fräulein Hottinger, in a foul mood because the results of some referendum didn't accord with his wishes. I told him the news. He said: 'That proves it, I always predicted Matthäi would go out of his mind, and now it's happened.' He was suddenly in the best of spirits, ate two steaks, while his wife kept talking about some show where she knew some of the actors.

"Thereupon, a few days later, the phone rang. During a meeting. With the municipal police again, naturally. It was the director of an orphanage. The old lady told me in great excitement that Matthäi had appeared at her door, solemnly dressed in black, evidently in order to impress her with his seriousness, and asked her whether he might adopt a certain girl from among her 'charges' as he put it. It had to be that particular child; he had always wanted a child, he said, and now that he was running a garage in Graubünden by himself, he was in a position to raise one. Naturally she had rejected his request, politely referring to the statutes of the orphanage; but my former first lieutenant made such a peculiar impression on her that she considered it her duty to inform me. Then she hung up. Now this was indeed a strange state of affairs. I drew on my Bahianos, completely bewildered. But what made Matthäi's behavior impossible for us at headquarters was an entirely different affair. We had arrested a highly questionable character, an unofficial pimp and official hairdresser who had ensconced himself in a handsome villa by the edge of a lake in a village favored by many poets. At any rate, traffic in that direction got pretty lively—taxis and private cars, everything. Now, no sooner had I started questioning him than he popped out with an answer I didn't expect, beaming with pleasure as he rubbed the news under our noses. Matthäi, he said, was shacking up with the Heller girl in his gas station. I immediately called the police in Chur; the story was true. I was dumbstruck. The hairdresser sat gloating in front of my desk, chewing his gum. I gave up. I gave orders to let the old sinner go in the name of God. He had outplayed us.

"The situation was alarming. I was perplexed, Henzi was outraged, the district attorney disgusted, and when the federal councilor heard about it, he used the word 'disgrace.' Lotte Heller had once been our guest at headquarters. A colleague of hers—a lady well known all over the city—had been murdered. We suspected that Heller knew more than she was telling us, and eventually she was summarily expelled from the canton of Zürich, even though, apart from her profession, there was no evidence against her. But there are always people in the administration who have their prejudices and feel the need to act on them.

"I decided it was time to intervene, to drive out there. I sensed that Matthäi's actions had something to do with Gritli Moser, but I couldn't imagine how. My ignorance infuriated me; it also made me unsure of myself. But aside from that, I felt a detective's curiosity. As a law and order man, I wanted to know what was going on."

24

"I set out in my car, alone. It was a Sunday again, and it seems to me, looking back, that many of the crucial moments in this story took place on Sunday. Bells ringing all around, the whole country seemed to be clanging and chiming; and somewhere in Schwyz canton I got held up by a procession. One car after another on the road, and on the radio, one sermon after the other. Later, the sounds of guns banging, whistling, clattering, booming away at shooting booths in every village. A monstrous, senseless commotion—the whole of eastern Switzerland seemed to be on the move; somewhere an automobile race was being held, and droves of cars came rolling in from the west, whole families, clans. It was the noisiest day of rest I had ever experienced. By the time I reached the gas station—the one you saw earlier—I was exhausted. I looked around. The place wasn't as run-down as it is today. It looked friendly, everything clean, geraniums in the windows. There was no tavern yet. The whole thing had a solid, reliable, lower-middle-class look about it. There were various objects, too, alongside the street, that indicated the presence of a child: a swing, a large doll-house on a bench, a doll's carriage, a rocking horse. Matthäi himself was just attending a customer who hastily took off in his Volkswagen as I stepped out of my Opel. Next to Matthäi stood a seven- or eight-year-old girl with a doll tucked under one arm. She had blond braids and was wearing a red skirt. She looked familiar, but I couldn't remember where I had seen her; she didn't resemble Lotte Heller at all.

"'That was Red Meier, wasn't it?' I said, pointing at the Volkswagen as it moved away. 'He was let out a year ago.'

"'Regular?' Matthäi asked indifferently. He was dressed in a pair of blue mechanic's overalls.

"'Super.'

"Matthäi filled the tank, washed the windshield.

"'Fourteen thirty.'

"I gave him fifteen. 'Keep the change,' I said. Then I blushed. 'Excuse me, Matthäi, that just slipped out.'

"'That's all right,' he said, slipping the bills in his pocket. 'I'm used to it.'

"Embarrassed, I looked at the little girl again.

"'Sweet little thing,' I said.

"Matthäi opened the door of my car. 'I wish you a pleasant ride.'

"'Come on now,' I muttered. 'I'm really here to talk to you. For Pete's sake, Matthäi, what's all this about?'

"'I promised not to bother you any more with the Gritli Moser case, Chief. Now I must ask you to do the same for me,' he replied and turned his back on me.

"'Matthäi,' I said, 'let's stop fooling around.'

"He said nothing. I heard some loud popping and whistling nearby, probably a shooting booth. It was shortly before eleven. I watched him attend to an Alfa Romeo.

"'He served three and a half years,' I said as the car took off. 'Can't we go inside? All this shooting makes me nervous. I don't like it.'

"He led me into the house. In the hallway we encountered Lotte Heller. She was coming up from the cellar with potatoes. She was still an attractive woman, and as a policeman I was a little embarrassed—a bad conscience. She gave us a quizzical look, a little disturbed, it seemed, but then she gave me a friendly greeting. She made an altogether good impression.

"'Is that her child?' I asked, after she had left the kitchen.

"Matthäi nodded.

"'Where did you find her?' I asked. 'Lotte Heller, I mean.'

"'Near here. She was working in the brickyard.'

"'And why is she here?'

"'Well,' Matthäi said, 'someone has to do the housework.'

"I shook my head.

"'I need to talk to you in private,' I said.

"'Annemarie, go to the kitchen,' Matthäi said.

"The little girl went out.

"The room was poorly furnished but clean. We sat down at a table by the window. A loud series of bangs erupted outside, one salvo after the other.

"'Matthäi,' I said, 'what's this all about?'

"'Very simple, Chief,' my former first lieutenant replied. 'I'm fishing.'

"'What do you mean?'

"'Detective work, Chief.'

"Annoyed, I lit a Bahianos.

"'I'm not a beginner, but I still don't understand.'

"'Let me have one of those.'

"'Help yourself,' I said, shoving the box over to his side.

"Matthäi put a bottle of kirsch on the table. We were sitting in the sun; the window was half open. Outside, the geraniums, mild June weather, and banging guns. Whenever a car stopped—which happened more rarely now, since it was around noon—Lotte Heller worked the pump.

"'You got Locher's report on our conversation,' Matthäi said after carefully lighting the Bahianos.

"'That didn't get us anywhere.'

"'But it did me.'

"'How so?' I asked.

"'The child's drawing reflects the truth.'

"'I see. And what are those hedgehogs?'

"'That I don't know yet,' Matthäi replied, 'but I do know what that beast with the strange horns was supposed to be.'

"'Well?'

"'It's an ibex,' Matthäi said, with a leisurely draw at his cigar. Then he puffed the smoke into the room.

"'That's why you went to the zoo?'

"'For days,' he replied. 'I also had children draw ibexes. Their versions are like Gritli Moser's.' I understood.

"'The ibex is the emblem of Graubünden,' I said. 'It's the old heraldic beast of this region.'

"Matthäi nodded. 'It appears on the license plates issued here. It caught Gritli's eye.'

"The solution was simple.

"'We should have thought of that right away,' I muttered.

"Matthäi watched the ash growing on his cigar, the faint curling of the smoke.

"'The mistake we all made,' he said, 'you, Henzi, and I, was to presume that the killer was operating from Zürich. He's actually from Graubünden. I checked the scenes of the other murders—they're all on the route from Graubünden to Zürich.'

"I reflected on that.

"'Matthäi, there may be something to that,' I had to admit.

"'There's more.'

"'Well?'

"'I met some anglers.'

"'Anglers?'

"'Well, boys who were fishing.'

"I didn't know what to make of that.

"'You see,' he said, 'the first thing I did after my discovery was drive out to the Graubünden canton. Logical. But I soon realized how pointless it was. Graubünden canton is so big—how are you going to find a man about whom you only know that he's big and that he drives a black American car? More than seven thousand square kilometers, more than a hundred and thirty thousand people scattered around countless valleys—it's simply impossible. So there I was, at the end of my tether. One cold day, then, I was sitting by the Inn river, in the Engadine, watching some boys by the water. I was about to turn away when I noticed that the boys had become aware of me. They looked frightened, as if put on the spot. One of them was holding a homemade fishing rod. "Go ahead and fish," I said. The boys eyed me suspiciously. "Are you from the police?" one of them asked, a redhead with freckles. "Is that what I look like?" I replied. "Well, I don't know," the boy said. "I'm not from the police," I said. Then I watched them toss the bait into the water. There were five boys, all absorbed in their activity. "No bites," the freckled boy finally said with a resigned shrug, and climbed up the bank to where I was sitting. "Do you have a cigarette?" he asked. "At your age?" I replied with amusement. "You look as if you'd give me one," the boy declared. "In that case, I'll have to," I replied and held out my pack of Parisiennes. "Thanks," the boy said, "I've got my own matches." Then he blew out the smoke through his nose. "That sure feels good after a total bust with the fishes," he said grandly. "Well," I said, "your friends aren't giving up as quickly as you are. I bet they'll catch something soon." "They won't," the boy said. "Or at most a grayling." "I guess you'd prefer a pike," I teased him. "I'm not interested in pike," the boy replied. "Trout. But that's a question of money." "How come?" I wondered. "When I was a kid, I used to catch them by hand," I said. He shook his head disparagingly. "Those were young ones. Just try and catch a full-grown trout with your hand. They're predators, just like pike, but they're harder to catch. And you need a permit, and," the boy added, "a permit costs money." "Well, you and your buddies are doing it without money," I laughed. "But the disadvantage," the boy said, "is that we can't get to the right places. That's where the guys with the permits are." "What's a right place?" I asked. "You obviously don't know a thing about fishing," the boy noted. "I'll admit that," I said. We had both sat down on the embankment. "You think you just drop your bait any old place and wait?" he said. I thought about that and finally said: "What's wrong with that?" "Typical beginner," the freckled boy said, blowing smoke out through his nose again: "To get anywhere with fishing, you have to have two things before anything else: the right place and the right bait." I listened attentively. "Let's say you want to catch a trout," the boy continued, "and I mean one that's full-grown. Remember, the trout needs prey, he's a predator. The first thing you have to figure out is where the fish likes to be. Naturally that would be a place that's protected against the current, but near a strong current, because that's where a lot of animals come swimming along. So I'm talking about a place downstream behind a big rock, or even better, downstream behind a bridgehead. And unfortunately those places are taken by the guys with the permits." "The stream has to be blocked," I said. "You got it," he said proudly. "And the bait?" I asked. "Well, that depends on what you're after, a predator or a grayling, or a burbot, which are vegetarians," he replied. "A burbot you can catch with a cherry. But for a predator like a trout or a bass you need something that's alive. A mosquito, a worm, or a little fish." "Something alive," I said thoughtfully, and stood up. "Here," I said, giving the boy the whole packet of Parisiennes. "You've earned these. Now I know how to catch my fish. First I have to find the place and then the bait."'

"Matthäi fell silent. For a long time I said nothing, drank my schnapps, stared out into the lovely late spring day, listened to the rifles popping, and relit my cigar.

"'Matthäi,' I finally said, 'now I understand what you meant by fishing before. This gas station is the propitious spot, and the road is the river, right?'

"Matthäi's face was impassive.

"'Whoever wants to get from Graubünden to Zürich has to use this road,' he quietly replied. 'Otherwise he has to go out of his way through the Oberalp Pass,' he quietly replied.

"'And the girl is the bait,' I said. My own words frightened me.

"'Her name is Annemarie,' Matthäi replied.

"'And now I know who she reminds me of,' I said. 'Gritli Moser.'

"We both fell silent again. It had grown warmer outside, the mountains were shimmering in the haze, and the shooting continued. There must have been some kind of contest.

"'Isn't that a rather devilish scheme?' I finally asked hesitantly.

"'Possibly,' he said.

"'You intend to wait here until the murderer comes along, sees Annemarie, and falls into the trap you laid out for him?'

"'The murderer *has* to come by here,' he replied.

"I thought about that. 'All right,' I said then, 'let's assume you're right. This murderer exists. Obviously, it's possible. Anything's possible in our profession. But don't you think your method is too risky?'

"'There is no other way,' he declared, and threw his cigarette butt out the window. 'I know nothing about the murderer. I can't search for him. So I had to search for his next victim, a girl, and use the child as a bait.'

"'Fine,' I said, 'but you adapted this method from the art of fishing. Those are two different worlds. You can't keep a little girl near the road as bait all the time. She has to go school, she'll want to get away from your damn highway.'

"'Summer vacation's coming,' Matthäi replied stubbornly.

"I shook my head.

"'I'm afraid you're getting obsessed,' I replied. 'You can't just stay here waiting for something you think should happen that may not happen at all. It's true, the murderer probably does pass through here, but that doesn't mean he'll reach for your bait—to use your comparison. And then you'll be waiting and waiting. . .'

"'Anglers have to wait too,' Matthäi replied stubbornly.

"I gazed out the window, watched the woman filling up Oberholzer's tank. Six years in Regensdorf jail altogether.

"'Does Lotte Heller know why you're here, Matthäi?'

"'No,' he replied. 'I told the woman I needed a housekeeper.'

"I felt very uneasy. The man impressed me: his method was certainly unusual, in fact there was something magnificent about it. I suddenly admired him, and wished him success, if only to humiliate that awful Henzi; but still I considered his undertaking to be hopeless, the risk too great, the chances of winning too small.

"'Matthäi,' I said, trying to reason with him, 'there's still time for you to assume that post in Jordan. If you don't, the guys in Bern will send Schafroth.'

"'Let him go.'

"I still wouldn't give up. 'Wouldn't you like to join us again?'

"'No.'

"'We would have you work in the office for the time being, at your old salary.'

"'Don't feel like it.'

"'You could switch to the municipal police. Consider that just from a financial point of view.'

"'At this point I'm almost making more money here than I did working for the state,' Matthäi replied. 'But here's a new customer, and Fräulein Heller is probably busy preparing her roast.'

"He stood up and walked out. Then another customer arrived. Pretty-boy Leo. When Matthäi was done with him, I was already in my car.

"'Matthäi,' I said, as I took leave, 'you're really beyond help.'

"'That's the way it is,' he replied, and signaled to me that the road was clear. Next to him stood the girl in the red skirt, and in the doorway stood her mother, wearing an apron, looking extremely mistrustful. I drove home."

25

"So he waited. Relentlessly, obstinately, passionately. He served his customers, did his work—pumping gas, checking the fluids, washing the windshields, always the same mechanical operations. The child was always next to him or playing with her doll's house when she came back from school, skipping, hopping, watching the goings-on with wondering eyes, talking to herself; or else she would sit on the swing in her red skirt, singing, pigtails flying. He waited and waited. The cars drove past him, cars of all colors and price ranges, old cars, new cars. He waited. He wrote down the license plates of vehicles from Graubünden canton, looked up their owners in the records, called the town registrars to inquire about them. Lotte Heller worked in a small factory near the village up toward the mountains, and would come back in the evening down the little incline behind the house, with her shopping bag and a mesh bag full of bread. Sometimes at night they heard footsteps around the house, and low whistles, but she never opened the door. Summer came, a shimmering, heavy, endless heat that frequently discharged its tension with thunderous downpours, and finally the schools closed and the long summer vacation began. Matthäi's chance had come. Annemarie was now always with him by the edge of the road and thus always visible to everyone who drove past. He waited and waited. He played with the girl, told her fairy tales, the whole Brothers Grimm, all of Hans Christian Andersen, *A Thousand and One Nights*, invented some stories of his own, desperately did everything he could to attach the girl to himself and to the road where he needed her to be. The child stayed, content with the stories and fairy tales. The drivers regarded the pair with wonderment or were touched by this idyll of father and child, gave the girl chocolate, chatted with her, while Matthäi lurked and watched, waiting for his moment. Was that big heavy man the killer? His car had Graubünden plates. Or that long tall thin one who was talking to the girl now? Owner of a candy store in Disentis, as Matthäi had found out long ago. 'Want your oil checked? At your service. I'll fill your tank. That'll be twenty-three ten. Have a pleasant trip, sir.'

"He waited and waited. Annemarie loved him, was content with him; he had only one thing in mind, the arrival of the killer. Nothing existed for him but this faith, this hope that he would arrive. He longed for no other fulfillment. He imagined how the fellow would look when he came—powerful, clumsy, childish, full of sweetness and bloodthirstiness; how he would keep coming back with a friendly grin, in his Sunday suit, a retired railroad man or customs official; how she would gradually respond to his luring advances, how Matthäi would follow them to the woods behind the station, treading softly, ducking low, and how at the crucial moment he would leap out, how they would fight then, man to man, a wild, bloody battle, then the deciding blow, the final resolution, the murderer lying before him, beaten to a pulp, whining, confessing. But then he had to admit to himself that all this was impossible because he was much too obviously keeping an eye on the child; that he would have to allow her more freedom if he wanted to see results. Then he allowed Annemarie to wander away from the street but secretly followed her, leaving the gas station unattended, while the cars angrily honked their horns. The girl would skip off to the village, a half hour away, and play with other children near the farm houses or by the edge of the woods, but always she would come back after a short time. She was used to solitude, and she was shy. And the other children avoided her. Then Matthäi changed his tactics again. He invented new games, new fairy tales, to draw Annemarie back to his side. He waited and waited. With unswerving, unbending resolution. And without explanation. For Annemarie's mother had long since noticed how much attention he gave the child. She had never believed that Matthäi had hired her as a housekeeper out of pure kindness. She sensed that he had some ulterior motive, but she felt safe with him, perhaps for the first time in her life, and so she gave it no further thought. Perhaps she was hopeful of further developments; who knows what goes on in a poor woman's mind. In any case, after a while she ascribed Matthäi's interest in her daughter to genuine affection, although from time to time her old distrust and her old realism returned.

"'Herr Matthäi,' she said once, 'this may be none of my business, but did the chief of the cantonal police come here on my account?'

"'Of course not,' Matthäi said. 'Why would he?'

"'People in the village are talking about us.'

"'Who cares?'

"'Herr Matthäi,' she began again, 'is your being here in some way connected with Annemarie?'

"'Nonsense,' he laughed. 'I just love her, that's all, Fräulein Heller.'

"'You're good to me and Annemarie,' she replied. 'I wish I knew why.'

"Then the summer vacation was over; fall came, the landscape turned red and yellow, everything sharply contoured as if under a huge magnifying glass. Matthäi felt as if a great opportunity had slipped away; but still he waited. Tenaciously, stubbornly. The child walked to school. Matthäi usually went to meet her at noon and in the evening, driving her home in his car. His plan was looking more and more senseless, impossible; his chances of winning were getting slimmer and slimmer, and he knew it. He wondered how often the murderer had driven past his gas station. Maybe every day. Certainly once a week. And yet nothing had happened. He was still groping in the dark, without a clue, without even a hunch; just drivers coming and going, occasionally chatting with the girl in a harmless, casual manner, nothing to pin a suspicion on. Which one of them was the one he was looking for? Was he one of them at all? Perhaps the reason he wasn't succeeding was that too many people knew about his old profession; here was an obstacle he hadn't reckoned with, though it couldn't have been avoided. But still he persevered, waited and waited. He could no longer turn back; waiting was the only method, even though it was wearing him out, even though there were times when he was ready to pack his bags and go anywhere, even to Jordan, just to get away, and other times when he was afraid of losing his mind. Then there were hours, days, when he became indifferent, apathetic, cynical, and let things take their course, sat on the bench in front of the gas station drinking one schnapps after the other, staring into space, littering the ground with cigarette butts. Then he would pull himself together again. But more and more he would sink into apathy, dozing away the days and weeks in a perpetual round of cruel, absurd waiting. But one day as he sat there, unshaven, weary, grease-stained, he was startled by the realization that Annemarie wasn't back from school yet. He set out to meet her, on foot. The unpaved, dusty country road rose slightly behind the house, then dipped down, crossing a barren plain and leading through the woods, from the edge of which one could see the village from afar, old houses huddled around a church, blue smoke over the chimneys. From here one could also see the whole stretch of road down which Annemarie had to come, but there was no sign of her. Matthäi turned back to the forest, suddenly tense and wide awake; low fir trees, bushes, rustling red and brown leaves on the ground, a woodpecker hammering somewhere in the background where larger fir trees blocked the sky except for slanting shafts of light that broke through their branches. Matthäi left the road, forced his way through briers and undergrowth; branches struck him in the face. He reached a clearing, turned around in surprise; he had never seen it before. From the opposite side, a wide path cut through the woods and ended in the clearing; evidently this was a road used to cart refuse out of the village, for a mountain of ashes was heaped up in the clearing. Along its edges lay tin cans, rusty wires, and similar junk, a regular garbage collection sloping down to a little brook that was bubbling through the middle of the clearing. Only then did Matthäi notice the girl. She was sitting by the bank of the silvery stream with her doll and her school bag beside her.

"'Annemarie,' Matthäi called.

"'I'm coming,' the girl replied, but she remained sitting where she was.

"Matthäi carefully climbed across the garbage and finally stood next to the child.

"'What are you doing here?' he asked.

"'Waiting.'

"'For what?'

"'For the wizard.'

"The girl had nothing but fairy tales in her head; one day she'd be waiting for an elf, the next it would be a wizard; it was like a mockery of his own waiting. Despair overcame him again, the realization of the futility of his actions, and the paralyzing knowledge that he had no choice but to go on waiting because there was nothing left for him to do but wait, wait, and wait.

"'Come on,' he said listlessly, took the child by the hand and walked back with her through the forest, sat down on the bench again, stared into space; twilight came, night; he had become indifferent to everything; he sat there, smoking, waiting and waiting, mechanically, with fixed determination, relentlessly. Once in a while he unconsciously whispered, as if to summon his enemy out of the night: 'Come already, come, come, come.' Then he sat motionless in the white moonlight, and suddenly fell asleep. He woke up stiff and frozen at dawn and crawled into bed.

"But the next morning, Annemarie came home from school earlier than usual. Matthäi had just risen from his bench to pick her up when she came walking along with her school bag on her back, singing quietly and hopping from one foot to another. The doll dangled from her hand, its little feet dragging on the ground.

"'Homework?' Matthäi asked.

"Annemarie shook her head and continued her song, 'Maria sat upon a stone,' and went into the house. He let her go; he was too desperate, too hopeless, too tired to tell new fairy tales, to draw her to himself with new games.

"But when Lotte Heller came home, she asked: 'Was Annemarie a good girl?'

"'What do you mean? She was in school all day,' Matthäi replied.

"Lotte looked at him with surprise. 'In school? But she had the day off, teachers' conference, or something.'

"Matthäi sat up straight. The disappointment of the past few weeks was suddenly dispelled. He sensed that the fulfillment of his hopes, of his mad expectation, was near. He controlled himself with difficulty. He asked no more questions of Lotte Heller. Nor did he probe the little girl. But the next afternoon he drove to the village and left the car in a side street. He wanted to watch the girl secretly. It was almost four. From the windows came singing, then screams and shouts, the children poured out of the building, boys were fighting and throwing stones, girls were walking arm in arm; but Annemarie was not among them. The teacher came out and subjected Matthäi to a moment of stern, stiff scrutiny before informing him that Annemarie had not been in school. 'Is she ill?' she asked. 'She was already absent day before yesterday, in the afternoon, and she brought no excuse.' Matthäi replied that the child was indeed sick, said good-bye and drove like a madman back to the woods. He rushed through the underbrush to the clearing, found nothing. Exhausted, breathing heavily, scratched and bleeding from the thorns, he returned to the car and drove home. But before he reached the gas station, he saw the girl skipping along the edge of the road. He stopped.

"'Get in, Annemarie,' he said pleasantly, after opening the door.

"Matthäi held out his hand to help the girl climb into the car. Then he noticed that her hand was sticky. And when he looked at his own hand, he saw traces of chocolate.

"'Who gave you the chocolate?' he asked.

"'A girl,' Annemarie replied.

"'In school?'

"Annemarie nodded. Matthäi said nothing. He pulled up in front of the house. Annemarie climbed out and sat down on the bench in front of the gas station. Matthäi watched her unobtrusively. The child put something in her mouth and started chewing. Slowly he went up to the girl.

"'Show me,' he said, and carefully opened the slightly clenched little hand, revealing a prickly brown ball, partly bitten off. A chocolate truffle.

"'Do you have any more?' Matthäi asked.

"The girl shook her head.

"The inspector reached into the pocket of Annemarie's skirt, pulled out her handkerchief, unfolded it, and found two more truffles in it.

"Annemarie was silent.

"Nor did the inspector speak. An enormous happiness had swept over him. He sat down on the bench next to the child.

"'Annemarie,' he finally asked, and his voice was quivering as he carefully held the prickly chocolate balls in his hand, 'did the wizard give them to you?'

"The girl said nothing.

"'Did he forbid you to tell anyone about you and him?' he asked.

"No answer.

"'You're right not to tell,' Matthäi said kindly. 'He's a nice wizard. You can go see him again tomorrow.'

"All at once the girl beamed as if in tremendous joy, embraced Matthäi, ardent with happiness, and ran up to her room."

26

"The next morning at eight—I had just arrived at my office—Matthäi laid the chocolate truffles on my desk. He was so excited that he hardly greeted me. He was wearing his former suit, but without a tie, and he was unshaven. He took a cigar from the box I offered him and started puffing away.

"'What's this chocolate about?' I asked, dumbfounded.

"'The hedgehogs,' Matthäi replied.

"I looked at him, still baffled, turning the little chocolate balls between my fingers. 'What do you mean?'

"'Very simple,' he explained. 'The murderer gave Gritli Moser chocolate truffles, and she turned them into hedgehogs. That's the secret of her drawing.'

"I laughed: 'How do you want to prove that?'

"'Well, the same thing has happened to Annemarie,' Matthäi replied, and gave me a complete report.

"I was instantly convinced. I summoned Henzi, Feller, and four policemen, gave them instructions, and informed the district attorney. Then we drove off. The gas station was orphaned. Lotte Heller had taken the child to school and gone on to the factory.

"'Does her mother know what happened?' I asked.

"Matthäi shook his head. 'She has no idea.'

"We went to the clearing. We searched it carefully but found nothing. Then we split up. It was close to noon; Matthäi returned to the gas station in order not to arouse suspicion. It was a favorable day, a Thursday, when the child had no school in the afternoon. Gritli Moser had also been killed on a Thursday—the realization shot through me. It was a bright autumn day, hot, dry, dense with the humming of bees, wasps, and other insects, and with the screeching of birds. From far away, you could hear the echoing blows of an ax. At two o'clock, the bells of the village rang out sharply, and then the girl appeared, broke through the shrubbery across from me, effortlessly hopping, jumping, ran to the little brook with her doll, sat down and gazed steadily toward the woods, attentive, tense, with shining eyes. She seemed to be waiting for someone, but she couldn't see us. We were hidden behind trees and shrubs. Then Matthäi cautiously came back and leaned against a tree trunk near me, as I was doing.

"'I think he'll be here within a half hour,' he whispered.

"I nodded.

"Everything had been meticulously organized. We were keeping an eye on the access road from the highway to the woods. We even had wireless equipment. We were all armed with revolvers. The child was sitting by the brook, almost motionless, full of wondrous, anxious, marveling expectation, the garbage heap at her back. At times she was in the sun, then in the shadow of one of the great dark firs; not a sound could be heard other than the humming of the insects and the trilling of the birds. Now and then the girl sang to herself with her thin voice: 'Maria sat upon a stone,' over and over, always the same words and verses; and heaped around the stone on which she sat were rusty tin cans, metal barrels, and wires; and sometimes abrupt gusts of wind came blowing across the clearing, rousing the leaves till they danced and rustled, until it was quiet again. We waited. Nothing was left of the world but this forest, enchanted by the colors of autumn, and the little girl with her red skirt in the clearing. We waited for the murderer, determined, avid for justice, retribution, punishment. The half hour had long since passed—two whole hours, in fact. We waited and waited; we ourselves now were waiting as Matthäi had waited for weeks and months. Five o'clock came; the first shadows, then the twilight, the dimming, the dulling of all the radiant colors. The girl skipped away. Not one of us said a word, not even Henzi.

"'We'll come back tomorrow,' I decided. 'We'll spend the night in Chur. At the Hotel Steinbock.'

"And so we waited on Friday and Saturday also. I really ought to have used the Graubünden police. But this was our affair. I didn't want to have to explain anything, didn't want any interference. The district attorney called on Thursday evening already, objected, protested, threatened, dismissed the whole thing as nonsense, flew into a rage, insisted we come back to Zürich. I remained firm, told him we would stay regardless of his objections, and compromised only to the degree of sending one officer back. We waited and waited. At this point we were no longer concerned about the child or the murderer; we were concerned with Matthäi. The man had to be proven right, had to reach his goal, otherwise there would be a disaster; we all felt it, even Henzi, who said he was convinced now. On Friday night he declared firmly that the unknown killer would be coming on Saturday; after all, he said, we had incontrovertible evidence—the hedgehogs—and besides, why would the girl keep coming back to sit in the same spot again and again? She had to be waiting for someone. And so we stood in our hiding places, behind our trees and shrubs, motionless, for hours, staring at the child, at the tin cans, at the tangles of wire, at the mountain of ashes, smoking in silence, never exchanging a word, listening to her perpetual singsong: 'Maria sat upon a stone.' On Sunday the situation was more difficult. The woods were suddenly full of hikers, on account of the long spell of sunny weather. Some sort of mixed chorus with a conductor broke into the clearing, noisy, sweating, shirt-sleeved, took up formal positions, and burst into mighty praise of the joys of wandering and the eternal glory of God on high. Thank heavens we weren't in uniform behind our shrubs. Later a couple came along and behaved rather shamelessly despite the presence of the child, who simply sat there, waiting with incomprehensible patience, in rapt anticipation, for the fourth afternoon in a row. We waited and waited. By now the three policemen had gone back with their wireless equipment. There were only four of us left: Henzi, Feller, Matthäi, and I. Strictly speaking, our stakeout was no longer justifiable, but Henzi pointed out that Sunday wasn't a safe day for the killer, so the day didn't really count. He was right about that, so we waited on Monday too. On Tuesday, Henzi went back to headquarters—somebody had to take care of business—but he was still convinced that we were on the verge of finding the murderer. We waited and waited and waited, constantly hiding, each of us independent of the others now, since we were too few to organize a cordon. Feller had posted himself near the forest path behind a bush where he lay in the shadow, dozing in the summery heat of that placid autumn and suddenly snoring so intensely that the wind wafted the sounds across the clearing; this happened on Wednesday. Matthäi was standing on the side of the clearing nearest to the gas station, and I was watching the scene from the opposite side. And so we waited in ambush for the murderer, the hedgehog giant, with the child between us, and were startled each time a car passed on the main road. Every day the girl came to the clearing by the little brook, singing 'Maria sat upon a stone,' stubbornly, mindlessly. It was incomprehensible; we began to detest her, hate her. Sometimes, of course, she took a long time to come. She would wander about near the village with her doll, staying clear of the houses, since she was playing hooky. That caused us some problems. I had to talk to her teacher in private to prevent the school from looking into the matter. I cautiously hinted at our reason for being there, identified myself, and obtained her somewhat hesitant consent. Then the child circled the forest. We followed her with our binoculars, but she always returned to the clearing—except for Thursday, when, to our despair, she stayed near the gas station. Whether we wanted to or not, we had to hope for Friday. Now I had to make a decision; Matthäi had long since fallen silent, and was standing behind his tree the next day when the girl came skipping along again with her red dress and her doll and sat down as she had on previous days. The glorious fall weather was still strong, radiant, bursting with presence before the long sleep of decay; but the district attorney couldn't take another half hour of this. He came at five p.m., in the car with Henzi, showed up completely unexpectedly, came over to me, who had been standing there since one o'clock, constantly shifting from foot to foot, staring at that child, red in the face, I'm sure, with anger at that ceaseless little voice: 'Maria sat upon a stone.' I was so sick of that song, and sick of that child, too, that horrible little gap-toothed mouth, those skimpy braids, that shoddy little red dress; she looked disgusting to me, vulgar, idiotic—I could have strangled her, killed her, torn her limb from limb, just to shut her up and put an end to that awful song. It was maddening. Everything was still as it always had been, viciously stupid, senseless, except that the dry leaves were piling up higher and the gusts of wind were perhaps more frequent, and the sun was pouring more gold than ever onto that vile heap of garbage. It was simply unbearable. And then all of a sudden the district attorney started running—it was like a release, a liberation—broke through the undergrowth, straight toward the child, ignoring the fact that his shoes were sinking into the ashes, and as we saw him stomping up to the girl, we, too, burst out of our cover; it was time to put an end to this.

"'Who are you waiting for?' the district attorney screamed at the girl, who sat on her stone, clutching her doll and staring up at him in terror.

"'Who are you waiting for, damn it, you answer me now!'

"And now we had all reached the girl and surrounded her, and she stared at us in utter horror and incomprehension.

"'Annemarie,' I said, and my voice was quivering with rage, 'a week ago someone gave you some chocolate. I'm sure you remember, little pieces of chocolate that looked like hedgehogs. Did a man in black clothes give them to you?'

"The girl did not answer. She just looked at me with tears in her eyes.

"Now Matthäi kneeled down before her and put his arms around her little shoulders. 'Look, Annemarie,' he explained, 'you must tell us who gave you the chocolate. You must tell us exactly what that man looked like. I once knew a girl,' he continued urgently, for now everything was at stake, 'a girl who wore a red dress just like yours, and a big man in black clothes gave her chocolate. The same spiky little chocolate balls you ate. And then the girl went to the woods with that big man, and the big man killed the girl with a knife.'

"He fell silent. The girl still did not reply. She stared at him with wide open eyes.

"'Annemarie,' Matthäi screamed, 'you must tell me the truth! All I want is to keep you from getting hurt!'

"'You're lying,' the girl quietly replied. 'You're lying.'

"Now the district attorney lost his patience for the second time. 'You stupid little thing,' he yelled, grabbing the child's arm and shaking her, 'now you tell us what you know!' And we all screamed with him, senselessly, because we had simply lost control of ourselves; we, too, shook her, and started to hit her, beat that little body lying there in ashes and red leaves among rusty tin cans, beat her cruelly, furiously, shouting and yelling.

"The girl let our fury pass over her for what seemed an eternity, though it must have lasted only a few seconds, and made no sound at all. But then suddenly she screamed with such an unearthly, inhuman voice that we stood frozen to the spot. 'You're lying! You're lying! You're lying!' Appalled, we let her go. Her screams had brought us back to our senses, and we were filled with horror and shame at what we had done.

"'We're animals,' I gasped. 'We're beasts.'

"The child ran across the clearing to the edge of the forest. 'You're lying! You're lying! You're lying!' she shrieked again, so horribly we thought she had lost her mind, but she ran straight into the arms of her mother. For Lotte Heller—as if things hadn't gone from bad to worse already—had just at that moment stepped into the clearing. That was all we needed. She had been informed about everything; the teacher had talked after all when Lotte walked past the school; I knew it, I didn't have to ask. And now this poor woman stood there, hugging her sobbing child, and staring at us with the same look her daughter had given us before. Naturally she knew every one of us—Feller, Henzi, and unfortunately the district attorney too; the situation was grotesquely awkward; we were all embarrassed and felt plainly ridiculous; the whole thing was nothing but a lousy miserable comedy. 'Lies! Lies! Lies!' the child was still screaming, beside herself. 'Lies! Lies! Lies!' Then Matthäi went up to the two of them, head bowed, with uncertain steps.

"'Fräulein Heller,' he said politely, humbly in fact, which made no sense at all, because there was only one thing left to do, and that was to put an end to the whole thing, finish, case closed, cut loose from the whole bloody puzzle, no matter whether the murderer existed or not. 'Fräulein Heller, I noticed that Annemarie was given chocolate by an unknown person. I have reason to suspect that this is the same person who lured a little girl into a forest a few weeks ago and killed her.'

"He spoke precisely and in such an officious manner I could have laughed out loud. The woman calmly looked into his eyes. Then she spoke just as formally and politely as Matthäi. 'Lieutenant,' she asked softly, 'did you take me and Annemarie into your gas station just so you could find this person?'

"'There was no other way, Fräulein Heller,' the inspector replied.

"'You are a swine,' the woman quietly replied, without moving a muscle in her face. Then she took her child and went through the woods in the direction of the gas station."

27

"We stood there in the clearing, in the lengthening shadows, surrounded by old tin cans and tangled wire, our feet in ashes and leaves. It was all over, our whole undertaking had turned into a senseless, ridiculous mess, in fact nothing less than a catastrophe. Matthäi was the only one who had regained his composure. He looked downright stiff and dignified in his blue mechanic's outfit. He performed a tight little bow before the district attorney—I could hardly believe my eyes and ears—and said: 'Doctor Burkhard, now we must keep on waiting. There is no other way. We must wait, wait, and wait again. If you would give me six more men and the radio equipment, that would be enough.'

"The district attorney eyed my former subordinate with alarm. He had come prepared for everything but this. Just a moment ago, he had firmly intended to give us all an earful; now he gulped a few times, passed a hand over his forehead, and then abruptly turned on his heels and stomped with Henzi through the woods in the direction of the gas station. At a sign from me, Feller also left.

"Matthäi and I were alone.

"'Now you listen to me,' I screamed, determined to bring the man to his senses at last, and furious at myself for supporting his nonsense, indeed for making it possible. 'The operation has failed, we have to admit that. We waited more than a week and no one showed up.'

"Matthäi did not answer. He just looked about, peering, listening. Then he went to the edge of forest, walked around the clearing, and returned. I was still standing on the garbage heap, up to my ankles in ashes.

"'The girl was waiting for him,' he said.

"I shook my head. 'No,' I said. 'The girl came here to be by herself, to sit by the brook, to dream with her doll, and to sing "Maria sat upon a stone." We just imagined that she was waiting for someone.'

"Matthäi listened attentively to my words.

"'Someone gave Annemarie the hedgehogs,' he said stubbornly, still firmly convinced.

"'Someone gave Annemarie some chocolate,' I said. 'That's true. Anyone could give chocolate to a child! But that those chocolate truffles were the hedgehogs in Gritli Moser's drawing—I'm sorry, Matthäi, that, too, is your interpretation, and there's nothing to prove it.'

"Again Matthäi gave no response. He walked back to the edge of the forest, circled the clearing again, searched a spot where fallen leaves had accumulated, then gave up and returned to me.

"'This is the site for a murder,' he said. 'You can feel it. I will keep waiting.'

"'But that's nonsense,' I replied, suddenly filled with horror and disgust. I was shivering, exhausted.

"'He will come here,' Matthäi said.

"I screamed at him, beside myself: 'Poppycock! Bullshit! This is idiotic!'

"He seemed not to be listening. 'Let's go back to the gas station,' he said.

"I was more than glad to turn my back on that accursed place. The sun stood low now, the shadows were tremendous, the wide valley lay steeped in a strong golden glow, and the sky above was a pure blue; but I hated everything. I felt as though I had been banished to some immense kitschy postcard. Then the highway appeared—rolling cars, convertibles with colorfully dressed people, the wealth of life surging and rushing past. It was absurd. We reached the gas station. Feller was waiting in my car next to the pumps. He was half asleep again. Annemarie was sitting on her swing, singing in a tinny, somewhat tearful voice, 'Maria sat upon a stone,' and there was a fellow standing there, leaning against the doorpost, probably a worker from the brickyard, with an open shirt and a hairy chest, a cigarette in his mouth, grinning. Matthäi ignored him. He went into the little room, to the table where we had sat before; I trotted after him. He put a bottle of schnapps on the table and poured himself one glass after the other. I couldn't drink, I was too disgusted by everything. Lotte Heller was nowhere in sight.

"'It'll be hard,' he said, 'but the clearing isn't that far. Or do you think I'd better wait here, by the gas station?'

"I didn't answer him. Matthäi walked back and forth, drank, and ignored my silence.

"'It's too bad Annemarie and her mother found out,' he said. 'But we'll fix that.'

"Outside, the noise of the road and the child's whiny voice: 'Maria sat upon a stone.'

"'I'm leaving now, Matthäi,' I said.

"He went on drinking, didn't even look at me.

"'Good-bye,' I said, left the room, stepped outside, walked past the man and the little girl, and waved to Feller, startling him out of his half-sleep. He opened the door of the car for me.

"'Back to headquarters,' I ordered."

28

"That's the story as far as poor old Matthäi figures in it," the former chief of the cantonal police continued. (This is probably the right place to mention the fact that the old man and I had long since finished our drive from Chur to Zürich and were now sitting in the Kronenhalle, the restaurant he had mentioned and praised so often in his account, being served by Emma of course, under the painting by Gubler—which had replaced the Miró—all in accord with the old man's habits and preference. I should mention, too, that we had already eaten—off the trolley, *bollito milanese;* this, too, was one of his well-known traditions, why not go along with it; it was nearly four o'clock already, and after the 'Café Partagas,' as the chief called his passion for smoking a Havana along with his espresso and following these up with a Réserve du Patron, he offered me a second charlotte. I should also add, as a purely technical point, in defense of my craft and for the sake of literary honesty, that I have of course not always reproduced that immense verbal outpouring precisely as it was delivered, and I'm not just referring to the fact that we spoke in Swiss dialect; I mean those parts of the old man's story that he did not relate from his own point of view, as his own experience, but described objectively, as events in themselves—for example, the scene when Matthäi gave his solemn promise. At such moments I had to intervene, shape and reshape, though I tried as hard as I could not to falsify anything but only to take the material the old man supplied and rework it according to certain laws of literary craft; in short, to put it into publishable form.)

"Naturally," he continued, "I went back to visit Matthäi a few times, more and more convinced he had been mistaken about the peddler's innocence, because in the following months, and eventually years, no new murder took place. Well, I don't have go into further detail; the man fell apart, drank himself into a perpetual stupor, degenerated; there was no way to help him or bring about a change; at night, the young fellows no longer slinked and whistled around the gas station in vain; things took a nasty turn, the Graubünden police made a number of raids. I had to fill them in on the whole story; once my colleagues in Chur understood, they looked the other way. They've always been more sensible up there than we are. So everything continued on its downhill course, and you saw the results yourself a few hours ago. It's a sad story. Especially because the little girl, Annemarie, didn't turn out any better than her mother. Possibly just because various organizations immediately set about rescuing her. The child was taken care of, but kept running away and coming back to the gas station, where Lotte Heller set up that shabby bar two years ago. God only knows how she wangled the license; at any rate, for the girl that was the final touch. She pitched in. In every respect. Four months ago she came back after a year of reform school, to tell you the truth. Not that she learned anything from it. You saw the evidence with your own eyes, let's not dwell on it. But I imagine you've been wondering all this time what my story has to do with the criticism I made of your lecture, and why I called Matthäi a genius. A very reasonable question. Your objection is probably that a daring or unconventional idea isn't necessarily right, let alone inspired. That, too, is correct. I can even imagine what you're cooking up in your literary brain. All we need—I can imagine you making some sly calculation like this—all we need is for Matthäi to be on the right track, let him capture the murderer in the end, and bingo, we've got a terrific novel or movie script. After all, what's the purpose of writing if not to give things a certain twist that'll make them transparent, so that the higher idea shines through just enough for the reader to sense it, infer it; in fact, by this little twist, by making Matthäi succeed, my degenerate detective would become not just interesting, he'd be a character of Biblical dimensions, a sort of modern Abraham of hope and faith, and my senseless story—of someone who goes after a nonexistent murderer because he believes in the innocence of a guilty man—would be full of meaning; the guilty peddler would become innocent in the realm of poetic vision, the nonexistent murderer would become a real one, and a course of events that tends to make a mockery of human faith and human reason would instead glorify these powers. Who cares what actually happened, and how; the main thing is that this version is equally possible. That, more or less, is how I imagine your train of thought. I think this variant of my story is so uplifting and positive that I predict it will just have to be published or turned into a film in the near future. You will tell it all pretty much the way I tried to, but you'll make it more understandable. After all, you're a pro. You won't let the murderer show up until the very end; that way, hope is rewarded, faith triumphs, and the story becomes acceptable for the Christian world. I could imagine a few other softening touches. For example, I would suggest that as soon as Matthäi discovers the truffles, he is shocked into awareness of Annemarie's dangerous situation and is no longer able to continue with his plan of using the child as a bait—either out of mature altruism or out of paternal love, whereupon he could take Annemarie and her mother out of harm's way and put a big doll next to the little brook. Then a huge, solemn figure would come striding out of the forest in the light of the setting sun, straight up to the look-alike doll—Annemarie's wizard, lusting for this new chance to apply his straight razor; then, realizing he has fallen into a fiendish trap, he would fly into a rage, a fit of madness, there'd be a fight with Matthäi and the police, and then perhaps at the end—please bear with me, I'm just trying to imagine—there'd be a deeply moving conversation between the wounded inspector and the child, not long, just a few half sentences. Why not? You could have the girl slip away from her mother to meet her beloved wizard, race through the woods toward her great happiness; that way, after all those horrors, you could pierce the darkness with a ray of gentle humanity, sweet renunciation, and poetic tenderness; or else, more likely, you'll fabricate something very different; I know you a little by now, even though, to be perfectly frank, I prefer Max Frisch;* it'll be the very senselessness of my story that appeals to you, the fact that someone believes in the innocence of a guilty man and now sets out to find a murderer who cannot exist, as we have defined the situation accurately enough. But now you become crueler than reality, just for the hell of it and to make us policemen look completely ridiculous: now Matthäi would actually find a murderer, one of your comical saints, some sectarian preacher with a heart of gold who is of course actually innocent and utterly incapable of doing anything evil, and just for that reason, by one of your more malicious inventions, he would attract every shred of suspicion the plot has to offer. Matthäi would kill this pure, simple soul, all his proofs would be confirmed, whereupon we at headquarters would take the happy detective back into our fold and celebrate him as a genius. That's another conceivable version. You see, I'm onto you. But I expect you won't just ascribe all my talk to the Réserve du Patron—though we're into our second liter, admittedly; no, I presume you have a feeling that I have yet to tell the end of the story; with some reluctance, I must say, because unfortunately—I don't have to hide this from you—unfortunately this story has a point, and as you no doubt already suspect, that point is a thoroughly shabby one, so shabby that it simply can't be used in any decent novel or film. It is so ridiculous, stupid, and trivial, you would just have to skip it. It would ruin the story if you wanted to set it to paper. However, it would be dishonest not to admit that this point is, for now at least, thoroughly in Matthäi's favor, puts him in the proper light, and

*Max Frisch (1911–1991), Swiss novelist, dramatist, and diarist.

makes him a genius, a person so deeply in touch with factors of reality that are hidden from us that he broke through the hypotheses and assumptions that obstruct our vision and penetrated close to those laws that keep the world in motion, and which usually elude our grasp. He came close, I said, but no nearer than that. For this gruesome point which, I'm very sorry to say, is a real part of my story—this factor of the incalculable, this randomness, if you will—makes all his genius, his plans, and his actions appear even more painfully absurd in hindsight than was the case before, when in the opinion of all of us at headquarters he was mistaken: there is no greater cruelty than a genius stumbling over something idiotic. But when something like that happens, everything depends on the stance the genius takes toward the ridiculous thing that tripped him; whether he can accept it or not. Matthäi couldn't accept it. He wanted reality to conform to his calculations. Therefore he had to deny reality and end in a void. So my story ends on a particularly sad note—it's just about the most banal of all the possible 'solutions.' Sometimes that just happens. Sometimes the worst possible thing *also* takes place. We are men, we have to reckon with that, armor ourselves against it, and above all, we have to realize that the only way to avoid getting crushed by absurdity, which is here to stay and will necessarily show itself more and more clearly and strongly, and the only way to make a reasonably comfortable home for ourselves on this earth, is to humbly include the absurd in our calculations. Our rational mind casts only a feeble light on this world. In the twilight of its borders live the ghosts of paradox. Let us beware of taking these figments as things existing 'in themselves,' independently of the human mind; or, even worse: let us not make the mistake of regarding them as an avoidable error, which could tempt us to execute the world in a fit of defiant morality by trying to establish a flawless rational structure, for the very perfection and flawlessness of such a scheme would be a deadly lie and a sign of the most terrible blindness. But forgive me for injecting this commentary into my lovely story. Philosophically not quite up to par, I know, but you have to grant an old man like me a few thoughts about what he's experienced, crude though they may be; I'm just a policeman, but still I do make an effort to be a man and not an ox."

29

"Anyway, it was last year—on a Sunday again, naturally—that I received a telephone call from a Catholic priest and had to pay a visit to the cantonal hospital. It happened just before my retirement, in the last days of my term in office. My successor was already on the job—not Henzi, who fortunately didn't make it, despite his well-connected wife—but a man of substance and rigor, endowed with a civil decency that could only be of benefit to the office he held. The telephone call had reached me in my apartment. The only reason I acceded to the request was that it was supposed to be something important a dying woman wanted to tell me, which is something that happens now and then. It was a sunny but cold December day. Everything bare, forlorn, melancholy. At such moments our city can reduce you to tears. What a day! As if visiting a dying woman wasn't sad enough. That's why I walked around Aeschbacher's *Harp* in the park several times, in a rather gloomy mood, but finally I pulled myself together and walked into the building. Frau Schrott, medical clinic, private ward. The room, with a view to the park, was full of flowers, roses, gladioli. The curtains were half drawn. Slanting rays of light fell on the floor. By the window sat a huge priest with a rough red face and a gray untended beard, and in the bed lay a little old woman, delicately wrinkled, her hair thin and snow-white, extraordinarily gentle, apparently very rich, to judge by the care she was receiving. Next to the bed stood a complicated apparatus, some sort of medical contraption with various hoses that led under her blanket. The machine had to be repeatedly checked by a nurse who kept walking in and out of the room, silent and observant. I might as well mention these regular interruptions from the start.

"I said hello. The old woman looked at me attentively and very calmly. Her face was waxen, unreal, but still curiously animated. In her wrinkled yellowish hands she was holding a little black gilt-edged book, evidently a psalter, but it was almost impossible to believe that this woman was about to die; such a vital, unbroken force emanated from her, despite all those tubes crawling out from under her blanket. The priest remained seated. With a gesture as majestic as it was awkward he indicated a chair next the bed.

"'Sit down,' he said, and when I had taken the seat, his deep voice sounded again from the window, before which he towered as a mighty silhouette. 'Tell the chief what you have to report, Frau Schrott. At eleven we'll have to proceed with Extreme Unction.'

"Frau Schrott smiled. 'I'm sorry to put you to so much trouble,' she said with great charm, and her voice, although quiet, was still very clear, in fact quite lively.

"'It's no trouble at all,' I lied, convinced now that the old woman was going to inform me of some bequest for needy policemen or something like that.

"'It's a rather unimportant and harmless story I have to tell you,' the old woman continued, 'the sort of thing that probably happens in all families once or several times, which is why I forgot it, but now that eternity is drawing near, I suppose it had to come up again. I mentioned it in my general confession, purely by chance, because a moment before, a granddaughter of my only godchild had come with flowers and wearing a little red skirt, and Father Beck got all upset and told me to tell you the story, I really don't know why, it's all in the past, but if Reverend Beck thinks . . .'

"'Tell him what happened, Frau Schrott,' said the deep voice by the window, 'tell him.' And in the city the church bells started ringing the end of the sermon, a dark, distant clanging.

"'Well, I'll try,' the old woman began again, and started to chatter. 'It's been such a long time since I've told a story. I used to tell stories to Emil, my first husband's son, but then Emil died of consumption, there was nothing anyone could do. He would have been as old as I am now. Or rather, as old as Reverend Beck. But now I'll try to imagine that you're my son, and that Reverend Beck is my son too. Because right after Emil, I gave birth to Markus, but he died three days after he was born, premature. He was a six-month baby, and Dr. Hobler thought it was best for the poor little thing.' And on and on she went in this scattered manner.

"'Tell the story, Frau Schrott, tell it,' the priest admonished her in his bass voice, sitting immobile by the window except for an occasional Moses-like movement of his hand as he stroked his wild gray beard, emitting, all the while, a distinct odor of garlic that met my nostrils in a succession of mild, steady waves. 'We don't have much time. We have to proceed with Extreme Unction!'

"Now she suddenly became proud, downright aristocratic. She even raised her little head a bit, and her eyes flashed. 'I am a Stänzli,' she said. 'My grandfather was Colonel Stänzli, who led the retreat to Escholzmatt in the Sonderbund War,* and my sister married Colonel Stüssi of the Zürich General Staff in the First World War, who was General Ulrich Wille's best friend and knew Kaiser Wilhelm personally, as I'm sure you remember.'

"'Of course,' I said, feeling bored, 'naturally.' What did I care about old Wille and Kaiser Wilhelm. Spit it out already, I said silently in my thoughts, to whom do you want to bequeath your money? If only I could smoke, a Suerdieck cigarillo would be just the right thing to blow some jungle air into this hospital atmosphere and these damn garlic waves. And the priest droned on like the bass register of a giant organ, stubbornly, relentlessly: 'Tell the story, Frau Schrott, tell the story.'

"'You should know,' the old lady continued, and now her face took on a strangely fierce, almost hateful expression, 'you should know that my sister

*Swiss civil war of 1847 over religion and states' rights.

with her Colonel Stüssi were to blame for the whole thing. My sister is ten years older than I, she's ninety-two now, she's been a widow for forty years, she's got a villa on the Zürichberg, she's got Brown-Boveri stock, she owns half the Bahnhofstrasse*...' And then suddenly, out of the mouth of this little old lady on her deathbed, came a muddy stream, or let's put it this way: such a filthy, squalid flood of profanity that I wouldn't dare to reproduce it. At the same time, the old creature raised herself slightly, and her little ancient head with the snow-white hair wiggled back and forth with astonishing vigor, as if mad with joy over this burst of rage. But then she calmed down again, because fortunately the nurse came in—now, now, Frau Schrott, let's not get upset, nice and easy now. The old woman obeyed, and made a feeble movement with her hand when we were alone again.

"'All these flowers,' she said, 'they're from my sister. She sends them just to annoy me. She knows very well I don't like flowers. I hate to see money wasted like that. But we never had a falling out, as you probably imagine. No, no, we have always been sweet and kind to each other. All the Stänzlis have this politeness, even though we can't stand one another. You see, we use our politeness to hurt each other. Oh, if we could draw blood with politeness, we would. And a good thing it is, this discipline in the family, because otherwise all hell would break loose.'

"'The story, Frau Schrott,' the priest urged again for a change. 'Extreme Unction is waiting.' By now, in my wish for something to smoke, I had replaced the little Suerdieck with one of my big Bahianos.

"The endless babbling flood continued: 'Back in ninety-five, I married Dr. Galuser, God bless his dear departed soul, he was a physician in Chur. That fact alone was an affront to my sister with her colonel, my husband wasn't a fine enough gentleman for them, I could definitely tell, and when the colonel died of influenza later, right after the First World War, my sister got more and more unbearable. She practically sainted her fancy militarist, it was disgusting.'

"'Tell the story, Frau Schrott, the story,' the priest kept after her, but not at all impatiently; at most, he betrayed a faint sadness at so much confusion. I was drifting. Once in a while his voice startled me out of my stupor: 'Extreme Unction, Frau Schrott, think about it, get to the point, tell the story.'

"There was nothing to be done, the old woman went on nattering away on her deathbed, sliding from one subject to the next, inexhaustibly, despite her feeble, high-pitched voice and the tubes beneath her blanket. To the extent that I was still able to think, I vaguely expected some banal story about

*The main traffic artery of Zürich, and Switzerland's financial center.

a helpful policeman, and then the announcement of a bequest of a few thousand francs, just to annoy the ninety-nine-year-old sister; I prepared some warm words of gratitude, resolutely suppressed my unrealistic dreams of a good smoke, and turned my desires, in order not to succumb to despair altogether, in the direction of my customary aperitif and the traditional Sunday dinner in the Kronenhalle with my wife and daughter.

"'And then,' the old woman continued, 'after the death of my dear departed husband, the late Dr. Galuser, I married the late Herr Schrott, who used to be our chauffeur and gardener and general handyman; yes, he did all the things that have to be done in a big old house and that really ought to be done by men, like heating, fixing the shutters, and so forth, and even though my sister made no comment about it and even came to Chur for the wedding, I know she was angry about this marriage. Not that my sister would ever show it, oh no, she wouldn't give me that pleasure. Anyway, that's how I became Frau Schrott.'

"She sighed. Outside, somewhere in the corridor, the nurses were singing. Christmas carols. 'Well, it was quite a harmonious marriage with my dearly beloved,' the dying woman continued after listening to a few bars of the song. 'Even though it was probably harder for him than I can imagine. My blessed Albert was twenty-three when we married—since he had been born in 1900 exactly—and I was already fifty-five. But I'm sure it was the best thing he could do. You see, he was an orphan; his mother was, oh, I don't want to even say what she was, and as for his father, nobody knew who he was, not even his name. My first husband had taken the boy in when he was sixteen; he couldn't cope with school, you know, he never was much good at reading and writing. Marriage was simply the cleanest solution. As a widow, you see, you get talked about; not that there was ever anything between me and Bertie, bless his dear soul, not when we were married either, how could there have been, with such a great difference in age; but my assets were limited, I had to keep a budget in order to get by with the rent I collected from my houses in Zürich and Chur; but imagine my blessed Bertie, with his limited mental capacities, having to go out and fend for himself in the struggle of life—he would have been lost, and as a Christian one does have certain obligations. So we lived together honorably; he did this and that in the house and the garden, a good-looking man, I have to say, a big, firm fellow, always dressed in a dignified way, as if for a formal occasion; I never had cause to be ashamed of him, even though he hardly said anything, except maybe "Yes, Mumsy, of course, Mumsy," but he was obedient and temperate in his drinking; not with food though, he loved to eat, especially noodles, all sorts of pasta in fact, and chocolate. That was his passion, chocolate. But for the rest, he was a good, decent man and stayed that way all his life, so much nicer and so much more obedient than the chauffeur my sister married four years later, despite her colonel. He too was only thirty.'

"The old woman fell silent, apparently exhausted, while I innocently awaited the bequest for needy policemen.

"'Tell the story, Frau Schrott,' the priest's voice wafted from the window with relentless indifference.

"Frau Schrott nodded. 'You see, Chief,' she said, 'in the forties my life with Bertie gradually started to go downhill, I'm not sure what was wrong with him, but something must have been damaged in his head; he got more and more blank and quiet, stared into space a lot, didn't speak for days at a time, only did his work, always properly so I had no reason to scold him, but he would drive around for hours on his bicycle. Maybe the war confused him, or the fact that the army hadn't taken him; who's to say what goes on in a man's head! Also, he was eating a tremendous amount; fortunately we had our chickens and rabbits. And then that thing happened to my dear departed Albert, the thing I'm supposed to tell you about. The first time was near the end of the war.'

"She stopped talking because once again the nurse and a doctor had entered the room. They busied themselves in part behind the medical contraption, in part behind the old woman. The doctor was German, blond, straight out of a picture book, cheerful, peppy, on his routine round as the doctor on Sunday service, how are you, Frau Schrott, chin up, my, my, you've got excellent results, don't give up now; then he strode away, followed by the nurse, and the priest admonished the patient: 'Tell the story, Frau Schrott, Extreme Unction's at eleven,' a prospect that did not seem to alarm the old biddy in the least.

"She resumed her tale: 'Every week my poor little Bertie, God bless his soul, had to bring eggs to my militarist sister in Zürich. He would tie the little basket to the back of his bicycle and come back in the evening, because he would start out early, at five or six in the morning, always dressed up in black, with a round hat. Everyone gave him a friendly greeting when he pedaled through Chur and then out into the country, whistling his favorite song, "I am a Switzer lad and love my country dear." This time it was a hot midsummer day, two days after the national holiday, and this time it was past midnight when he came home. I heard him fussing and washing in the bathroom for a long time, went there and saw my dear Bertie all covered with blood, his clothes too. "My God, Bertie," I asked, "what happened to you?" He just stared, and then he said, "An accident, Mumsy, I'll be all right, go to sleep, Mumsy," so I went to sleep, even though I wondered because I hadn't seen any wounds. But in the morning when we were having breakfast and he was eating his eggs, always four at a time, and his slices of bread with marmalade, I read in the newspaper that a little girl had been murdered in the canton of St. Gallen, probably with a straight razor, and then it occurred to me that in the bathroom the night before, he had been cleaning his razor, even though he always shaved in the morning, and then I suddenly realized what had happened, it came like revelation, and I got very serious with Bertie, God bless his soul, and said, "Bertie dear, you killed that girl in St. Gallen canton, didn't you?" Then he stopped eating his eggs and bread and marmalade and pickles and said, "Yes, Mumsy, it had to be, it was a voice from heaven," and then he went on eating. I was all confused that he could be so sick; I felt sorry for the girl, I also thought of calling Doctor Sichler, not the old one but his son, who is also very capable and very sympathetic; but then I thought of my sister, she would have been tickled pink, it would have been the best day of her life, so I was just very stern and firm with my blessed Bertie and told him plainly: "This must never, never happen again," and he said, "Yes, Mumsy." "How did it happen?" I asked. "Mumsy," he said, "I kept meeting a little girl with a red skirt and blond braids when I drove to Zürich by way of Wattwil, a big detour, but ever since I met this girl near a little patch of woods I always had to take the detour, the voice from heaven, Mumsy, and the voice told me to share my chocolate with her, and then I had to kill the girl, it was all the voice from heaven, Mumsy, and then I went into the woods nearby and lay under a shrub until night came, and then I came back to you, Mumsy." "Bertie," I said, "you're not going to drive your bicycle to my sister any more; we'll send the eggs by mail." "Yes, Mumsy," he said, smeared some jam on another slice of bread and went into the courtyard. "I suppose now I really should go to Father Beck," I thought, so he'd give my blessed Bertie a serious talking-to, but then I looked out the window, and seeing my blessed Bertie so faithfully doing his duty out there in the sun, quietly and a little sadly mending the rabbit hutch, and seeing how spick and span the whole courtyard was, I thought, "What's done is done, Bertie is a good, decent fellow, and basically such a kind soul, and besides, it won't happen again."'

"Now the nurse came back into the room, checked the instrument, rearranged the tubes, and the little old woman lying back in her pillow seemed exhausted again. I hardly dared to breathe. The sweat was running down my face; I ignored it. I was suddenly cold and felt doubly ridiculous for having expected a bequest from the old woman. And then this enormous array of flowers, all those red and white roses, flaming gladioli, asters, zinnias, carnations, obtained God knows where, a whole vase full of orchids, senseless, blatant, and the sun behind the curtains, and that huge motionless priest, and the smell of garlic; I felt like flying into a rage, arresting the woman, but it would have been pointless, she was about to receive Extreme Unction, and there I sat in my Sunday suit, all spiffed up and useless.

"'Go on with the story, Frau Schrott,' the priest admonished impatiently, 'get on with it.' And she went on. 'And so my dear blessed Albert really did get better,' she expounded in her calm, gentle voice, and it really was as if she were telling two children a fairy tale in which evil and absurdity happen as something just as wonderful as the good. 'He no longer went to Zürich; but when the Second World War was over, we could use our car again, the one I had bought back in thirty-eight, because the car of Dr. Galuser, God bless his soul, was really out of fashion, and so Bertie, God bless his soul, drove me around in our Buick again. Once we even went to Ascona, and then I thought, since he gets so much pleasure from driving, why not let him go to Zürich again, it's not so dangerous with the Buick, he'll have to keep his eye on the road and won't hear any voices from heaven, and so he was driving out to my sister again and faithfully delivering the eggs, as was his wont, and every once in a while he delivered a rabbit. But then unfortunately one day he didn't come home until after midnight. I immediately went to the garage; I sensed it right away, because he had suddenly started taking chocolate truffles from the candy box, and sure enough I found Bertie, God bless his soul, washing the inside of his car, and everywhere I looked there was blood. "Did you kill a girl again, Bertie?" I said, in a very serious tone. "Mumsy," he said, "don't worry, it wasn't in the St. Gallen canton, it was in Schwyz canton, the voice from heaven wanted it, the girl had a red dress and blond braids again." But I *was* worried, and I was even sterner with him than the first time; I almost got angry. He wasn't allowed to drive the Buick for a week, and I wanted to go to Father Beck, I really intended to; but my sister would have been just delighted to hear that, I couldn't let that happen, and so I kept even stricter watch over Albert, God bless his soul, and then for two years things went really well, until he did it again, because he just had to obey the voice from heaven, my Bertie, God bless his soul, he was crushed, he cried, but I noticed it right away because there were truffles missing from the bonbon box. This time it was a girl in the Zürich canton, again with a little red skirt and yellow braids. It's unbelievable, how carelessly mothers dress their children.'

"'Was the girl's name Gritli Moser?' I asked.

"'Her name was Gritli, and the ones before were Sonya and Eveli,' the old lady replied. 'I noted all the names; but Bertie, God bless his soul, got worse and worse, he started to get absent-minded, I had to tell him everything ten times, all day long I had to scold him like a schoolboy, and it was in 1949 or '50, I'm not sure any longer, a few months after Gritli, that he started getting restless again, and jumpy; even the chicken coop was a mess, and the chickens were cackling wildly because he wasn't feeding them properly, and he kept driving around in our Buick and staying away for whole afternoons, just saying he was out for a ride, and suddenly I noticed there were truffles missing in the bonbon box. Then I watched him closely, and when he stole into the living room, my Bertie, God bless his soul, with his razor tucked into a pocket like a fountain pen, I went up to him and said: "Bertie, you found another girl." "The voice from heaven, Mumsy," he replied, "please let me do it just this one time; it's commanded by heaven, I have to obey, and she has a red skirt too and blond braids." "Bertie," I said sternly, "I can't allow this, where is the girl?" "Not far from here, near a gas station," Bertie said, God bless his soul, "please, please, Mumsy, let me obey." Then I put my foot down: "Absolutely not, Bertie," I said, "you gave me your promise; now clean the chicken coop and give the chickens a decent feeding." Then Bertie, God bless his soul, got angry, for the first time in our marriage, which was so harmonious otherwise, he shouted: "All I am is your servant," that's how sick he was, and ran out with the truffles and the razor to the Buick, and just fifteen minutes later I received a call telling me he had collided with a truck and died. Reverend Beck came and Police Captain Bühler, he was particularly sensitive, which is why in my testament I have bequeathed five thousand francs to the police in Chur, and five thousand more will be going to the Zürich police, because I have houses here in the Freistrasse, and of course my sister came with her chauffeur, just to annoy me. She spoiled the whole funeral for me.'

"I stared at the old woman. There it was, the bequest I had been waiting for. It felt like a mockery.

"But now finally the chief doctor came with an assistant and two nurses; we were sent out, and I took leave of Frau Schrott.

"'Good-bye, get some rest,' I said stupidly, feeling embarrassed and wanting nothing more than to get away as quickly as possible, whereupon she started to giggle and the chief doctor gave me a peculiar look; the scene was awkward, to say the least; I was glad to leave the old woman, the priest, the whole assembly behind me and finally step out into the hallway.

"Everywhere I looked, there were visitors with packages and flowers. Everything smelled of hospital. I fled. The exit was near; in my mind, I was already outside in the park. But then a very large man in dark, formal clothes with a round, childish face and a hat came down the corridor pushing a wheelchair in which sat a wrinkled, trembling old woman in a mink coat, holding flowers in both arms, enormous bundles of them. Maybe this was the ninety-nine-year-old sister with her chauffeur, what did I know? I looked after them in horror until they vanished in the private ward. Then I almost ran. I rushed out of the building and through the park, past patients in wheelchairs, past convalescents, past visitors, and only began to calm down in the Kronenhalle. Over the liver dumpling soup."

30

"I drove straight from the Kronenhalle to Chur. Unfortunately I had to take my wife and daughter along: it was Sunday and I had promised them the afternoon, and I didn't want to get embroiled in explanations. I didn't say a word, drove way above the speed limit; maybe something could still be salvaged. But my family didn't have to wait long in the car outside the gas station. The tavern was positively hopping. Annemarie had just come back from reform school; the place was swarming with some pretty unsavory characters; despite the cold, Matthäi was sitting on his bench in his mechanic's overalls, smoking a cheroot, stinking of absinthe. I sat down beside him and told him the story in a few words. But it was too late. He didn't even seem to be listening. For a moment I was undecided; then I went back to my Opel Kapitän and drove on to Chur. My family was impatient, they were hungry.

"'Wasn't that Matthäi?' my wife asked; as usual, she had no idea.

"'Yes.'

"'I thought he was in Jordan,' she said.

"'He didn't go, dear.'

"In Chur we had trouble parking. The pastry shop was crammed full of people from Zürich and their screaming children, all stuffing their bellies and sweating. But finally we found a table, ordered tea and pastry. But my wife called the waitress back again.

"'And please bring us half a pound of chocolate truffles.'

"She was only slightly surprised when I didn't want to eat any truffles. Not for the life of me.

"And now, my dear sir, you can do what you want with this story. Emma, the bill."

Greek Man Seeks Greek Wife

A Prose Comedy

1

It had been raining for hours, nights, days, and weeks. The streets, the avenues, the boulevards gleamed with wetness; rivulets, brooks, minor rivers flowed along the curbs, cars swam about, people walked under umbrellas, shrouded in raincoats, their shoes soaked, their socks perpetually damp; the giants, putti, and Aphrodites supporting the balconies of mansions and hotels clung to the walls, trickling and dripping ropes of water mixed with dissolving bird droppings, while under the Grecian gables of the House of Parliament pigeons sought shelter between the legs and breasts of the patriotic statuary. It was a miserable January. Then came the fog, which also lasted days and weeks, and with it a flu epidemic, no real threat to decent, respectable people of means, though it did carry off a few rich old uncles and aunts, to the delight of their heirs, and a couple of venerable statesmen; it was the bums under the bridges by the river who died like flies. And intermittently it rained. Again and again.

His name was Arnolph Archilochos, and Madame Bieler behind her counter would say: "That poor boy. Imagine living with a name like that.* Auguste, bring him another glass of milk."

And on Sundays she said: "Bring him another Perrier."

Auguste, however, her husband, slender, winner of a legendary Tour de Suisse and runner-up in an even more legendary Tour de France, who served his customers in his tournament gear, his *maillot jaune*† (for the benefit of a small group of cycling fans who showed up regularly)—Auguste did not

*The name, pronounced in German, sounds like "Arschloch," meaning "asshole."

†Literally, "yellow jersey"; the shirt worn by the current lead bicyclist in the Tour de France.

agree. "Georgette, this love of yours," he would say getting up in the morning, or still in bed, or behind the stove after everyone had left and he could warm his thin hairy legs, "Georgette, your love for Mr. Archilochos is something I can't understand. He's not a man, he's all bottled up. How can a guy go through life drinking nothing but milk and mineral water!"

"There was a time when you drank nothing else either," Georgette would reply then in her deep voice, setting her arms akimbo, or, if she was still in bed, crossing them over her mountainous bosom.

"True," Auguste Bieler admitted after long reflection, massaging his legs again and again. "But that was in order to win the Tour de Suisse, and I won it, up mountain passes *this* high, and almost the Tour de France. That's abstinence with a purpose. But this Monsieur Archilochos? He's never even slept with a woman. And he's forty-five years old."

That bothered Madame Bieler too, and she always became embarrassed when Auguste raised the issue in his *maillot jaune* or in bed. As a matter of fact there was no denying that Monsieur Arnolph, as she called Archilochos, had certain principles. For example, he didn't smoke either. Swearing was even more unthinkable. Nor could Georgette imagine him in a nightshirt, let alone naked—that's how buttoned-up, how perpetually (though poorly) dressed he looked.

His world was structured, punctual, ethical, hierarchic. Way above, enthroned at the apex of this moral order, this edifice of cosmic law, sat the President.

"Believe me, Madame Bieler," Archilochos would say, staring reverently at the portrait of the President hanging in an edelweiss frame above the horizontally stacked schnapps and liqueur bottles behind the counter, "believe me, our head of state is a sober man, a philosopher, almost a saint. Doesn't smoke, doesn't drink, a widower for thirty years, no children. You can read it in the newspapers."

Madame Bieler did not dare to contradict him straight out. She, too, like everyone in the country, had some respect for the President, since he was the only stable pole in the welter of politics, the passing succession of governments, even though such consummate virtue made her uneasy. She preferred not to believe it.

"It's in the newspapers," Georgette therefore said hesitantly. "To be sure. But who knows the real story? Newspapers lie. Everyone says so."

"That is a fallacy," Archilochos replied. "The world is fundamentally moral." With solemn sips he imbibed his Perrier as if it were champagne.

"Auguste also believes in the newspapers."

"No," Georgette said. "I know better. Auguste doesn't believe a word he reads in the papers."

"What about the sports pages, doesn't he believe in the results?"

Madame Bieler couldn't argue with that.

"Virtue is visible," Archilochos continued, cleaning his rimless, slightly bent glasses. "It shines in this face and it shines in the face of my Bishop."

And he turned to the portrait that hung over the door.

"The Bishop is pretty fat," Madame Bieler protested. "He can't be all that virtuous."

Archilochos' faith was unshakable.

"It's his nature," he replied. "If he didn't live virtuously, philosophically, he would be even fatter. Look at Fahrcks, on the other hand. How unrestrained, how intemperate, how conceited. Sinful in every respect. And vain."

He pointed with his thumb over his right shoulder at the portrait of the notorious revolutionary.

Madame Bieler maintained her position. "You can't call that vain," she declared. "Not with that bush on his lip and that wild hair. And with his feeling for the oppressed."

"That's just a special kind of vanity," Arnolph insisted. "I don't understand why you would have that demagogue hanging here. And he just got out of jail!"

"Oh, you never know," Madame Bieler always replied, draining a glass of Campari in one draught. "You never know. You have to be careful in politics too."

The Bishop—let us return to his portrait, opposite Fahrcks—the Bishop was Number Two in Mr. Archilochos' vertically graduated world. He was not a Catholic bishop, although, in her own way, Madame Bieler was a good Catholic who went to church—when she went—in order to cry her heart out (but she cried just as passionately at the movies); nor was he a Protestant bishop, since Auguste Bieler ("Gödu" Bieler's "Gusti"), an immigrant from German Switzerland, the first Helvetian titan of the highway (*Sports*, September 9, 1929), could not, as a Zwinglian* (in his own particular way as well; he had no idea that he was a Zwinglian) recognize any bishop at all; no, the Bishop was head of the Old New Presbyterians of the Penultimate Christians, a perhaps somewhat hazy and peculiar sect imported from America, and he was only hanging over the door because Archilochos had introduced himself to Georgette with that portrait under his arm.

*A follower of Swiss religious reformer Ulrich Zwingli (1484–1531).

Nine months ago. It was May. Great puddles of sunlight on the street, slanting bundles of rays in the little restaurant, Auguste's golden jersey gilded anew, along with his sad cyclist's legs, his hair a shimmering aureole.

"Madame," Archilochos said timidly, "I have come because I noticed the picture of our President in your establishment. Above the counter, in a prominent place. I am a patriot and reassured. I am looking for a place to eat my meals. A home. But it must always be the same place, preferably in a corner. I am alone, a bookkeeper, live righteously, and am a strict teetotaler. I don't smoke either, and you won't hear any swearing from me."

Then they settled on a price.

"Madame," he said again, handing her the picture and gazing dolefully at her through his dusty little glasses, "Madame, may I ask you to hang this Bishop of the Old New Presbyterians of the Penultimate Christians. Preferably next to the President. I can no longer eat in a room where he is not hung. That is why I left the Salvation Army restaurant, where I used to eat. I revere my bishop. He is a sterling example, an absolutely sober, Christian person."

And so Georgette hung up the Bishop of the Penultimate Christians, not next to the President, but still over the door, and there he hung, contented and silent, a man of honor, only occasionally disowned by Auguste, whose clipped reply to the rare inquiries about the portrait was "A racing fan."

Three weeks later Archilochos came with a second picture. A personally autographed photo portrait of Petit-Paysan, owner of the Petit-Paysan Engineering Works. It would give him great pleasure, Archilochos said, to see Petit-Paysan hanging in Madame Georgette's establishment, perhaps in place of Fahrcks. It turned out that in the edifice of cosmic law, the owner of the engineering works was in third place.

Madame Georgette was against it.

"Petit-Paysan makes machine guns," she said.

"So?"

"Tanks."

"So?"

"Atomic cannon."

"You're forgetting the Petit-Paysan electric razor and the Petit-Paysan obstetric forceps, Madame Bieler, purely humanitarian objects."

"Monsieur Archilochos," Georgette solemnly declared, "I warn you against any further dealings with Petit-Paysan."

"He is my employer," Arnolph replied.

Georgette laughed. "Then it doesn't do you a bit of good," she said, "to drink milk and mineral water, abstain from meat" (Archilochos was a vegetarian), "and avoid sleeping with women. Petit-Paysan supplies the army, and when the army's supplied, there's a war. It's always that way."

Archilochos didn't agree.

"Not here!" he cried. "Not with our President!"

"Oh, him!"

"Evidently you don't know Petit-Paysan's shelter for expectant working mothers," Archilochos continued undeterred, "and his home for disabled workmen. You don't realize what an ethical, in fact downright Christian person he is."

But Madame Bieler would not be swayed, and as a result, Mr. Archilochos (pale, shy, and somewhat chubby in his corner among the racing fans) consumed his meals in contemplation of his two supreme idols and the very lowest creature in the cosmic order, its negative principle, Fahrcks, the communist who had instigated the coup in San Salvador and the revolution in Borneo. For he hadn't been able to persuade Georgette of the merits of Number Four either.

"You could hang the picture under Fahrcks," he suggested as he handed her a reproduction—a cheap one, incidentally.

"Who painted this?" Georgette asked, staring in dismay at the triangular rectangles and dented circles.

"Passap."

It turned out that Monsieur Arnolph worshipped the world-famous painter, but Georgette still didn't know what the picture was supposed to represent.

"Right living," Archilochos declared.

"But down there it says 'Chaos,'" Georgette exclaimed, pointing to the lower right-hand corner of the painting.

Archilochos shook his head. "Great artists create unconsciously," he said. "I simply know that the picture represents right living."

Georgette remained unmoved. Archilochos was so offended that he didn't show up for three days. Then he returned, and eventually Madame Bieler learned about Monsieur Arnolph's life, to the extent that one can call such a punctilious, well-ordered, skewed construction a life. For example, there were four more ranking figures in Archilochos' world, Numbers Five to Eight.

Number Five was Bob Forster-Monroe, the U.S. Ambassador. Though not an Old New Presbyterian of the Penultimate Christians, he was an Old Presbyterian of the Penultimate Christians, a painful though not a hopeless difference, which Archilochos, who was not at all intolerant in matters of religion, could discuss for hours on end. (The only church he rejected outright was the New Presbyterians of the Penultimate Christians.)

Number Six in the cosmic order was Maître Dutour.

Number Seven was Hercule Wagner, Rector Magnificus of the university.

Dutour had defended a sex murderer who was eventually decapitated, a curate of the Old New Presbyterians (it was but the flesh that violated the curate's spirit, his soul remained separate, unstained, and saved); the Rector Magnificus, on the other hand, had visited the students' dormitory of the Penultimate Christians and had spent five minutes talking with Number Two (Bishop).

Number Eight was Bibi Archilochos, his brother, a good person, Arnolph stressed, unemployed, which surprised Georgette, since, thanks to Petit-Paysan, there was plenty of work to be found.

Archilochos lived in a garret not far from Chez Auguste, as the champion's little restaurant was called, and it took him more than an hour to reach his place of work in the white, twenty-story, Corbusier-designed administrative building of the Petit-Paysan Engineering Works, Inc. As for the garret: fifth floor, smelly corridor, small, slanted ceiling, indeterminate wallpaper, a chair, a table, a bed, a Bible, behind a curtain his Sunday suit. On the wall: first, President; second, Bishop; third, Petit-Paysan; fourth, reproduction of a picture by Passap (rectangular triangles); and so on all the way down to Bibi (family picture with little kiddies). View: a dirty facade six feet away, fantastically splotched in white, yellow, and green, with regularly spaced rows of small, open, stinking windows, belonging to the next door building's bathrooms, the wall dark except for occasional midsummer transfigurations at high noon, and an acoustic accompaniment of perpetually flushing toilets. As for his place of work: one of fifty other Bookkeepers in a large room partitioned with glass, labyrinthine, traversable only by a zigzag course, seventh floor, Obstetrical Forceps Division, elbow patches for the protection of sleeves, pencil behind his ear, gray smock; lunch in the cafeteria, where he was unhappy because neither the President nor the Bishop hung there, only Petit-Paysan (Number Three). Archilochos was not a Bookkeeper proper, just an Assistant Bookkeeper. Or, more precisely, the Assistant Bookkeeper of an Assistant Bookkeeper. In short, one of the lowest Assistant Bookkeepers, insofar as it is possible to speak of a lowest one: the number of Bookkeepers and Assistant Bookkeepers in Petit-Paysan, Inc. was virtually infinite; but even in this modest job somewhere near the bottom of the heap he was still far better paid than the garret seemed to proclaim. The cause of his banishment to that dark den surrounded by toilets was Bibi.

2

Madame Bieler made the acquaintance of Number Eight (brother) as well.

On a Sunday. Arnolph had invited Bibi Archilochos to dinner. Chez Auguste.

Bibi came with his wife, two mistresses, and seven kiddies, the oldest of whom, Théophile and Gottlieb, were almost grown up. Magda-Maria, thirteen, brought along a lover. Bibi proved to be a godforsaken drinker. His wife was accompanied by a man she called "Uncle," a retired sea captain, indestructible. They created a hullabaloo that was too much even for the racing fans. Théophile boasted of his time in prison, Gottlieb of a bank robbery, Matthäus and Sebastian, twelve and nine, went at each other with knives, and the two youngest, twins, six years old, Jean-Christophe and Jean-Daniel, fought over a bottle of absinthe.

"What awful people!" Georgette cried after this hellish crew had left.

"They're children," Archilochos placated her, and paid the bill (half a month's salary).

"Listen," Madame Bieler said indignantly, "your brother seems to be supporting a bunch of criminals. And you give him money? Almost everything you earn?"

Archilochos' faith was unshakable. "One must look at the inner core, Madame Bieler," he said, "and the core is good. In every human being. Appearances are deceiving. My brother, his wife, and his little ones are noble beings, but perhaps not quite able to meet the challenges of this life."

But now—it was a Sunday again, though a good deal earlier, half past nine—he entered the restaurant for a different reason, with a red rose in his lapel, impatiently awaited by Georgette. None of this would have happened were it not for the endless rain, the fog, the cold, the perpetually damp socks, and the flu epidemic, which in the course of time turned into an intestinal virus, as a result of which Archilochos was kept awake in his room for nights on end by the constant hydraulic roaring. All this had deflected Arnolph's will, by degrees, as the flood rose in the gutters, until he finally yielded to Madame Bieler's pressure on the particular point she found so annoying.

"You should get married, Monsieur Arnolph," she had said. "What sort of life is that in your garret. And hanging around with racing fans isn't for a man with higher interests either. You need a wife to take care of you."

"You take care of me, Madame Bieler."

"No, no, getting a wife is something very different. A nice cozy warmth, you'll see."

And finally she got his agreement to place a personal ad in *Le Soir*. Immediately she brought paper, pen, and ink.

"Bachelor, bookkeeper, forty-five, Old New Presbyterian, refined, seeks Old New Presbyterian . . ." she suggested.

"That's not necessary," Archilochos said. "I'll convert my wife to the right faith."

Georgette consented. "Seeks a loving, cheerful wife, same age, widow not excluded . . ."

She would have to be a maiden, Archilochos objected.

Georgette firmly shook her head. "Forget about a maiden," she said forcefully. "You have never been with a woman. One of you has to know how to do it."

Monsieur Arnolph ventured an objection: the ad he had in mind would be different, he said.

"What's your idea?"

"Greek man seeks Greek wife!"

"Good Lord," Madame Bieler exclaimed, "are you Greek?" And she stared at the rather plump, ill-appointed, northern-looking figure before her.

"You know, Madame Bieler," he said shyly, "I know that most people's idea of a Greek is very different from what I happen to be, and it's a long time since my ancestor came to this country to die by the side of Charles the Bold in the Battle of Nancy.* That's why I don't quite look like a Greek. I admit it. But now, Madame Bieler, in this fog, in this cold and this rain, I long to go back, as I usually do in the winter, back to my homeland, which I have never seen, to the Peloponnesus with its ruddy cliffs and its blue sky (I read about it in *Paris Match*), and that's why the girl I'll marry will have to be Greek, because she'd feel as lonely as I do in this country."

"You talk just like a poet," Georgette had replied, drying her eyes.

And sure enough, Archilochos had received an answer just two days later. A small, fragrant envelope, a little card, blue as the sky of the Peloponnesus. Chloé Saloniki had written to say that she was lonely and to ask when she might see him.

Following Georgette's advice, he made an epistolary arrangement with Chloé: Chez Auguste, Sunday, January so and so. Identification: a red rose.

Archilochos put on his dark blue confirmation suit and forgot his coat. He was restless. He wondered whether he shouldn't turn back and hide in

*Charles the Bold, duke of Burgundy, was defeated by the Swiss in the Battle of Nancy in 1477.

his garret, and for the first time he minded the sight of Bibi waiting in front of Chez Auguste, almost unrecognizable in the fog.

"Give me a couple of hundreds and a ten," Bibi said, holding out his cupped fraternal hand: "Magda-Maria needs English lessons."

That surprised Archilochos.

"She's got a new suitor," Bibi explained. "Swell guy, but he only speaks English."

Archilochos with his red rose handed over the money.

Georgette, too, was excited. Only Auguste sat in his cyclist's outfit by the stove, as he always did when there were no customers, rubbing his bare legs.

Madame Bieler cleared off the counter. "I wonder what she's like," she said. "Nice and chubby, I bet. Not too old, I hope, since she didn't mention her age. But who likes to do that?"

Archilochos, freezing, ordered a cup of hot milk.

And while he was cleaning his glasses, which had fogged over from the steam of the milk, Chloé Saloniki stepped into the restaurant.

Archilochos, nearsighted, at first saw Chloé only as a vague shadow with a large red dot somewhere to the right below the oval of the face—the rose, he presumed, but the silence that suddenly reigned in the pub, this ghostly silence in which not the tinkle of a glass nor the sound of a breath could be heard, was so disquieting that he was unable to put on his glasses straightaway. But as soon as he did, he took them off and excitedly set about polishing them again. It was unbelievable. A miracle had happened, in a little neighborhood joint, amid fog and rain. To this pudgy bachelor and timid lover of mankind, locked up in a stinking garret, barricaded behind his milk and his mineral water, laden with principles and burdened with inhibitions, to this Assistant Bookkeeper of an Assistant Bookkeeper, with his eternally damp and torn socks and his unironed shirt, his much too tight-fitting clothes, his worn-out shoes and preposterous opinions, there had come such an enchanting creature, such a marvel of beauty and grace, so picture-perfect a little lady, that Georgette did not dare to move and Auguste, abashed, hid his cyclist's legs behind the stove.

"Monsieur Archilochos?" a soft, hesitant voice inquired. Archilochos stood up, knocking the cup with his sleeve, which caused the milk to run over his glasses. Finally he had them on again, and through streaks of milk he blinked at Chloé Saloniki, rooted to the spot.

"Another cup of milk," he finally said.

"Oh," Chloé laughed, "for me too."

Archilochos sat down, unable to take his eyes off her or to invite her to join him, although he would have liked to. He was afraid, the unreality of the situation depressed him, and he didn't dare think of his ad; bewildered, he removed the rose from his jacket. At any moment he expected her to turn in disappointment and leave. Perhaps, too, he thought he was only dreaming. He felt utterly defenseless, at the mercy of this girl's beauty and the miracle of this moment, which was incomprehensible, and which he dared not hope would last more than a moment. He felt ridiculous and ugly; suddenly his garret and its surroundings loomed enormously in his mind, the desolation of the working-class district in which he lived, the monotony of his work as a bookkeeper; but she simply sat down at the table opposite him and looked at him with big black eyes.

"Oh," she said happily, "I didn't imagine you would be so nice. I'm glad we Greeks have found each other. But come, your glasses are full of milk."

She took them from his nose, wiped them—apparently with her scarf, or so it seemed to Archilochos—and breathed on the lenses.

"Mademoiselle Saloniki," he finally said with a strangled voice, as if pronouncing his own death sentence: "It may be that I am no longer quite a real Greek. My family emigrated in the days of Charles the Bold."

Chloé laughed: "Once a Greek, always a Greek."

Then she put the glasses back on his nose, and Auguste brought the milk.

"Mademoiselle Saloniki . . ."

"Just call me Chloé," she said. "Now that we're going to get married. And I want to marry you, because you're Greek. I just want to make you happy."

Archilochos blushed. "This is the first time I've ever talked with a maiden, Chloé," he finally said. "It's only been Madame Bieler before this."

Chloé said nothing. She seemed to be thinking about something, and they both drank the hot, steaming milk.

After Chloé and Archilochos had left the restaurant together, Madame Bieler recovered her speech.

"What a dish," she said. "Unbelievable. And that bracelet she had, and that necklace, hundreds of thousands of francs. She must have worked hard. And did you see the coat on her? Some fur! A man couldn't wish for a better wife."

"And so young," said Auguste, still dazed.

"What are you talking about?" Georgette replied, mixing herself a glass of Campari and soda. "She's past thirty. But well put together. She gets a massage every day."

"So did I," Auguste said, "when I won the Tour de Suisse," and gazed mournfully at his skinny legs.

"And what a perfume!"

3

Chloé and Archilochos stood in the street. It was still raining. The fog was still there, too, a dark, gloomy presence, and the cold that pierced through one's clothing.

"There's a teetotalers' restaurant opposite the World Health Office," he finally said. "Very reasonable."

He was freezing in his damp and frayed confirmation suit.

"Let me have your arm," Chloé requested.

The Assistant Bookkeeper was at a loss. He did not quite know how this was done. He scarcely dared to look at the creature tripping along by his side through the fog with a silvery blue scarf thrown over her black hair. He was slightly embarrassed. It was the first time he had walked through the city with a girl, and so he was actually grateful for the fog. A church bell struck half past ten. They walked through vacant suburban streets whose houses were mirrored in the wet asphalt. Their steps echoed from the walls. It was as though they were in an underground vault. There wasn't a person in sight. A half-starved dog trotted toward them out of the darkness, a dirty spaniel, black-and-white, dripping wet, his ears and tongue drooping. The red traffic lights shimmered dimly through the gloom. Then a bus rolled past, senselessly honking its horn, evidently headed for the North Station. Archilochos, overwhelmed by the empty street, by Sunday, by the weather, snuggled into the soft fur of her coat to find room under her little red umbrella. They were walking in step, almost like regular lovers. Somewhere the tinny voices of a Salvation Army choir sounded through the mist, and once in a while the Telediffusion Sunday morning concert could be heard coming from the houses—some symphony, Beethoven or Schubert, mingling with the tooting of automobiles lost in the fog. Walking through uniform streets, stretches of which became visible as the day brightened, then dissolved back into grayness, they sensed that they were approaching the river. They walked down an endless boulevard with perpetually identical, boring facades (which could be made out clearly now), villas of long-since-ruined bankers and faded cocottes, with Doric and Corinthian columns at the doors, with stiff balconies and tall windows on the second floor, most of them lit, most of them damaged, spectral, dripping.

Chloé began to tell him about herself. The story of her youth, which was as wondrous as she was. She told it hesitantly, often haltingly. But to the Assistant Bookkeeper, everything that was untrustworthy appeared natural, for wasn't he experiencing a fairy tale himself?

She was an orphan (according to her story), the child of Greek immigrants from Crete who had frozen to death in the terrible winters. In a barracks. Then came the great desolation. She had grown up in a slum, filthy, ragged, just like that black-and-white spaniel before, stealing fruit and robbing the poor boxes. The police chased her, pimps pursued her. She slept under bridges among vagrants and in empty barrels, shy and suspicious as a wild animal. Then she was picked up, literally, by an archaeological couple out for an evening walk, and put in a school, with nuns, and was now living with her benefactors as a maid, decently dressed, decently fed, a touching story, all in all.

"An archaeological couple?" Arnolph wondered. He had never heard of anything like it.

"A couple who studied archaeology," Chloé Saloniki specified, "and made excavations in Greece. They discovered a temple with precious statues buried in the moss, and golden pillars."

What was their name?

Chloé hesitated. She seemed to be searching for a name.

"Gilbert and Elizabeth Weeman."

"The famous Weemans?"

(An article with color photographs of them had just appeared in *Paris Match.*)

"Yes, those."

He would incorporate them in his ethical world order, Arnolph said. As numbers Nine and Ten, or perhaps as numbers Six and Seven, in which case Maître Dutour and the Rector Magnificus could occupy numbers Nine and Ten, which was still an honor.

"You have an ethical world order?" Chloé asked, surprised. "What is that?"

A person needs something to hold on to in life, ethical models, Archilochos said. He hadn't had it easy either, he continued, though he hadn't grown up among murderers and vagabonds as she had, but with his brother Bibi in an orphanage; and he began describing his universal moral edifice.

4

The weather had changed, unnoticeably at first for Arnolph and Chloé. The rain had stopped, the fog was lifting. It had turned into ghostly figures, long, stretched-out dragons, hulking bears, and giant men that slid over the villas, banks, government houses, and palaces, blending into each other, rising, and dissolving. Blue sky shimmered through the masses of fog, indistinct at first, delicate, the merest intimation of spring, which was still far away, a hint of sunlight, infinitely subtle, then ever more clear, bright, and powerful. On the wet asphalt you could see the shadows of buildings, of lanterns, of monuments, of people, and all at once every object stood out with extraordinary clarity, shining in the sudden burst of light.

They were on the quay in front of the President's palace. The river was brown and hugely swollen. Bridges with rusty iron railings arched across it, empty barges moved along, hung with diapers, their freezing skippers pacing to and fro with pipes in their mouths. The streets were swarming with Sunday strollers, solemn grandfathers with their dolled-up grandchildren, families forming rows on the sidewalks. Policemen stood about, reporters, journalists, evidently waiting for the President, who promptly came bursting out of the palace in his historic carriage drawn by six white horses, accompanied by his mounted bodyguards with their golden helmets and white plumes, off to perform some political act, dedicate a monument, pin a medal on a chest, or open an orphanage. Trampling hooves, blaring trumpets, hurrahs, and hats filled the air, which was now clear of mist and rain.

Then the incomprehensible happened.

At the moment when the President drove past Chloé and Archilochos, and Arnolph, delighted by this unexpected meeting with Number One in his world order (which he had just begun to explain), peered at His goateed, gray-haired Excellency (who, spangled with gold and framed by the window of his carriage, looked exactly like the picture that hung over Madame Bieler's Pernod and Campari bottles), the President suddenly greeted the Assistant Bookkeeper by waving His right hand as if Archilochos were an old acquaintance. And so conspicuous was this fluttering of a white glove, and so clearly was it intended for him, that two policemen with commanding moustaches snapped to attention.

"The President greeted me," Archilochos stuttered incredulously.

"Why shouldn't he greet you?" asked Chloé Saloniki.

"But I'm just an insignificant citizen!"

"As President, he is a father to all of us," was how Chloé explained the strange occurrence.

Then another event took place that Archilochos was also unable to understand, but that filled him with fresh pride.

He was on the verge of telling her about Number Two in his world order, Bishop Moser, and about the extremely important differences that had developed between the Old New and the Old Presbyterians of the Penultimate Christians, after which he would have briefly touched on the New

Presbyterians (that scandal within the Presbyterian Church), when they met with Petit-Paysan (Number Three in the world order, actually out of turn), who may have come from the World Bank, five hundred meters from away from the President's palace, or from St. Luke's Cathedral, which stood next to the World Bank. He was dressed in a splendid coat, top hat, and white scarf, rustling with elegance. His chauffeur had already opened the door of the Rolls-Royce when Arnolph caught sight of him. Arnolph faltered. The event was unique and, in view of the explanations he was giving Chloé concerning his world order, instructive. The great industrialist did not know Archilochos, nor could he have known him, a mere Assistant Bookkeeper in the Obstetrical Forceps Division, a fact that in turn gave Archilochos the courage to point out this exalted being, though not the courage to greet him (you don't greet a god). And so Archilochos, though frightened, felt secure in the knowledge that he could pass by this mighty man unnoticed, when for the second time, as in the case of the President's passing, the incomprehensible happened: Petit-Paysan smiled, lifted his top hat, waved it, performed a courteous bow before a paling Archilochos, then dropped into the soft seat of his limousine, waved again, and roared off.

"But that was Petit-Paysan," Archilochos panted.

"So?"

"Number Three in my world order!"

"So?"

"He greeted me!"

"I should hope so."

"But I'm just an Assistant Bookkeeper working with fifty other Assistant Bookkeepers in the most insignificant subsection of the Obstetrical Forceps Division," Archilochos exclaimed.

"Then he must be a man with a social conscience," Chloé decided, "worthy of holding third place in your universal moral edifice." Evidently she did not yet comprehend the astonishing nature of this encounter.

But that Sunday's miracles would not cease: the weather, in the middle of winter, grew steadily warmer and more brilliant, the sky steadily bluer and more unreal; the whole enormous city seemed suddenly to be greeting Archilochos as he walked with his Greek fiancée across the bridges with their wrought-iron railings and through the old parks outside the half-decayed palaces. Arnolph became prouder, more confident, his gait freer, his face more radiant. He was more than an Assistant Bookkeeper. He was a happy human being. Elegant young men greeted him, waving from cafés, buses, and Vespas, well-groomed gentlemen with graying temples, even a Belgian general with many decorations, evidently from NATO headquarters, stepping out of a jeep. In front of the American Embassy, Ambassador Bob Forster-Monroe, accompanied by two Scotch sheepdogs, clearly called out to him: "Hello!" while Number Two (Bishop Moser, even more well-nourished than he was on the picture at Madame Bieler's) encountered them between the National Museum and the crematorium on his way to the teetotalers' restaurant opposite the World Health Office. Bishop Moser, too, saluted him—this seemed somehow quite natural by now—even though their previous acquaintance was not at all personal but restricted to Arnolph's presence, one day, among a flock of hymn-singing ladies attending an Easter sermon given by the Bishop (whose biography, however, Archilochos had read at least a hundred times in a pamphlet on this exemplary subject that was distributed among the congregation). Yet the Bishop seemed even more confused than the greeted member of the Old New Presbyterian Church, for with noticeable suddenness and haste, and for no apparent reason, he dashed into a side street.

Then they dined together in the teetotalers' restaurant. They sat by a window and gazed out across the river at the World Health Office with the monument of a famous World Health official in front of it, on which gulls rested, from which they rose, around which they circled, upon which they settled again. They were both tired from their long walk and held hands even after the soup had been placed before them. The restaurant was mainly frequented by Old New Presbyterians (just a few Old Presbyterians among them), mostly spinsters and eccentric bachelors who came to dine here on Sundays in support of the struggle against alcoholism, even though the host, an intractable Catholic, stubbornly refused to hang Bishop Moser's portrait; on the contrary, the man hanging next to the President was the Archbishop.

5

Later they sat, two Greeks beneath two Greeks, moving ever more closely together under a moldering statue in the old municipal park that, according to the travel guides and city maps, was supposed to represent Daphnis and Chloé.* They watched the sun setting behind trees, a red child's balloon. Here, too, Archilochos was greeted. This inconspicuous man (pale, bespectacled, somewhat paunchy), who was ordinarily noticed only by cycling

*Hero and heroine of a famous Greek pastoral romance.

fans and Assistant Bookkeepers, seemed suddenly to interest the city, to be the center of society. The fairy tale continued. Number Four passed by (Passap), accompanied by a gaggle of art critics, some of them distraught, others enthusiastic, for the master had just abandoned his rectangular period with the circles and the parabolas and was now painting only sixty-degree angles with ellipses and parabolas, and using cobalt blue and ochre in place of red and green. Surprised, the master of modern painting stopped in his tracks, growled, scrutinized Archilochos thoroughly, nodded, and ambled on, continuing with his lecture. The former Numbers Six and Seven (now Nine and Ten), on the other hand, Maître Dutour and the Rector Magnificus, greeted Archilochos with a barely perceptible wink, for they were walking at the side of mightily proportioned wives.

Archilochos told Chloé about his life. "I don't earn much," he said. "The work is monotonous; reports about forceps, and it has to be done with precision. The boss, a Vice Bookkeeper, is strict, and I also have to support my brother Bibi and his little children, lovable people, perhaps somewhat wild and natural, but honest. We will save, and in twenty years we'll go to Greece together. The Peloponnesus, the islands. That's been my dream for a long time, and now that I know I'll be traveling with you, the dream is even more beautiful."

She was delighted. "It'll be a lovely trip," she said.

"On a steam ship."

"On the *Julia*."

He gave her a questioning look.

"A luxury liner, Mrs. and Mr. Weeman travel on it."

"Of course," he remembered, "that's what it said in *Paris Match*. But the *Julia* will be too expensive for us, and twenty years from now it will have been scrapped. We'll go on a coal boat. That's cheaper."

He often thought of Greece, he went on, observing the fog, which was beginning to return, drifting along the ground like fine white smoke. He could see the old temples clearly, he said, their half-shattered forms, the ruddy cliffs shining through the olive groves. Often he felt as if he were an exile in this city, like the Jews in Babylon, and the meaning of his life was to go home some day to the land his ancestors had left long ago.

Now the fog lurked behind the trees by the banks of the river like huge heaps of cotton, embracing the slow-moving barges, whose foghorns blared like rutting beasts. Then the whiteness rose, flared violet, and began to spread as soon as the large, red sun had set. Archilochos accompanied Chloé to the boulevard where the Weemans lived—a rich and elegant neighborhood, he noticed. They passed wrought-iron fences, large gardens with stately old trees that shielded the villas and mansions from public view. Poplars, elms, beeches, black fir trees towered into the silvery evening sky and vanished among the thickening banks of fog. In front of an iron gate with putti and dolphins, strange leaves and spirals and two huge stone pillars, Chloé stopped, illumined by a red lamp above the portal.

"Tomorrow evening?"

"Chloé!"

"Will you ring?" she asked, pointing to an archaic contraption. "At eight?"

Then she kissed the Assistant Bookkeeper, wrapping both arms around his neck, kissed him again, and a third time.

"We will go to Greece," she whispered, "to our ancient homeland. Soon. And on the *Julia*."

She opened the garden gate and vanished among the trees and into the mist, waving back once more and calling out some phrase, tenderly, like a mysterious bird, as she walked toward some building that presumably stood invisibly somewhere in the garden.

Archilochos, on the other hand, marched back to his working-class district. He had a long way to go, trotting along all the paths he had taken with Chloé. He thought back on all the phases of this magical Sunday, stopped in front of the deserted bench under Daphnis and Chloé, then in front of the teetotalers' restaurant, which the last Old New Presbyterian spinsters were just leaving, one of whom greeted him and perhaps waited for him at the next corner. Then he went to the crematorium, the National Museum, and walked along the quay. The fog was dense, but not dirty as it had been on previous days; it was tender, milky, a miraculous fog, it seemed to him, with rays of light bundled into long golden sheaves, and delicate, finely spiked stars. He reached the Ritz, and as he passed the pompous portal with the six-foot doorman in a green coat and red trousers holding a long silver staff, there stepped out of the hotel Gilbert and Elizabeth Weeman, the world-famous archaeologists, whose pictures he had seen in the newspapers. These were English persons, she too more man than woman, with the same haircut as his, both of them equipped with golden pince-nez, Gilbert with a red moustache and a short pipe (the only features that distinguished him clearly from his wife).

Archilochos plucked up his courage. "Madame, monsieur," he said. "My respects."

"Well," the scientist said, amazed by the sight of the Assistant Bookkeeper in his worn-out shoes and frayed confirmation suit, while Mrs. Weeman peered at him through her pince-nez: "Well," and then he added, "yes."

"I have appointed you Numbers Six and Seven in my ethical world order."

"Yes."

"You have given a home to a Greek maiden," Archilochos continued.

"Well," Mr. Weeman said.

"I, too, am Greek."

"Oh," said Mr. Weeman and drew out his wallet.

Archilochos made a gesture of refusal. "No, sir, no, madam," he said. "I know I don't look trustworthy, and perhaps not exactly Greek either, but my salary at the Petit-Paysan Engineering Works will suffice for me to set up a modest household with her. Yes, we will even be able to consider having children, though perhaps just three or four, since the Petit-Paysan Engineering Works maintain a socially progressive maternity clinic for its employees."

"Well," said Mr. Weeman, putting his wallet back in his pocket.

"Farewell," Archilochos said. "God bless you, and I will pray for you in the Old New Presbyterian Church."

6

But at the door of his house he met Bibi with the cupped fraternal hand.

"Théophile ripped off the National Bank," he said. "The cops picked up on it."

"So?"

"He has to go south till the heat's off. I need a couple of hundreds. You'll have 'em back by Christmas."

Archilochos gave him money.

"What's up, brother?" Bibi demurred, disappointed. "A dime-note, that's it?"

"It's all I can do, Bibi," Archilochos apologized, embarrassed and, to his surprise, a little annoyed. "Really. I sat with a maiden in the teetotalers' restaurant opposite the World Health Office. The menu and a bottle of grape juice. I want to start a family."

Brother Bibi was alarmed.

"What do you want with a family?" he cried out indignantly. "I've already got one! Does she have any money at least?"

"No."

"What's her line?"

"She's a maid."

"Where?"

"Boulevard Saint-Père number twelve."

Bibi whistled through his teeth.

"Go hit the sack, Arnolph, but hand me another ten."

7

After reaching his garret, on the sixth floor, he undressed. He lay down on his bed. He would have liked to open the window. The room was stuffy. But the toilets were more noticeable than usual. He lay in semidarkness. In the little windows across the shaftway, the lights went on and off, now here, now there. The flushing never stopped. Alternately, on the wall of his garret, one or the other picture of his world order lit up: first the Bishop, then the President, now Bibi with his little dears, next the triangular rectangles in Passap's painting, now one of the other numbers.

"Tomorrow I must get myself a picture of the Weemans and have it framed," he thought.

The air was so stale, so thick, that he could hardly breathe. Sleep was out of the question. He had gone to bed happy, but now worries beset him. It would be impossible for him to live in this garret with Chloé, to found a household, to find room for the three or four children he had planned on his way home. He would have to find a new apartment. But he had no money for that, no savings. He had given all he had to his brother Bibi. Now he owned nothing. Not even the wretched bed, the miserable table, and the rickety chair. He lived in a furnished room. Only the various pictures of his universal moral edifice belonged to him. His poverty depressed him. Chloé's delicacy and beauty needed a delicate, beautiful setting, he sensed. She must never return to the bridges by the river and the empty barrels in the garbage dumps. The roaring cascades outside his window sounded more and more malignant, more and more odious. He vowed to leave this garret; tomorrow, he decided, he would look for another place. But as he thought about how he might accomplish this goal, he felt helpless. He saw no way. He realized that he was trapped in a pitiless machine, and that he had no chance to make a reality of the marvel that had presented itself to him on this Sunday. Disheartened and helpless, he lay awake waiting for morning, which eventually announced itself with an increased tumult of flushing toilets.

Toward eight now, as on every Monday morning, and in the dark, for it was that time of the year, Archilochos trotted along with the armies of Bookkeepers, secretaries, and Assistant Bookkeepers into the administrative offices of the Petit-Paysan Engineering Works, an inconspicuous particle in the gray stream of humanity that poured out of the subways, the buses, the streetcars and suburban trains, and bleakly flowed on in the light of the street lamps toward the gigantic steel-and-glass cube that swallowed, divided, sorted them, shoved them up and down elevators and escalators, squeezed them through corridors, first floor: Tank Division; second floor: Atomic Cannon; third floor: Machine Gun Division, and so forth. Archilochos, wedged in among the crowds, pushed and driven, worked on the seventh floor, Obstetrical Forceps Division, Office 122-OF, in one of many bare, colorless rooms partitioned with glass, but had to first step into the Hygiene Room, gargle, take a pill (against the intestinal flu), a measure required by Social Welfare. Then he put on his gray working smock, still freezing, because now, for the first time that winter, a great, cutting cold had attacked the city, overnight, covering all things with a smooth sheen. He had to hurry, for it was already one minute to eight, and lateness was not tolerated (time is money). He sat down at a desk, also made of steel and glass, which he shared with three Assistant Bookkeepers numbered AB122-OF28, AB122-OF29, and AB122-OF30, and uncovered his typewriter. The number on his working smock was AB122-OF31. He began to type. His fingers were still stiff. The hand of the big clock had advanced to eight. It was his task, this morning, to tabulate the rise in obstetrical forceps sales in the canton of Appenzell Innerrhoden. Like himself, the three other Assistant Bookkeepers clattered away at their typewriters, the forty-six others in the room, the hundreds, thousands in the building, from eight to twelve, from two to five, with meals in the Community Canteen, all of them integrated in Petit-Paysan's model company, visited by cabinet ministers, by foreign delegations, by bespectacled Chinese and lecherous Hindus, who, being interested in social welfare, floated through the rooms with their silken wives.

But sometimes (though rarely) the miracles of Sunday continue on Monday.

8

An announcement came through the loudspeaker, telling Archilochos to report to Bookkeeper B121-OF. For a moment there was a deathly silence in Room 122-OF. Not a breath could be heard. Not even the most timid clatter of some typist continuing his chore. The Greek stood up. Pale, reeling. He feared the worst. Dismissals were impending. But Bookkeeper B121-OF received him in his office next to Room 122-OF in a manner that was nothing less than cordial, as Archilochos, who had hardly dared to enter, noticed with amazement, for he had heard some awful accounts of B121-OF's fits of rage.

"Monsieur Archilochos," B121-OF exclaimed, walking forward to meet the Assistant Bookkeeper and even shaking his hand, "I have long been aware of your exceptional talent, I must say."

"Oh, please," said Archilochos, surprised at the praise but still suspicious.

"Your presentation," smiled B121-OF, rubbing his hands (small, nimble, fiftyish, with nearsighted eyes, in a white Bookkeeper's smock with gray elbow patches), "your presentation of the status and maintenance of obstetrical forceps in the Canton of Appenzell Innerrhoden is exemplary."

"I'm glad to hear that," Archilochos said, still convinced that he had fallen prey to a cruel whim on the Bookkeeper's part, and taking his friendliness for a ruse.

The Bookkeeper offered his suspicious Assistant Bookkeeper a chair and excitedly paced back and forth in his office.

"In view of your excellent work, my dear Monsieur Archilochos, I am planning to take certain steps."

"This is a great honor for me," stammered Archilochos.

"I'm thinking of a Vice Bookkeeper's position," B121-OF purred. "I have just sent the proposal to the Chief of Personnel in charge of the section that includes our office."

Gratefully Archilochos rose to his feet, but the Bookkeeper had a second request. He looked anxious and unhappy as he came out with it, as if *he* were an Assistant Bookkeeper.

"I almost forgot," B121-OF said softly, trying to keep his composure. "Chief Bookkeeper CB9-OF wishes to speak to Monsieur Archilochos. This morning."

The Bookkeeper wiped the sweat from his brow with a red checked handkerchief.

"Right now the Chief Bookkeeper wants to talk to you," he continued. "Sit down again, my dear friend, we have another minute. Above all, collect yourself, don't lose your nerve, take courage, see that you rise to the occasion."

"Certainly," Archilochos said, he would try.

"Good Lord," said the Bookkeeper, sitting down behind his desk. "Good Lord, Monsieur Archilochos, I'm sure you don't mind my calling you that, my good friend, in confidence and just between the two of us—my name is Rummel, Erwin Rummel—this is an event the like of which I have never seen, and I've been working in the Petit-Paysan Engineering Works for thirty-three years. A Vice Bookkeeper asking to see an Assistant Bookkeeper, just like that—I have never experienced such a blatant violation of standard protocol. I am close to fainting, my dear friend, I mean I believed in your brilliant qualities, but still! All my life I've never stood in the presence of a Chief Bookkeeper, and I'd tremble like an aspen leaf if I did, because Bookkeepers deal with Vice Bookkeepers only! And now you! Directly summoned by a Chief Bookkeeper! I'm sure he's got his reasons, some secret purpose, I foresee a promotion, you'll get my job, that's it . . ." (here B121-OF dried his eyes) ". . . perhaps you'll even get to be Vice Chief Bookkeeper, as happened recently in the Atomic Canon Division to a Bookkeeper who had the honor of getting quite closely acquainted with the spouse of a Chief Personnel Director—not you, my friend, not you, in your case it's just your achievements, that consummate report on the Canton of Appenzell Innerrhoden, I know. But, dear friend, just between you and me: it was just by chance that my recommendation for your promotion to Vice Bookkeeper and the summons from the Chief Bookkeeper came at the same moment, so to speak, I give you my word of honor! My request concerning your promotion was already written when out of a clear blue sky the telephone call from the secretary of our esteemed Chief Bookkeeper reached me—but it's high time, my good friend—incidentally, my wife would love to have you for dinner—as well as my daughter—quite charming, quite pretty, takes singing lessons—whenever you wish—you would do us an honor—fifth corridor southeast, sixth office—my God, all this when my heart's ailing—and my kidneys are acting up too."

9

CB9-OF, fifth southeastern corridor, sixth office, a portly man with neatly trimmed black beard, flashing gold teeth, cologne scent, and paunch, the photograph of a seminude dancer in a platinum frame on his desk, received the Assistant Bookkeeper courteously, shooed flocks of secretaries out of his office, and with a generous sweep of his hand offered him a comfortable easy chair.

"My dear Monsieur Archilochos," he began, "we Chief Bookkeepers have long been aware of your superb contributions, and your reports on the introduction of the obstetrical forceps in the far north, with special regard to Alaska, have, especially, caused quite a stir; in fact, I dare say they have raised waves of the highest admiration. Your works are discussed within our circles, and the Alaskan report is said to have greatly impressed the Directors."

"There must be some mistake, sir," Arnolph interjected. "I only work on the canton of Appenzell Innerrhoden and the Tyrol."

"Just call me Petit-Pierre," said CB9-OF. "After all, we're among ourselves and not among philistines. Whether or not you wrote the report on Alaska, it was inspired by you, it breathes your spirit, the incomparable style of your classical reports on the canton of Appenzell Innerrhoden, on the Tyrol. One more happy sign that your work is bearing fruit, that others are following in your footsteps. I always exclaimed to my colleague, Chief Bookkeeper Schränzle: Archilochos is a poet, a great prose stylist. Schränzle sends his regards, incidentally. So does Chief Bookkeeper Häberlin. I have always been pained by the subordinate position you occupy in our highly respected organization, a post that isn't at all commensurate with your extraordinary abilities. By the way, may I offer you a glass of vermouth?"

"Thank you, Monsieur Petit-Pierre," said Archilochos, "but I am a teetotaler."

"It strikes me as particularly scandalous that you should be working under Bookkeeper B121-OF, that truly mediocre factotum, Rummler or whatever his name is."

"He just proposed my promotion to Vice Bookkeeper."

"That's typical of him," CB9-OF said angrily. "Vice Bookkeeper! He'd like that! A man of your ability! Why, the Petit-Paysan Engineering Works owes the rise in obstetrical forceps production during the last quarter exclusively to you."

"But Monsieur Petit-Pierre . . ."

"Let's not be too modest now, my dear sir, not too modest. There's a limit to everything. Here I've waited patiently for years, hoping that you would turn to me in confidence as your most faithful friend and admirer, and you simply keep holding out under that intolerable Bookkeeper, carrying on as an Assistant Bookkeeper among Assistant Bookkeepers, in an environment that couldn't be more unsuitable for you. Instead of pounding your fist on the table! It must have been nerve-wracking, spending your days with that riffraff. I just had to put a stop to this. I may just be a powerless little Chief Bookkeeper in the labyrinth of our administration, a nothing, a midget. But I took my heart into both hands. Someone had to stand up for your talents no matter what the consequences, even if the world came to an end, even if it cost him his own head. The courage of our convictions! If we don't have that, my friend, it's all over with the ethical value of the Petit-Paysan Engineering Works, and what we'll have is the pure dictatorship of bureaucracy, as I've been proclaiming for years. I rang up the Chief Personnel Director of our division (who, incidentally, asked me to convey his regards to you): I wanted to propose you as Vice Director; frankly, I couldn't think of anything more satisfying than continuing to work under you, dear Monsieur Archilochos, for our worthy enterprise, the continual refinement and expanding distribution of the obstetrical forceps, but Petit-Paysan himself, God the Father, so to speak, or fate, if you wish, has, alas, alas, anticipated me—a small personal setback, which of course, from your point of view, represents a great though not undeserved good fortune."

"Petit-Paysan?"

Archilochos thought he was dreaming.

"But that's impossible!"

"He wishes to see you today, this very morning, this very hour, Monsieur Archilochos," CB9-OF said.

"But . . ."

"No buts."

"I mean . . ."

"Monsieur Archilochos," the Chief Bookkeeper said earnestly, stroking his well-tended beard, "let us speak frankly. Man to man, friend to friend. Take my word for it: this is an historic day, a day of candor, of clarification. From the bottom of my heart I assure you, on my word of honor, that the fact that I have proposed you for Vice Director and the fact that our revered Petit-Paysan, hats off to him, wishes to speak to you, have nothing whatsoever to do with each other. On the contrary. I had just dictated the formal request for your promotion when Director Zeus called for me."

"Director Zeus?"

"The man in charge of the Obstetrical Forceps Division."

Archilochos apologized for his ignorance. He had never heard this name.

"I know," the Chief Bookkeeper replied, "the names of our Directors have not filtered down to the circles of Bookkeepers and Assistant Bookkeepers. What would be the purpose? Those coolies are supposed to keep writing, churning out bunk about the canton of Appenzell Innerrhoden or God knows what holes in the wall, all of which, just between you and me, my dear Monsieur Archilochos, holds not the slightest bit of interest for anyone—with the exception of your works, of course, which we Chief Bookkeepers positively devour as soon as we can get our hands on them: your reports on the canton of Basel, for instance, or the one about Costa Rica, which are superb, classical, as I've already said; but the others—overpaid useless clowns, these Bookkeepers and Assistant Bookkeepers, I've been piping and preaching about this to the gentlemen of the Administration for ages. I could run this joint with my secretaries alone. Let's face it, the Petit-Paysan Engineering Works isn't a home for the mentally retarded. Incidentally, Director Zeus sends his kind regards."

"Thank you."

"Unfortunately he's in the hospital now."

"Oh."

"Nervous breakdown."

"I'm sorry to hear that."

"You see, my dear friend, you have plunged the Obstetrical Forceps Management into complete catastrophe. Sodom and Gomorrah were a harmless flash in the pan by comparison. Petit-Paysan wishes to see you! Very well, it's his right, God the Father can put horns on a full moon if he wants, but we'd be very surprised nonetheless if he did that. Petit-Paysan and an Assistant Bookkeeper! It's really no less miraculous. So we shouldn't be surprised that some unfortunate Director hears the bell tolling. And the Vice Director? He broke down too."

"But why?"

"Because, my dear sir, you are going to be appointed Obstetrical Forceps Director, any infant can see that. Otherwise none of this would make any sense. Anyone summoned to Petit-Paysan's office gets to be a Director, that's something we know from experience. Firing is done by the Chief Personnel Director."

"Director? Me?"

"Certainly. Chief Personnel Director Feuz has already been notified of the promotion. He, too, sends his regards, incidentally."

"Of the Obstetrical Forceps Division?"

"Possibly of the Atomic Cannon as well, who knows. Chief Personnel Director Feuz thinks anything is possible."

"But why?" shrieked Archilochos, who couldn't make sense of any of this.

"My dear, good friend! You forget your excellent reports on Upper Italy..."

"My work is exclusively on Eastern Switzerland and the Tyrol," the Assistant Bookkeeper obstinately corrected him.

"Eastern Switzerland and Tyrol, I get mixed up about landscapes, I'm not a geographer."

"But that can't be a reason for making me the Obstetrical Forceps Director."

"Oh, come now."

"But I don't have the ability to be a Director," Archilochos protested.

CB9-OF shook his head, gave Archilochos a quizzical look, smiled, revealing his gold teeth, and folded his hands over his pampered belly. "The reason," he said, "my dear, most esteemed friend, the reason why you have been appointed Director is something you must know, not I, and if you don't know, don't try to find out. It's better that way. Take my advice. This is probably the last time we will sit face to face. Directors and Chief Bookkeepers don't commonly associate, it would go against the unwritten rules of our exemplary firm. After all, I myself saw Director Zeus in person today for the first time, in the hour of his downfall, to be sure, just as poor Vice Director Stüssi, who is my proper superior and who alone associates with the Chief Bookkeepers, was being carried out on a stretcher. Truly a twilight of the gods. Let us pass over this impressive scene in silence. Your scruples: You're afraid you don't have any executive ability. My dearest friend, just between the two of us, everyone has executive ability, any fool can do it. All you have to do is be a Director, exist as a Director, assume the dignity, represent the company, lead Indians, Chinese, and Zulu Kafirs through the halls, members of UNESCO and the medical association and whoever else in God's great world has an interest in the noble obstetrical forceps. The practical business, the plant, the technology, the calculations, the planning, all this gets worked out by the Chief Bookkeepers, to put it somewhat frankly in the presence of an esteemed friend. No need for your hair to turn gray over that. What will be important, of course, is whom you select from the ranks of the Chief Bookkeepers to be Vice Director. Stüssi's finished now, and high time, too, he was too closely linked to Director Zeus, His Lordship's minion—well, I don't want to comment on Zeus's professional qualifications, it wouldn't be proper. He's had a nervous breakdown. Far be it from me to criticize. It was a cross working under him, just between the two of us, because, you see, he was incapable of merely comprehending the reports on Dalmatia that you, my esteemed friend and patron, had written, and was altogether without a glimmer—I know, I know, it wasn't Dalmatia, it was Toggenburg or Turkey: forget it, you were born for higher aspirations. Like an eagle you soar above us into the blue empyrean, and we Chief Bookkeepers can only stand in amazement. At any rate, once again between you and me: we Chief Bookkeepers are glad to have you as our Director! That I especially as your best friend will cry hallelujah and hosanna . . ." (here CB9-OF's eyes grew moist) ". . . is something I don't wish to stress again, it would really be quite inappropriate, it would look as if I, of all people, were asking to be appointed Vice Director, although frankly I do hold a senior position. Whatever your choice among us Chief Bookkeepers, whomever you appoint to be your deputy, I shall accept that choice with humility, will remain your greatest admirer—my colleague Spätzle still wants to see you, and then Schränzle, but I'm afraid, I'm afraid, I must now escort you as fast possible to Petit-Paysan and deliver you undamaged to his waiting room, the hour is getting late. So come now, carry your head proudly, enjoy your good luck, you deserve it, you're the worthiest, most talented of any of us, true as gold, so to speak, a brilliant child of fortune, the Obstetrical Forceps Division will yet surpass the Machine Gun Division with vigor, I foresee it, my dear, most highly esteemed Director, as I had best call you from now on, may I, please, it's my privilege, it is my great pleasure, we might as well take the Directors' elevator right away."

10

With CB9-OF, Archilochos entered rooms he had never imagined, realms of glass and unknown materials, gleaming with cleanliness, marvelous elevators that raised him to the upper, mysterious stories of the administration building. Lovely secretaries floated fragrantly past him, smiling, their hair colored blond, brunette, black, and in one case a glorious vermilion, male secretaries stepped aside for him, Directors bowed, General Directors nodded to him, plush corridors received him, the little lamps lighting up over their doors, now red, now green, the only signs of discreet administrative activity. They walked soundlessly on soft rugs, for all noise, even the slightest clearing of a throat, the most guarded little cough, would have seemed out of place. French Impressionists glowed on the walls (Petit-Paysan's collection of paintings was famous), a Degas dancer, a bathing beauty by Renoir, flowers in tall vases exuded their scents. The higher the two men floated, the fewer people they encountered. The corridors and rooms lost their cold, hypermodern, functional sobriety without changing their proportions, and became more fantastical, warmer, more human; Gobelins hung on the walls now, golden Rococo and Louis XIV mirrors, some Poussins, some Watteaus, a Claude Lorrain, and when they reached the top floor (CB9-OF, who was just as intimidated as Archilochos, for he had never penetrated this far, took his leave now), the Assistant Bookkeeper was received by a dignified gray-haired gentleman in an impeccable tuxedo, no doubt a secretary, who led the Greek down serene corridors and rooms bathed in light, with antique vases and Gothic madonnas, Asian idols and Indian wall hangings. There was nothing here to remind one of the production of atomic cannon and machine guns, though perhaps the sight of a few cherubs and putti smiling down at the Assistant Bookkeeper from a Rubens painting might evoke a thought of obstetrical forceps. A serene calm prevailed in these heights. The sun shimmered through the windows, a warm, cheerful disc, even though in reality it stood in an ice-cold sky. Comfortable armchairs and couches stood about, a bright laugh rang out somewhere, reminding Archilochos in his gray working smock of Chloé's laughter, of that radiant Sunday and its continuing wonders. Somewhere music trembled, Haydn or Mozart, no clattering of typewriters could be heard, no walking back and forth of agitated Bookkeepers, there was nothing to remind him of the world he had just risen out of and that now lay far below him like a bad dream. Now they were standing in a bright room with red silk covering the walls and a large painting representing a naked woman, probably the famous Titian people were talking about, whispering its fabulous price wherever you went. Delicate little pieces of furniture stood about, a small desk, a little wall clock with a silver pendulum, a diminutive gaming table surrounded by dainty armchairs, and flowers, roses, camellias, tulips, orchids, gladioli in lavish profusion, as though there were no seasons, no cold, no fog, and no winter. No sooner had they entered than a small side door opened and Petit-Paysan came in, dressed like the secretary, in a tuxedo, an India-paper edition of Hölderlin's poems in his left hand, his index finger parting the pages.* The secretary left the room. Archilochos and Petit-Paysan stood face to face.

"Well," said Petit-Paysan, "my dear Monsieur Anaximander—"

"My name is Arnolph Archilochos," the Assistant Bookkeeper corrected him, bowing.

"Archilochos. Very good. I knew your name had something Greek or Balkan about it, my dear Chief Bookkeeper."

"Assistant Bookkeeper," Archilochos said.

"Assistant Bookkeeper, Chief Bookkeeper, it amounts more or less to the same thing," said the industrialist, smiling, "doesn't it? At least, I don't make any distinction. How do you like my abode up here? Nice view, if I may say so myself. You can see the whole city, the river, and even the President's palace, not to mention the cathedral, and out there in the distance, North Station."

"Very beautiful, Monsieur Petit-Paysan."

"You're the first one of the Atomic Cannon Division to enter this floor," the industrialist said, as if congratulating Archilochos for an athletic feat.

Archilochos replied that he was from the Obstetrical Forceps Division, and that his area was Eastern Switzerland and the Tyrol, currently the canton of Appenzell Innerrhoden.

"My goodness," Petit-Paysan said in surprise. "You're from the Obstetrical Forceps Division. I had no idea we built that sort of thing. What is it?"

The obstetrical forceps, Archilochos explained, was a set of tongs used as an aid in childbirth and designed to grasp the child's head during parturition in order to speed up the delivery. The Petit-Paysan Engineering Works, Inc., produced forceps in several models, he said, but in all of them one could distinguish between different parts: first the two fenestrated blades, which

*Friedrich Hölderlin (1770–1843), German romantic poet.

were curved to hold the head and were also equipped with a second curve, the so-called pelvic bend, and a third one, the perineal bend, to facilitate the introduction of the instrument; next, the handles, which could be long or short, made of metal or wood, with or without special holds and cross-grips; and finally, the lock, that is, the mechanism by means of which both blades could be set to function as tongs at the moment of use. The prices . . .

"You certainly have a grasp of your subject," the captain of industry said with a smile. "But let's spare ourselves the question of price. Now, my dear Monsieur—"

"Archilochos."

"Archilochos, to make it brief and not keep you in suspense any longer, I have appointed you Director of the Atomic Cannon. To be sure, you just confessed to me that you belong to the Obstetrical Forceps Division, the existence of which was truly unknown to me. That surprises me a bit, something must have gotten mixed up somewhere, there are always mix-ups in a huge enterprise like this. All right, it doesn't matter, let's simply combine the two divisions, consider yourself from now on Director of the Atomic Cannon and Obstetrical Forceps Division. I'll have the respective directors put on retirement pension. I am very pleased to have the opportunity to inform you personally of your promotion, and I wish you the best of luck."

"Director Zeus of the Obstetrical Forceps Division is already in the hospital."

"Oh, what's wrong with him?"

"Nervous breakdown."

"Goodness, then my intention must have already come to his notice." Petit-Paysan shook his head in wonder. "And yet I only meant to discharge Director Jehudi of the Atomic Cannon Division. There's always a leak somewhere, and then it trickles down, too much gossip. Very well, Director Zeus anticipated me with his nervous breakdown. I would have had to dismiss him anyway. Let us hope that Director Jehudi will absorb the news of his removal with greater composure."

Archilochos pulled himself together and for the first time dared to look directly at Petit-Paysan with his India-paper volume. "May I ask," he said, "what all this means? You send for me, you appoint me Director of the Atomic Cannon and Obstetrical Forceps Divisions. I have to confess I'm feeling uneasy, because I don't understand any of this."

Petit-Paysan regarded the Assistant Bookkeeper calmly, placed the Hölderlin volume on the little green gaming table, sat down, invited Archilochos with a gesture to sit down also. They sat facing each other in the sunlight, on soft cushions. Archilochos scarcely dared to breathe, so awed was he by the solemnity of the occasion. At last he would learn the reason for these mysterious events, he thought.

"Monsieur Petit-Paysan," he therefore began anew, in a shy, halting voice: "I have always revered you, you are Number Three in my moral world edifice, which I built myself in order to have some moral stability. You come immediately after our revered President and Bishop Moser of the Old New Presbyterian Church, let that be confessed right away; all the more urgently I beg you to explain to me the reason for your actions: Bookkeeper Rummel and Chief Bookkeeper Petit-Pierre have tried to make me believe it's on account of my reports on Eastern Switzerland and the Tyrol, but I'm sure nobody reads them."

"My dear Monsieur Agesilaos," said Monsieur Petit-Paysan solemnly.

"Archilochos."

"Dear Monsieur Archilochos, you were a Bookkeeper or Chief Bookkeeper—as I said, the difference escapes me—and now you are Director; that seems to confuse you. You see, my dear friend, you must look at all these events, peculiar as they may seem to you, in a worldwide context, as a part of the manifold activities that my dear Engineering Works is involved in. After all, it produces—as I have heard with pleasure for the first time today—even obstetrical forceps. I hope this line brings in some profit as well."

Archilochos beamed.

In the canton of Appenzell Innerrhoden alone, he reported, sixty-two obstetrical forceps had been sold in the last three years.

"Hm, that's not much. But so be it. I suppose it's more like a humanitarian division. It's good to think that, in addition to things that remove human beings from the world, we also manufacture things that bring them into it. There has to be a certain balance, even if it's not always profitable. So let us be thankful."

Petit-Paysan paused and looked thankful.

"In his poem 'Archipelagos,' Hölderlin calls the merchant—and hence the industrialist—a 'far-intentioned' man," he finally continued, with a slight sigh. "A phrase that stirs me to the depths. A company like this is enormous, my dear Monsieur Aristipp, the number of workers and employees, of Bookkeepers and secretaries, is vast beyond all comprehension. Why, I scarcely know the Directors, and just very peripherally the General Directors. The nearsighted lose their way in this jungle. Only a man farsighted enough to train his eye, not on details and individual destinies, but on the whole; a man who does not lose sight of the distant goal, who is far-intentioned, as the poet says—you know his works, of course—only the man who knows how to forge ever-new plans, launch ever-new enterprises, in India, in Turkey, in the Andes, in Canada, will not drown in the swamps of competition and cartels. Far-intentioned: I'm about to merge with the Rubber and Lubricating Oil Cartel. It'll be the killing to end all killings."

Petit-Paysan paused again and looked far-intentioned.

"That is how I plan, how I labor," he said then, "adding my part to the patterns spun on the whirring loom of time. A modest part, to be sure. What are the Petit-Paysan Engineering Works beside the Steel Trust or the All-Joy Foundries, Inc., the Pestalozzi Plants, or Hosler-LaBiche! Nothing! But what about my workers and white-collar employees? What about all the individual destinies I have to oversee in order to keep my eye on the whole? This question preoccupies me often. Are they happy? The freedom of the world is at stake; are my workers free? I have established social services, maternity and paternity homes, vacation centers, gymnasiums, swimming pools, canteens, health pills, theatrical performances, concerts. But isn't the world I employ still caught up in material concerns, in filthy lucre? A question that gives me an almost painful discomfort. A Director suffers a collapse, only because another man replaces him. This is revolting. How can anyone take money so seriously? Only the spirit counts, my dear Monsieur Artaxerxes, nothing is more contemptible, more insignificant than money."

Petit-Paysan paused once again and looked concerned.

Archilochos scarcely dared to move.

But now the magnate straightened up; his voice sounded mighty and cold.

"You ask why I appointed you Director. So be it, I shall give you an answer: In order to practice freedom and not just preach it. I do not know my employees, I don't comprehend them, they don't appear to have struggled all the way through to a purely spiritual understanding of things, Diogenes, Albert Schweitzer, St. Francis do not seem to be their ideals, as they are mine. They would forgo meditation, helpful service, the joys of poverty for the frippery and illusions of society. Very well, give the world what it wants. I have always followed this rule of Lao-Tse. That, precisely, is why I appointed you Director. So that justice may prevail in this regard also. The man who has risen from the ranks, who knows the cares and sufferings of employees from the bottom, ought to be a Director. I plan the enterprise as a whole, but the man who comes into contact with the Bookkeepers and Chief Bookkeepers, with the stenographers and secretaries, with the errand boys and cleaning women of this administration, should be from their ranks. Director Zeus and Director Jehudi do not come from their ranks, I bought them as ready-made Directors from competitors who have since gone bankrupt. Let there be an end to that. It is time we radically re-create our Western world. The politicians have failed. If industry should also fail, everything will go to ruin, my dear Monsieur Agamemnon. Only as a creative being is man wholly human. Your appointment represents a creative act, an act of creative socialism, which we *must* oppose to uncreative communism. That is all I have to tell you. From now on you are a Director, a General Director. But first take a vacation," he continued with a smile, "there's a check waiting for you at the payroll office. Set yourself up. I saw you recently with an adorable woman—"

"My fiancée, Monsieur Petit-Paysan."

"You are about to marry. Congratulations. Do so. Unfortunately I have not been allotted such happiness. I have had a General Director's annual salary made out to you, which now will be doubled, since you are taking over the Obstetrical Forceps Division along with the Atomic Cannon Division—I have an important call to Santiago coming up—good-bye, my dear Monsieur Anaxogoras . . ."

11

No sooner had General Director Archilochos, once AB122-OF31, descended from the administration building's most holy precinct (after being escorted to the elevator by the secretary) than he was received like a prince, effusively embraced by General Directors, greeted with obeisances by Directors, flattered from all sides by cooing secretaries. From a distance Chief Bookkeepers padded in his direction. Somewhere, CB9-OF lurked, dripping with subordination, while from the Atomic Cannon Division, Director Jehudi was carried out on a stretcher, apparently in a straitjacket, exhausted and unconscious. It was said that he had smashed all the furniture in his office. But the only enticing thing, for Archilochos, was the check, of which he promptly took possession. "At least this much is certain," he thought, still distrustful, went on to promote CB9-OF to Vice Director of the Obstetrical Forceps Department, numbers AB122-OF28, AB122-OF29, and AB122-OF30 to Bookkeepers, gave a few instructions concerning the advertisements for obstetrical forceps in the canton of Appenzell Innerrhoden, and left the administration building.

Now he sat in a taxi, for the first time in his life, exhausted, hungry, bewildered by his lightning-swift rise to power and eminence, and had himself driven to Madame Bieler's.

The city lay in an icy cold under a clear sky. All things were inordinately clear in the glaring light: the palaces, the churches, the bridges. The big flag above the President's palace was immobile, as if frozen stiff. The river was like a mirror. The colors lay side by side without blending. The shadows on streets and boulevards, too, were hard-edged, as if drawn with a compass.

Archilochos stepped into the little restaurant. The door tinkled as always, and he took off his shabby winter coat.

"My God," said Georgette behind her counter, pouring herself a Campari, surrounded by bottles and glasses, which sparkled in the cold sunlight: "My God, Monsieur Arnolph! What's the matter with you? You look pale and worn, as though you've had no sleep, and you're visiting us at a time when you should be engaged in your drudgery. Is something wrong? Have you slept with a woman for the first time, or drunk wine? Have you been fired?"

"On the contrary," Archilochos said and sat down in his corner.

Auguste brought him his milk.

"What does that mean, 'on the contrary'?" Georgette asked, lighting a cigarette and blowing smoke into the slanting rays of sunlight.

"This morning I was appointed General Director of the Atomic Cannon and Obstetrical Forceps Department. By Petit-Paysan personally," Archilochos reported, still short of breath.

Then Auguste brought a bowl of applesauce, noodles, and salad.

"Hm," Georgette muttered. She did not seem particularly overwhelmed. "And why?"

"For reasons of creative socialism."

"What do you know. And how was it with the Greek girl yesterday?"

"We got engaged," Archilochos said, blushing.

"That makes sense," Madame Bieler said, with praise in her voice. "What does she do for a living?"

"She's a maid."

"Must be a remarkable job," said Auguste, "if she can afford a coat like that."

"Shush!" said Georgette.

They had gone for a walk, Arnolph told them, and everything had been so strange, so peculiar, almost like a dream. Everyone had suddenly started greeting him, waving from cars and buses, the President, Bishop Moser, the painter Passap, and the American Ambassador, who had called out "hello" to him.

"Aha," said Georgette.

"Maître Dutour greeted me too," Arnolph continued, "and Hercule Wagner, though he did it just with a wink."

"With a wink," Georgette repeated.

"She's that sort," Auguste muttered.

"Shut up!" Madame Bieler snapped at him, so sharply that he crept behind the stove and pulled in his shimmering legs. "Keep your remarks to yourself, this isn't the sort of thing men understand. So now you'll want to marry your Chloé right away, I guess," she said, addressing Archilochos again and draining her glass of Campari.

"As soon as possible."

"That's smart. When it comes to women, it's action that counts, especially when they're named Chloé. And where do you intend to live with your Greek wife?"

"I have no idea," Archilochos sighed, busy with his applesauce and his noodles. "Not in my garret, of course, on account of the flushing water and the bad air. In a boardinghouse, for the time being."

"Come on, Monsieur Archilochos," Georgette laughed, "a man with your cash reserves. Go to the Ritz, that's where you belong. And from now on, you're paying double here. General Directors are there to be fleeced, otherwise they're of no use to anyone."

Then she poured herself another Campari.

After Archilochos left, there was silence for a while at Chez Auguste. Madame Bieler washed the glasses, and her husband sat motionless behind the stove.

"That sort," Auguste finally said, rubbing his skinny legs. "When I came in second in the Tour de France, I had a chance to have one like that too, with a fur coat, expensive perfume, and she had an industrialist—the guy owned coal mines in Belgium. I'd probably be General Director now too."

"Nonsense," Georgette said, drying her hands. "You weren't born for higher things. That sort wouldn't marry you. There's nothing to awaken in you. Archilochos was born under a lucky star, I've always felt that, and he's Greek. Just wait and see how he develops. He'll thaw out yet, and how! That woman's top-notch. It's only natural she'd want to get out of her business. It tires you out in the long run, and believe me, it's not always pleasant. All of them want to get married. I did, too. Of course the majority don't make it, they really do end up in the gutter, just as everyone preaches. And some manage to land an Auguste with bare legs and a yellow bicycle racer's outfit—*eh bien,* not that I'm complaining, now that we're talking about those days, and I never had an industrialist. I didn't have the professional caliber for that. My clients were lower middle class, a few were with the Revenue Service, and once I had an aristocrat for two weeks, Count Dodo von

Malchern, the last of his family, long buried. But that Chloé, she'll make it. She's got her Archilochos, and things will turn out just fine."

12

Archilochos, meanwhile, took a taxi to the World Bank and then to a travel bureau on the Quai de l'État. He entered a large room with maps and colorful posters on the wall: "Visit Switzerland. The Sunny South Beckons. Air France to Rio. Green Ireland." Clerks with polite, smooth faces. Clattering typewriters. Neon lights. Foreigners speaking strange languages.

He wanted to go to Greece, Archilochos said. To Corfu, to the Peloponnesus, to Athens.

The clerk said that, regrettably, his agency did not book freighters.

He wanted to go on the *Julia*, Archilochos objected. He would like a first-class cabin for himself and his wife.

The clerk leafed through a timetable and gave a Spanish pimp (Ruiz) a train schedule. The *Julia* was fully booked, he finally said, and turned to a businessman from Cairo.

Archilochos left the travel bureau and returned to his waiting taxi. He sat for a few moments, thinking. Then he asked the driver who was the best tailor in town.

The driver was surprised. "O'Neill-Papperer on the Avenue Bikini and Vatti on the Rue St. Honoré," he replied.

"The best barber?"

"José on the Quai Offenbach."

"The top haberdasher?"

"Goschenbauer."

"Where does one buy the best gloves?"

"At De Stutz-Kalbermatten."

"Good," said Archilochos. "Take me to those stores." So they drove to O'Neill-Papperer on the Avenue Bikini and to Vatti on the Rue St. Honoré, to José on the Quai Offenbach and to De Stutz-Kalbermatten for gloves and to Goschenbauer for a hat. As he passed through a thousand fussing, measuring, cleaning, cutting, and polishing hands, he began to change noticeably, looking more dapper and smelling more fragrant each time he stepped into the taxi. After Goschenbauer's he wore a silver-gray Anthony Eden hat, and late in the afternoon he again drove up to the travel bureau on the Quai de l'État.

He would like a first-class cabin with twin beds on the *Julia*, he said in an unchanged voice to the clerk who had turned him away, and laid his silver-gray Anthony Eden hat on the glass counter.

The clerk started filling out a form. "The *Julia* sails next Friday. Corfu, the Peloponnesus, Athens, Rhodes, and Sámos," he said. "May I have your name?"

But after Arnolph had paid for the two tickets and left, the clerk turned to the Spanish pimp, who was still lounging about, leafing through travel folders and now and then receiving visits from several ladies who (likewise studying travel folders) slipped money into his long, suave hands.

"It's a scandal, Señor," the clerk said with disgust and in night-school Spanish. "Some street cleaner or chimney sweep comes in asking for two tickets on the *Julia*, which is really reserved for the aristocracy and the best sort of people." (He bowed to Don Ruiz). "I mean, the Prince of Hesse's going to take part in the next cruise, Mr. and Mrs. Weeman, Sophia Loren—and when I hold him off, out of decency, really, out of pure kindness, because he would just make a fool of himself, the guy has the nerve to come back dressed like a lord, rich as an oil baron, and I'm forced to hand out the tickets—what can I do against the power of money? Three hours it takes a bastard like that to make his career. I figure it's bank robbery, rape, felonious assault, or politics."

"Truly outrageous," Don Ruiz replied in night-school Spanish.

Archilochos, meanwhile, was driving across the new bridge—it was growing dark and the lights were going on in the city—to the Boulevard Künnecke and the residence of the Bishop of the Old New Presbyterians of the Penultimate Christians, but in front of the small Victorian villa he found Bibi, with a crushed hat, ragged and dirty, sitting on the curb, stinking of whiskey and leaning against a street lamp, reading a newspaper he had found in the gutter.

"Hey, what's that you're wearing, Brother Arnolph?" he asked, whistling through his teeth, clicking his tongue, blowing his nose with his fingers, and carefully folding the dirty newspaper. "Boy, what an outfit! Super."

"I've become a General Director," Arnolph said.

"No kidding!"

"I'll hire you as a Bookkeeper in the Obstetrical Forceps Division if you promise to pull yourself together. You can't go on like this."

"No, Arnolph, I'm not made for office work. Can you spare a couple of grand?"

"What's wrong now?"

"Gottlieb fell off a building, broke his arm."

"What building?"

"Petit-Paysan's."

Archilochos lost his temper, for the first time in his life.

"Gottlieb has no business burgling Petit-Paysan's house," he barked at his surprised brother. "He's got no business burgling anywhere. Petit-Paysan is my benefactor. For reasons of creative socialism he appointed me General Director, and now you come asking me for money, money that comes from Petit-Paysan, when you get right down to it."

"It won't happen again, Brother Arnolph," Bibi replied with dignity. "It was just for practice, and Gottlieb miscalculated. He was looking for some moolah in the Chilean Embassy, they've got an easier facade. He had the wrong number; look, he's still an innocent child. So how about a couple of grand?"—and he held out his cupped fraternal palm.

"No," said Archilochos, "I can't support such wrongdoing. I must see the Bishop now."

"I'll wait for you, Brother Arnolph," Bibi said, unperturbed, and unfolded the newspaper again. "I've got to see what the world's up to."

13

Bishop Moser, fat and rosy, in black ministerial garb and stiff white collar, received Archilochos in his study, a small, steep, smoke-stained room lit by one little lamp, spiritual and secular books lining the walls, with a high window behind heavy curtains, through which fell the light of the streetlamp under which brother Bibi was waiting.

The visitor introduced himself. He was actually an Assistant Bookkeeper, he said, but had just become General Director of the Atomic Cannon and Obstetrical Forceps Division in the Petit-Paysan Engineering Works.

Bishop Moser regarded him with mild satisfaction.

"I know that, my good friend," he mumbled. "You attend Preacher Thurcker's services at the Heloise Chapel, don't you? I know a few things about our dear Old New Presbyterian congregation. Welcome, my friend."

The Bishop vigorously shook the General Director's hand.

"Sit down," he said, offering him a comfortable armchair and sitting down behind his desk.

"Thank you," Archilochos said.

"Before you pour out your heart to me, I would like to pour out mine to you," the Bishop mumbled. "May I offer you a cigar?"

"I'm a nonsmoker."

"A glass of wine? Schnapps?"

"I'm a teetotaler."

"Do you mind if I permit myself a cigar? For intimate talk and delightful confession there's nothing like a good Dannemann. Sin bravely, Luther said, and I would like to add: smoke bravely, and add: drink bravely. Will you permit?"

He filled a small glass with schnapps that he kept in an old bottle behind the books.

"Oh, of course," Archilochos said, somewhat perturbed. He was sorry that his Bishop was not quite the model of excellence he had always imagined.

Bishop Moser lit a Dannemann.

"You see, dear brother, as I believe I may call you, it has long been my heart's desire to chat with you" (he ejected the first puffs of Dannemann smoke). "But, good God, the things a Bishop has to take care of: visiting old-age homes, organizing youth camps, finding Christian homes for fallen girls, inspecting Sunday schools and confirmation classes, examining candidates, lambasting the New Presbyterians, giving our preachers a much-needed talking-to. There are a thousand big and little things to do, and somehow nothing important gets accomplished. Our dear friend Thurcker has always talked about you; he says you've never missed a single service and that you display a truly rare zeal for our congregation."

"For me, attending services is a heartfelt need," was Archilochos' simple reply.

Bishop Moser poured himself a second glass of schnapps.

"Exactly. I've been hearing this about you for a long time, with pleasure. And now our venerable member of the Old New Presbyterian World Church Council went home to his heavenly father two months ago, and I have been considering whether you would not be the right man for this honorific post, which I'm sure could be combined with your duties as General Director—we would just have to minimize the Atomic Cannon Division a bit. We are in need of men who stand with both feet in the midst of the hard and often gruesome struggle of life, Monsieur Archilochos."

"But, Bishop . . ."

"Well, do you accept?"

"This is a most unexpected honor . . ."

"Then may I propose you to the World Church Council?"

"If you think . . ."

"I don't want to conceal from you the fact that the World Church Council tends to be quite willing, sometimes only too willing, to follow my recommendations. It's only too often I live in the popish odor of being self-willed and despotic. They're all amiable gentlemen and good Christians, to be sure, I'll say that much for the World Church Council; they're happy to let me relieve them of organizational burdens and occasionally do their thinking for them, which, sadly, isn't everyone's strong point, not the World Church Council's either. The next meeting you would have to attend as a candidate will take place in Sidney. In May. It's really a gift from God, a little trip like that, one gets to know a country and its people, foreign manners, foreign customs, the sorrows and needs of our dear humanity in regions far from our own. The expenses, of course, would be carried by the Old New Presbyterian Church."

"You put me to shame."

"This is my entreaty," the Bishop lisped. "Now let us hear yours. From man to man, sir. For I can already guess what it is. You are considering marriage, you wish to tie the knot with a dear little woman. I saw the two of you yesterday between the crematorium and the National Museum, and greeted you, but just had to quickly dash off into a dismal little side street to see an old woman who's dying and dear to my heart—one of those silent saints in our midst."

"Of course, Your Grace."

"Well, have I guessed it?"

"It is as you say."

Bishop Moser closed the Greek Bible that lay before him.

"Quite a spruce little lady," he said. "I congratulate you. When shall the wedding be?"

"Tomorrow. In the Heloise Chapel, if possible—and I would be happy if you could perform the ceremony."

The Bishop looked somewhat embarrassed.

"That's really the officiating minister's job," he said. "Thurcker performs weddings splendidly, and he has a truly mellifluous instrument."

"Won't you please make an exception," Archilochos pleaded, "now that I'm going to be a World Church Councilor?"

"Hm. Do you think you can get the legal formalities settled?"

"I'll ask Maître Dutour to take care of that."

"In that case, yes," the Bishop finally gave in. "Let's say tomorrow at three p.m., in the Heloise Chapel? May I have the name of the bride and her personal data?"

The Bishop wrote down the needed details.

"Your Grace," Archilochos said, "my intended marriage may be a sufficient reason for taking up your time, but it's not the most important one, if I may say so, if it's not a sin to even suggest such a thing, because I'm sure there can't be many things more important than it is for a man to enter on the obligation to live with a woman for a whole lifetime. Nevertheless, at this moment there is something much more important to me, because it lies so heavily on my heart."

"Say all that you need to say, my dear General Director," the Bishop replied amiably. "Courage. Relieve your soul of its cares, its human or perhaps all too human burden."

"Your Grace," Archilochos said timorously, straightening up in his easy chair and crossing his legs, "forgive me if what I say sounds confused. This morning I was still dressed quite differently; shabbily, to be honest; and the suit I was wearing when you saw me on Sunday was my confirmation suit; and suddenly I'm walking around in expensive clothes by O'Neill-Papperer and Vatti. I am embarrassed, Your Reverence. You must think I'm completely in thrall to the world and its glittering illusions, as Preacher Thurcker always says."

"On the contrary," the eminent cleric smiled. "A pleasant exterior, attractive clothing, are only commendable, especially nowadays when it has become fashionable in certain circles that emulate a Godless philosophy to dress in a blatantly sloppy, almost beggarly manner, with gaudy shirts hanging outside the trousers and similarly weird monstrosities. Decent attire and Christianity are by no means mutually exclusive."

"Your Grace," Archilochos continued, more boldly, "a Christian person might very well feel disturbed, I think, to find himself suddenly struck by one misfortune after another. He might feel like a Job whose sons and daughters have perished, who is reduced to poverty and covered with sores; but he will be all the more deeply consoled if he regards his misfortune as the consequence of his sins. But when the opposite happens, when one stroke of luck follows another, it seems to me there is very serious cause for concern, for there is no way to explain it: where is there a person who would deserve all this?"

"My dear Monsieur Archilochos." Bishop Moser smiled. "The Creation happens to be constituted in such a way that a case like this hardly ever occurs. The whole creation groaneth, as Paul says, and so do we all groan under misfortunes that do tend, more or less, to accumulate, and which of course we must not take too tragically, but rather understand in the sense of Job, as you so correctly and beautifully said, almost as well as Preacher Thurcker. A case like the one you indicated before, this accumulation of every conceivable good fortune, is not at all likely to be found and evidenced anywhere."

"I am such a case," Archilochos said.

It was very quiet in the study, and the light had darkened since Archilochos had entered. Outside, the day was completely extinguished, blackest night reigned, and from the street scarcely a sound penetrated into the room, only the occasional hum of a passing car or the diminishing footsteps of a pedestrian.

"I am experiencing one stroke of luck after the other," the former Assistant Bookkeeper continued softly, in his impeccable suit, a chrysanthemum in his lapel (the silver-gray Anthony Eden hat, the brilliantly white gloves, and the elegant fur coat were in the closet). "An ad in the personal columns of *Le Soir* is answered by the most charming maiden, who loves me at first sight, and whom I love at first sight, everything happens like in a bad movie, I'm almost ashamed to talk about it, the whole city starts to greet me as I walk through the streets with this maiden, the President, you, all sorts of important celebrities, and today I find myself raised to the most improbable heights both in worldly terms and in the realm of our church, a rise out of nothing, from the miserable existence of an Assistant Bookkeeper to General Director and World Church Councilor—it's all inexplicable and upsets me deeply."

For a long time the Bishop did not say a word. He suddenly looked old and gray, staring into space. He had even laid the Dannemann in the ashtray, where it remained, useless and cold.

"Monsieur Archilochos," the Bishop finally said, suddenly no longer mumbling and speaking in a different, firm voice: "Monsieur Archilochos, all these events you are describing to me in private on this quiet evening are, to be sure, strange and extraordinary. Whatever the underlying causes may be, it is my belief that it is not these unknown causes . . ." (here his voice quivered, and for a moment his lisp reappeared) ". . . that are important, let alone pivotal for us, since they lie in the human sphere, and here we are all sinners; no, what is important is the meaning of all this: that you are a blessed person upon whom the proofs of grace are being heaped in the most visible manner. It is not the Assistant Bookkeeper Archilochos who must stand his ground now, but the General Director and World Church Councilor Archilochos, and the purpose of it all must be that you prove whether you are deserving of this grace. Accept these events as humbly as you would if they were misfortunes, that is all I am able to tell you about it. Perhaps you are destined to walk an especially difficult path, the path of good fortune, which is not imposed on most people for the sole reason that they would know even less how to walk it than they know how to walk the path of misfortune, which as a rule is the path we must travel in this life. Farewell now." He stood up. "We will meet again tomorrow in the Heloise Chapel. By then,

I presume, many things will look clearer to you, and I can only pray that you will not forget my words, no matter what happens to you in the future."

14

After the conversation with Bishop Moser in his smoke-stained room with his classics and Bibles lining the walls, its desk and heavy curtains, and after his brother Bibi, reading the newspaper (*Le Soir*) under the Bishop's window, had received his money, the World Church Councilor would have liked to go straight to the Boulevard Saint-Père; but the clock on the Jesuit church by the Place Guillaume was just striking six, so he decided to wait until eight, as they had agreed, even though he was painfully aware that this meant prolonging Chloé's life as a maid for two unnecessary hours. He resolved to move into the Ritz with her before the day was done, and proceeded to make the necessary arrangements, reserving two rooms, one on the first and one on the fifth floor, so as not to embarrass the maiden or place the World Church Councilor in an improper light. Then he tried to reach Maître Dutour, unfortunately in vain. He was told that the lawyer and notary had gone out to execute the transfer of title of a house. So he had more than an hour and a half to wait. He prepared himself, bought flowers, inquired about a suitable restaurant. He didn't want to go back to his old teetotalers' restaurant opposite the World Health Office, nor could he imagine going to Chez Auguste, for he felt with secret pain that with his elegant clothes he had excluded himself from the little restaurant. A suit by O'Neill-Papperer next to Monsieur Bieler's *maillot jaune*! Therefore he decided, though with a bad conscience, to dine at the Ritz itself (without alcohol, of course), reserved a table, and went in a happily expectant mood to the Passap exhibition, which he had happened to notice at the Nadelör Gallery, right across the street from the Ritz, and which was being kept open in the evening to accommodate the great number of visitors. Among the paintings were Passap's most recent works (sixty-degree angles, ellipses, and parabolas), which Archilochos contemplated with reverence and enthusiasm as he wandered through the bright rooms with his flowers (white roses), surrounded by American women, journalists, and painters. But he stopped short in front of a picture in cobalt blue and ochre, even though it showed nothing but two ellipses and a parabola. Convulsively clutching his flowers, he stared aghast at the picture, blushing deeply, suddenly dashed off, terrified, sweating and shivering as if in a fever, stopped briefly at the cash register, where Herr Nadelör stood in a black tuxedo, smiling and rubbing his hands, asked for the painter's address, and leaped into a taxi; whereupon the art dealer, without taking a coat, immediately hailed another taxi and followed Archilochos, determined to secure his percentage, for he suspected a secret sale. Passap lived in the Rue Funèbre in the old part of the city. The taxi (closely followed by Nadelör's cab) reached the house by way of the Marschall-Voegeli Allée, but with great difficulty, since the followers of Fahrcks were holding a mass rally, with pictures of the anarchist on long poles, with red flags and huge banners bearing slogans like "Down With the President!" and "Prevent the Treaty of Lugano!" and the like. Somewhere Fahrcks himself was making a speech. Thunderous roars and shrieks filled the air, whistles shrilled, hooves clattered, and as the police began wielding nightsticks and fire hoses, water poured over the cab containing the General Director and into the one containing the art dealer, who had unfortunately opened a window to satisfy his curiosity. But at that moment both vehicles with their cursing drivers turned into the old city. The badly paved streets rose steeply past ramshackle houses and dives. Whores stood around in droves like black birds, waving and hissing, and it was so cold that the wet cars were already covered with ice. And so it came to pass that Archilochos, still cradling his bouquet of white roses, stepped out in front of no. 43 (where Passap lived), in the badly lit Rue Funèbre, from an enchanted vehicle adorned with glittering, tinkling icicles. Besieged by street urchins who clung to his trouser legs, he asked the driver to wait, and then pressed on past a malicious and drunken concierge into the interior of the tall old house, and began climbing endless flights of stairs, which were so rotted that his foot broke through the steps several times and he found himself hanging in space, clinging to the wooden banister. Wearily, he climbed from story to story, splinters in his aching hands, virtually in the dark, searching the old doors for Passap's name, ignoring the sound of Nadelör's heavy breathing behind him. It was bitterly cold in the stairwell, somewhere a piano was tinkling, and somewhere a window banged open and shut. Behind a door, a woman shrieked and a man yelled, and there was a smell of orgies. Archilochos climbed higher and higher, sank again through a rotten board to his knee, walked into a spider web, felt a fat, half-frozen bug crawl over his forehead, irritably wiped it off. Finally, with Vatti's fur coat and the lovely new suit by O'Neill-Papperer covered with dust and his trousers already ripped, but with the flowers intact, he discovered, at the end of a steep and narrow attic staircase, Passap's name scrawled diagonally across a rickety door in huge chalk-drawn letters. He knocked. Two steps further down, Nadelör waited in the icy cold. No answer. He knocked a second, a third, a fourth time. No one. The World Church Councilor pressed the latch, the door was unlocked, and he stepped in.

It was a boundless attic he had entered, almost a barn, a tangle of beams with several floors. Everywhere African idols stood about, piles of paintings, empty frames, sculptures, strangely bent wire constructions, a glowing iron stove with an outsized, grotesquely twisted pipe, wine and whiskey bottles everywhere, squeezed-out tubes, cans of paint, brushes, cats everywhere, and towering heaps of books on the chairs and all over the floor. In the middle of the room stood Passap in an apparently once-white painter's smock, now brilliantly spattered with color, dabbing away with a spatula at a picture on an easel, parabolas and ellipses, while in front him, near the stove, a fat girl sat on a wobbly chair, stark naked, with long blond hair, her arms crossed behind her neck. The World Church Councilor stood petrified (this being the first time he had seen a naked woman), scarcely daring to breathe.

"Who are you?" Passap asked.

Archilochos introduced himself, somewhat surprised by the question, since the painter had greeted him on Sunday.

"What do you want?"

The Greek choked out his reply: "You painted my fiancée, Chloé, naked."

"You mean the painting *Venus, July 11*, which is hanging at the Nadelör gallery now."

"That's it."

"Get dressed," Passap snapped at the model, who vanished behind a screen. Then for a long time, with a pipe in his mouth, its smoke curling in the tangle of beams, he stood staring attentively at Archilochos.

"So?"

"Sir," Archilochos replied with utmost dignity, "I am an admirer of your art. I have followed your work with enthusiasm, in fact I have raised you to Number Four in my world order."

"World order? What sort of nonsense is this?" Passap asked, heaping new mounds of color (cobalt blue and ochre) on his palette.

"I have compiled a list of the worthiest representatives of our time, a list of my moral exemplars."

"Well?"

"Sir, in spite of the enthusiasm I feel for you, in spite of my profound respect, I must ask you to supply an explanation. It is certainly not an everyday occurrence for a bridegroom to see his bride depicted naked as Venus. Even though it is an abstract painting, a sensitive viewer cannot fail to recognize the subject."

"Not bad," Passap said. "My critics aren't capable of that."

Thereupon he scrutinized Archilochos again, stepped up to him, felt him over like a horse, stepped back a few steps, and squinted.

"Take off your clothes," he said then. He poured himself a glass of whiskey, drank it, and stuffed his pipe.

"But . . ." Arnolph tried to protest.

"No buts," Passap snapped at him, with such angry, black, piercing little eyes that Archilochos fell silent. "I want to paint you as Ares."

"Ares?"

"The Greek god of war," Passap explained. "I've been looking for a suitable model for years, the pendant to my Venus: You're the one. The type that flies into a frenzy, in love with the heat of battle, fomenter of bloodbaths. Are you Greek?"

"Certainly, but . . ."

"There you go."

"Monsieur Passap." Archilochos resumed talking at last. "You are mistaken. I don't fly into frenzies, I don't love the heat of battle, and I don't foment bloodbaths. I am a peace-loving man, World Church Councilor of the Old New Presbyterian Church, a strict teetotaler, and I completely refrain from smoking. In addition I am a vegetarian."

"Nonsense," Passap said. "What is your profession?"

"General Director of the Atomic Cannon Division and the . . ."

"There we have it," Passap interrupted him. "A war god after all. And prone to frenzy. You are merely inhibited and haven't arrived at the way of life that suits you. You are also a born drinker and erotic genius, the most magnificent Ares I have ever encountered. So get undressed and make it snappy. My business is painting, not babbling."

"Not if that young lady you were just painting is still in the room," Archilochos protested.

"Get out, Catherine. He's embarrassed," the painter shouted. "I won't need you again till tomorrow, chubs."

The fat girl with the blond hair, now with her clothes on, said good-bye. When she opened the door, Nadelör stood before her, shivering and covered with ice.

"I must protest," the art dealer cried hoarsely. "I must protest, Monsieur Passap, we had an agreement . . ."

"Go to hell!"

"I'm cold," the art dealer cried out desperately. "We had an agreement . . ."

"Go freeze."

The girl closed the door. They could hear her descending the stairs.

"Well," the painter asked Archilochos impatiently, "aren't you out of your pants yet?"

"All right," the General Director replied, undressing. "The shirt too?"

"Everything."

"The flowers? You see, they're for my fiancée."

"Put them on the floor."

The World Church Councilor laid his clothes neatly over a chair, dusted them (for they were covered with dust from the arduous climb up the stairs), and finally stood there naked.

He was cold.

"Move the chair over to the stove."

"But . . ."

"Stand on the chair and assume a boxer's stance, holding your arms at a sixty-degree angle," Passap commanded. "That's exactly the way I've always imagined the god of war."

The chair was quite unsteady, but Archilochos obeyed.

"You're fat," the painter growled, pouring himself another whiskey. "I don't go for that except with certain women, but we can eliminate that. The main thing is the face and chest. All that hair on you is good, a strong martial touch. The thighs are still okay. But take off your glasses, they spoil the whole illusion."

Then he began to paint, sixty-degree angles, ellipses, and parabolas.

"Sir," the World Church Councilor began again (in his boxer's pose), "you owe me an explanation . . ."

"Shut up," Passap thundered. "If anyone talks here, it's me. The fact that I painted your fiancée is the most natural thing in the world. A superb woman. I'm sure you know what I mean when I mention her breasts."

"Sir . . ."

"And her thighs, her navel."

"I simply must . . ."

"Get back into a decent boxer's pose, damn it," the painter snarled, applying thick mounds of ochre and then cobalt blue. "You don't even know your fiancée in the nude and you get engaged."

"You're stepping on my flowers. White roses."

"So what. A revelation. Your naked fiancée, I had to force myself not to become the most banal naturalist or one of those here-we-go-gathering-nuts-in-May Impressionists, faced with such splendid flesh, such breathing skin. Pull in your belly, damn it! Never have I had a more divine model than Chloé with her glorious back, her perfect shoulders, and those plump round buttocks, like the two halves of the world edifice; seeing that sort of thing tends to put cosmic ideas in your mind. I enjoyed painting as I hadn't for a long time. Usually I don't care to paint women at all, just once in a while a fat one like the one that just left. Artistically, they don't yield much of anything special. A man's different: there the deviations from the classical ideal are what's interesting. But with Chloé! In her everything is still a unity, as in paradise, her legs, her arms, her neck grow out of her body with perfect naturalness, and her head is still a woman's head. I've also done a sculpture of her: here!"

He pointed to a construction of tangled wire.

"But . . ."

"Back to the boxer's pose," Passap admonished the World Church Councilor. Then he stepped back several times, examined his painting, changed an ellipsis, lifted the canvas off the easel, and screwed another one into place.

"All right," he commanded. "Now kneel. Ares after the heat of battle. Bend forward more. Come on, I don't have you available every day."

By now Archilochos, confused and half roasted by the stove, was putting up only weak resistance.

"I would really like to ask you," he said, but was interrupted by Nadelör, who barged shivering into the attic, a walking, tinkling lump of ice, full of suspicion that a painting was being sold.

Passap went wild.

"Get out!" he shouted, and the art dealer crept back into the arctic cold of the stairwell.

"Art is my explanation," the painter finally said, drinking whiskey, painting, and simultaneously stroking the tomcat that had climbed on his shoulders. "And I don't give a hoot whether this explanation satisfies you or not. I made something out of your naked fiancée, a masterpiece of proportion, of artfully distributed planes, of rhythm, of color, of pictorial poetry, a world of cobalt blue and ochre! You on the other hand want to make something very different out of Chloé, once you have her at your disposal in the nude. A little mama with children, I suppose. It is you who destroy a masterpiece of Creation, sir, not I, who glorify this masterpiece, raise it to the level of the Absolute, the Definitive, the Dream."

"It's quarter past eight," Archilochos exclaimed in alarm, at the same time relieved by the painter's explanation.

"So?"

"I'm supposed to meet Chloé at eight," Arnolph explained anxiously, cats purring around his legs, and made motions to step off his chair. "She's waiting for me at the Boulevard Saint-Père."

"Let her wait. Keep your pose!" Passap yelled. "Art is more important than your love affair!" and went on painting.

Archilochos groaned. The tomcat, gray with white paws, had climbed onto his shoulder now, and was hurting him with its claws.

"Quiet," Passap commanded. "Don't move."

"The cat."

"The cat's all right, but you're not," the painter said angrily. "How can anyone develop such an enormous belly without even drinking?"

Nadelör appeared in the doorway again (numb, covered with ice). He was frozen through, he lamented, his voice so hoarse it was almost inaudible.

"No one told you to wait in front of my door, and I don't want you in my studio," Passap roughly replied.

"You're in business with me," the art dealer croaked. Then he had to sneeze, but was unable to get his hand out of his pocket because his sleeves were frozen to his trousers.

"On the contrary, you're in business with me," the painter thundered. "Out!"

The art dealer withdrew for a third time.

Archilochos no longer dared to say another word. Passap drank whiskey, painted sixty-degree angles, parabolas, and ellipses, heaped cobalt on ochre and ochre on cobalt, and after half an hour the General Director was permitted to put on his clothes.

"Here," Passap said, pressing the wire construction into his arms, "put this next to your marriage bed, my wedding present. So you'll remember the beauty of your bride when it fades. And I'll send you one of your portraits once it's dry. And now get the hell out of here. I hate World Church Councilors and General Directors almost as much as art dealers. Your luck that you look like the Greek god of war, otherwise I'd have thrown you out long ago, naked, you'd better believe it!"

15

After Archilochos had left the painter, the white roses in one arm and in the other the wire construction that was supposed to represent his naked fiancée, he approached the steep, narrow stairway, actually more of a ladder, and encountered the art dealer Nadelör, under whose nose lumps of ice had formed, standing flush against the wall in the icy draught, chilled to the bone and utterly miserable.

"You see," the ice-covered man lamented almost inaudibly as if from a crevasse, "just as I thought. You bought something, I protest."

"It's a wedding gift," Arnolph explained and began cautiously descending the stairs, hampered by the flowers and the sculpture, annoyed at himself for his senseless adventure, for it was almost nine o'clock; but the stairs did not permit a more rapid descent.

The art dealer followed him.

"You should be ashamed," Nadelör remonstrated, to the extent that his words could be made out at all. "I heard you tell Passap that you're a World Church Councilor. Scandalous. Modeling in your profession! Stark naked!"

"Would you be so kind as to hold the sculpture for me?" Archilochos was forced to ask after some time (between the fourth and third floors, where the woman was still shrieking and the man still yelling). "Just for a moment," he added, "my foot has gone through the board."

"Impossible," Nadelör whisper. "I never touch a sculpture unless I get a percentage."

"Then the flowers."

"I can't," the art dealer apologized, "my sleeves are frozen solid."

Finally they reached the street. The car with the icicles gleamed like silver. Only the radiator was free of ice, and the motor was running. It was cold inside. The heater wasn't working, the shivering driver explained.

"Boulevard Saint-Père number twelve," Archilochos said, happy at the prospect of seeing his fiancée soon.

The car was about to start when the art dealer knocked on the window.

"I must ask you to take me along." These were the words that emerged indistinctly from the icy mass as Arnolph lowered the window and leaned toward the glimmering figure. "I can't take another step," the art dealer continued, "and very few taxis come to the Old Town."

"Impossible," Archilochos said. "I have to go to the Boulevard Saint-Père, it's urgent and I'm already much too late."

"You as a Christian and World Church Councilor can't just abandon me," Nadelör replied indignantly. "I'm beginning to freeze to the pavement."

"Get in," Archilochos said, opening the door.

"A little warmer here, it seems to me," the art dealer said when he was finally sitting next to Archilochos. "I hope I'll thaw out."

But when they turned into the Boulevard Saint-Père, Nadelör had not thawed yet. On top of that, he had to get out of the cab with Archilochos. The driver did not want to go back to the quay. He had had enough of the cold and drove off. So the two men stood in front of the wrought-iron gate with the putti and the dolphins, with the red lamp, which was extinguished now, and the two large stone pillars. Archilochos tugged at the archaic contraption. No one came. The boulevard was deserted, and the only sound was the distant shouting of the demonstrating followers of Fahrcks.

"Sir," Archilochos said, upset by his lateness, holding the flowers and the wire sculpture in his arms, "I must leave you now."

Resolutely he opened the gate, but Nadelör followed him into the garden.

Annoyed that he couldn't get rid of the ice-coated art dealer, Arnolph asked him what more he wanted.

He had to call for a cab, the gallery owner replied.

"I have only a passing acquaintance with the people here—"

"You as a World Church Councilor—"

"All right," said Archilochos. "Fine. Come along—" The cold was merciless. The art dealer tinkled like a glockenspiel as he walked. The fir and elm trees stood motionless, huge stars sparkled in the sky, red and yellow, and the silver ribbon of the milky way. Through the spaces between the tree trunks came the muted gold glow of the windows of a villa which, as they approached it, turned out to be a small rococo palace, somewhat ornate, with slender columns, the whole thing covered with the interwoven vines of wild grape, plainly visible in the clear night. A gently curving staircase led up to the entrance. It was brightly lit and had no nameplate, only a heavy hand-bell, but again no one came to open the door.

One more minute in this cold, the art dealer moaned, and he would freeze to death.

Archilochos pressed the latch. The door was unlocked. He would go and see, he said.

Nadelör went in with him.

"Are you crazy?" Archilochos hissed.

"I can't very well stand outside in this cold . . ."

"I don't know this house."

"You as a Christian . . ."

"Then wait here," Arnolph commanded.

They had entered a large room. Furniture that reminded Archilochos of Petit-Paysan's quarters, flowers and little mirrors. Everything exuded a snug, homey warmth. The art dealer began thawing immediately, and little streams of water ran down him.

"Don't stand on the rug," the World Church Councilor snapped, worried by the sight of the dripping gallery owner.

"All right," Nadelör said, posting himself next to the umbrella stand. "If I may just use the phone soon."

"I'll ask the master of the house."

"As soon as possible."

"At least hold the wire sculpture," Archilochos suggested.

"Only for a percentage."

Arnolph placed the work of art next to Nadelör and opened a door, peered into a small salon with a couch, with a little tea table, with a spinet and delicate little armchairs. He cleared his throat. The salon was empty, but he heard footsteps behind a double door. Evidently Mr. Weeman. He crossed the salon, knocked.

"Come in!"

To his amazement, he found himself facing Maître Dutour.

16

Maître Dutour, a short, sprightly man with a black moustache and a dramatic shock of white hair, stood next to a large and beautiful table, in a room lined with high golden mirrors and illuminated by a chandelier full of lit candles, radiant as a Christmas tree.

"I have been expecting you, Monsieur Archilochos," said Maître Dutour, bowing. "May I ask you to take a seat."

He indicated an armchair and sat down facing the World Church Councilor. A document was spread out on the table.

"I don't understand," Archilochos said.

"My dear General Director," the lawyer smiled, "I have the pleasure of transferring this house to you as a gift. There is no mortgage on it and it is in superb condition, except for the west side of the roof, which ought to be repaired some day."

Archilochos, surprised but by now somewhat jaded by his various strokes of good fortune, said that he failed to understand. "Would you mind explaining . . ."

"The former owner of the house does not wish his name to be mentioned."

"I know his name nonetheless," Arnolph declared. "It is Mr. Weeman, the famous archaeologist and excavator of Greek antiquities. He found an ancient temple with precious statues, hidden away in some mossy grove, with golden pillars."

Startled, Maître Dutour looked at Archilochos and shook his head. He was not permitted to dispense any information, he finally said; the previous owner had wanted his house to be in Greek hands and was glad to have found in Archilochos a man who met these conditions. In a time of corruption and immorality, he continued, in a time when the most unnatural crimes appear to be the most natural, in which legal thinking is in decay and one and all are reverting to the fist-and-club jurisdiction of primitive eras, a man of law would despair of ever seeing any meaning in his striving for order, for justice, if he did not find occasion, here and there, to prepare and execute a purely charitable act such as the transfer of this little palace. The documents were ready, the General Director had only to quickly peruse them and sign his name. The tax required by the state—Moloch demanded his victims—had also been paid.

"Thank you," Archilochos said.

The lawyer read the documents aloud, and the World Church Councilor signed his name at the bottom.

"The little palace now belongs to you," the lawyer said, and rose to his feet.

Archilochos likewise rose. "Sir," he said solemnly, "permit me to express my joy at meeting a man I have always revered. You defended that poor curate. It was only the flesh overpowering the spirit, you cried out at the time; the soul remained unsullied. Those words impressed me profoundly."

"Oh, I beg you," Dutour said, "I was only doing my duty. Unfortunately the curate was beheaded, which still leaves me disconsolate, since I had pleaded for a twelve-year sentence. However, we did succeed in averting the worst: he wasn't hanged."

Archilochos asked whether he might trouble the Maître for another moment.

Dutour bowed.

"May I ask you, sir, to prepare the papers for my marriage?"

"They are prepared," the lawyer replied. "Your dear fiancée has already asked me to."

"Oh," Arnolph joyfully exclaimed, "you know my dear bride!"

"I have had the pleasure."

"Isn't she marvelous?"

"Quite."

"I am the happiest man in the world."

"Whom do you propose as witnesses?"

He hadn't thought of that yet, Archilochos admitted.

"I would recommend the American Ambassador and the Rector of the University," Dutour suggested.

Arnolph hesitated.

"I have already secured their consent," Maître Dutour said. "No further steps are needed. The marriage is creating a sensation in society, for word of your astonishing career has gotten around, my dear Monsieur Archilochos."

"But those gentlemen don't know my fiancée!"

The little lawyer tossed back his artistic shock of hair, stroked his moustache, and contemplated Arnolph with an almost malicious gaze.

"Oh, I believe they do," he said.

"I understand," Archilochos realized. "The gentlemen have been guests of Gilbert and Elizabeth Weeman."

Again Maître Dutour started and looked surprised. "In a manner of speaking," he said then.

Arnolph was not really enthusiastic. "It's true I have great admiration for the Rector of the University."

"There you are."

"But the American Ambassador . . ."

"You have political reservations?"

"Not that," Archilochos replied, embarrassed. "Mr. Forster-Monroe does after all occupy the fifth place in my universal moral edifice, but he belongs to the Old Presbyterian Church, whose dogma of universal atonement I cannot share, since I believe unshakably in the eternity of hellfire."

Maître Dutour shook his head. "I don't want to offend against your faith," he said, "but you needn't trouble your mind. Surely the eternity of hellfire and your marriage don't have much in common."

Archilochos sighed with relief. "I must say I agree," he said.

"May I bid you good-bye then," the lawyer said, closing his briefcase. "The civil ceremony will take place at two o'clock sharp in the Hôtel de Ville."

Arnolph wanted to see him to the door.

"I prefer to walk through the garden," the little lawyer said, pushing aside a red curtain, and opened a glass door: "This is the shortest way."

Icy air streamed into the room.

"He must have been a frequent guest here," Archilochos thought as he stood on the terrace outside the glass door and the lawyer's quick footsteps faded into the night. He gazed at the twinkling of the stars above the trees. Shivering, he stepped back into the room and closed the door. "The Weemans must have entertained a great deal," he murmured.

17

Archilochos started wandering through the little rococo palace that now belonged to him. He thought he had heard light footsteps from an adjoining room, but he found no one. Everything was illuminated, either by large white candles or by small lamps. He walked through family rooms and small salons, over soft carpets, past delicate furniture. On the walls hung old, sometimes rather frayed, precious tapestries with pale gold lilies against a silvery background and splendid pictures, which, however, he was afraid to really look at, but on whose account he blushed several times, for most of them showed naked women who were occasionally joined by gentlemen in the same natural condition. He didn't find Chloé anywhere. If at first he had wandered about planlessly, he now followed a colored trail of paper cutouts, blue, red, and gold stars that lay on the soft rugs and were evidently meant to represent a path he was supposed to pursue. And so he eventually arrived at a narrow unexpected winding staircase, which he reached through a secret door in the tapestry, and climbed it to the top floor (for a long time he had stood irresolutely in front of the wall where the stairs ended, until he discovered the door); on every step lay either a paper star or a paper comet, at one point the planet Saturn with its ring, then the moon, then the sun. From step to step, Archilochos grew more and more tentative, his courage had left him, and his old fearfulness had overcome him again. He breathed heavily, clutching the white roses, which he had never let out of his hand, not even during his conversation with Maître Dutour. The winding staircase ended in a round room with a large desk and three tall windows, a globe of the world, a high-backed chair, a tall standing lamp, a chest, all the furniture with a distinctly medieval cast, as in Faust's study on the stage, and a yellowed sheet of parchment on the armchair: "Arnolph's study" was inscribed on it, with lipstick. At the sight of the telephone on the desk, Arnolph thought for a moment of the waiting and dripping gallery owner next to the umbrella stand in the hall down below, who perhaps had finally completely thawed out, but when he opened the second door of the study, where the stars and comets led him, he forgot Nadelör again, for now he saw before him a bedroom with a huge old canopy bed, "Arnolph's bedroom," as it said on the sheet of parchment on top of a small renaissance table. The next room—he continued following the trail of stars—changed back to rococo and was not, strictly speaking, a room but a charming boudoir, lit by little red lamps, with all the appropriate furniture and objects: "Chloé's boudoir," it said here, and the parchment with the lipsticked inscription lay on a little armchair over which some articles of clothing had been tossed in hasty disorder, much to Archilochos' bewilderment: a brassiere, a girdle, a bodice, a slip, panties, all gleaming white, stockings and shoes on the floor, and through a half-opened door you could see in a black-tiled bathroom a tub set into the floor and filled with green, fragrant, and slightly steaming water; but all the comets on the floor pointed not only to the bathroom but through it to another door, which he opened, holding the flowers before him like a shield. He entered a bedchamber at the center of which stood a delicate but nonetheless vast canopied bed, and there the path of stars and moons came to an end, except for a few that were pasted onto the wooden frame; but there was no one to be seen, since the curtains of the bed were drawn. Some logs were burning in the fireplace; they cast Arnolph's shadow, huge and flickering, against the scarlet curtains of the bed, which were embroidered with strange golden emblems. Tentatively, he approached the bed. Peering through the crack between the curtains, all he saw in the darkness was the white cloud of the linen. But it seemed to him that he could hear breathing, and so he whispered softly and in a thousand fears: "Chloé." No one answered. He had to act, much though he would have preferred to withdraw, away from the room, from the little palace itself, back to his garret where he was safe and not bewildered by stars. And so at last with heavy heart he drew the curtain aside and found her lying in the bed, circled by the black curls of her loosened hair, sleeping.

Archilochos was so confused that he sat down on the edge of the bed and shyly looked at Chloé, though he didn't dare look for more than moments at a time. He was tired, too; his ceaseless luck hadn't given him a chance to rest and reflect, and so his shadow projected against the sheer vermilion curtain on the other side of the bed sagged closer and closer to the sleeping Chloé. But suddenly he noticed that Chloé had opened her eyes slightly and was studying him from under her long lashes, and had probably been doing so for a long time.

"Oh," she said, as if awakening, "Arnolph. Did you find the way all right, through all those rooms?"

"Chloé," he exclaimed, still frightened, "you are lying in Mrs. Weeman's bed."

"But the bed is yours now," she laughed, stretching.

"You confessed our love to Mr. and Mrs. Weeman, right?"

She hesitated with the answer. "Of course," she said then.

"Whereupon they gave us this little palace."

"They have several more in England."

"I don't know," he said, "I still can't quite grasp it all. I had no idea the English were so socially open-minded and would simply give a castle to their maid as a present."

"Seems to be a custom there in certain families," Chloé explained.

Archilochos shook his head: "And I've also become General Director of the Atomic Canon and Obstetrical Forceps Division."

"I know."

"With an enormous salary."

"So much the better."

"And also World Church Councilor. In May I have to take a trip to Sidney."

"That'll be our wedding trip."

"No," he said, "this!" He took two tickets from his pocket. "We're going to Greece on Friday. On the *Julia*."

But then he hesitated.

"How come you know all about my career?" he asked.

She sat up and was so beautiful that Archilochos lowered his eyes. She seemed to want to say something, but then gave it up with a sigh after looking at Arnolph for a long and pensive moment, and sank back into the pillows. "The whole city is talking about it," she finally said with a peculiar voice.

"And tomorrow you want to marry me," he stammered.

"Don't you?"

Archilochos still did not dare to look, for she had thrown aside the blanket. It was altogether difficult to look anywhere in this room, because there were pictures of naked gods and goddesses everywhere—something he would not have expected of skinny Mrs. Weeman.

"These Englishwomen," he thought. "Fortunately they are good to their maids, so one can forgive them their sensuousness," and more than anything he wanted to lie down, take Chloé in his arms, and simply sleep, for hours, a deep, dreamless sleep in the warm glow of the fireplace.

"Chloé," he said softly, "everything that has happened is so confusing to me, and I suppose to you also, that sometimes I hardly feel myself any longer and think I must be somebody else and in reality I'm still in my garret, with the spots on the wall, and that you never really existed either. It's much harder to endure good fortune than misfortune, Bishop Moser said today, and now there are moments when I think he's right. Misfortune is not surprising, it happens because it has to, but good fortune happens by chance, and so I'm afraid our good fortune, our happiness, will end as quickly as it began, and that this is all a game people are playing with you and me, with a housemaid and an Assistant Bookkeeper."

"You don't have to brood about all this now, darling," Chloé said. "I've waited for you all day, and now you're here. And how handsome you are. Won't you take off your coat? I bet it's made by O'Neill-Papperer."

But as he started to take it off, he realized that he was still holding the flowers in his hands.

"Here," he said, "white roses."

He wanted to give her the flowers and had to lean far across the bed, but was embraced by two soft white arms and pulled down.

"Chloé," he barely managed to gasp, "I never got to explain to you the fundamental dogmas of the Old New Presbyterian Church." But at that moment someone cleared his throat behind him.

18

The World Church Councilor shot up to a sitting position and Chloé crept under the blanket with a cry. It was the gallery owner, who stood before the canopied bed, shivering, with clattering teeth and wet as a corpse freshly pulled from the river, thin strands of hair in his forehead, his moustache dripping, his sopping clothes glued to his body, Passap's wire sculpture in his hands. A puddle, gleaming in the candlelight, stretched from his feet all the way to the door, with a few paper stars floating in it.

"I have thawed out," the art dealer said.

Archilochos stared at him.

"I have brought the sculpture," the gallery owner said.

"What do you want?" Arnolph finally asked, blushing.

He had no intention of intruding, Nadelör replied, shaking his sleeves, from which water ran to the floor as if from pipes; but he had to beg Monsieur Archilochos as a Christian and a World Church Councilor to call for a doctor at once, since he had an extremely high fever, stabbing pains in his chest, and a terrible backache.

"All right," Arnolph said, straightening his clothes and standing up. "Perhaps you had best put the sculpture over here."

As the gentleman wished, Nadelör replied, and he put the sculpture next to the bed, not without groaning; he had an inflamed bladder too, he added.

"My fiancée," Archilochos said by way of introduction, gesturing toward the mound beneath the blanket.

"You should be ashamed of yourself," the art dealer said, while fresh fountains bubbled out of him. "You as a Christian . . ."

"She really is my fiancée!"

"You may count on my discretion."

"May I request now, sir," Archilochos said, ushering Nadelör out of the room; but in the boudoir, next to the chair with the brassiere, the corset, and the panties, the gallery owner stopped again.

"A bath would do me good," he said, shivering and pointing at the open bathroom door and the steaming green water in the sunken tub.

"Impossible."

"You as World Church Councilor . . ."

"As you wish," Archilochos replied.

Nadelör undressed and stepped into the bath.

"Don't go away," he begged, naked and soft in the tub, drenched in sweat, with large, pleading, feverish eyes: "I might faint."

Then Archilochos had to massage him.

The gallery owner became fearful.

"What if the master of the house shows up?" he lamented.

"I am the master of the house."

"But you yourself said . . ."

"The house was just turned over to me."

The man had a high fever and his teeth were chattering. "Owner or not," he said, "I'm not leaving this house."

"It's really true," Archilochos said. "You can believe me. Why don't you trust me?"

"I still have some of my sanity left," Nadelör gasped, climbing out of the tub. "You as a Christian! I am enormously disappointed! You aren't any better than the rest of them."

Archilochos wrapped him in a blue-striped bathrobe that hung in the bathroom.

"Take me to a bed now," the art dealer moaned.

"But . . ."

"You as a World Church Councilor . . ."

"All right."

Archilochos led him to the canopied bed in the Renaissance room. And there he lay. "I'm calling the doctor now," Arnolph said.

"First a bottle of cognac," the gallery owner requested, shivering, with a croaking voice. "That always helps me. You as a Christian . . ."

He would look in the cellar, Archilochos promised, and wearily began to descend the stairs.

19

But as he reached the cellar stairs, which he found after some wandering about, he heard a distant yelling and hooting from below. Also, everything was lit up, and when he reached the vaulted cellar he found his presentiment confirmed: brother Bibi was lying on the floor with the twins Jean-Christophe and Jean-Daniel, surrounded by emptied bottles, singing folk songs.

"See what's coming from on high!" Bibi sang enthusiastically when he caught sight of his brother. "Uncle Arnolph!"

"What are you doing here?" Arnolph asked anxiously.

"Digging up schnapps and practicing harmony; a-hunting we will go."

"Bibi," Arnolph said with dignity, "I must ask you not to sing. This is the cellar of my house."

"Well," Bibi laughed, "you hit the jackpot, all right. Congratulations.

Plop yourself down there, brother Arnolph, smack on the couch," and offered his brother an empty keg that stood in a puddle of red wine.

"Come on, kiddies," he urged the twins, who were climbing about on Arnolph's knees and shoulders like monkeys, "sing a mighty psalm for your uncle."

"Be faithful, honest, true, and good," Jean-Christophe and Jean-Daniel sang with screeching voices.

Archilochos tried to shake off his weariness. "Brother Bibi," he said, "I have to talk to you once and for all."

"Cut the music, twins! Listen good," Bibi said with a thick tongue. "Uncle Arnolph wants to make a speech!"

"Not that I'm ashamed of you," Arnolph said. "You are my brother, and I know that at the bottom of your heart you are a good and quiet man, of noble disposition. But because of your weakness I now have to be strict with you, like a father. I have supported you, and the more money I gave you, the worse things have gotten with you and your family, and now you're even lying drunk in my cellar."

"Pure oversight, Brother Arnolph, I thought it was the War Minister's cellar. Pure oversight."

"So much the worse," Arnolph replied sadly. "It's wrong to break into other people's cellars. You'll end up in prison. Now you go home with your twins, and tomorrow you'll start in your job at Petit-Paysan in the Obstetrical Forceps Division."

"Home? In this cold?" Bibi asked with alarm.

"I'll order you a taxi."

"You want my delicate twins to freeze to death," Bibi protested indignantly. "In our windy barracks they'll die in this temperature. Minus twenty degrees Celsius."

From an adjoining vault came rumbling sounds. Matthäus and Sebastian, twelve and nine years old, rushed in, pounced on their uncle, and climbed up his knees and shoulders to join the twins.

"Throw away those daggers when you're climbing on your uncle, Matthäus and Sebastian," brother Bibi commanded.

"My God," Arnolph asked from beneath his four nephews, "who else have you got here?"

"Just Mom and the Captain," Bibi said, opening a bottle of vodka. "And Magda-Maria with her new beau."

"The Englishman?"

"What Englishman?" Bibi said in a tone of wonderment. "That's water under the bridge. This one's Chinese."

But when he finally returned to Nadelör, the art dealer was asleep, though wildly delirious, and it was too late to call a doctor. Archilochos was exhausted. The sounds of singing voices still resounded from the cellar. Not daring to follow the trail of comets and stars to Chloé's bedroom a second time, he lay down on the couch, not far from the chair with the brassiere and the girdle, where, after finally taking off his O'Neill-Papperer coat and covering himself with it, he fell asleep at once.

20

In the morning he was awakened toward eight o'clock by a chambermaid in a white apron.

"Hurry up, sir," the chambermaid said, "take your coat and leave, before the master of the house wakes up." She opened a door that he had noticed previously that led out to a wide hallway.

"Nonsense," Archilochos said, "I am the master of the house. The man in the bed is the gallery owner Nadelör."

"Oh," the girl said, and made a curtsey.

"What is your name?" he asked.

"Sophie."

"How old?"

"Sixteen, sir."

"Have you been here long?"

"Half a year."

"Mrs. Weeman hired you?"

"Mademoiselle Chloé, Monsieur."

Archilochos thought there must be some confusion somewhere, but he felt embarrassed and refrained from asking further questions.

"Would the gentleman like some coffee?" the girl asked.

"Is Mademoiselle Chloé up yet?"

"She sleeps till nine."

In that case he would ask to see her at nine, Archilochos said.

"Mon Dieu, Monsieur." Sophie shook her head: "That's when Mademoiselle takes her bath."

"And at nine thirty?"

"She has a massage."

"At ten?"

"Monsieur Spahtz comes."

Who was that, Archilochos wanted to know.

"The dressmaker."

So when could he see his bride, Arnolph cried out in despair.

"*Ah non*," Sophie said firmly. "The wedding is being prepared, Mademoiselle is much too busy."

Archilochos submitted. "Show me the way to the breakfast room, please," he replied. At least he would have something to eat.

He breakfasted in the room where Maître Dutour had transferred the house to him, served by a stately, gray-haired butler (the whole place was suddenly swarming with servants and maids). Eggs, ham (which he didn't touch), mocha, orange juice, grapes, and fragrant rolls with butter and jam were served, while outside the tall windows, behind the trees in the garden, day was breaking and wedding presents began pouring into the palace. Flowers, letters, telegrams, mountains of packages. Mail trucks came driving in, horns tooting, jamming up in front of the house, and the heaps of presents kept growing until they were piled high in the entrance hall, in the salon, even in front of the bed and on the blanket of the forgotten gallery owner, who lay, mute and dignified, still shivering in his fever.

Archilochos wiped his mouth with the napkin. He had dined for almost an hour, earnestly, silently, for since his noodles and applesauce at Georgette's he hadn't had anything to eat. On the sideboard stood bottles of aperitifs and liqueurs, boxes of cigars, brittle fragrant Partagas, Dannemanns, Costa Pennas, a colorful array of cigarette boxes, and for the first time, the temptation to try something like that arose in him, until, alarmed, he fought down the feeling. He was enjoying this early hour as master of the house. To be sure, the singing and howling of Bibi's clan, which at times sounded only too distinctly from the cellar, upset him somewhat: the fat cook, who had gone down there, came back badly disheveled; she had almost been raped by the Captain.

A band of robbers had broken in, the butler remarked fearfully, and wanted to call the police. Archilochos made a dismissive gesture with his hand:

"It's just my family."

The butler bowed.

Arnolph asked his name.

"Tom."

"How old?"

"Seventy-five, sir."

"Have you been here long?"

"Ten years."

"Mrs. Weeman hired you?"

"Mademoiselle Chloé."

Another misunderstanding, Archilochos thought, but for the second time he refrained from asking further questions. He felt a little embarrassed before this seventy-five-year-old butler.

O'Neill-Papperer would be coming at nine, the butler said. To prepare the tuxedo for the wedding. Goschenbauer had already sent the top hat.

"All right."

"At ten the registrar. There are still some formalities to settle."

"Fine."

"At half past ten Monsieur Wagner will call to bring the honorary doctorate of the Medical Faculty, for Monsieur's accomplishments with regards to the Obstetrical Forceps."

"I shall be expecting him."

"At eleven the American Ambassador is coming with a letter of congratulations from the President of the United States."

"Delighted."

"At one there will be a small lunch with the witnesses, and at twenty minutes to two departure for the Registry Office. After the Heloise Chapel, dinner at the Ritz."

Who had organized all this? Archilochos wanted to know.

"Mademoiselle Chloé."

"How many guests?"

Mademoiselle desired an intimate celebration. Exclusively the closest friends.

"Precisely my sentiments."

"Therefore we have invited only two hundred."

Archilochos was somewhat bewildered. "Very well," he finally said, "I don't know about these things. Have a cab come for me at half past eleven."

"Shouldn't Robert drive you?"

"Who is that now?" Archilochos asked.

"The chauffeur," the butler replied. Monsieur's red Studebaker, he said, was the finest in the whole city.

"Strange," Archilochos thought, but at that moment O'Neill-Papperer arrived.

And so, shortly before half past eleven, he drove to the Ritz to call on Mr. and Mrs. Weeman. He found the two in the hotel lobby, in a magnificent room with plush sofas and all sorts of armchairs, with such dark paintings on the walls that the objects depicted in them—various fruits, assorted game—

were all but invisible. The couple were sitting on a sofa, reading magazines: he the *New Archaeological Survey*, she the *Journal of Antiquities*.

"Mr. and Mrs. Weeman," he addressed them, intensely moved, handing the Englishwoman two orchids as she looked up in astonishment: "You are the finest people I have ever known."

"Well," said Mr. Weeman, drawing on his pipe and laying aside the *New Archaeological Survey*.

"I am raising you to Numbers One and Two in my ethical world order!"

"Yes," said Mr. Weeman.

"I revere you even more than the President and the Bishop of the Old New Presbyterians."

"Well," said Mr. Weeman.

"He who gives from the heart deserves thanks from the heart."

"Yes," said Mr. Weeman, staring at his wife.

"Thank you very much!" Arnolph added in English.

"Well," said Mr. Weeman, and then again, "Yes," and pulled out his wallet, but Archilochos had already vanished.

"Lovely people, these Englishmen, but a little reserved," he thought in his red Studebaker (the finest in the city).

It was not just a few little old ladies from the Old New Presbyterian congregation that awaited the wedding procession in front of the Heloise Chapel. Huge masses of people stood half-frozen on Emil Kappeler Street and formed long rows along the sidewalks. The windows of the run-down, dirty quarter were filled with bodies. Ragged urchins clung like lime-spattered grapes to the lampposts and to the few pathetic trees that stood about. Now the procession of automobiles turned from the Boulevard Merkling, on its way from City Hall, to the chapel. Leading the procession was the red Studebaker, from which Chloé and Archilochos emerged. The crowd screamed and roared with enthusiasm, "Hail Archilochos," "Evviva Chloé," the bicycle-racing fans shouted themselves hoarse, and Madame Bieler and her Auguste (this time not in his cyclist's outfit) both wept. A little later, the President's ornate carriage drove up, six white horses, the bodyguards with their golden helmets and white plumes mounted on prancing black chargers. A throng of bodies filled the Heloise Chapel. It was not exactly a beautiful building, more like a small factory, without a tower, its once white walls badly damaged, an altogether unfortunate product of modern ecclesiastical architecture, surrounded by a few sad cypresses; and since, in exchange for a pittance, the Heloise had once acquired the furnishings of an extremely old church that was demolished to make room for a movie theater, its interior was correspondingly drab and barren, with rough wooden benches and a bulky pulpit that jutted, crude and solitary, into the room. Opposite the entrance stood a large, half-rotted cross. The wall behind the cross, with its yellow and greenish stains, reminded Archilochos of his former garret, as did the high windows, like arrow slits in a fort, through which rays of light filled with dancing particles of dust fell at a slant to the floor. But as the wedding guests began to populate this poor, devout, stagnant world with its odor of little old women, cheap perfume, and probably a slight whiff of garlic as well, it took on a resplendent brilliance, became friendly and warm; the sparkle of jewelry and pearl necklaces filled the room, shoulders and breasts glowed, and clouds of the finest perfume rose upward into the half-charred rafters (the church had once nearly burned down). Bishop Moser mounted the pulpit, dignified in his black Old New Presbyterian robe. He laid the Bible with its lustrous gilt edging on the knotty wood of the lectern, clasped his hands, and looked down, somewhat embarrassed, it seemed, his pink face drenched with sweat. Right below him sat the bridal couple: Chloé with big, black, reverent eyes, shining with joy from behind a filmy veil in which a ray of sunlight quivered, and Archilochos stiffly at her side, now also embarrassed, scarcely recognizable in his tuxedo (O'Neill-Papperer), for all that remained of his former apparel were the rimless, dusty glasses, which now perched somewhat askew on his face. His top hat (Goschenbauer) and white gloves (De Stutz-Kalbermatten) rested on his knees. Behind the pair, but somewhat apart from the others, sat the President, goateed, his face covered with a filigree of wrinkles, white-haired, gold-spangled, dressed in the uniform of a cavalry general, his long sword dangling between skinny legs that were encased in shining boots; and behind the President sat the witnesses: the American Ambassador with medals on the breast of his white formal jacket, the Rector Magnificus decked out in all the pomp of his official dignity; then the guests, rather uncomfortably seated on wooden benches; Petit-Paysan; Maître Dutour at the side of his enormous wife, who towered in the room like a mountain covered with pearls instead of snow; Passap—he, too, in tails, his hands still stained with cobalt blue; in addition, gentlemen (mainly gentlemen) of the upper one thousand, the capital's crème de la crème, with solemn faces; and just as the Bishop was about to begin his oration, even Fahrcks came in, although late: Fahrcks the revolutionary, the last and bottommost in Arnolph's ethical world order, his huge head with the bristly moustache and fiery red locks massively set between mighty shoulders, the double chin touching the breast of his tailcoat, from which dangled a gold decoration studded with rubies: the Kremlin Medal.

21

"The words," Bishop Moser began his address in a low, lisping voice, shifting back and forth in his pulpit with visible discomfort; the words of which he wished to remind the dear congregation assembled for this happy event were to be found in the Seventy-Second Psalm, a psalm of Solomon, where it was written, Blessed be the Lord, the God of Israel, who alone does wondrous things. His task today, the Bishop continued, was to bind together for life two human beings who had become dear and precious not only to him but undoubtedly to all who had gathered in the Heloise Chapel. There was, first of all, the bride (here Bishop Moser stammered a little), whom all those present had surely locked in their hearts with great tenderness, a bride who (here Bishop Moser waxed poetic) had so gracefully bestowed upon all those assembled here so much love, so much beauty and sublimity, in short, so many beautiful hours, that no sufficient thanks could be given her (the Bishop wiped the sweat from his brow), and there was the bridegroom, the Bishop continued with relief, also a dear, noble soul who would now partake of all the love that his bride was capable of giving so lavishly, a citizen of our town who in a few days had attracted the attention of the world, rising from humble estate to the eminence of General Director, World Church Councilor, Honorary Doctor of the Medical Faculty, and Honorary Consul of the United States of America. True though it might be that everything Man undertakes, and all that he achieves, all his titles and merits, are transitory, chaff in the wind, a nothingness in the face of the Eternal, nevertheless this precipitate rise showed that grace had intervened (here Fahrcks audibly cleared his throat). But this grace was not of the kind bestowed by men (now Petit-Paysan cleared his throat), it was the grace of God, as our passage from Scripture teaches; not the favor of men had elevated Archilochos, but the Lord alone, who of course had employed human hearts that He guided, who indeed had made use of human weakness, human fallibility, for His ends, wherefore the glory was His alone.

Thus preached Bishop Moser, and his voice grew more powerful, more emphatic, his words more splendid, more unctuous, the further he was able to move from the particular to the general, from his original point of departure, namely the bridal couple, to the infinite and divine, unfolding an image of a cosmos that was really at bottom so very excellently and wisely ordered, and in which God's appointment ultimately turns all things to the good. But now that the Bishop had finished, now that he had stepped down from the pulpit and completed the ceremony, the two having breathed their "I do's," and Archilochos stood there, his lovely wife, with her large, black, happy eyes, holding his arm, and, as if awakening, looked at the festive throng through which he now had to pass—the dignified President, these ladies and gentlemen loaded with medals and jewels, these powerful, influential, and famous persons in the land—and as he noticed Fahrcks with his shaggy red hair scrutinizing him with a mocking smile, his face twisted in a malignant grimace, and as the little organ above the choir began its squeaking rendition of Mendelssohn's "Wedding March"—suddenly, at the climax of his joy, envied by the crowd outside, the Greek understood. He grew pale, he reeled. Sweat poured down his face.

"I have married a courtesan," he cried out desperately, like a fatally wounded animal, tore himself away from his wife, who anxiously pursued him to the portal with her veil waving behind her, and ran out of the Heloise Chapel, where the crowd, seeing the groom appearing alone, immediately realized what had happened and received him with whoops and gales of laughter. Archilochos hesitated for a moment among the wretched cypresses, afraid, for only now did he realize the vast number of spectators. Then he ran past the President's carriage and the waiting line of Rolls-Royces and Buicks and frantically, like an animal chased by a pack of dogs, ran down Emil Kappeler Street, taking a zigzag course to escape the menacing bodies of people who stepped in his way.

"Long live the biggest cuckold in town!"

"Down with him!"

"Tear his clothes off!"

Whistles shrilled in his ear, shouted insults, stones were thrown at him, street urchins ran after him, tripped him, several times he fell, until, covered with blood, he was able to hide under the stairs in the entrance of a tenement house, cowering in the darkness, the resounding steps of the mob above his head, his face buried in his arms, until after a while his pursuers dispersed, since they had not been able to find him.

For hours he cowered under the stairs, freezing, sobbing quietly, while the unheated corridor of the tenement grew darker and darker. She slept with all of them, he whimpered; with every one of them, with the President, with Passap and Maître Dutour, all of them. His entire ethical world order had collapsed, crushing him under its enormous weight. Finally he struggled to his feet. He staggered down the hallway, fell over a bicycle, and stepped out on the street. It was already night. He sneaked down to the river, through badly lit, dirty alleys, stumbled through crowds of squawking beggars who lay wrapped in newspaper under the bridges. A dog, ghostlike in the darkness, snapped at him, squeaking rats flitted past him, gurgling water lapped at his feet. Somewhere a ship howled.

"That's the third one this week," a beggar's voice squawked. "Go ahead, jump in!"

"Nonsense," another man gasped. "It's much too cold."

Laughter.

"Hang yourself, hang yourself," the beggars barked in chorus. "That's the most pleasant way to go, that's the most pleasant way to go."

He left the river, wandered blindly through the Old Town. Somewhere the Salvation Army was tooting away. He strayed into the Rue Funèbre, where Passap lived, started to run, trudged for hours through quarters he had never entered before, through elegant residential streets, through working-class housing projects filled with the noise of radios, past vicious dives from which the satirical songs of the Fahrcksists resounded, through factory districts with ghostly foundries, and reached his old garret toward midnight. He did not turn on the light; he stood leaning against the door, which he had closed behind him, trembling, filthy, in the shredded remnants of O'Neill-Papperer's tuxedo; he had long lost Goschenbauer's top hat. The flushing toilets still roared, and the lights from the little windows in the facade across the shaftway fell through the dusty windowpanes, illuminating now the curtain (with his old Sunday suit behind it), now the iron bed, now the chair and the rickety table with the Bible, now the pictures of his former ethical world order on the indistinctly patterned wallpaper. He opened the window and was met by a blast of stench and amplified roaring. He ripped one picture after the other from the wall and violently threw the President, the Bishop, the American Ambassador, even the Bible into the dark depths of the shaft. Only brother Bibi with his little brood was left hanging. Then he slunk into the attic, where long rows of wash hung indistinctly, untied a rope, left some family's linen lying on the floor, and groped his way back to his garret. He put the table under the lamp, climbed on top of it, attached the rope to the hook from which the lamp was suspended, tested the hook's firmness. Then he knotted the noose. The window blew open and shut, an icy draft touched his forehead. There he stood, with his head in the noose, about to throw himself off the table when the door opened and the light was turned on.

It was Fahrcks, still in the tuxedo he had worn at the wedding, a fur-lined coat thrown over it, his massive face immobile, gigantic above the Kremlin Medal, his tousled hair a furious flame. Two men accompanied him. One of them was Petit-Paysan's secretary, who now bolted the door, while the other, a man-mountain in the uniform of a taxi driver, shut the window, chewing gum, and put the chair in front of the door. Archilochos stood on the swaying table, his head in the noose, with the spectral light of the lamp upon him. Fahrcks sat down on the chair and folded his arms. The secretary sat down on the bed. The three men remained silent, the roar of the flushing toilets was somewhat muted, and the anarchist scrutinized the Greek attentively.

"Well, Monsieur Archilochos," he finally began, "you really should have expected a visit from me."

"You too have slept with Chloé," Archilochos hissed down at him from the table.

"Of course," Fahrcks replied. "After all, that is the lovely lady's profession."

"Get out!"

The revolutionary did not move. "Each of her lovers gave you a wedding present," he said. "Now it's my turn: Luginbühl, hand him my present."

The giant in the chauffeur's uniform stepped to the table, chewing, and placed a round, egglike object between Arnolph's feet.

"What is that?"

"Justice."

"A hand grenade?"

Fahrcks laughed: "Precisely."

Archilochos took his head out of the noose, cautiously climbed down from the rickety table, and hesitantly picked up the grenade. It was cold and sparkled in the light.

"What am I supposed to do with it?"

The old radical didn't reply immediately. Immobile, lurking, he sat on the chair, his huge hands spread out over his knees.

"You wanted to kill yourself," he said. "How come?"

Archilochos said nothing.

"There are two ways to deal with this world," Fahrcks said slowly and dryly. "Either one is destroyed by it or one changes it."

"Be quiet!" Archilochos screamed.

"All right. Then hang yourself."

"Speak."

Fahrcks laughed. "Give me a cigarette, Schubert," he said, turning to Petit-Paysan's secretary. Luginbühl gave him fire from an unwieldy lighter, and so he sat, smoking at his leisure, puffing out big, bluish clouds.

"What should I do?" Archilochos shouted.

"Accept what I am offering you."

"What for?"

"The social order that made a fool of you has to be overthrown."

"That is impossible."

"Nothing is easier," Fahrcks replied. "You are to assassinate the President. The rest I'll take care of myself." And he tapped the Kremlin Medal.

Archilochos reeled.

"Don't drop the bomb," the old incendiary warned him. "It could explode."

"I'm supposed to become a murderer?"

"Well, what's wrong with that? Schubert, show him the plan."

Petit-Paysan's secretary stepped up to the table and unfolded a sheet of paper.

"You're in league with Petit-Paysan!" Archilochos exclaimed, horrified.

"Nonsense!" Fahrcks said. "I bribed the secretary. You can get guys like this for small change."

Here was the floor plan of the President's palace, the secretary began explaining in a businesslike manner, running his finger over the drawing. This wall here surrounded the palace on three sides. The front of the building was closed off by an iron fence thirteen feet high. The wall was seven feet nine inches high. To the left was the Ministry of Commerce, to the right the Nuncio's residence. And right where the courtyard of the Ministry of Commerce met with the wall, there stood a ladder.

Was that ladder always there, Archilochos wanted to know.

"It is there tonight, that's all you need to know," the secretary replied. "We will drive you as far as the quay. You climb up the wall, draw the ladder after you, and use it to climb down. On the other side you will be standing in the shade of a fir tree. Step behind the tree and wait until the guard has passed. Then go to the back of the palace. You will find a small door with several steps leading up to it. The door is locked; here is the key."

"And then?"

"The President's bedroom is on the first floor; you reach it from the little door by way of the main staircase. It's in the back. Throw the hand grenade on his bed."

The secretary fell silent.

"And after I've thrown the bomb?"

"Go back the way you came," the secretary said. "The guards will rush into the palace through the main portal, and you'll have time to escape across the courtyard of the Ministry of Commerce, in front of which our car will be waiting for you."

It was silent in the garret, and cold. Even the flushing of toilets had stopped. Pinned to the dirty wallpaper, brother Bibi with his little brood hung in solitude.

"Well?" Fahrcks interrupted the silence. "What do you say to this presentation?"

"No," Archilochos screamed, pale, shaking with horror. "No!"

The old man dropped his cigarette to the floor, which was primitive (splintery wood with large knotholes); there it continued to smolder.

"They all scream like that at first," he said. "As if this world could be changed without murder."

Next door, awakened by Arnolph's cries, a maid thumped on the wall of the garret. Archilochos saw himself, Chloé on his arm, walking through the wintry city. Fog over the river, with large shadowy ships and lights. He saw the people waving from the streetcars, from automobiles—young, handsome, elegant men; then he saw the wedding guests, all spangled with gold and studded with diamonds, black tuxedos and evening dresses, scarlet decorations, white faces in golden sunlight, with the dancing particles of dust, and everywhere benevolent smiles that were in truth so malicious; he felt again the sudden, cruel moment of recognition, of shame, saw himself rushing out of the Heloise Chapel, emerging from among the cypresses, saw himself faltering and finally starting out on his zigzag dash through Emil Kappeler Street, straight through the roaring, laughing, jubilant crowd, saw the shadows of his pursuers grow to gigantic size on the pavement, felt once again his body pitching forward, felt the impact of his fall on the hard ground, which reddened with blood, and the stones, the fists that struck him like hammers, and how he quivered as he crouched under the stairs of the hallway, with footsteps pounding above him.

"I'll do it," he said.

22

Archilochos, determined to avenge himself upon the world, was taken by Fahrcks and his associates in an American car to the Quai Tassigni. From there it was only a ten-minute walk to the Quai de l'État (where the President lived). It was a quarter after two. The quay was deserted, and a quarter moon had risen behind St. Luke's cathedral. The ice floes in the river and the bizarre spikes and beards on the frozen St. Cecilia's fountain shimmered in its light. He moved in the shadows of the mansions and hotels, passed by the Ritz with its freezing doorman pacing in front of the entrance; but otherwise he met no one. Only Fahrcks drove by several times, as if by chance, checking to see whether Archilochos was carrying out his orders, stopping to ask the policeman in front of the Ministry of Commerce some feigned question, so that

Archilochos could reach the courtyard without being noticed. There he found the ladder against the wall. He put his hand to the pocket of his old, patched coat, which he had brought with him from the garret, felt the bomb, climbed the ladder, sat down on top of the narrow wall and drew the ladder after him, lowered it to the other side and descended. He was standing on a lawn in the shadow of a fir tree, as the secretary had said; the ground was frozen. Bright lights fell on the lawn from the quay side of the building, and a car's horn tooted somewhere; perhaps it was Fahrcks. The quarter moon emerged from behind the presidential palace, a ponderous, profusely ornamented baroque building (reproduced in all art books and praised by all the explainers of art). Close to the moon a large star twinkled, and the lights of an airplane passed by far above. Then footsteps resounded on the paved path that wound along outside the palace. He pressed close against the trunk of the fir, hidden behind its branches, which reached down to the ground, surrounding him with their resinous scent and scratching his face with their needles. Two guards were approaching in step, visible at first only as dark silhouettes, with shouldered rifles and fixed bayonets, their white plumes swaying in the moonlight. They stopped in front of the fir. One of them pushed the branches aside with his rifle. The Greek held his breath, thought himself discovered, and was already prepared to throw the hand grenade. But they hadn't seen him after all, and moved on. Now they were brightly lit by the moon, so that their golden helmets and the cuirasses of their historical uniforms flashed. They turned the corner of the palace. He slipped away from the tree and hurried to the back of the building. Here everything lay in the glare of the moonlight—tall firs and bare weeping willows, an ice-coated pond and the Nuncio's palace. He found the door immediately. The key fit. It turned, but the door did not open. It must have been barred from the inside. Archilochos hesitated; the guards might return at any moment. He stepped back into the yard and looked up the rear wall of the building. The back door was embedded between two nude marble giants, evidently Castor and Pollux, who carried a curving balcony on their shoulders. According to his calculations, the President's bedroom must be behind this balcony. Filled with a sudden mad resolve to carry out the assassination, come what may, he started to climb up, tackling a thigh, then a belly, a chest, digging his fingers into a marble beard, holding on to a marble ear, hoisting himself up over a marble head, and reached the balcony. In vain. The door would not open, and he didn't dare smash the windows, for he could already hear the guards' footsteps. He lay down on the cold floor of the balcony, the guards passed by beneath him, marching in step as before. The door of the balcony was surrounded by various nude men and women, larger than life, with horses' heads among them, all brightly illumined by the moon, fighting and savaging each other in the most gruesome and complicated postures, as he noted, still pressed to the floor of the balcony—a battle with Amazons, evidently—and in the midst of this turmoil of bodies he spotted the open cavern of a round window. He ventured up into the world of marble gods, found himself in a welter of huge breasts and thighs, fearing all the while that the bomb in his coat pocket might explode, crawled past the bellies of heroes, along arched and twisted backs, managed to hang on to the drawn sword of a warrior just as he thought himself already fallen, and pressed himself anxiously into the arms of a dying Amazon whose moonlike face regarded him with tenderness, while far below him the guards completed their round for the third time, and stopped.

Archilochos saw the guards step back into the lighted garden to look up at the wall of the palace.

"Someone's climbed up there," one of them said after a long stare.

"Where?" the other asked.

"There."

"Nonsense, that's just a shadow between the gods."

"Not gods, they're Amazons."

"What's that?"

"Women with only one breast."

"But they've got two."

"The sculptor forgot," the first guard suggested. "But there's a body stuck in there. I'll bring him down."

He took aim with his rifle. Archilochos didn't move.

The other man objected: "You want to wake the whole neighborhood with your shooting?"

"But someone's there."

"No, there isn't. No one could get up there anyway."

"You've got a point."

"You see? Let's go!"

The two marched off, in step, their rifles shouldered again. Arnolph climbed on, reached the window at last, crawled through it. He was on the second floor, in a steep, bare latrine, filled with moonlight that fell through the open window. He was dead tired, covered with dust and bird droppings, and sobered by the abrupt change from the world of marble gods to his present location. He was breathing heavily. He opened the door and found himself in an ample hall that opened out on both sides into drawing rooms, which were moonlit as well, with statues between the columns; vaguely he made out a wide curving staircase. He descended cautiously to the second floor, reached the hallway the secretary had told him about, peered through the tall windows facing the quay, and shrank back, blinded by the lights of the city. In the courtyard below him, the guard was being changed, a solemn ceremony with salutes, clicking heels, standing at attention, and goose-stepping. He glided back into the darkness, crept toward the bedroom door at the other end of the hallway and opened it quietly, with the bomb in his right hand. Shimmering moonlight fell through the high balcony door—the same door he had stood in front of outside. He entered the room, intent on searching for the bed and throwing the hand grenade, but there was no bed in the room, no sleeping President, only a basket full of plates and dishes. Otherwise the room was empty. Everything was wrong. Evidently even anarchists were misinformed sometimes. He withdrew in bewilderment and began defiantly searching for his victim. He went up to the third floor again, holding the bomb ready, then to the fourth, traversed sumptuous reception rooms, conference rooms, corridors, small lounges, looked into office rooms with covered typewriters, wandered through picture galleries and a small weapons room with ancient armor, cannon, and hanging banners, where a halberd ripped his sleeve. Finally, as he climbed to the fifth floor, pressed close to the wall, he saw a shimmer on the marble surface. Someone must have turned on a light. He plucked up his courage and walked on. The hand grenade gave him a feeling of power. He entered the corridor. His exhaustion was gone. He peered down the hallway, which ended at a door. It was half open. A light was burning in the room. He hurried across the soft rug, but when he tore open the door, holding the hand grenade over his head, the President stood before him in his bathrobe, so surprisingly that Archilochos barely managed to conceal the bomb in his coat pocket.

23

"Excuse me," the assassin stammered.

"Why, there you are, my revered Monsieur Archilochos," the President exclaimed joyfully, grasping the bewildered Greek's hand and shaking it: "I've been expecting you all evening, and then I happened to look out the window and saw you climbing over the wall. Good idea. My bodyguards are much too pedantic. Those fellows would never have let you in. But here you are, and I'm awfully glad. How did you ever get into the house? I was just about to send my valet down. I just moved to the fifth floor a week ago, it's so much more comfortable than on the second floor, although, of course, the elevator doesn't always work."

"The back door was unlocked," Archilochos stammered, realizing that he had missed the right moment; besides, he was standing too close to his victim.

"How nice," the President said. "My valet, good old Ludwig, or Ludovigo, as I call him (he really looks more like a President than I do), has improvised a little dinner."

"Oh, please," Archilochos said, blushing. "I don't mean to intrude."

He wasn't intruding at all, the goateed old gentleman assured him. "At my age one doesn't sleep much. Cold feet, rheumatism, worries—personal ones and, as President, professional worries too, what with the current tendency of states to collapse; so I often have a bite to eat during the long nights in my lonely palace. Fortunately we had central heating installed last year."

"It really is pleasantly warm," Archilochos observed.

"But look at you!" the President exclaimed: "All covered with dust. Ludovigo, why don't you brush him off a bit."

"Permit me," the valet said, and removed the dust and bird droppings from the assassin's clothing. Archilochos, who didn't dare to fend him off, was afraid the bomb might explode in his pocket as a result of the brushing. He was relieved when the valet helped him out of his coat.

"You resemble my butler at the Boulevard Saint-Père," he said.

"That's because he's my half-brother," the valet remarked. "Twenty years younger than I."

"We have a great deal to chat about, I'd say," the President said, leading his murderer along the corridor, which was now brightly lit.

They stepped into a small, candlelit room facing the quay. In a window recess stood a small table set with precious china and sparkling crystal on a white linen cloth.

"I'll strangle him," Archilochos thought defiantly. "That's the simplest way."

"Let us sit down, my dear good fellow," said the courteous old President, lightly touching Arnolph's arm. "From here, if we wish, we can look down into the courtyard at the gentlemen of the guard with their white plumes, who would be surprised to know that someone had sneaked in to find me. The idea of the ladder is excellent and pleases me all the more in that I, too, sometimes climb over the wall with a ladder, in the middle of the night, as you have just done, but that's just between you and me. An old President has to resort to such means, for there are certain matters in life that concern a man of honor but not the gentlemen of the press. Ludovigo, pour us the champagne."

"Thank you," Archilochos said. "But I'll murder him anyway," he thought.

"And some chicken," the old man said with pleasure. "We always have that in the kitchen, Ludovigo and I, champagne and chicken at three o'clock in the morning. A nice solid snack. I assume your climb over the wall has made you good and hungry."

"Somewhat," Archilochos said honestly, remembering his arduous climb up the facade. The valet served them with great dignity, though with alarmingly tremulous hands.

"Don't worry about Ludovigo's shaking," the President said. "He has already served six of my predecessors."

Arnolph cleaned his glasses with his napkin. The bomb would have been more convenient, he thought. He still didn't know how to proceed. He couldn't very well say "excuse me" and begin strangling the President; besides, the valet would have to be killed to prevent him from summoning the guards, which would have complicated matters. So he ate and drank, at first to gain time and adapt to the new conditions, and then because he was enjoying himself. The dignified old man made him feel good. It was as though he were sitting with a father to whom he could confess everything.

"The chicken is superb," the President declared.

"It really is," Archilochos admitted.

"The champagne's not bad either."

"I never thought there was anything so delicious," Archilochos confessed.

"Let us chat while we eat, and let's not shy away from each other. Let's talk about your lovely Chloé, who is on your mind, after all, and who confuses you," the old man proposed.

"I was very shocked today in the Heloise Chapel," Archilochos said, "when I suddenly realized the truth."

"I rather had that impression myself," the President confirmed.

"When I saw you sitting there," Arnolph confessed, "in the church, with all your medals, it suddenly occurred to me that you had only come to the wedding because you and Chloé . . ."

"You had a high opinion of me?" the old man asked.

"You were my model. I thought you were a strict opponent of alcohol," Archilochos shyly remarked.

"The press did that to me," the President grumbled. "The government is waging a campaign against alcoholism, so they always photograph me with a glass of milk."

"It was also said that you were extremely strict in regard to morals."

"According to the Women's Federation. You're a teetotaler?"

"Vegetarian as well."

"And drinking champagne now, and eating chicken?"

"I've lost my ideals."

"I'm sorry to hear that."

"They're all hypocrites."

"Chloé too?"

"You know perfectly well what Chloé is."

"The truth," remarked the President, laying down a gnawed drumstick and pushing the candelabrum aside from where it stood between them, "the truth is always an embarrassing thing when it comes to light, not only for women but for all people and especially for a government. There are times when I feel like dashing out of my palace—which I find revolting just from an architectural point of view—as you did from the Heloise Chapel, but frankly, I don't have the courage, so I secretly climb over the wall. I don't wish to defend any of the persons involved," he continued, "least of all myself. This is altogether an area that's hard to discuss in a decent way, and if at all, then only at night, tête-à-tête, because any sort of talk tends to bring in views and moralities that are out of place, and because the virtues, passions, and faults of people lie so close together that contempt and hatred easily arise where only love and respect would suggest themselves as appropriate. I shall therefore say only one thing to you, my dear good fellow: If there is one person whom I envy, it is you, and if there is one person for whose safety I fear, it is you as well. . . . I had to share Chloé with many," he said after a while, settling back in his Biedermeier chair and regarding Archilochos almost with tenderness. "She was the queen of a dark, elemental realm. She was a courtesan. The most famous in the city. I don't want to prettify the fact, and I am too old to do that. I am grateful that she gave me her love, and there is no other human being I think back on with more gratitude. Now she has turned away from all of us and come to you. Therefore her day of rejoicing was for us a farewell ceremony and a thanksgiving feast."

The aged President fell silent. Dreamily, he stroked his well-tended goatee. The valet poured champagne. From outside came the sharply shouted commands and goose-stepping of the guards. Archilochos, too, had leaned back in his chair, and was thinking with consternation of the now so useless bomb in his coat pocket, when, peering through the window, he saw Fahrcks's car waiting in front of the Ministry of Commerce.

"Now as for you, my dear good fellow," the President continued softly after a while, lighting a small light cigar that the valet had offered him (Archilochos, too, was smoking), "I understand your tempestuous emotions. What man in your situation would not be offended? But it is precisely these perfectly natural feelings that must be combated, since they do the greatest harm. I cannot help you. Who could do that? I can only hope that you find a way to accept a fact that no one can deny, and that will only become void and insignificant if you have the strength to believe in the love that Chloé is offering you. The miracle that happened between the two of you is only possible and believable through love, and outside that love, it turns into a farce. Thus you are walking on a narrow bridge, across dangerous abysses, on the edge of a sword like the Muslims when they enter paradise, at least that's what I read somewhere; but have some more chicken," he urged his thwarted assassin. "It is really excellent and always a consolation." Archilochos sat there, enveloped by the glow of candlelight, entranced by the mellow warmth of the room. On the walls, in heavy gold frames, hung earnest, long-deceased statesmen and heroes who had passed into eternity and gazed at him with a thoughtful, remote, and lofty expression. A calm such as he had never experienced entered his soul, an incomprehensible serenity, produced not only by the President's words—what did words amount to, anyway—but by his kindly, paternal, courteous manner.

"A grace has befallen you," the old gentleman added. "There are two possible reasons for this grace, and it depends on you which one it is: love, if you believe in this love, or evil, if you do not believe in this love. Love is a miracle that is always possible; evil is a fact that is always present. Justice condemns evil, hope wants to improve it, and love overlooks it. Only love is capable of accepting grace as it is. There is nothing more difficult, I know. The world is terrible and meaningless. The hope for a meaning behind all this nonsense, behind all this terror, can be preserved only by those who love, despite everything."

He fell silent, and for the first time Archilochos was able to think of Chloé again, without dread, without horror.

24

Then, when the candles had burned down, the President helped Archilochos into the coat with the now useless bomb and accompanied him, since the elevator happened to be out of order, down to the main entrance, because, he said, he did not want to inconvenience Ludovigo, who had fallen asleep, standing, stiff and proper, next to his master's chair—a feat that, the old man declared, ought to be respected under any conditions. So the two walked down the wide, curving staircase through the empty palace, Archilochos consoled, content with the world, yearning for Chloé, the President more like a museum curator, turning on the lights in this or that hall and furnishing the necessary explanations. This here, he would say, pointing into a vast splendid hall, was where he gave formal receptions; and here was where he accepted the Prime Minister's resignation twice a month; and here in this intimate salon with the almost genuine Raphael he had had tea with the Queen of England and her prince consort, and had nearly fallen asleep when the prince consort began talking about the navy; nothing bored him more than navy stories, and only the adroitness of his Chief of Protocol had prevented a mishap by awakening him at the decisive moment and whispering a properly naval reply in his ear. Otherwise they had been very nice, these English folk.

Then they took leave of each other, two friends who had heard each other out and made peace. The old man smiled back once more from the main entrance, smiling, serene. Archilochos looked back. The palace loomed into the cold night, dark now, like a huge chest of drawers covered with sumptuous ornaments. The quarter moon was no longer visible. He walked between the saluting bodyguards and arrived at the Quai de l'État, but then, seeing Fahrcks's car rushing toward him from the direction of the Ministry of Commerce, he turned into the narrow Ruelle Etter between the Nuncio's residence and the Swiss embassy, arrived at Rue Stabi in front of Pfyffer's Bar, and took a taxi; he didn't want to meet up with Fahrcks again. Then he ran through the garden, possessed by the single thought of taking Chloé in his arms. The little rococo palace was brightly lit and resounded with raucous singing. The door was open. Dense yellow swathes of cigar and pipe smoke filled the air. Brother Bibi with his brood had now taken possession of the whole house. Everywhere, members of the gang were sitting or lying around, drunk and babbling, on the couches, under the tables, wrapped in curtains that had been torn down. All the city's vagrants, pimps, and drag queens seemed to be assembled, women were screeching in the beds, bare breasts gleamed, gallows birds sat in the kitchen, eating, smacking their chops, guzzling the dregs of the liquor cabinets and the cellar, Matthäus and Sebastian were playing hockey with two wooden legs in the dining room, in the hallway the Captain and Mom were practicing knife throwing, while Jean-Christophe and Jean-Daniel played marbles with Jean-Daniel's glass eye and Théophile and Gottlieb slid down the banisters with hookers on their laps; full of foreboding, Arnolph ran to the top floor, past the gallery owner Nadelör, who still lay delirious in his bed, through the boudoir, where, from the bathroom, the sound of singing men, splashing water, and Magda-Maria's shrill voice could be heard, and when he burst into the bedroom, brother Bibi was lying in the bed with a mistress (nude). After searching and rummaging through the whole house, there was no sign of Chloé.

"Where is Chloé?"

"What's this, brother," Bibi said reproachfully, puffing a cigar: "Never enter a bedroom without knocking."

Bibi was unable to continue his speech. His brother was transformed. Having rushed into his palace with the most tender feelings, full of love, full of longing for Chloé, these emotions now turned to wrath. The inanity of having supported this family for years, the audacity with which they had taken over his palace, the fear that he had lost Chloé through his own fault, brought out the berserker in him. He became an Ares, a Greek war god, as Passap had predicted, and it was with Passap's wire sculpture that he proceeded to bear down upon his comfortably lounging, cigar-smoking brother, striking him with such force that Bibi leaped to his feet with a cry and, receiving a blow to the jaw, staggered off to the door, where Arnolph pounded him again, then turned his attention to the mistress, whom he dragged by her hair into the hallway and threw at the Captain, who, alarmed by Bibi's roars, had come rushing to his aid, whereupon the two tumbled together down the stairs. From all the doors, cutthroats, pimps, and other rabble came rushing toward Arnolph, some of them members of his family, like Théophile and Gottlieb, whom he dashed down the winding staircase, together with Nadelör in his Renaissance bed, now Sebastian and Matthäus, whom he gave a second beating, now Magda-Maria with her admirer (Chinese), whom he tossed naked through the shattering windowpanes into the garden, now all sorts of unknown riffraff. Artificial limbs whirred through the air, chair legs, blood spurted, hookers fled, Mom fainted, drag queens and counterfeiters scrambled away with their heads pulled in, whistling like rats in their terror. He flailed his fists, strangled, scratched, kicked, smashed, broke skulls, pounded foreheads together, raped a hooker, wooden legs, brass knuckles, truncheons, and bottles raining down on him, rose again, freed himself, foaming, covered with debris, used a round table as a shield and vases, chairs, oil paintings, Jean-Christophe, and Jean-Daniel as missiles, and, steadily advancing, trampling and tearing everything in his path, spewing out immense curses, drove the whole vicious lot of them out of his house, in which the wallpaper now hung in shreds, waving like banners in the icy draft, in the thinning clouds of tobacco smoke, and threw the hand grenade after the howling mob, adding a brilliant flash to the first light of dawn that was just beginning to illuminate the garden.

Then he stood for a long time at the entrance of his demolished palace and stared into the morning as it rose, gleaming like silver behind the elms and firs of the garden. Warm gusts of wind surged through the trees, lashing them, shaking them. A thaw was setting in. The ice on the roof was melting;

water gurgled in the gutter. Everything was dripping, huge cloud banks swept over the roofs and gardens, heavy, pregnant; rain drizzled down in thin veils. Bruised, scantily dressed, shivering, Nadelör limped past him into the damp morning.

"You as a Christian."

Archilochos ignored him. He stared into space through swollen eyes, covered with caked blood, his wedding tuxedo in shreds, the lining hanging out, his glasses lost.

End of Part I

(The following is the end for lending libraries.)

24a

He began to search for Chloé.

"Oh my God, Monsieur Arnolph," Georgette cried when he stood before the counter demanding a Pernod. "My God, what happened to you?"

"I can't find Chloé."

The restaurant was full of customers. Auguste was serving. Archilochos drained his glass of Pernod and demanded a second one.

"Have you looked everywhere?" Madame Bieler asked.

"At Passap's, at the Bishop's, everywhere."

"She'll turn up," Georgette consoled him. "Women don't get lost so easily, and often they're exactly where you wouldn't expect them."

Then he poured himself a third Pernod.

"At last," Auguste said with relief to the cycling fans: "Now he's drinking."

Archilochos kept searching. He forced his way into convents, boarding houses, apartment buildings; Chloé was not to be found. He wandered through his empty palace, through the empty garden, stood in the wet leaves. There was only the wind surging in the trees, only the clouds racing above the roofs. A sudden nostalgia overcame him, a longing for Greece, for ruddy cliffs and dark groves, for the Peloponnesus.

Two hours later he embarked, and the car full of Fahrcks's bandits that came racing into the harbor as the *Julia* glided, howling, into the fog, wrapped in her own smoke, sent a few bullets after the ship that were meant for the deserting assassin but merely slashed the wearily waving green-gold national flag.

Among the passengers were Mr. and Mrs. Weeman, who regarded him anxiously when he approached them one afternoon.

The Mediterranean. The deck full of sunlight. Deck chairs everywhere. Archilochos said:

"I have had the honor of speaking with you several times."

"Well," Mr. Weeman muttered.

Arnolph apologized. It was just a misunderstanding, he said.

"Yes," said Mr. Weeman.

Then Archilochos asked if he might help with the excavations in his old homeland.

"Well," Mr. Weeman replied, folding the *Journal of Antiquities*. Then, stuffing his short pipe, he said: "Yes."

And so Archilochos dug for antiquities in Greece, in a part of the Peloponnesus that did not in the least correspond to the picture he had conceived of his homeland. He shoveled under a merciless sun. Rubble, snakes, scorpions, and a few crippled olive trees against the horizon. Low, barren hills, dried-up springs, not even shrubs. A circling vulture over his head, stubborn, impossible to scare away. For weeks he chipped away at a hill, streaming sweat, gradually hollowing out the hard earth, until finally sand appeared inside some shabby walls he had excavated; sand that became hot as fire in the sun, crept under his fingernails, inflamed his eyes. Mr. Weeman hoped they had uncovered a temple of Zeus, Mrs. Weeman presumed it was a sanctuary of Aphrodite. Their quarreling could be heard for miles. The Greeks had long since gone home. Mosquitoes hummed, flies covered his face, crawled over his eyes. Dusk fell, a mule's cries rang out in the distance, shrill and plaintive. The night was cold. Archilochos lay in his tent next to the excavation site, Mrs. and Mr. Weeman in the district capital, a miserable hole some seven miles away. Night birds and bats fluttered around the tent. Some unknown animal howled nearby, a wolf perhaps; then it was quiet again. He fell asleep. Toward morning he thought he heard a few soft steps. He slept on. As soon as the sun, burning red above the senseless barren hills, touched his tent, he got up. He staggered to his solitary work site, to the walls. It was still cold. High above, the vulture was still circling. Inside the walls it was still almost dark. His limbs ached. He set to work with the shovel. Before him lay a longish heap of sand, shimmering in the semidarkness, but the very first cautious stab met with resistance. The goddess of love or Zeus, he thought, curious as to which of the two archaeologists was right, reached in with both hands, scraping away the sand, and unearthed Chloé.

He scarcely dared to breathe. He stared at his beloved.

"Chloé," he cried, "Chloé, how did you get here?"

She opened her eyes, but remained lying in the sand.

"Very simple," she said. "I followed you. We had two tickets."

Then they sat on the wall and gazed out into the Greek landscape with its low, barren mountains and the tremendous sun above them, the crippled olive trees in the distance and the white gleam of the district capital on the horizon.

"This is our homeland," she said, "yours and mine."

"Where were you?" he asked. "I looked for you all over the city."

"At Georgette's. Upstairs in the apartment."

Two dots moved in the distance, approaching. Mr. and Mrs. Weeman.

Then she delivered to him her discourse on love, somewhat like Diotima's to Socrates*—not quite as profound, of course, since as the child of a Greek businessman (we note this by way of correcting the question of her origins) Chloé Saloniki was the more robust and practical of the two.

"You see," she said, while the wind played with her hair and the sun rolled higher and higher in the sky and the English couple came steadily nearer on their mules, "now you know what I was, that's cleared up between us. I was tired of my profession, which was hard work, like any honest work. But it made me sad. I had a longing for love, for having someone to care for, to be there not just for his pleasure, but also for his sorrow; and one morning when my little palace was hidden in fog, a wintry morning, dark, as it had been for weeks, I read in *Le Soir* that a Greek man wanted a Greek wife, and I made up my mind to love *this* Greek, only him and nobody else, no matter what happened, no matter what he was like. So I came to you, on that Sunday morning at ten, with the rose. I didn't want to pretend to you. I came in my best clothes. Just as I would accept you as you were, I wanted you to accept me as I was, and when I saw you sitting at the table, embarrassed, awkward, with the steaming milk, cleaning your glasses, it happened: I loved you. But since you thought I was still a girl, since you showed so little knowledge of the world that you were unable to guess my profession, as Georgette and her husband guessed it, I did not dare to destroy your dream. I was afraid of losing you and only made everything worse. Your love became ridiculous, and when in the Heloise Chapel you recognized the truth, your love was shattered along with your world. It was good that that happened. You couldn't love me without the truth, and only love is stronger than the

*In Plato's *Symposium*.

truth that threatened to destroy us. The love of your blindness had to be destroyed for the sake of the love that sees, which is the only one that counts."

24b

But it took some time before Chloé and Archilochos could return. The government collapsed. Fahrcks with the Kremlin Medal under his double chin took the rudder, the night sky turned red. Everywhere flags, everywhere choruses chanting "Yankee go home"; everywhere banners, everywhere giant portraits of Lenin and the Russian Prime Minister not yet fallen out of favor. But the Kremlin was far, the dollar needed, and power of one's own an enticing prospect. Fahrcks moved into the Western camp, had the chief of the secret police (Petit-Paysan's secretary) hanged, and resided in the most dignified manner in the presidential palace on the Quai de l'État, protected like his predecessor by the same bodyguards with the golden helmets and the white plumes, his red hair carefully trimmed, his moustache cropped. He relaxed his regime, his ideology faded, and one lovely Easter day he visited St. Luke's cathedral. Civil order returned, but Chloé and Archilochos no longer felt at ease in it. They tried it for a while. They opened a boardinghouse in their little palace. Passap rented a room, having become passé (in matters of art Fahrcks clung to the doctrine of Socialist Realism); Maître Dutour, also down at the heel; Hercule Wagner with his enormous wife, he too deposed; and the overthrown President, polite, observing the course of things; finally Petit-Paysan (ruined by his merger with the Rubber and Lubricating Oil Cartel), doing housework: bankrupt, all of them. Only the Bishop was missing. He had gone over to the New Presbyterians of the Penultimate Christians. The boarders drank milk and on Sundays Perrier, lived quietly, spending their summers dreaming under the trees in the garden, adrift in their mellow world. Archilochos was dismayed. He went to see his brother, who was running a plant nursery in a suburb with Mom, the Captain, and the kiddies—the great brawl with Arnolph had worked wonders (Matthäus had passed the teacher's exam, Magda-Maria the exam for kindergarten teachers, the others worked in factories or for the Salvation Army). But he did not stay there for long. The stolid atmosphere, the pipe-smoking Captain, Mom's knitting, it all bored him, and so did Bibi, who was now attending services at the Heloise Chapel in his stead. Four times a week.

"You look pale, Monsieur Arnolph," Georgette said one day as he stood at her counter (behind her, above the schnapps and liqueur bottles, Fahrcks in the edelweiss frame). "Are you unhappy?"

She handed him a glass of Pernod.

"Everyone's drinking milk," he muttered. "The cycling fans and now your husband."

"What can little guys like us do," Auguste said, still in his *maillot jaune*, rubbing his shimmering legs: "The government has launched a new anti-alcohol campaign. And besides, I'm a sportsman."

Then Archilochos noticed Georgette opening a bottle of Perrier.

"She too," he thought sorrowfully. And lying next to Chloé in the canopied bed, behind the red curtains, logs burning in the fireplace, he said: "It's all very nice in our little palace with our satisfied, aging boarders, I don't wish to complain, but this virtuous world we are living in feels uncanny to me. It looks to me as if I had converted the world and the world had converted me, so that it all amounts to the same thing and it was all pointless."

Chloé had sat up.

"I keep thinking of our ruined walls, back in our homeland," she said. "When I covered myself with sand in order to surprise you and lay there on that dark morning and looked out for that vulture that circled over the walls, I felt something hard beneath me, something stony, like two big hemispheres."

"The goddess of love," Archilochos cried and leaped out of bed. So did Chloé.

"We must never stop searching for the goddess of love," she whispered, "otherwise she will leave us."

They got dressed, soundlessly, packed a valise, and the next morning around eleven, when Sophie, accompanied by the concerned boarders, entered the bedroom after knocking in vain for a long time, she found it empty.

End of Part II

Traps A Still Possible Story

Part One

Are there any possible stories left, stories for writers? If a man doesn't want to write about himself, doesn't intend romantically, lyrically to universalize his ego, if he feels no compulsion to speak—with perfect truthfulness, to be sure—of his hopes and defeats and his way of lying in bed with women, as if candor transposed all these things into universality rather than into medical or, at best, psychological subject matter; if instead he prefers to step back discreetly and politely keep his privacy, handling his materials much as a sculptor treats wood or stone, working on them, and in the process developing himself, trying, in a sort of classical spirit, not to fall into despair over the undeniable nonsense that keeps cropping up on all sides; if this is his aim, then the business of writing becomes more difficult, more lonely, and more meaningless, too. Getting a good grade in literary history is of no interest, considering the dunces who have gotten top grades and the junk that has been honored with prizes—the demands of the day are more important. But here, too, a dilemma presents itself, and an unfavorable market. Mere entertainment is supplied by life, and in the evening by the movies, poetry can be found in the arts section of the newspaper, and for anything more than a franc the reader wants soul, true confessions, higher values and moral instruction, quotable pronouncements, something has to be overcome or affirmed, Christianity or else some fashionable despair, in short what is wanted is literature. But what if the author refuses to produce this, persistently, more and more stubbornly, because, though he knows that his writing is based in varying proportions on his own conscious and unconscious life, on his faith and his doubts, he also believes that these are none of the public's business, that forming and shaping the surface of things is sufficient and altogether more appetizing, and that, for the rest, his job is to keep his mouth shut and refrain from both comment and gossip? Having arrived at this insight, he will hesitate, falter, he can hardly avoid it. A suspicion arises that there are no stories left to be told, and he seriously entertains the thought of resigning. Perhaps a few sentences are still possible, but for the rest he'll turn to biology, a way of coping, at least conceptually, with the explosion of humanity, the advancing billions, the ceaselessly delivering wombs, or to physics, or astronomy, in order to render an account—for the sake of order, if nothing else—of the structure within which we oscillate. The rest is for the magazines, for *Life, Paris Match*, and *Quick:* the president under his oxygen tent, Uncle Bulganin in his garden, the princess with her super-duper flight captain, movie celebs and dollar faces, interchangeable, passé the moment their names are dropped. In addition there is everyone's everyday life, Western European in my case, more precisely Swiss, bad weather, the ups and downs of the market, worries and tribulations, upheavals in the private realm, but unrelated to the world, to the course of things meaningful and absurd, to the unfolding or unraveling of necessity. Fate has left the stage and lurks in the wings, outside the conventions of dramaturgy, while in the foreground everything becomes a matter of accident, all the sicknesses, for instance, the crises. Even war now depends on whether the electronic brains forecast a profitable outcome, but this, we know, can never happen (presuming, of course, that the computers work), for nowadays only defeats are mathematically conceivable. Let's just hope no one fudges the figures, illicitly tampers with the artificial brains; but an even more awkward possibility is that of a screw coming loose, a spring getting caught, a keyboard malfunctioning, apocalypse by a short circuit, a technical snafu. So it is no longer a God who threatens us with divine justice, no fate knocks on the door as in the Fifth Symphony, what we're up against are traffic accidents, dams bursting as a result of faulty construction, the explosion of an atom bomb factory set off by a distracted technician, a wrongly set dial on an incubator. As we advance into this world of smash-ups and breakdowns, a few possible stories still take place by the dusty edge of the road, among billboards promoting shoes, cars, and ice cream, among tombs commemorating the victims of traffic; stories in which humanity gazes out from some dime-a-dozen face, and an ordinary mishap unintentionally widens into universality, and judgment and justice come into view, maybe grace as well, accidentally caught and reflected in the monocle of a drunken man.

Part Two

An accident, too—just a harmless mechanical breakdown, but an accident nonetheless: Alfredo Traps, employed in the textile industry, forty-five, still far from stout, pleasant appearance, not educated so much as trained to exhibit adequate manners, a certain primitivity shimmering through, the crude gregariousness of a door-to-door salesman—this man of our time had just been traveling in his Studebaker along one of the great highways of this land, with reasonable prospects of getting home to his fair-sized city within an hour, when his car went on strike. It simply stopped. Helpless, the gleaming red car lay at the foot of a hill, while the road swung itself across the modest summit. A cumulus cloud had formed in the north, and in the west the sun still stood high, with an almost afternoonish persistence. Traps smoked a cigarette and then did what he had to do. The mechanic who finally came to tow away the Studebaker declared that he would not be able to repair the defect before the next morning—a fault in the fuel line. Whether or not this was true could not be determined, nor was it advisable to try; we are at the mercy of mechanics as we once were of robber knights, and earlier, of local gods and demons. Too phlegmatic to walk a half hour to the next train station and then take the short if somewhat complicated trip home to his wife and four children, all boys, Traps decided to spend the night where he was. It was 6:00 p.m., hot, just a few days before the longest day of the year. The garage stood by the edge of a friendly village, its houses straggling off toward wooded hills, with a little knoll supporting a church, a parsonage, and an ancient oak with mighty iron rings and props. Everything was neat and proper; even the heaps of manure in front of the farmhouses were carefully stacked and trimmed. There was also a small factory standing around somewhere, and several taverns, and some inns, the praises of which Traps had often heard, but their rooms had been claimed by a poultry farmer's convention, and our traveling textiles man was directed to a private house that was known to take in an occasional guest. Traps hesitated. It was still possible to take the train home, but he was tempted by the hope of experiencing an adventure. Sometimes there were girls in the villages, as in Grossbiestringen recently, who knew how to appreciate traveling salesmen. With his spirits revived, he set out toward the house. A clangor of bells from the church. Cows trotting toward him, mooing. The two-story house stood in a large garden, its walls dazzling white, a flat roof, green shutters, half hidden by shrubs, beech, and firs, flowers near the street, mainly roses, among them an aged little man wearing a leather apron, possibly the master of the house, puttering in his garden.

Traps introduced himself and asked for lodging.

"Your profession?" asked the old man, who had come to the fence, smoking a Brissago. He was so small that his head scarcely reached above the gate.

"I'm in textiles."

The old man examined Traps closely, peering over small rimless glasses in the manner of farsighted people: "Sure, the gentleman may spend the night here."

Traps asked for the price.

He was not in the habit of charging, the old man replied. He was alone, for his son had left for the United States. He had a housekeeper, Mademoiselle Simone, who took good care of him, so he enjoyed putting up a guest now and then.

Traps thanked him. He was touched by the old man's hospitality and remarked that evidently here, in the countryside, the ways of our ancestors had not yet died out. The garden door was opened. Traps looked around. Gravel paths, a lawn, large shaded areas, patches of sunlight.

When they reached the flowers, the old man stopped to carefully clip a rosebush and remarked that he was expecting some gentlemen that night, friends from the village and from the hills further off. Pensioners, all of them, like himself. They had moved to his neighborhood because of the mild climate and because the föhn wasn't felt in those parts. All of them were lonely, widowed, eager for something new, fresh, and lively, so he would be delighted if Herr Traps would join them for dinner and spend the evening with them.

The traveling salesman hesitated. He had intended to eat in the village, at that celebrated inn, but he felt obligated to accept the invitation. After all, he had accepted an offer to spend the night free of charge. He did not want to be seen as a rude city dweller. So he pretended to be pleased. The master of the house showed him up to the second floor. A friendly room. Running water, a wide bed, a table, a comfortable chair, a picture by Hodler on the wall,* old leather-bound volumes in a bookcase. Traps opened his little valise, washed, shaved, swathed himself in a cloud of eau de cologne, stepped up to the window, lit a cigarette. The sun, a large orange disc, was sliding down toward the hills, framing the beeches in a halo. Quickly he ran over the day's business, the order from Rotacher Inc., not bad, the difficulties with Wildholz, five percent he wanted, boy oh boy, he'd wring his neck yet. Then memories rose to the surface. A jumbled mess of everyday stuff, a planned adultery in the Touring

*Ferdinand Hodler (1853–1918), noted Swiss artist, whose most famous paintings portrayed everyday life.

Hotel, whether or not to buy an electric train for his youngest and favorite son, the question of whether it would not be polite and actually his duty to call his wife and inform her of the unwanted delay. But he didn't call her. Not for the first time. She was used to it, and besides, she wouldn't believe him. He yawned, granted himself another cigarette. He watched three elderly gentlemen marching along the gravel path, two of them arm in arm, and a fat, bald one following in tow. Greetings, handshakes, hugs, conversations over the roses. Traps withdrew from the window and went to the bookcase. To judge by the titles, he was in for a tedious evening: Hotzendorff, *Homicide and the Death Penalty;* Savigny, *System of Contemporary Roman Law;* Ernst David Holle, *The Praxis of Interrogation.* The traveling salesman saw clearly: his host was some kind of legal expert, maybe a former attorney. He braced himself for an evening of convoluted discussion. "These university types," he thought, "what do they know about real life? Nothing, and their laws prove it." And then he foresaw another unpleasant possibility: the conversation could turn to art or something like that, in which case he might easily make a fool of himself. "Oh, well," he thought, "if I wasn't caught up in the struggle of life, I'd be familiar with higher things too." So it was without great pleasure that he went downstairs, where the old men had settled down in the open, still sunlit veranda, while the sturdy housekeeper set the table in the adjoining dining room. But when he saw the company that was awaiting him, he stopped short. Fortunately the first to approach him was the master of the house, who looked almost dandyish now, dressed in an outsized frock coat, his sparse hair carefully brushed. The old man welcomed Traps with a little speech. That gave him time to conceal his astonishment. "The pleasure is all mine," he murmured, with a cool, aloof little bow, playing the worldly expert in textiles, but meanwhile he was thinking, with tears in his heart, that the only reason he had stayed in this village was because he had hoped to pick up a girl for the night. No hope of that now. Facing him in the summery room with its wicker chairs and airy curtains, filling it with their presence, were three ancient, sloppy, disheveled men in black frock coats, three monstrous crows come to visit their owlish host. But those frock coats were of the finest quality, Traps immediately noted. On closer inspection that bald fellow (Pilet was his name, seventy-seven years old, as the host informed Traps in the course of the introductions that now began) was downright neat, sitting there with such rigid dignity on an extremely uncomfortable stool, even though several soft armchairs stood nearby, his whole garb and bearing hypercorrect, a white carnation in his buttonhole, constantly stroking his black-dyed, bushy moustache, obviously retired, perhaps a former sexton or chimney sweep who had lucked into some money, or possibly a railroad engineer. The two others looked all the more slovenly. One of them (Herr Kummer, eighty-two), even fatter than Pilet, immense, an assemblage of lardlike bulges and mounds, sat in a rocking chair, his face bright red, with a mighty drinker's nose, jovial frogs' eyes behind a golden pince-nez; and in addition, presumably due to an oversight, he was wearing a nightshirt under his black suit and had newspapers and letters stuffed in all his pockets. The other man (Herr Zorn, eighty-six), long and gaunt, a monocle clamped into his left eye, dueling scars on his face, hooked nose, snow-white mane, a sunken mouth, all in all an antediluvian appearance, had buttoned his vest askew and was wearing socks of different colors on his feet.

"Campari?" asked the host.

"Yes, please," replied Traps and lowered himself into a chair, while the tall thin man scrutinized him through his monocle.

"I trust Herr Traps will take part in our little game?"

"Oh, sure. I enjoy games."

The old gentlemen smiled, wagging their heads.

"Our game is possibly a little strange," remarked the host cautiously, almost hesitantly. "It consists of our spending an evening playing at our old professions."

The old men smiled again, politely, discreetly.

Traps didn't know what to make of this.

"Well," explained the host, "I used to be a judge, Herr Zorn was a prosecutor, and Herr Kummer was a defense attorney, and so we play court."

"I see," Traps said. It didn't sound like a bad idea. Maybe it wasn't a wasted evening after all.

The host regarded the salesman solemnly. "Generally," he explained in a mild voice, "we go through the famous historical trials—the trial of Socrates, the trial of Jesus, the trial of Joan of Arc, the trial of Dreyfuss. Recently we did the Reichstag Fire.* Another time we found Frederick the Great *non compos mentis*."

Traps was amazed. "You do this every evening?"

The judge nodded. But it was most fun, he continued, when they had a chance to play with living material. That made for particularly interesting situations. Day before yesterday, for instance, they had tried a member of Parliament who had given an election speech in the village and missed his last train. They had sentenced him to fourteen years for extortion and bribery.

*A pivotal event in the establishment of Nazi Germany, the 1933 fire at the Reichstag building in Berlin (which housed the German Parliament) was alleged by Nazi leaders—who, historians believe, actually instigated the arson—to be the work of communists.

"A tough court!" Traps noted with amusement.

"And proud of it!" the old men beamed.

"So what part can I play?" Traps asked.

Smiles again, almost laughter.

His host explained that they already had a judge, a prosecutor, and a counsel for the defense. "These posts," he said, "require knowledge of the subject and of the rules of the game. The only vacant role is the defendant's. However, let me emphasize again, Herr Traps, you really don't have to play."

The traveling salesman felt his good mood restored. The evening was saved. There would be no boring highbrow talk; on the contrary, this game actually promised to be entertaining. Traps was a simple man, not greatly endowed with intellectual vigor and hence not inclined to exert himself mentally. He was a businessman who could think on his feet if he had to, wholehearted in his line of work, but also fond of food and drink, with a weakness for crude amusements. "I'll play," he said. "And I'll be honored to adopt your orphaned post of defendant."

"Bravo!" squawked the prosecutor, clapping his hands. "Bravo! That's a man's word you're giving us, that's what I call courage!"

The traveling salesman inquired curiously what crime would be attributed to him.

"An insignificant point," replied the prosecutor, cleaning his monocle. "A crime can always be found."

They all laughed.

Herr Kummer rose. "Come, Herr Traps," he said almost paternally, "let's sample the port they've got here; it's old, you really must try it."

He led Traps into the dining room. The large round table was festively set. Old chairs with high backs, dark pictures on the walls: everything was old-fashioned and solid. From the veranda, Traps heard the old men's conversation. The evening light shimmered through the open windows. Birds were twittering. On a small table stood a large number of bottles, more were assembled on top of the fireplace. Bottles of Bordeaux had been placed in baskets. The defense attorney took an old bottle of port and carefully, tremulously, filled two small glasses to the brim. Then, very cautiously, lest any of the precious liquid be spilled, he touched the salesman's glass with his.

Traps tasted the wine. "Superb," he said.

"I am your attorney, Herr Traps," said Herr Kummer. "I say we should drink to good friendship!"

"To good friendship!"

It would be best, the attorney said, moving his red face with its drinker's nose and pince-nez closer to Traps, so that his enormous belly touched him, an unpleasant soft mass—it would be best if the gentleman confided his crime to him right away. That would give the defense the best chance of prevailing in court. The situation was not exactly dangerous, but neither should it be underestimated. The prosecutor—that tall, thin fellow—was still well in command of his mental powers, they would have to watch out for him. And their host was inclined to be strict and perhaps even pedantic, a tendency that, unfortunately, had worsened with age. "Let's face it," he said, "the man is eighty-seven." Nevertheless, the lawyer continued, he had managed to win most of his cases, or at least prevent the worst from happening. There was really only one defendant he hadn't been able to help at all—a case of combined robbery and homicide. But Herr Traps did not strike him as the sort of man who would resort to robbery and homicide—or was he mistaken?

"I'm sorry," Traps said, laughing, "I haven't committed any crime." Then he raised his glass: "*Prosit*!"

"Confess it to me," the lawyer encouraged him. "You needn't be ashamed. I know life. Nothing surprises me any longer. The destinies that have crossed my path, Herr Traps, the depths that have opened up before me . . . believe me."

"I'm truly sorry," the traveling salesman smiled, "I'm afraid what you have here is a defendant without a crime. And besides, it's the prosecutor's job to come up with a crime. He said so himself, I'll take his word for it. A game is a game. I'm curious to see what happens. Will there be a real interrogation?"

"I'd say so!"

"I look forward to it."

The defense attorney looked doubtful.

"You feel yourself to be innocent, Herr Traps?"

The traveling salesman laughed: "Thoroughly," he said. He found the whole conversation extremely amusing.

The defense attorney cleaned his pince-nez.

"Mark my words, young friend. Whether you're innocent or not, what counts are the proper tactics. To plead not guilty before this court is nothing short of reckless, to put it mildly. The smart thing is to accuse yourself of a crime from the start. A good choice for businessmen, for example, is fraud. Then, in the course of interrogation, it may turn out that the defendant is exaggerating, that no fraud was in fact committed, just some harmless obfuscation, the sort of thing that's commonly done in business, an advertising gimmick, say. The road from guilt to innocence is difficult but not impossible; on the other hand, it is virtually hopeless to try to preserve one's innocence, and the result can be devastating. You will lose where you might have won, and moreover you will have your guilt imposed on you instead of choosing it freely."

Amused, the traveling salesman shrugged. "I'm sorry I can't oblige," he said. "I am not aware of any misdeed that would have brought me into conflict with the law."

The defense attorney put on his pince-nez. "It won't be easy," he said thoughtfully. "Be prepared for a struggle. But above all," he said, by way of conclusion, "please weigh each word before you say it, don't just chatter. Otherwise you may find yourself suddenly sentenced to years of hard labor, and there won't be anything I can do about it."

Then the others came in. They sat down at the round table, chatted amiably, exchanged witty remarks. First various hors d'oeuvres were served, cold cuts, eggs à la Russe, snails, turtle soup. Everyone was in a marvelous mood, spooning away and slurping at leisure.

"Well, defendant, what do you have to offer us?" the prosecutor croaked. "I hope it's a nice solid murder."

The defense attorney protested: "My client is a defendant without a crime, a jurisprudential rarity, as it were. Claims to be innocent."

"Innocent?" The prosecutor cocked an eyebrow. His red dueling scars lit up. His monocle dropped, nearly fell into his plate, and dangled like a pendulum from its black cord. The dwarfish judge, who had been breaking bread into his soup, halted his hands, cast a reproachful look at the traveling salesman, and shook his head. The bald, taciturn fellow with the white carnation stared at Traps in astonishment. The silence was frightening. Not a clink of a fork or spoon could be heard, not a sniff, not a slurp. Only Simone giggled softly in the background.

"We'll have to look into this," said the prosecutor, pulling himself together. "What can't be, doesn't exist."

"Go right ahead," Traps laughed. "I'm at your disposal!"

Wine was served with the fish, a light, zesty Neuchâtel. "Well now," said the prosecutor as he dissected his trout, "let's see. Married?"

"For eleven years."

"Any kids?"

"Four."

"Occupation?"

"I'm in textiles."

"Traveling salesman, eh, my dear Herr Traps?"

"Sales manager."

"Fine. Little mishap with your car?"

"It just so happened. For the first time in a year."

"Hm. And a year ago?"

"Oh, back then I still had my old car," Traps explained. "A Citroën 1939, but now I have a Studebaker, the red one, limited series."

"Well, well, a Studebaker, how interesting. And you just got it recently. I suppose you weren't sales manager before that?"

"Just a plain ordinary traveling salesman."

"Boom times," the prosecutor nodded.

Next to Traps sat the defense attorney. "Watch out," he whispered.

Unconcerned, the traveling salesman—the sales manager, we may call him now—squeezed lemon juice onto his beefsteak tartare (his own recipe), and added a dash of cognac, paprika, and salt. "I've never had a pleasanter meal," he said, beaming. "I always thought our get-togethers at the Cockaigne Club were the finest entertainment a guy like me could hope to enjoy, but this is even more fun."

"Aha," said the prosecutor. "So you're a member of the Cockaigne Club. What is your nickname there?"

"Marquis de Casanova."

"Lovely!" the prosecutor croaked joyously, as though this information were highly important. He put his monocle back in place. "We're all delighted to hear that. Does your nickname permit us to draw some conclusions about your private life, my dear sir?"

"Careful," hissed the defense attorney.

"Only to a limited degree, sir," replied Traps. "When something extramarital happens in my life, it's only by accident and without ambition."

"Would Herr Traps have the kindness," said the prosecutor as he refilled the glasses with Neuchâtel, "to give the assembled company a brief summary of his life? Since we have decided to sit in judgment over our dear guest and sinner and possibly have him locked up for years, it's only appropriate that we should learn something personal, private, intimate, about his dealings with women. And do make it nice and spicy, if you don't mind."

"Tell us, tell us!" the old gentlemen giggled.

"We had a pimp at our table once," the judge said. "He told us all sorts of racy stories about his business, and still we only sentenced him to four years."

"Oh, well," said Traps, joining in their laughter, "there's not a whole lot to tell about me. I lead an ordinary life, gentlemen, a common life, I might as well admit it. Cheers!"

"Cheers!"

The sales manager raised his glass and warmly gazed into the birdlike eyes of the four old men, who were peering at him as if at a particularly dainty morsel. Then they touched glasses.

Outside, the sun had finally set and the furious clamor of the birds had subsided, but the countryside was still drenched in daylight—gardens, red roofs among trees, wooded hills, and in the distance the foothills of the Alps and a few glaciers: a landscape of peace, of bucolic tranquility, of imponderable promise, divine benediction, and cosmic harmony.

While Simone changed the plates and brought in a huge, steaming bowl of mushrooms à la crème, Traps told the old men that his early years had been difficult. His father had been a factory worker, he said, a proletarian, and had fallen prey to the views of Marx and Engels, a bitter, joyless man who had never cared for his only child. His mother, a washerwoman, had faded prematurely.

"The only education I was allowed to receive was primary school, just primary school," he said with tears in his eyes, feeling both angered and moved by his meager past. He raised his glass of Réserve des Maréchaux for a toast.

"Curious," said the prosecutor, "curious. Just primary school. You've certainly worked your way up in the world, haven't you?"

"I'd say so," boasted Traps, inflamed by the Réserve des Maréchaux, elated by the congenial cheer of his company and the lordly splendor of the view through the windows. "I'd say so. Ten years ago I was nothing but a door-to-door salesman traipsing from house to house with a little valise. Hard work, lots of hiking, sleeping in haylofts, questionable inns. I started way down at the bottom of my line, way down. And now, gentlemen, if you could see my bank account! I don't want to brag, but does any one of you own a Studebaker?"

"Be careful," the defense attorney whispered anxiously.

"How did this come about?" asked the prosecutor.

"Watch out and don't talk so much!" warned the defense attorney.

"I became the sole agent for Hephaeston on this continent," Traps announced, looking around triumphantly. "Except for Spain and the Balkans—that's someone else's turf."

"Hephaestus," giggled the little judge, heaping mushrooms on his plate, "Hephaestus was a Greek god, a great metalsmith, who trapped the goddess of love and her paramour, Ares, the god of war, in a net that was so finely forged and invisible that the other gods were tickled pink by this catch. But Hephaeston, this enterprise of which you, my dear Herr Traps, are the sole agent, must have another meaning, a meaning that is still veiled in mystery."

"And yet you are close to that meaning, my dear host and judge," Traps replied, laughing. "You yourself said 'veiled,' and this Greek god you just told me about, whose name is almost the same as my product's name, spun a fine and invisible net. You have heard of nylon, gentlemen of the court, you have heard of perlon, myrlon. Well, there is another synthetic, Hephaeston, the king of synthetics, tear-proof, transparent, a veritable balm for people with rheumatism, equally useful in industry and in fashion, in wartime and in peacetime. The perfect material for parachutes and at the same time the sheerest cloth you can find for a lady's nightgown, as I know from my own research."

"Hear, hear," croaked the old men, "his own research, that's a good one," and Simone changed the plates again and brought in a roast loin of veal.

"A regular banquet," beamed the sales manager.

"I'm glad you can appreciate it," said the prosecutor, "and right you are! We couldn't be served better fare, and there's plenty of it, too, a menu fit for the last century, when people still had the courage to eat. Let us praise Simone! Let us praise our host! He does his own shopping, old gnome and gourmet that he is. As for the wines, we owe them to Pilet, who runs the Ox Tavern in the next village. Praise to him too! But where do things stand with you, my industrious young fellow? Let us take a closer look at your case. We know about your life, it was a pleasure to be given a glimpse of it, and we also have a pretty clear idea of the nature of your work. There is only one minor point that is still unclear: how did you arrive at such a lucrative position? Just by discipline and hard work?"

"Careful," the defense attorney whispered. "Now it's getting dangerous."

"It wasn't so easy," Traps replied, watching greedily as the judge began to carve the roast. "First I had to win against Gygax, and that was hard."

"I see, and Gygax, who's that now?"

"My former boss."

"You mean he had to be pushed out?"

"He had to be canned," Traps replied as he reached for the gravy. "That's putting it in the rough terms we use in the business. I hope, gentlemen, you will not be offended if I speak plainly. It's a harsh life, being a businessman, tit for tat, and nice guys finish last. I'm raking in the money, but I also work like ten elephants. Every day I travel four hundred miles in my Studebaker. I wasn't exactly playing fair when it came to putting a knife to old Gygax's throat and then jamming it in, but I had to get ahead. What can you do? Business is business."

The prosecutor looked up from his veal, cocking an eyebrow.

"'Canned,' 'putting a knife to his throat,' 'jamming it in'—those are rather violent expressions, my dear Traps."

The sales manager laughed: "They're figures of speech."

"And how is Herr Gygax these days?"

"He died last year."

"Are you mad?" hissed the defense lawyer. "You must be out of your mind!"

"Last year," said the prosecutor, putting on a regretful face. "I'm sorry to hear that. How old was he?"

"Fifty-two."

"Still in his prime. And what did he die of?"

"Some illness."

"After you took his job?"

"Shortly before."

"Good, that's all I need to know for now," said the prosecutor. "We've been lucky. We've turned up a corpse, and that's the most important thing."

Everyone laughed. Even Pilet, the bald man, who had been shoveling enormous quantities of food into his mouth with a kind of reverent, pedantic constancy, looked up.

"Nice," he said, stroking his black moustache.

Then he went on eating.

The prosecutor solemnly raised his glass. "Gentlemen," he declared, "let us celebrate this find with the Pichon-Langueville 1933. A good Bordeaux to go along with a good game!"

They clinked glasses again and drank to one another.

"Gosh, gentlemen!" exclaimed the sales manager, emptying the Pichon in one draught and holding out his glass to the judge. "This is delicious!"

Dusk had fallen and the faces in the room could scarcely be distinguished. The first stars had begun to appear in the windows. The housekeeper lit three large, heavy candelabra, and the shadows of the men assembled in a circle were painted on the walls like the chalice of a fabulous flower. The mood was cozy, congenial, relaxed, and informal.

"Like a fairy tale," said the amazed Traps.

The defense attorney wiped the sweat from his brow with a napkin. "*You* are the fairy tale, my dear Traps," he said. "I have never seen an accused man make such careless remarks with such equanimity."

Traps laughed. "Have no fear, my good neighbor! Once the interrogation begins, I won't lose my head."

Once again a deathly silence filled the room. No more slurping, no more smacking of lips.

"You poor fool!" groaned the defense attorney. "What do you mean: Once the interrogation begins?"

"Well," said the sales manager, heaping salad on his plate, "it hasn't started yet, has it?"

The old men smiled, leered, snickered, and finally cackled with glee. The silent, calm, bald-headed man giggled: "He didn't notice! He didn't notice!"

For a moment Traps was disconcerted. There was something uncanny about this burst of roguish amusement. But the impression quickly passed, and he joined in their laughter: "Forgive me, gentlemen," he said, "I had expected our game to be more solemn, more dignified and formal, more like a court of law."

"My dear Herr Traps," the judge informed him, "the expression on your face is priceless. I can see that our way of holding court strikes you as peculiar, too lively perhaps. But, my dear, the four of us at this table are in retirement, and we have rid ourselves of the needless welter of formalities and verbatim reports and scribblings and laws that bog down our official courts. We dispense justice without regard for law books and legal paragraphs."

"That's bold," replied Traps, his tongue beginning to thicken, "really bold. Gentlemen, I'm impressed. No legal paragraphs, that's a bold idea."

The defense attorney laboriously rose to his feet. "I'm going out for some fresh air," he said, "before the fowl and the rest of our meal is served. It's time for a little constitutional and a cigar." Then, turning to Traps, he said, "Would you care to join me?"

They stepped out from the veranda into a warm and majestic night, for darkness had finally fallen. From the windows of the dining room, golden bands of light fell onto the lawn, reaching all the way to the rose beds. The sky was full of stars, moonless; the trees had become a single dark mass. The two men could barely discern the gravel path on which they were walking. They had linked arms. Heavy with wine, they staggered and swayed here and there, though they tried to walk straight. They were smoking Parisienne cigarettes, red dots in the darkness.

"My God," said Traps, gasping for breath, "what a ball we had in there," pointing at the illuminated windows just as the massive silhouette of the housekeeper became visible. "This is fun, really a lot of fun."

"Dear friend," said the defense attorney, tottering and leaning on Traps, "before we return and attack our capon, allow me to give you a word of serious advice, which you would do well to take to heart. I like you, young man, I feel a certain tenderness toward you, I want to speak to you like a father: we are well on the way to losing our case lock, stock, and barrel!"

"That's too bad," replied the sales manager, carefully steering his attorney along the gravel path and around the large, black, spherical mass of a shrub. They came to a pond, divined the presence of a stone bench, found it, and sat down. The water mirrored the stars. A cool air wafted their way.

From the village came the sounds of singing voices and an accordion, and then the melodious blast of an alp horn. The poultry farmers' association was celebrating.

"You must pull yourself together," the attorney admonished Traps. "The enemy has taken some important bastions; that dead man, Gygax, who turned up completely unnecessarily as you kept babbling away—this is a tremendous threat. An unpracticed defense attorney would have to throw in the towel. But if I'm stubborn enough and exploit every chance we get, and if you, especially, are careful and maintain the greatest discipline, I may be able to salvage something."

Traps laughed. "This is a hilarious parlor game," he said. "I've got to introduce it at the next meeting of the Cockaigne Club."

"Isn't it?" said the defense attorney in warm agreement. "It has the most enlivening effect. I was wasting away, my dear friend, after I suddenly found myself retired, deprived of my old profession, with nothing to do but enjoy my twilight years in this village. What's there to enjoy? Nothing, just that the föhn doesn't blow here. Healthy climate? A joke, without intellectual stimulation. The prosecutor was dying, our host was believed to have stomach cancer, Pilet was suffering from diabetes, I had trouble with my blood pressure. That's what retirement brought us. A dog's life. Once in a while we'd sit together and talk nostalgically about our old professions and our successes—that was our one scant little pleasure. Then the prosecutor struck upon the idea of this game. The judge supplied his house, and I provided my financial resources. You see, I'm a bachelor, and for the past forty years I've worked for the upper crust. That adds up, my friend, you wouldn't believe the munificence of an acquitted robber knight, opulence isn't the word for it. At any rate, this game has become our fountain of youth; our hormones, our stomachs, our pancreas have all started working again, our boredom has disappeared, our energy, youthfulness, elasticity, and appetites have been restored. Look at this . . . "

And indistinctly in the darkness, Traps saw his attorney performing a few gymnastic exercises, despite his voluminous belly.

"We play with the judge's guests, they're the defendants," the old man continued after sitting down again. "All sorts of people: salesmen, vacationers . . . two months ago we even had the opportunity to give a German general a twenty-year sentence. He came wandering through here, hiking with his wife. It was only thanks to my skill that he was spared the gallows."

"Amazing," marveled Traps. "So productive! But what you said about gallows—it seems to me that you're exaggerating a little. Capital punishment has been abolished."

"In the official system of justice it has," the attorney corrected him, "but this is a private judiciary, and we have reinstated it. It is precisely the risk of a death penalty that makes our game so exciting and unique."

"And I suppose you have an executioner too?" said Traps, laughing.

"Naturally," the defense counsel proudly replied. "Pilet."

"Pilet?"

"You're surprised, eh?"

Traps swallowed several times. "But he runs the Ox Tavern, doesn't he? He supplies the wines we've been drinking."

"He's always been an innkeeper," the attorney smiled benignly. "His work for the government was just a sideline. Almost an honorary post. One of the best of his trade in his own country. He's been retired twenty years, but I dare say he's kept up with the state of his art."

A car drove past, and the headlights illuminated the smoke of their cigarettes. For a second, Traps saw the defense attorney, his corpulent figure in a stained frock coat, his fat, satisfied, complacent face. Traps shivered. He felt a cold sweat on his forehead.

"Pilet."

The defense attorney looked surprised. "What's the matter, dear Traps? I believe you're trembling. Are you all right?"

The image of the bald man rose up before him, silently chewing in a rather stupid absorption. It was an imposition, really, having to share one's meal with someone like that. But that was unfair, how could you blame the poor man for his profession. The mildness of the summer night and the even greater mellowness of the wine had inclined Traps to be humane, tolerant, free of prejudice. After all, he was a man who had seen many things and who knew the world. He was not a coward or a prig, but a first-rate expert in textiles. In fact, it now seemed to Traps that without an executioner, the evening would have been a good deal less enjoyable. He looked forward to telling the guys at the Cockaigne Club all about his adventure. Why not invite the executioner to come there some time, in exchange for a small fee and expenses? Relieved, he finally laughed out loud: "Got me there! I was scared for a moment! This game is getting better all the time!"

"I confided in you, please now do the same for me," said the defense attorney. They rose to their feet and, blinded by the light from the windows, groped their way, arm in arm, back toward the house. "How did you knock off Gygax?"

"What do you mean, knock off?"

"Well, since he's dead."

"But I didn't kill him."

The defense attorney stopped walking. "My dear young friend," he replied sympathetically, "I understand your reservations. Murders are the most embarrassing crimes to confess. The accused is ashamed, doesn't want to face what he has done, forgets his deed, pushes it out of his mind. You might say he is deeply prejudiced toward the past, burdens himself with exaggerated guilt feelings, and doesn't trust anyone, not even his fatherly friend, his defense attorney, which is the biggest mistake he can make, because a real defense attorney loves murder. Bring him a murder and he's in ecstasy. Let's have it, dear Traps! I'm not fully at ease till I'm faced with a real challenge, like an alpinist before a difficult climb. I know what I'm talking about, I'm an old mountain climber myself. It's only then that your brain starts to bubble and boil and strain and stretch, and thinking becomes a pleasure. So you're making a big mistake not trusting me. In fact, I dare say it's your decisive mistake. So let's have your confession, old boy!"

"But I have nothing to confess," the sales manager insisted.

The defense attorney was taken aback. He stood in the glare of the window, gaping at Traps, while the clinking of glasses and ever more mirthful peals of laughter resounded from the dining room.

"Damn it, my boy," the attorney growled reproachfully, "what are you up to now? Are you still clinging to those wrongheaded tactics? Still pretending to be innocent? Haven't you caught on? You have to confess, whether you want to or not, and there's always something to confess. Hasn't that dawned on you yet? So let's get to it, my friend, no more shilly-shallying, spit it out: how did you kill Gygax? In a fit of emotion, right? In which case we'll have to prepare ourselves for a charge of manslaughter. I bet that's where the prosecutor's heading. It's my hunch. I know him."

Traps shook his head. "My dear, most esteemed counsel for the defense," he said, "the special appeal of our game—if, as a beginner, I may be allowed to express my humble opinion—is that it gives you the creeps. The game threatens to flip over into reality. You suddenly ask yourself: am I a criminal or not, did I kill Gygax or didn't I? As you were talking, I almost felt myself reeling. And so, to reciprocate your trust: I am innocent of the old bastard's death. Truly." With that, they stepped back into the dining room, where the capon had already been served and a Château Pavie 1921 was sparkling in the glasses.

Traps, in high spirits, walked up to the grave, taciturn, bald-headed man and pressed his hand. "My lawyer told me about your former profession," he said. "I want you to know that I can't imagine a greater pleasure than sharing a meal with such a worthy man as you. I have no prejudices whatsoever. On the contrary!" Pilet blushed, stroked his dyed moustache, and mumbled, somewhat embarrassed, and in an awful dialect: "Pleased, very pleased, I'll do my best."

After this touching display of mutual goodwill, the capon tasted superb. "A secret recipe of Simone's," the judge announced. The men smacked their lips, ate with their hands, praised the masterpiece, drank, toasted one another's health, licked the sauce from their fingers, and leisurely, amiably, continued with the trial. The prosecutor, a napkin tied under his chin, holding the capon in front of his beaklike, audibly chewing mouth, expressed the hope that, after the fowl, they might be served a tasty confession. "Surely, my dearest, most honorable defendant," he probed, "surely you poisoned Gygax?"

"No," laughed Traps, "nothing of the sort."

"Well, let's say: shot?"

"Not that either."

"Arranged a secret car accident?"

Everyone laughed, and the defense counsel hissed another warning: "Watch out, that's a trap!"

"Sorry, my dear prosecutor, I'm truly sorry," Traps cried exuberantly. "Gygax died of a heart attack, and it wasn't even his first. He'd had one years before, so he had to be careful. He was always making a show of how fit he was, but the slightest upset could set off his heart again. I know it for a fact."

"Oh? And who told you?"

"His wife, sir."

"His wife?"

"Careful, for heaven's sake," whispered the defense attorney.

The Château Pavie 1921 surpassed everyone's expectations. Traps was already on his fourth glass, and Simone had put an extra bottle near him. The prosecutor still looked astonished. The sales manager raised his glass to the old men: "Gentlemen," he said, "I don't want the high court to have the impression that I am concealing something. I want to tell the truth and nothing but the truth, even when my counsel whispers at me to be careful. Yes, I had a little affair with Frau Gygax. You see, the old bastard was out of town a lot, off on some trip or other, cruelly neglecting his nicely built and very tasty little dish of a wife. She needed consoling. That job fell to me, first on the couch in Gygax's living room and later, occasionally, in their matrimonial bed. That's the way of the world."

At these words, the old gentlemen froze in their seats. But then, all of a sudden, they screeched with pleasure, and the bald man, who normally held his tongue, tossed his white carnation in the air, shouting: "A confession, a confession!" Only the defense attorney drummed his fists despairingly against his temples.

"Such madness!" he cried. "Gentlemen, my client has quite obviously lost his mind. His testimony cannot and must not be taken at face value!" Indignantly, amid renewed applause, Traps protested. This gave rise to a long argument between the defense attorney and the prosecutor, a stubborn dispute, half comic, half serious, about the word *dolus*, the meaning of which was unknown to the sales manager. The dispute grew steadily louder, more intense, and more incomprehensible. The judge joined in the fulminations of the two opponents. At first Traps made an effort to listen and guess at the meaning of the debate. Then he sighed with relief as the housekeeper came in with various cheeses—Camembert, Brie, Emmentaler, Gruyère, Tête de Moine, Vacherin, Limburger, Gorgonzola. To hell with *dolus*, he thought, raising his glass to the bald man, who was sitting by himself, silent and perhaps as uncomprehending as Traps, who was now reaching for the cheese—when suddenly, unexpectedly, the prosecutor addressed him again: "Herr Traps," he said, with his lion's mane standing on end and his face flushed, holding his monocle in his left hand, "are you still on friendly terms with Frau Gygax?"

All eyes gaped at Traps, who had just shoved a piece of white bread with Camembert into his mouth and was now complacently chewing. He took another sip of Château Pavie. Somewhere a clock was ticking, and from the village came once again the sound of a distant harmonica and the voices of men singing in unison.

"I've stayed away from the lady," Traps explained, "ever since Gygax's death. I wouldn't want to damage the good widow's reputation."

To his surprise, this explanation gave rise to a new burst of incomprehensible hilarity. There was something eerie about their delight. The prosecutor screamed, "*Dolo malo, dolo malo!*" and roared Greek and Latin verses, cited Schiller and Goethe, while the little judge blew out all the candles except one, which he used to project shadow images against the wall—goats, bats, devils, and goblins—twisting his fingers behind the flame and bleating and hissing, while Pilet drummed on the table until the dishes, glasses, and platters danced: "There will be a death sentence, there will be a death sentence!" Only the defense attorney abstained from the general merriment. He shoved the cheese platter in Traps's direction. "Take," he said. "Enjoy. You might as well. There's nothing else left to do."

A Châteaux Margaux, vintage 1914, was brought in, and peace was restored. Everyone stared with bated breath as the judge cautiously and meticulously employed a curious old-fashioned corkscrew that would enable him to draw the cork from the dusty bottle as it lay in the basket. Since the label had not survived the four decades of the bottle's existence, the cork was the only proof that the vintage was indeed 1914; but to establish that proof, the cork had to be extracted with the least possible damage. The cork did not come out whole, and the remainder had to be carefully removed. But the date was still legible. The rare object was handed around the table, smelled, admired, and was then solemnly given to the sales manager—"As a memento of a wonderful evening," the judge said. It was the judge, then, who tasted the wine, smacked his lips, and filled the glasses, whereupon the others first sniffed, then sipped the precious substance, and broke out into cries of delight and gratitude. The cheese was passed around, and the judge asked the prosecutor to hold his "little speech" charging their guest with his crime. The prosecutor asked for new candles first. "This moment calls for solemnity," he said, "for reverence, concentration, inner composure." Simone brought the candles. All eyes were fixed on the judge. The sales manager felt uncomfortable; once again he felt there was something eerie about these old men and their game. But what a wonderful adventure he was having! He wouldn't have missed it for anything in the world. Only his attorney did not look pleased.

"All right, Traps," he said, "let's listen to the prosecution's case. You'll be amazed by the damage you've done with your careless answers, your foolish tactics. Your situation was bad before—now it's catastrophic. Nevertheless: chin up. I'll get you out of this mess. Just don't lose your head. Don't give them another inch, if you want to come out of this in one piece."

The moment had come. There was a general clearing of throats, some coughing, another toast, and amid grins and giggles the prosecutor began his speech.

"The special pleasure of this gathering of ours," he said, raising his glass but remaining seated, "and the unique satisfaction it has given us, are no doubt due to our having uncovered a murder so cunningly prepared that of course it has brilliantly escaped our official system of justice."

At this, Traps balked. For the first time, he was annoyed. "Are you saying I've committed a murder? Listen, this is going too far, I've already heard this baloney from my lawyer . . . " But then he reflected, and started to laugh so hard that it took him minutes to regain his powers of speech. "A wonderful joke!" he gasped. "Oh, now I understand—you're trying to talk me into admitting to a crime! This is hilarious, simply hilarious!"

The prosecutor gazed at Traps with a dignified air, polished his monocle, inserted it back in his eye.

"The accused," he said, "doubts his own guilt. How human. Who among us knows himself, who among us knows his own crimes and secret misdeeds? But let me stress one thing in advance, before the passions of our game flare up again: if Herr Traps is a murderer, as I maintain and fervently hope, then we are standing at the threshold of an uncommonly solemn hour. And rightly so. It is a most joyful event, the discovery of a murder, an event that makes our hearts beat higher, that confronts us with new tasks, decisions, and duties. And so, before all else, I take the liberty of congratulating our dear prospective culprit, for without a culprit it is not possible to uncover a murder and let justice prevail. A very special toast then to the health of our friend, our modest Alfredo Traps, whom a friendly fate has brought into our midst!"

The old men cheered, rose from their chairs, drank to the health of the sales manager, who in turn thanked them with tears in his eyes, assuring them that this was the most wonderful evening of his life.

Now the prosecutor also had tears in his eyes. "Gentlemen," he said, "hear the words of our esteemed guest: his most wonderful evening! A profoundly moving statement. Think of the gloomy functions we used to perform in the service of the State. The accused stood before us, not as a friend, but as an enemy—whom we now can take to our hearts, whereas once we were forced to eject him from our midst. To my heart, then, friend!"

With these words he rushed over to Traps, yanked him to his feet, and embraced him fervently.

"Prosecutor, my dear, dear friend," the sales manager stammered.

"Defendant, dear Traps," sobbed the prosecutor. "Let us drop these wretched formalities. My name is Kurt. To your health, Alfredo!"

"To yours, Kurt!"

They kissed, caressed and patted each other, toasted each other again. Deeply stirred, the other men contemplated this tender blossoming of a new friendship. "How everything has changed!" the prosecutor cried, his voice singing with joy. "Where once we rushed from case to case, from crime to crime, from verdict to verdict, we now build our cases, argue, contend, speak and reply at leisure, pleasantly, joyfully, learn to appreciate the defendant, love him, feel the waves of his sympathy coming toward us—a fraternal embrace where there used to be fear and loathing. Once this is established, everything is easy, crime has no weight, and judgment can be pronounced with a smile. Let me, then, express my admiration for the murder that has been committed. [An interjection from Traps, in the best of spirits: "Prove it, Kurt, prove it!"] Yes, admiration, for what we have here is a perfect, a beautiful murder. Now our charming culprit may find my use of this word glib and cynical. That is not the spirit in which I am using it. His deed may be characterized as 'beautiful' in two respects: first philosophically, and second, in praise of its technical virtuosity. You see, my dear friend Alfredo, all of us at this table have shed the prejudice that regards crime as something ugly and terrible, and justice as a thing of beauty, of terrible beauty perhaps, but beautiful nonetheless. No, we realize that there is beauty in crime as well, for without it, justice would not be possible. That is the philosophical side. Now let us render homage to the technical beauty of the deed. Homage. I believe that is a fitting word, for my speech of indictment is not intended to terrify our young friend, or embarrass or confuse him; no, it is meant to extend to him our sincerest respect for his achievement, and in doing so, reveal to him the nature of his crime, make it flower in his consciousness: only on the pure pedestal of understanding can the seamless monument of justice be erected."

Exhausted, the eighty-six-year-old prosecutor paused. In spite of his age, he had spoken in a loud, rasping voice, underscoring his words with grandiloquent gestures, and copiously eating and drinking all the while. Now he used his spotted bib to wipe the sweat from his brow and dry his wrinkled neck. Traps was moved. He sat slumped in his chair, sluggish from the meal. He was full, but he did not want to be outdone by these four old men, even though he had to admit to himself that he found their huge appetite and enormous thirst daunting. He was a prodigious eater himself, but never in his life had he encountered such vitality and such voracity. Amazed and stupefied, he gaped across the table, flattered by the prosecutor's heartfelt tribute, and listening as the church bell solemnly struck twelve, followed by the distant, droning chorus of the poultry farmers singing: "Our life is like a voyage . . . "

"Like a fairy tale," the sales manager thought to himself, "just like a fairy tale," and then: "Me, a murderer? I, of all people? I'd just like to know how."

The judge, meanwhile, had uncorked another bottle of Château Margaux 1914, and the prosecutor, refreshed, began again.

"Now what has happened?" he said. "How did I discover that our dear friend has a murder to his lasting credit, and not just an ordinary murder, but a superb piece of work, committed without bloodshed, without poison, pistols, or anything of the sort?"

He cleared his throat. Traps, his mouth full of Vacherin cheese, stared at him in fascination.

"My professional practice has taught me," continued the prosecutor, "to suspect a crime behind every event and every person. My first inkling that Herr Traps is one of those rare men favored by destiny and graced with a crime came to me when I learned that a year ago he was still driving an old Citroën, and that today he is proudly coasting along in a new Studebaker.

Now, I know that we live in boom times, so this inkling was still a vague one, comparable to the feeling of being on the verge of a joyous experience, in this case, of discovering a murder. That our dear friend took over his boss's position, that he had to displace the boss, that the boss died—all these facts were not proofs yet, just bits of supporting evidence for the validity of that feeling. Genuine suspicion, based on logical premises, did not arise until we learned what this legendary boss died of: a heart attack. From here on, real combinational skill was required, acuity, intuition, and a highly discreet approach, more like stalking the truth than a straightforward pounce; furthermore an ability to see the extraordinary in the ordinary, certainty in the uncertain, outlines in the fog, to believe in a murder precisely because it seemed absurd to presume a murder. Let us consider the available evidence. Let us sketch a picture of the deceased. We know little about him, and what we do know has been conveyed to us by our charming guest. Herr Gygax was the sales manager of the company producing Hephaeston, a synthetic textile that we willingly believe has all the agreeable qualities our dear friend Alfredo ascribes to it. We may deduce that this Gygax was the kind of man one would call a go-getter, who ruthlessly exploited his subordinates, who knew how to make a deal, even if the methods he used to close these deals were often more than questionable."

"That's right!" Traps cried enthusiastically. "You've got that scoundrel down to a T!"

"We may further conclude," the prosecutor continued, "that outwardly he liked to play the part of a powerful, robust man, a big bruiser who can deal with any situation and isn't fazed by anything. That is why Gygax kept his heart disease carefully secret—again we are citing Alfredo. Most likely he endured his illness with a sort of defiant fury, as if being sick constituted a loss of face."

"Wonderful!" exclaimed the sales manager. "This is almost uncanny! Kurt, you must have known him personally!"

"Hold your tongue!" the defense counsel snarled.

"In addition," declared the prosecutor, "to round off our portrait of Gygax, consider the fact that the deceased neglected his wife, whom we have to imagine as a nicely built and tasty little dish—at least that's how our friend put it, more or less. To Gygax the only thing that counted was success, business, externals, facades, and we may safely presume that he took his wife's fidelity for granted and that he was of the opinion that his own exceptional qualities as a man would not allow even the thought of adultery to occur to his wife. So it would have been a hard blow for him if he had learned of his wife's infidelity with our Casanova of the Cockaigne Club."

Everyone laughed, and Traps slapped his thighs. "And it was!" he cried, beaming. "It finished him off when he found out."

"You're completely out of your mind," the defense attorney groaned.

The prosecutor had risen to his feet and was happily gazing across the table at Traps, who was scraping away at the Tête de Moine with a knife. "I see," he asked, "how did he find out, the old sinner? Did his tasty little wife tell him?"

"She didn't have the courage for that, Prosecutor," Traps replied; "that hoodlum had her scared out of her mind."

"Did Gygax figure it out himself?"

"He was too conceited for that."

"Was it you who confessed to him, my dear friend and Don Juan?"

Traps blushed. "But no, Kurt," he said, "how could you think that? One of his upstanding business friends told the old crook."

"How come?"

"Wanted to harm me. Nothing new, he was always after me."

"The things people do," said the prosecutor. "But how did this man of honor find out about your affair?"

"I told him."

"Told him?"

"Well, yes—over a glass of wine. People say all sorts of things when they're drinking."

"Granted," said the prosecutor, nodding, "but you just said that this business friend of Herr Gygax was an enemy of yours. Wasn't it absolutely predictable *from the beginning* that the old crook would hear about your adultery with his wife?"

Now the defense attorney vigorously intervened. He even rose to his feet, bathed in sweat, the collar of his frock coat soaked through. "I want to advise you, Herr Traps," he declared, "that you needn't answer this question."

Traps disagreed.

"Why not?" he said. "It's a perfectly harmless question. After all, I didn't care whether Gygax found out or not. The old crook had treated me with such disregard, I really didn't see why I should show any regard for him."

For a moment the room was quiet again. Dead silence. Then a tumult of shrieks and shouts broke out, homeric laughter, a storm of jubilation. The bald-headed, taciturn fellow embraced Traps, kissed him, the defense attorney laughed so hard he lost his pince-nez ("Marvelous!" he cried, "you just can't be mad at a defendant like this!"), while the judge and the prosecutor danced around the room, pounded the walls, shook each other's hands, climbed up on chairs, and smashed bottles, beside themselves with joy.

"The defendant has confessed again," squawked the prosecutor, filling the room with his voice. He was sitting on the arm of his chair now. "We can't praise our guest highly enough, he is playing the game beautifully. The case is clear, proof is established beyond reasonable doubt." He sat perched on the swaying chair like a weatherworn baroque monument. "Consider our dearest, revered Alfredo! There he was at the mercy of that hoodlum boss of his, driving around the country in his Citroën. Just a year ago! He could have been proud of that, our friend, this father of four, the son of a factory worker. And rightly so. He'd been a door-to-door salesman during the war, but not even that, because he didn't have a license, he was a tramp, a little black market huckster dealing in illegitimate textiles, traveling by train from village to village or by foot along country lanes, often for miles through dark forests to some faraway farm, with a dirty leather bag strapped on his back, or even a basket, a disintegrating suitcase in his hand. Now he had bettered himself, built himself a nest in a regular business, was a member of the Liberal party, in contrast to his Marxist father. There he was, well above the ground, after a long and difficult climb. But who would stop to rest on this branch when above, nearer the treetop (poetically speaking), he sees further branches with even finer fruit? True, he was earning good money, was flitting from one textile shop to another in his Citroën, the car wasn't bad, but our dear Alfredo saw new models popping up right and left, soaring by, racing toward him, passing him from behind. Prosperity was on the rise all around him, who would not want to partake of it?"

"That's exactly how it was, Kurt," Traps beamed. "Exactly."

The prosecutor was in his element, happy, content as a child with his Christmas presents.

"That was easier to decide than it was to accomplish," he explained, still perched on the arm of his chair. "His boss refused to promote him. Instead he used him viciously, gave him advances only in order to tie him up in his lowly position more and more tightly!"

"Quite right," the sales manager cried indignantly. "You have no idea, gentlemen, how that old hoodlum put the screws on me!"

"So it was do or die now, all or nothing," said the prosecutor.

"Damn right!" Traps confirmed.

The defendant's interjections inspired the prosecutor. He was standing on the chair now, waving his napkin like a flag, his vest stained with wine, salad, tomato sauce, and bits of meat. "Our dear friend took the business route first—not always playing fair, as he himself admits. We can more or less imagine how he went about it. He secretly got in touch with his boss's suppliers, sounded them out, promised better conditions, planted seeds of confusion, conferred with other salesmen, made alliances and, at the same time, counter-alliances. But then he had an idea for another approach."

"Another approach?" Traps asked in surprise.

The prosecutor nodded. "This approach, gentlemen, led via the couch in Gygax's apartment to his matrimonial bed."

Everyone laughed, especially Traps. "Boy, oh boy," he confirmed, "that was really a nasty trick I played on the old hoodlum. But you know, thinking back on it, the situation was just too funny. I've been ashamed of looking into this until now. Who likes to see his own mind clearly? There's always some dirt that comes out with the wash, no matter who you are. But in the company of such understanding friends, shame becomes ridiculous, unnecessary. Strange! I feel understood and am starting to understand myself, as if I were meeting a person who is myself and whom I used to vaguely know as a sales manager in a Studebaker, with a wife and children somewhere."

"We note with pleasure," said the prosecutor warmly and cordially, "that a light is glimmering in the mind of our friend. Let us continue helping him, so that the glimmer may turn bright as day. Like a band of cheerful archaeologists, let us zealously track down his motives till we hit upon the buried splendor of a crime. He began an affair with Frau Gygax. How did it happen? He saw the tasty little dish, as we can well imagine. Perhaps late in the evening one day, maybe in wintertime, around six [Traps: "At seven, dear Kurt, at seven!"], when the city was nice and dark, with golden street lamps, the shop windows all illuminated and movie theaters with green and yellow marquees lit up in neon wherever you looked, a cozy hour, voluptuous, alluring. He had driven his Citroën along slippery streets to the elegant district where his boss lived [an enthusiastic comment from Traps: "Elegant district, you can say that again!"], a briefcase under his arm, orders, swatches. An important decision had to be made, but Gygax's limousine was not parked in its usual place by the curb. Nevertheless he crossed the dark lawn, rang the bell, Frau Gygax opened the door. She was wearing an evening dress, or better, a dressing gown. Her husband would not be home tonight, she said, and her maid was out, but still, if Traps would like to come in for a drink he was more than welcome. That's how they came to sit next to each other in the salon."

Traps was amazed. "The things you know about, Kurt. What are you, a magician?"

"Practice," the prosecutor explained. "All destinies follow the same course. It wasn't even a seduction on Alfredo's part or the woman's, it was simply an opportunity that he turned to account. She was alone, she was bored, had nothing on her mind, she was glad to have someone to talk to, the house was pleasantly warm, and beneath her dressing gown with its colorful floral design she was wearing nothing but her nightgown. And when Traps, sitting next to her, saw her white throat and the curve of her breasts, and heard in her talk how angry she was at her husband, how disillusioned, our friend realized that now he must make his move, and was in fact making that move when he realized it, and then he soon learned everything there was to know about Gygax, how precarious his health was, how any great upset could kill him, his age, how rough and mean he was with his wife, and how firmly convinced he was of her fidelity. For a woman who wants to take revenge on her husband will tell you anything you want to know. And so he continued the affair, quite intentionally now, for his newly formed plan was to ruin Gygax by any means available, no matter what the consequences. And then came the moment when he had all his boss's assets in hand—his business partners, his suppliers, and at night his white, fulsome, naked wife—and then he pulled the noose tight, provoked a scandal. Deliberately. We're already informed about this: evening again, another intimate twilight hour. We find our friend in a restaurant, let's say a tavern in the old part of town, somewhat overheated, everything solidly homespun, patriotic, genuine, the prices too, bull's-eye windows, the hefty proprietor [Traps: "It was the Rathauskeller, Kurt!"], correction, the hefty proprietress, surrounded by the portraits of faithful customers now dead, a newspaper vendor wandering through the place and leaving, later the Salvation Army singing 'Let the sunshine in,' some students, a professor, on a table two glasses and a good bottle, no small expense, this one, but so be it, and in the corner finally, pale, fat, beads of sweat on his face, open collar, as apoplectic as the intended victim, we see the upstanding business friend wondering what this is all about, why Traps has invited him all of a sudden, see him listening attentively, hearing about the adultery from Traps's own lips, and a few hours later, predictably, and as our dear Alfredo expected, rushing off, impelled by duty, friendship, and common decency, to enlighten the unfortunate Gygax about the disastrous state of his affairs."

"The hypocrite!" Traps cried, listening intently with round, shining eyes to the prosecutor's description, happy to be learning the truth, his proud, audacious, solitary truth.

Then:

"And so fate finally struck, the precisely calculated moment when Gygax found out everything. We can imagine the old hoodlum managing to drive home, filled with rage, sweating intensely in the car, pains in his chest, hands quivering, policemen angrily blowing their whistles, he's ignoring the traffic signs, a laborious walk from the garage to the front door, collapse, perhaps in the hallway as the wife steps toward him, that luscious, tasty little dish; it didn't last long, the doctor administered morphine, and then, finally, he's over the edge, finished, one more insignificant rattle, a sob on the part of the wife, our dear Alfredo, at home in the circle of his loved ones, picks up the telephone, dismay, inner rejoicing, a sense of 'I've made it,' finally, hurrah. Three months later—the Studebaker."

Another round of laughter. Traps, buffeted from one astonishment to the next, laughed along with the others, though slightly embarrassed, scratching his hair, giving the prosecutor a nod of respectful acknowledgment, but not at all unhappily. He was in a good mood. It had been a perfect evening; the fact that they considered him capable of murder had upset him a little and put him in a pensive mood, but this unfamiliar state was pleasant, for it gave him a dawning sense of higher things, of justice, of guilt and atonement, and filled him with wonder. The fear that had attacked him in the garden, and later during those bursts of hilarity at the table, and which he had not forgotten, now seemed to him without foundation and even amusing. It was all so human. He was eager to see how the game would continue. The company moved to the salon for coffee, staggering, with the stumbling defense attorney in tow. The room was crammed full of knickknacks and vases. Enormous engravings hung on the walls, views of towns, historical moments, the Rütli Oath, the Battle of Laupen, the massacre of the Swiss Guard,* scenes from the tales of Gottfried Keller,† a stucco ceiling, a piano in the corner, comfortable armchairs, low and huge, and on the chairs, doilies embroidered with pious sayings: "Blessed is he who walks in the ways of righteousness," "A good conscience is an easy pillow." Through the open windows one could dimly make out the highway, submerged in darkness, mysteriously still, and once in a while a pair of headlights floating past.

"That was the most thrilling speech I have ever heard," Traps declared. "I couldn't possibly improve on it, or correct it, except in small ways. The upstanding business friend, for instance, was short and skinny, with a stiff collar, and he wasn't sweaty at all. Frau Gygax didn't receive me in a dressing-gown but in a kimono, with a rather low décolleté, I might add, a very open person—just a little joke. Also, super-crook didn't get his well-deserved heart attack at home but in the warehouse, while the föhn was blowing. Then it was off to the hospital, cardiac arrest, and good-bye. But as I said, these are

*The Rütli Oath marked the foundation of the Swiss Confederation in 1291; the Battle of Laupen (June 21, 1339) was a victory for the Swiss Confederacy against feudal lords; the massacre of the Swiss Guards (August 10, 1792) took place at the Tuileries Palace in Paris, which the guards were defending against a revolutionary mob.

†Gottfried Keller (1819–1890), Swiss writer of the Poetic Realism school.

just details. Essentially, everything Kurt, my dear friend and prosecutor, has said is exactly right. I only got involved with Frau Gygax in order to ruin the old bastard, in fact now I can remember clearly lying in his bed, on top of his wife, and staring at a picture of him, a photograph of this unpleasant fat face with horn-rim glasses, behind them those big stupid frog's eyes, and feeling a sort of wild joy at the thought—really a presentiment—that what I was doing with such eagerness and pleasure was actually killing my boss, knocking him off, in cold blood."

When Traps delivered this explanation, the five men were already seated in the soft chairs with the pious sayings, reaching for their demitasses, stirring the hot brew with little spoons, and sipping an 1893 cognac, Raffignac, from large, wide-bellied glasses.

"I will now propose the sentence," the prosecutor announced, sitting athwart a monstrous wing chair, his legs with their unmatched socks (gray and black checks on one foot, green on the other) pulled up over one of the chair's arms. "Our friend Alfredo did not act *dolo indirecto,* as if the death had occurred accidentally, but *dolo malo,* with malice aforethought, as is clear from the fact that on the one hand he himself provoked the scandal and that on the other hand after the super-crook's death he no longer visited the tasty little dish—definitive proof that the wife was just an instrument for his bloodthirsty plans, the delightful murder weapon, so to speak, so that what we have here is a psychologically executed murder, so expertly planned that, aside from the adultery, it appears that no law was broken—appears, I say; but now that this veil of apparent innocence has been lifted, now that our dear defendant has been kind enough to confess, I have the pleasure as prosecutor—and this brings me to the end of my homage—to demand of our high judge that he impose the death penalty on Alfredo Traps, as a reward for a crime that deserves admiration, astonishment, and respect, and may rightfully be considered one of the most extraordinary crimes of the century."

They laughed, applauded, and fell upon the pie that Simone was brining in. "The crown jewel of the evening," she said. Outside, as an additional adornment, a late moon rose, a narrow crescent. Aside from a mild rustling in the trees, there was silence. Once in a long while a car passed by, then some late pedestrian walking home carefully, on a slightly zigzag course. The sales manager felt secure and sheltered, sitting next to Pilet on a soft, plush couch, in their backs the embroidered words: "Birds in their little nests agree." He laid an arm around the taciturn old man, whose only utterance was the repeated word "fine," pronounced with a windy, hissing F, and snuggled up to him, savoring his phlegmatic elegance, tenderly, with affection.

Cheek to cheek. The wine had made him heavy and placid. He reveled in the pleasure of being his true self in this understanding company, in no longer having to keep a secret because secrecy was no longer needed, in being appreciated, respected, loved, understood; and the idea that he had committed a murder felt more and more convincing to him, in fact it was changing his life, making it more difficult, more heroic, more precious. He felt exalted. He had planned the murder and carried it out—that was how he saw it now—in order to get ahead, but not professionally, not for financial reasons, or because he wanted a Studebaker, but to—what was the word—to become a person of substance, a deeper person, a . . . (here he reached the limits of his intellect) . . . someone worthy of the admiration and love of learned, educated men, who now seemed to him (even Pilet did) like those ancient Magi of whom he had once read in *Reader's Digest*, except that these men knew not only the secret of the stars, but also the secret of Justice—sublime Justice (the word intoxicated him), which in his life in the textile trade he had only known as an abstract nuisance, and which was now rising like a huge, incomprehensible sun over his limited horizon, an idea that he couldn't quite grasp and that for that reason sent shudders up and down his spine; and so, sipping his golden brown cognac, he listened, first with profound wonderment and then more indignantly, as the fat counsel for the defense tried zealously to transform his deed back into some ordinary, pedestrian, everyday act.

"I have listened with pleasure to the prosecutor's highly inventive speech," said Herr Kummer, raising his pince-nez from the red, swollen lump of flesh that was his face and orating with small, delicate, geometric gestures. "To be sure, that old hoodlum Gygax is dead; my client did suffer greatly under his rule; he did indeed work himself into a pitch of animosity against him; he tried to overthrow him. Who would deny it? And where in the world do such things not occur? But it is pure fantasy to take this death of a businessman with an ailing heart and describe it as if it were a murder. ["But I did murder him!" Traps protested, flabbergasted.] Unlike the prosecutor, I consider the defendant innocent, in fact I consider him incapable of guilt. [Traps, embittered: "But I am guilty!"] The sales manager of Hephaeston represents many others like him. When I say he is incapable of guilt, I do not mean that he is without fault—on the contrary. Traps is guilty of all sorts of things, he commits adultery, he swindles his way through life, sometimes with a certain malice, but his life does not consist only of swindling and adultery, no, no, he has his positive sides as well, I daresay his virtues. Our friend Alfredo is hard-working, tenacious, a faithful friend to his friends, tries to ensure a better future for his children, he is politically reliable. In short, all things considered, he is like a slightly soured wine, a touch spoiled, as is the case with many an average life, unavoidably. But just for that reason he is not capable of guilt in the great, pure, proud sense of the word, not capable of a resolute deed, of unequivocal crime. [Traps: "Slander, pure slander!"] He is not a criminal but a victim of the age, of Western civilization, which, alas, has lost touch with the wellsprings of faith (evaporating, it seems), with Christianity, with binding values and general truths, a chaos that offers no guiding light to the individual, producing confusion, degeneration, the law of the jungle in place of true morality. So what really happened? This very average man has fallen unprepared into the hands of a cunning prosecutor. His instinctive wheeling and dealing in the textile industry, his private life, all the adventures of an existence consisting of business trips, of the struggle to fill one's larder with a little bread, of more or less harmless amusements, have now been X-rayed, analyzed, dissected; unrelated facts are now knotted together; a logical plan has been smuggled in where there was none before; incidents have been presented as having caused actions that might just as well have taken a different turn; coincidence has been dressed up as intention, thoughtlessness as premeditation; and the inevitable result, *mutatis mutandum*, is a murderer leaping from the interrogation like a rabbit from a magician's hat.* [Traps: "That is not true!"] If we consider the Gygax case soberly, objectively, without succumbing to the prosecutor's mystifications, we come to the conclusion that the old hoodlum died of his own accord, thanks to his own disorderly life, and because of a weak constitution. We have all heard of stress disorder, popularly known as the 'manager's disease.' Add to this a chronic restlessness, noise, a marriage on the rocks, shattered nerves. But the direct cause of the heart attack was surely the föhn, which according to Herr Traps was blowing at the time. We know about the föhn's effect on a weak heart. [Traps: "Ridiculous!"] Gygax's death was unquestionably an accident. Granted, my client behaved ruthlessly, but he is subject to the laws of the business world, as he himself repeatedly stressed. Of course there were times when he felt like killing his boss. People think all sorts of things, do all sorts of things in their mind, but only in the mind. We have no evidence of such a thought being carried out because in fact the deed was not done. It is absurd to assume that it was, and it is doubly absurd now that my client has been led to imagine that he has committed a murder. After the breakdown of his car he has now suffered a mental breakdown. Therefore, as counsel for the defense, I request that the defendant, Alfredo Traps, be acquitted of the charge. . . ."

**Mutatis mutandum*: Properly, *mutatis mutandis;* Latin for "having made the required changes."

The sales manager meanwhile was getting more and more irritated by this well-meaning fog in which his beautiful crime was being covered up, distorted, dissolved, made to look unreal and shadowy, the mere product of atmospheric pressure, as if you could measure crime on a barometer. He felt belittled, and so he flared up as soon as the lawyer had completed his defense. Rising indignantly to his feet, a plate with a new slice of pie in his right hand, his glass of Raffignac in his left, he declared that before the sentence was passed he wanted to attest with the utmost firmness that he agreed with the prosecutor's speech—and as he said that, tears came to his eyes: "It was a murder," he said, "a conscious murder, this is clear to me now. And I am very disappointed by my defense attorney's speech, in fact I am shocked. I thought I could count on him, especially on him, to understand me, and now I see how mistaken I was. So I ask for a verdict, a sentence, a punishment. And not because I need to grovel, but out of a feeling of joy and inspiration. Because in the course of this night I have realized what it means to lead a *true* life . . . " (here our good stalwart Traps got confused) ". . . for which the higher ideas of justice, of guilt and atonement, are needed, just as certain chemical elements and combinations are needed to produce our synthetic fabric, Hephaeston. This insight has been a rebirth for me. At any rate—I'm afraid my vocabulary outside my own field is rather limited, I hope you can forgive me for not being able to really express what I mean—at any rate, rebirth seems to me the right word for this tremendous happiness that I feel blowing through me like a whirlwind, like a huge raging storm."

It was time for the verdict. Amid laughter, screeches, cheers, and attempts at yodeling (on the part of Pilet), the diminutive and by now profoundly drunk judge announced his decision. This required a considerable effort, not only because he had climbed onto the grand piano in the corner—or into it, rather, since he had first opened it—but also because language itself presented him with stubborn obstacles. He stumbled over words, twisted or mutilated others, started sentences he could not finish, resumed phrases whose meaning he had long forgotten, but his overall train of thought was still more or less discernible. He began with the question of who was right, the prosecutor or the defense attorney, whether Traps had committed one of the most extraordinary crimes of the century or whether he was innocent. He said he could not quite agree with either of these two views. Traps had in fact been outwitted by the prosecutor, as the counsel for the defense maintained, and had for that reason confessed to many things that had not actually occurred in that form; but on the other hand he had committed a murder—not by hatching some devilish plot, but by acting in concert with the thoughtless world in which he, as sales manager of the

Hephaeston synthetic textile company, happened to live. He had killed because it was perfectly natural to him to drive another man into a corner, to apply ruthless pressure, no matter what the consequences. In the world through which he soared in his Studebaker, nothing would have happened to their dear Alfredo, nothing indeed could have happened, but now he had been so kind as to visit them in their quiet white house . . . (here the judge became nebulous, and was only able to blurt out the remainder of his speech as a series of joyful sobs that were interrupted, now and again, by a tremendous and deeply emotional sneeze into a vast handkerchief that enveloped the entirety of his little head, to the greatly increased amusement of the others) . . . to visit four old men who had illuminated his world with the pure ray of justice . . . "Which, to be sure, bears strange features," he said, "I know it, know it, know it—grinning out of four faces, withered and worn, mirrored in the monocle of an old prosecutor, in the pince-nez of a fat defense attorney, giggling from the toothless mouth of a drunken judge who's already starting to babble, gleaming from the bald pate of a discharged executioner [the others, impatient with this lyrical excursion: "The verdict! The verdict!"], this grotesque, crotchety, superannuated thing, this justice in retirement, is, nevertheless, as such, *justice itself* [the others, rhythmically: "The verdict! The verdict!"], in whose name I now sentence our dearest, most precious Alfredo to death [the prosecutor, the defense attorney, the executioner, and Simone: "Eureka!" and "Hurrah!" Traps, now sobbing with emotion: "Thank you, dear Judge, thank you!"], a verdict that is legally founded on one factor alone: the condemned man's confession—but that, after all, is the most important factor. So it gives me great joy," he continued, buoyed up by a final surge of lucidity, "to have delivered a verdict which the condemned man approves without reservation. The dignity of man does not ask for mercy, and it is with joy that our esteemed friend and guest accepts the crowning of his murder, in circumstances that, I hope, have been no less agreeable than the murder itself. Fate comes to the average man by chance, by accident, by mere natural imperative, by disease, by the clotting of a blood vessel, by a malignant growth; but fate as we witness it here arises as a necessary moral result. Here life is perfected with the beautiful logic of art. . . . Here the human tragedy becomes visible, radiates, shines, assumes a flawless form, finds its apotheosis [the others: "Finish! Finish!"], indeed, I dare say that it is only the act of judgment that transforms a defendant into a condemned man that truly confers the accolade of justice. There can be nothing higher, nobler, or greater than the moment when a man is sentenced to death. Such a moment, my friends, has just passed. Traps, our perhaps not quite legitimate lucky duck—since strictly speaking only a qualified death sentence applies, but

I will leave that out of account, so as not to disappoint our dear friend—in short, Alfredo is now our peer and worthy of being accepted into our assembly as a master player of the game [the others: "Champagne! Champagne!"]."

The evening had reached its climax. The champagne bubbled, their gaiety was unclouded, vibrant, fraternal, the defense attorney had been woven back into the net of sympathy. The candles had burned down, some were already extinguished. Outside, the first glimmering of dawn, of paling stars, distant sunrise, freshness and dew. Traps, elated but also tired, asked to be led to his room, lurched from one embrace to the next. Everyone was fantastically drunk, meaningless speeches filled the salon, thick-tongued monologues no one was listening to. Smelling of red wine and cheese, the old men stroked the happy, tired sales manager's hair, caressed him, kissed him. He looked like a child surrounded by grandfathers and uncles. The bald, taciturn man led him to his room. It was an arduous climb up a flight of stairs, on all fours. Halfway up they got entangled in each other and could go no further. A stony dawn fell from above through a window, mingling with the whiteness of the plaster walls. Traps could hear the first sounds of the new day—a distant whistle and sounds of shunting from the tiny railroad station, vague reminders of a missed opportunity to return home. He was happy, desireless. Never before in his circumscribed life had he felt like this. Pale images rose in his mind: the face of a boy, probably his youngest, favorite child, then the misty outlines of the village he had landed in as a result of his car's breaking down, the bright ribbon of the road swinging itself over a small rise, the knoll with the church, the great rustling oak with the iron rings and the props, the wooded hills, the endless glowing sky behind them, above them, everywhere, endless. But then the bald man collapsed, mumbling, "Sleep, want to sleep, tired, I'm tired," and then actually started to doze off. Half conscious, he still heard Traps crawling up the stairs. Later, a chair fell over, and the bald, taciturn man on the stairs woke up for a few seconds, full of dreams and memories of long-submerged terrors and moments of horror. Then a clutter of legs passed over the sleeping man as the others climbed the stairs. Squeaking and croaking, they had scribbled a death sentence on parchment, couched in the most laudatory terms, with witty locutions and academic phrases in Latin and archaic German. Then they had set out to lay the product on the sleeping sales manager's bed, so that when he awoke he would find a pleasant memento of their gargantuan drinking bout. Outside, the bright early light and the first bird cries, strident, impatient. And so they went up the stairs, trampling over the bald man in the shelter of his sleep, clutching one another, each supporting the next, staggering, progressing with extraordinary difficulty, especially on the landing, where a repeated pattern of congestion, retreat, renewed advance and failure had to be sorted out. Finally they stood at the door of the guest room. The judge opened it, and then the solemn group, the prosecutor still with his napkin tied around his neck, froze on the threshold: In the window frame hung Traps, motionless, a dark silhouette against the dull silver of the sky, in the heavy scent of the roses, in a silence so final and absolute that the prosecutor, in whose monocle the gathering power of the rising day was reflected, had to gasp for air before, in an access of sorrow and perplexity over his lost friend, he exclaimed with considerable grief: "Alfredo, my dear good Alfredo! For God's sake what were you thinking of? You've ruined the most beautiful gathering we've ever had!"

The Coup

TO FRED SCHERTENLEIB

A

B C

D E

F G

H J

K L

M N

O P

After the members of the Political Secretariat had consumed their usual cold buffet of deviled eggs, ham, toast, whiskey, and champagne in the banquet hall, N was the first to enter the conference room. Now that he had been made a member of the country's highest office, this was the only room he felt safe in, even though he was only a Minister of Postal Services and the stamps for the peace conference had appealed to A, as he had learned from rumors in D's circle and more definitely from E; but all his predecessors had disappeared, despite the relatively subordinate position of the post office in the machinery of government, and although the head of the secret police, C, treated him pleasantly enough, it was not advisable to make inquiries about the previous postal ministers. Before entering the banquet hall and before entering the conference room, he had already been frisked, first by the athletic lieutenant-colonel who always performed this function, and then by a man N had never seen before, a blond colonel; the colonel who usually frisked him outside the conference room was bald, presumably on vacation, or else he had been moved to another post, or dismissed, or demoted, or shot. N laid his attaché case on the conference table and sat down. L sat down next to him. The conference room was long and not much wider than the conference table. The walls were covered to half their height with brown wainscoting. The unpaneled parts of the walls and the ceiling were white. The seating order corresponded to the hierarchy of the system. A sat at the top. Above him, on the white part of the wall, hung the Party flag. The other end of the table, across from him, remained empty, and behind it was the only window in the conference room. The window was arched at the top, tall, divided into five panes, and had no curtains. B D F H K M sat (from A's point of view) on the right side of the table and across from them C E G J L N; next to N sat the head of the youth organizations, P, and next to M the

Minister of Nuclear Energy, O, but P and O were not entitled to vote. L was the oldest member of the council and had carried out the function now carried out by D before A had taken over the Party and the state. L had been a blacksmith before becoming a revolutionary. He was tall and broad-shouldered and as lean as ever. His face and his hands were coarse, his gray hair was still dense and cropped short. He was always unshaven. His dark suit resembled a worker's Sunday clothes. He never wore a tie. The collar of his white shirt was always buttoned. L was popular within the Party and was liked by the people as well, and his deeds during the June uprising had become the stuff of legends; but so much time had passed since then that A called him "the Monument." L was considered a just man and he was a hero; therefore his downward career was not a spectacular plunge, but a continual and gradual descent within the hierarchy. L lived in fear of some imminent allegation; this undermined his strength. He knew he would be overthrown some day. Like the two marshals H and K he was often drunk. Even at meetings of the Secretariat, he no longer showed up sober. On this day, too, he stank of whiskey and champagne, but his rough voice was calm, and there was a mocking expression in his watery, bloodshot eyes: "Comrade," he said to N, "we're finished. O hasn't come." N did not reply. He didn't even flinch. He pretended to be indifferent. Maybe O's arrest was a rumor, maybe L was mistaken, and even if L was not mistaken, N's position might still not be as hopeless as L's, who was in charge of transportation. If there were any snags in industry, agriculture, conventional energy, not to mention nuclear energy (and there was always a snag somewhere), the Minister of Transportation could always be blamed. Accidents, delays, bottlenecks. The distances were considerable, supervision cumbersome and slow.

Party Secretary D and Minister J arrived. The Party Secretary was fat, powerful, and intelligent. His suit was tailored in military style. In this he was copying A, out of servility, according to some, mockingly according to others. J was red-haired and slender. After A's accession to power, he had been Prosecutor General and a very enterprising fellow indeed. He had enforced the death sentences against the old revolutionaries during the first great purge, but he had made a mistake in the process. At A's behest, he had demanded a death sentence for A's son-in-law, and when A unexpectedly intervened to forgive his son-in-law after all, the son-in-law had already been shot, a lapse that not only cost J his position as Prosecutor General: worse, he came to power. He was made a member of the Political Secretariat and was thus placed on the most convenient of all hit lists. He had reached a position where he could only be done in on political grounds, and political grounds were not hard to find. In J's case, they were already present. Of course no one believed that A had intended to save his son-in-law. The son-in-law's execution had undoubtedly been of advantage to A (A's daughter was already going to bed with P at the time); but now A had a public excuse for eliminating J whenever he wanted, and since A had never missed an opportunity to eliminate someone, J was generally considered a goner. J knew this and acted as if he didn't know it, but it was an awkward performance. On that day as well. His efforts to hide his insecurity were much too obvious. He told the Party Secretary about a performance of the State Ballet. At every meeting, J aired his balletomania, tossing around technical terms from the world of dance, especially after his appointment as Minister of Agriculture, a field that he, as a lawyer, knew nothing about. Added to that, the Ministry of Agriculture was, if anything, even more precarious than the Ministry of Transportation. In the long run, everyone came to harm there; there was no way the Party could prevail in agriculture. The peasants were ineducable, selfish, and lazy. N, too, hated the peasants, not in and of themselves but for posing an unsolvable problem that foiled all efforts at planning, and since failure could cost him his life, N hated the peasants doubly, and in his hatred he even understood J's attitude: why would anyone want to talk about peasants? Only the Minister of Heavy Industry, F, who had grown up in a village and been a village grade school teacher like his father, possessing a partial education crudely and primitively hammered together at a rural teacher's college, looking like a peasant and sounding like a peasant, talked about peasants in the Political Secretariat, serving up peasant anecdotes that amused only himself, citing peasant proverbs only he understood, while the learned lawyer J, forced to squabble with peasants whose incomprehension was driving him to despair, kept rattling off ballet stories as a way to avoid the subject of peasants, boring everyone to distraction, most of all A, who called the Minister of Agriculture "our ballerina" (earlier he had called him "our counsel for the shooting squad"). Nevertheless N despised the former Prosecutor General, whose freckled barrister's mug revolted him. The fellow had shifted from brisk hangman to anxious underling much too quickly. On the other hand, N greatly admired D for his upright bearing. Despite his power within the Party, and despite his political intelligence, "the Warthog," as A called him, was probably also afraid that the rumor of O's not showing up for the meeting would prove to be true, but D controlled himself. He never lost his composure. Even in danger, the Party Secretary remained calm. But his position was precarious. O's arrest (if it wasn't just a rumor caused by his not showing up at the meeting) could be the beginning of an attack on D, because O was subordinate to D in the Party, but it could also be aimed at the Chief

Ideologue, G, who was considered to be O's personal protector: that O's liquidation (if it were to take place) threatened both D and G was logically possible, but hardly probable.

Chief Ideologue G had already entered the conference room. He was awkward, wore smudged rimless glasses, and held his professorial head with its white shock of hair at a slant. He had previously been a teacher at a provincial high school—A called him the "Tea Saint." G was the Party theoretician. He was a teetotaler and an ascetic, a haggard introvert who left his broad, soft shirt collar open and wore sandals even in winter. While Party Secretary D was full of vitality, a skirt-chaser and an epicure, Chief Ideologue G's every step was theoretically calculated and quite frequently led to absurdity and bloodshed. The two men were bitter opponents. Instead of complementing each other, they wore each other down, setting traps for each other, trying to bring about each other's downfall: the Party Secretary as a technician of power confronting the Chief Ideologue as a theoretician of the Revolution. D wanted to maintain power by any means necessary; G wanted, by any means, to preserve power in its purity, a sterilized scalpel in the hands of a taintless doctrine. The Warthog had Foreign Minister B, Minister of Education M, and Minister of Transportation L on his side, while the Tea Saint could count on Minister of Agriculture J, President K, and the Minister of Heavy Industry, F, who was quite the equal of D in the way of violence but disliked him for being as obsessed with power as he was himself, and who therefore gravitated to G's camp, even though the former village grade school teacher felt inferior to the former high school teacher and probably hated him in secret as well.

G had long since ceased to greet D. The fact that the Chief Ideologue greeted the Party Secretary now, as N noted with a start, was a sign that G feared that O's disappearance was leveled at him, just as D's reciprocal greeting suggested that he, too, felt threatened. But the fact that both men were afraid meant that O must have actually been arrested. However, the Tea Saint's greeting was cordial, and the Warthog's just friendly; this suggested that a threat to the Chief Ideologue was a touch more possible than a threat to the Party Secretary. N breathed a small sigh of relief. D's downfall would have caused N some embarrassment, too. It was on D's recommendation that N had been accepted as a voting member of the Secretariat, and he was considered D's personal protégé, a view that could become dangerous, even though it was not quite in accord with the truth: first of all, N was not aligned with any faction; secondly, the Chief Ideologue, who supported Nuclear

Minister O, had expected before the elections that the Party Secretary would recommend his own protégé, the head of the youth organizations, P. But the Warthog had realized that it was easier to elect a neutral applicant to the Secretariat than one of his own or his enemy's cohorts—and besides, A's daughter was no longer dating P but was now sleeping with a novelist who was highly respected by the Party—whereupon D dropped his candidate to recommend N, thereby outmaneuvering the Tea Saint, who now had to vote for N as well. Thirdly, N was nothing but a specialist in his department and therefore harmless for both D and G. He was so insignificant for A that he hadn't even been given a nickname.

Of course that was also true of Foreign Trade Minister E, who had entered the room behind G and sat down right away, while the Chief Ideologue still stood next to the casually grinning Party Secretary, polishing his round schoolmarmish glasses with an awkward smile as Minister of Agriculture J regaled him with gossip about the National Ballet's first soloist. E was elegant, a man of the world. He wore an English suit with a loosely bunched handkerchief in the breast pocket, and was smoking an American cigarette. Like N, the Foreign Trade Minister had unwillingly joined the Political Secretariat, he too had been automatically pushed toward the inner circle by the Party's internecine struggle, others who had been more ambitious had been crushed in the scramble for the front seats—their own victims, in effect; thus E, a specialist like N, had survived every purge, which earned him A's sobriquet: "Lord Evergreen." If N was involuntarily the thirteenth most powerful man, E was just as involuntarily the fifth most powerful man of the empire. There was no way back. One wrong move, one careless remark could mean the end, arrest, interrogations, death, which was why E and N had to butter up everyone who was more powerful than they or who could become equally powerful. They had to be clever, look out for opportunities, pull in their heads if necessary, and exploit their colleagues' human weaknesses. They were forced into many a ridiculous and undignified situation.

Quite naturally. The thirteen men of the Political Secretariat exercised enormous power. They determined the fate of the gigantic empire, sent countless people into exile, to prison, and to their deaths, interfered in the lives of millions, trampled entire industries into the dust, displaced families and nations, caused mighty cities to arise, levied boundless armies, decided on war and peace, but since their instinct for self-preservation forced them to keep a wary eye on each other, their mutual sympathies and antipathies influenced their decisions far more than the political conflicts and economic conditions confronting them. Their power, and with it their fear of each other, was too great for the conduct of pure politics. Reason was powerless against it.

Two more missing members stepped in, the marshals: Defense Minister H and President K, both of them bloated, both of them sallow, both of them stiff, both of them plastered with medals, both of them old and sweaty, both of them stinking of tobacco, whiskey, and Dunhill perfume, two sacks tightly stuffed with fat, flesh, urine, and fear. They sat down side by side simultaneously without greeting anyone. H and K always showed up together. A, referring to their favorite drink, called them the "Gin-gis Khans." Marshal K, the country's president and a hero of the civil war, sat dozing in his seat; Marshal H, a military nincompoop who had weaseled his way up to marshalhood by rigidly adhering to the Party line and by delivering his predecessors, one by one, to A's feigned credulity and bloody judgment, pulled himself together before sinking into a stupor, shouting: "Down with the enemies within the Party!" and thereby admitting that he, too, knew about O's arrest. But no one paid him any attention. People were used to it, fear had a way of pressing slogans out of him. At every meeting of the Political Secretariat he saw his downfall coming, launched into self-accusations, and made wild attacks on someone without ever specifying who it was.

N stared at Defense Minister H, whose forehead was glistening with sweat, and felt his own forehead becoming damp. He thought of the Bordeaux he had intended to give F as a present but had not yet been able to give him since he did not have it yet. It had started three weeks ago at the International Postal Ministers' conference in Paris, where N had been able to organize some wine shipments for Party Secretary D, who liked to drink Bordeaux, in exchange for some of his own country's whiskey, which was to his French colleague's liking. Not that N was the only one who supplied the mighty D with Bordeaux. Foreign Minister B did the same thing. But N's complaisance had resulted in B's sending him shipments of Bordeaux as well, for the simple reason that N, in order not to appear calculating, also pretended to be a lover of good Bordeaux, even though he didn't care for wine at all. But when N discovered that the great national whiskey drinker F, lord of heavy industry, nicknamed "the Bootblack" by A, was a diabetic and was therefore, on his doctors' recommendation, secretly consuming only Bordeaux, he hesitated for a long time before sending F a gift of Bordeaux as well, because that would be an admission that he, too, knew about F's sickness. But he told himself that other members of the Secretariat must know about it as well.

He had received his information from the head of the Secret Police, C, and it seemed improbable that others hadn't been told about it. Therefore he decided to pass on a box of Lafitte '45 to F. The Minister of Heavy Industry reciprocated the gift promptly. The Bootblack's presents were notorious. N carelessly opened the package at the dinner table in his family's presence. It contained a roll of film, which N, unaware of its content and misled by its title, "Scenes from the French Revolution," ran through his home movie projector at his wife's and children's request. It was a pornographic film. From time to time the other members of the Political Secretariat received similar presents from F, N learned later. And yet it was known that F did not care for pornography. Such a gift was an instrument of control in his hand. He would act as if the recipient loved pornography. "Well, how did you like that dirty movie?" he had said to N a few days later. "It's not my cup of tea, but I know you like that sort of thing." N did not dare to contradict him. To show his gratitude, he sent the Bootblack a box of Château Pape Clément '34. Thus the sober and erotically moderate N found himself accumulating pornographic material and was forced at the same time to acquire more Bordeaux, for shipments from Paris came only twice a year, and he did not dare send F bottles he had received from B. True, the Foreign Minister and the Minister of Heavy Industry were enemies, but the front lines could change. It had happened before: impersonal enemies could be brought together by a sudden commonality of interest and become inseparable friends. N was forced to take Foreign Trade Minister E into his confidence. It turned out that he, too, was sending the Warthog and the Bootblack gifts of Bordeaux. E would be able to assist N through his foreign connections, but not indefinitely. N suspected that others were also sending D and F presents and being rewarded by F with incriminating material.

The "Party Muse" M had taken her seat opposite N. The Minister of Education was blond and imposing. At a meeting of the Secretariat, A had once made a prophesy concerning her breasts: they were the mountain range from whose peaks the Party Secretary would some day fall to his death. At that time the Party Muse was dressed in particularly stylish getup, and A's crude remark was an implicit threat to the Warthog. D was reputed to be M's lover. From that day on, M came to the meetings of the Secretariat wearing only a plain gray tailored suit. The fact that on this day she was wearing a décolleté black cocktail dress confused N, all the more since she was wearing jewelry as well. There had to be a special occasion. She, too, must know about O's arrest. The only question was whether the Party Muse was wearing that dress to distance herself from D by a show of unconcern, or whether she intended with the courage of desperation demonstratively to proclaim herself his lover. N received no answer from Party Secretary D, for D seemed to be ignoring M. He was now seated in his chair, examining a piece of writing.

M's choice of apparel became even more ambiguous now that the Bootblack, F, the short fat Minister of Heavy Industry, entered the room. Without so much as a glance at the others, he hurried up to the Party Muse and exclaimed, "Gee whiz, what a dress, delightful, fantastic, a welcome change from the usual Party garb. To hell with uniforms." Everyone stared at F, who went on: "Why did we make a revolution in the first place? Why get rid of plutocrats and bloodsuckers? Why string up the rich farmers from their cherry trees? To introduce beauty, that's why!" he shouted, petting and kissing the Minister of Education as if she were a peasant wench: "Dior to the workers!"* whereupon he took his seat between D and H, who both moved their chairs away from his, for they had to conclude, as N did, that the Minister of Heavy Industry was acting out of gallows humor and was apparently convinced that O's disappearance was aimed at the Chief Ideologue and therefore at him as well, although it was also possible that F's exuberance was genuine and based on some reliable information portending the Party Secretary's imminent fall.

B stepped in. (Only now did N notice that the head of the youth organizations, P, had been sitting next to him all along, a pale, bespectacled, anxious, solicitous servant of the Party, who had arrived unnoticed.) B calmly went to his seat, placed his attaché case on the table, and sat down. The Chief Ideologue and the Minister of Agriculture J, who were still standing, also sat down. Foreign Minister B's authority was undisputed, even though everyone hated him. He was superior to all of them. N actually admired him. If the Party Secretary was the intelligent practitioner of organized violence and the Minister of Heavy Industry the instinctive and sly adept of the same art, if the Chief Ideologue was the theoretician, then the Foreign Minister represented a virtually imponderable element in the web of their collective power. He had something in common with E and N: perfect mastery of his field of expertise. He was an ideal foreign minister. But unlike E and N, he had risen to power within the Party, without, however, getting embroiled in internecine battles like D and G. His influence extended beyond the Party and he was only concerned with his specified task. That made him powerful. He was not disloyal, but he avoided committing himself; even on a personal

*Christian Dior (1905–1957), prominent French fashion designer.

level, he had remained a bachelor. He ate moderately and drank moderately, a glass of champagne at a banquet, no more. His German, his English, his French, his Russian, his Italian were perfect, his study of Mazarin and his depiction of the great powers of early India had been translated into many languages, as had his essay on the Chinese concept of number. Also, translations he had made of Rilke and Stefan George were circulating. But his most famous work was his "Doctrine of Upheaval," which was why he was called the Clausewitz of the Revolution. He was indispensable, and was hated for that reason. He was hated especially by A, who called him "the Eunuch," a label that had been adopted by all the others, but not even A dared to call him that to his face. He would call him "our friend B," or, if he was beside himself, "our genius." B, on the other hand, addressed the assembly with "dear lady, honored gentlemen," as if speaking before a social club. And so, no sooner had he sat down than, "Dear lady, honored gentlemen," he began to speak, unbidden, which was not his usual way. "Dear lady, honored gentlemen, it might be of some interest that Minister of Nuclear Energy O has not arrived." Silence. B took some papers out of his attaché case, began to peruse them and said no more. N sensed how afraid everyone was. O's arrest was not a rumor. B could not have meant anything else. President K announced that he had always known O was a traitor, that O was an intellectual, and that all intellectuals are traitors, and Marshal H roared once again: "Down with the enemies within the Party!" The two Gin-gis Khans were the only ones who reacted, the others pretended indifference, except for D, who said "idiots" loudly enough for everyone to hear him, but no one seemed to notice. The Party Muse opened her pocketbook and powdered herself. The Minister of Foreign Trade pondered some documents, the Minister of Heavy Industry studied his fingernails, the Minister of Agriculture stared into space, the Chief Ideologue took notes, and the Minister of Transportation, L, appeared to be what the others called him, a motionless monument.

A and C entered the conference room. Not through the door that was situated behind the Ministers of Heavy Industry and of Defense, but through the door behind the Chief Ideologue and the Minister of Agriculture. C was dressed in a casual blue suit, as always; A was in uniform, but without decorations. C sat down, A remained standing behind his chair, carefully stuffing his pipe. C had begun his career in the Youth Organization and risen in the ranks to become its leader; then he was removed from his post. Not for political reasons, the complaints were of a different order. Thereupon he disappeared. According to rumors, he was vegetating in a prison camp, no one knew anything definite: suddenly he was back, and not just in good standing but head of the

Secret Police. He was still involved in homosexual affairs, there was no doubt about that. A brutally called him his "Governess," but no one dared protest against C any longer. C was tall, slightly overweight, and bald. Originally he had been a musician, and had acquired the concert diploma. If B was the Secretariat's magnifico, C was its bohemian. His beginnings in the Party remained obscure. The cruelty of his methods was notorious, the terror he spread evident to all. He had countless lives on his conscience, the secret police under his direction were more powerful than ever before, their informants all but omnipresent. Many regarded him as a sadist, and many disagreed, claiming that C had no other choice, that A had him in his grip, that if C did not obey, he could be put on trial again. They said the head of the secret police was really an aesthete who despised his position and hated his profession and was forced to ply his craft in order to save his own life and that of his friends. Personally, C gave a likable, even amiable impression, and often he seemed to be shy. C, who carried out his task within Party and State more ruthlessly than anyone else, appeared to be the wrong man in the wrong place and perhaps for that very reason so useful.

A, on the other hand, was uncomplicated. His simplicity was his strength. Raised in the tundra, descended from nomads, power was no problem to him, and violence a natural thing. He had been living for years in a bunker-like, unadorned building hidden away in the woods outside the capital, guarded by a company of soldiers and served by an old cook who had all been recruited from his native region. He came to the government palace only to meet visiting heads of state or Party bosses from abroad, to give a rare audience, and to attend the meetings of the Political Secretariat, but each member of the Secretariat had to report alone three times a week at his residence, to be received by A on a verandah with wicker furniture in summertime and in winter in his studio, which contained nothing but a huge mural, representing his native village animated by a few peasants, and an even larger desk, behind which he sat while the visitor was made to stand before him. A had been married four times. Three of his wives had died; as for the fourth one, no one knew whether she was still alive, and if she was living, where. Except for his daughter, he had no children. Sometimes he summoned girls from the city to his place, with a simple nod in their direction; all they had to do was sit next to him and watch American movies for hours. Then he would fall asleep in his armchair and the girls could go home. He also had the city's National Museum shut down once a month so he could walk through its rooms alone for hours at a time. But he never looked at works of modern art. He would stand reverently in front of huge, late bourgeois, historical paintings of battles, of brooding emperors sentencing their sons to death, pictures of drunk and carousing Hussars and horse-drawn sleds whizzing across the steppes with wolves in murderous pursuit. His musical tastes were equally primitive. He loved sentimental folk songs, and had them performed each year for his birthday by a choir from his native village, dressed up in traditional costumes.

A puffed at his pipe and thoughtfully observed his seated subordinates. N was always amazed at how slight and unimposing A was in reality. On photographs and on television he looked broad and stocky. A sat down and began to talk, slowly, haltingly, circumlocutiously, repeating himself, logical to a fault. He began with a general observation. The twelve other members of the Political Secretariat and the candidate P sat in a state of tense immobility, waiting, their faces set like masks. They were forewarned. When A planned something, he always started with roundabout observations about the development of the Revolution. It was as if he had to reach far back before delivering one of his deadly blows. Once again he went through his familiar oration. The goal of the Party, he said, was to transform society, tremendous achievements had already been accomplished, the fundamental tenets of a new social order were firmly installed, however the people did not yet perceive them as natural, but still as something imposed and enforced, they were still thinking in old categories, held back by superstition and prejudice, infested with individualism, they were still trying to break out of the new order and install a new egotism, they were not educated yet, the Revolution was still the cause of a minority, still solely the cause of revolutionary minds and not sufficiently a cause for the masses, who, though they had taken the path of revolution, could just as easily stray from it. Nor could the revolutionary order prevail by force alone, or the revolution by the dictatorship of the Party alone, but the Party, too, would disintegrate if it had not been organized from the top down; therefore the creation of the Political Secretariat had been a historic necessity. A interrupted his discourse and turned his attention to his pipe, lighting it again. A's lecture, N thought to himself, consisted of popular Party doctrine, why was everything made to sound like a political orientation class before the real, dangerous contents were brought up, he wondered. Everything ran according to formula, no matter where you were. It was like an endless prayer, this tedious recitation of all the political maxims by which A justified his power in the name of the Party. But meanwhile A was getting to the point. He was preparing his blow. Every success, he proclaimed, still sounding quite harmless, his tone of voice unchanged, every advance toward the ultimate goal, demanded a change within the Party. The new state had met its challenges, the ministries were functions of their respective administrative provinces, the new state was progressive in its content, dictatorial in its form. The state, he said, was the expression of all the practical necessities confronting it from within and from without; but the Party, as an ideological instrument confronted with practical challenges, had the mission of transforming the state at the appropriate time. For the state, as an objective given, could not revolutionize itself: only the Party, which controlled the state, could do that. Only the Party could enforce a transformation of the state in accord with the needs of the Revolution: precisely for that reason, the Party could not afford to be immutable, its structure had to be adjusted, phase by phase, to the level of revolutionary development. Presently, he said, the Party structure was still hierarchic and steered from above, which corresponded to the era of struggle; but the era of struggle had passed, the Party had won, it was in possession of power, therefore the next phase was to democratize the Party, as a first step toward the democratization of the new state: but the Party could only be democratized by getting rid of the Political Secretariat and delegating its power to an expanded Party Parliament, for the Political Secretariat's only purpose had been to apply the Party as a deadly weapon against the old order, a task that had already been accomplished, the old order no longer existed, which was why at this point the Political Secretariat could be liquidated.

N recognized the danger. Indirectly, everyone was threatened; directly, no one in particular. A's motion was surprising. There had been no previous indication that A would make such a motion; the motion corresponded to a tactic that worked with the unexpected. A's comments were ambiguous, his intentions not at all. His speech had been seemingly logical, delivered in the traditional revolutionary style, honed at countless secret and public meetings during the era of struggle. But actually the speech had contained a contradiction, and in that contradiction, the truth was concealed: A wanted to disempower the Party by democratizing it, a process that would enable him to overthrow the Secretariat and install himself once and for all as the country's sole ruler. Camouflaged by a pseudoparliament, he would be more powerful than before, which was why at the beginning he had spoken about the necessity of violence. A new purge did seem imminent, but you couldn't be sure. The Political Secretariat could be dissolved without a purge. But A had a tendency to liquidate elements he suspected, or who were under suspicion, of resisting his absolute authority. That A suspected the presence of such elements within the Political Secretariat was probable in view of O's arrest. But before N had time to consider whether or not he himself represented a threat to A and to what extent the dissolution of the Political Secretariat would make his fall as Minister of Postal Services likely—all he could summon up in his favor at the moment were the stamps for the peace conference—something unexpected happened.

A had just knocked the ashes out of his pipe, which was always a sign that he considered the meeting of the Political Secretariat to be closed and did not want any discussion, when Transportation Minister L spoke up without having first raised his hand. The Transportation Minister rose to his feet with an effort. His intoxication had apparently increased. With a thick tongue, after two false starts, he pointed out that O was missing and that therefore the meeting of the Political Secretariat could not have properly begun. It was too bad for A's splendid speech, but bylaws were bylaws, and that held true for revolutionaries as well. All the others stared dumbfounded at the Monument as he leaned over the table, supporting himself on both arms but swaying nonetheless, fixing a combative stare on A, his face with the white, bushy eyebrows and the gray stubble on his cheeks pale and masklike. L's objection was nonsense, although formally correct. It was nonsense because it was superfluous, A's extensive speech had set the meeting into motion; it was nonsense also because with his protest, the Transportation Minister was acting as if he knew nothing of O's and of his own possible imminent arrest. But what gave N pause was the swift glance A cast at C as he stuffed his pipe again. There was a peculiar astonishment in A's glance, which made N suspect that A was the only one who did not know that everyone else knew about O's arrest, a thought that immediately gave rise to the question whether the news of O's arrest had not been disseminated against A's will by the head of the Secret Police himself, but also whether Foreign Minister B, who had mentioned O's nonappearance to all the other members of the Political Secretariat, had not formed an alliance with C. N's suspicions were not completely refuted by A's retort. It made no difference, A replied, calmly expelling clouds of his English tobacco, Balkan Sobranie Smoking Mixture, it made no difference whether O was showing up or not, nor did the reason for his absence matter, for O was only a candidate and as such not entitled to vote, and the present meeting had no other purpose than to pass a resolution to dissolve the Political Secretariat, and that this resolution had indeed been passed, since no negative votes had been registered, a resolution for which O's presence was not required.

L, suddenly discouraged and tired, as tends to happen when one is drunk, was about to sink back into his chair when the head of the Secret Police, C, dryly remarked that the Minister of Nuclear Energy had not come because, obviously, he was sick, a shameless lie that, if C had in fact spread the news of O's arrest, could only have been intended to provoke L again, in order to prepare his arrest. "Sick?" L promptly exclaimed, leaning on his left forearm and banging the table with his right fist. "Sick, really sick?" "Probably," C replied cold-bloodedly, while sorting some papers. L stopped banging the table and sat down, speechless with rage. Now the colonel appeared in the doorway behind F and H, a complete anomaly, no one had the right to enter the room during a meeting of the Political Secretariat. The colonel's appearance had to portend something special, an alarm, a misfortune, some extremely important announcement. It was all the more surprising, therefore, when it turned out that the colonel had only come to ask L to step out for an urgent personal matter. "Get the hell out of here," L barked at the colonel, who obeyed, with some hesitation and not without casting a glance at the head of the Secret Police, but C was still occupied with his papers. Laughing, A remarked that once again L appeared to be plastered. It was the sort of good-natured, jovial, rough language he used when he was in a good mood. L himself, he suggested, should get the hell out and take care of his personal business. "Is one of your girlfriends pregnant?" Everyone laughed uproariously, not because A's words were found so amusing, but to relieve the enormous tension; and unconsciously, too, L's colleagues wanted to clear a path of retreat for him. Through the intercom, A summoned the colonel back in. The colonel reappeared. "What happened?" A asked. "The Transportation Minister's wife is dying," the colonel replied with a salute. "Now get back out," A said. The colonel left the room. "Go, L!" A said. "That crack about your girlfriends was in bad taste, I take it back. I know your wife was important to you. Go to her, the meeting is over anyhow." As humane as A's words sounded, the Transportation Minister's fear was too great, he didn't believe them. In his despair and drunkenness, the Monument saw only one way out: meet the danger head-on. "I am an old revolutionary," he shouted, propping himself up again, and as for his wife, she was in the hospital, everyone knew that, but she had survived the operation, he wasn't walking into this trap. He had been in the Party from the beginning, he said, before A, before C and B, who were nothing but miserable upstarts. He had worked for the Party when it was still dangerous to be in the Party, when it could cost you your life. He had been locked up in miserable stinking prisons, chained like an animal, with rats snapping at his bloody ankles. Rats, he shouted again and again, rats! He had ruined his health in the service of the Party, he had been sentenced to death for the Party. "The firing squad was already set up, comrades," he howled, "I was already facing them." After his escape, he continued, still slurring his words, after his escape he had gone underground, again and again he had gone underground, until the great Revolution, until at the head of the revolutionaries he stormed the palace with a gun and a hand grenade. "With a gun and a hand grenade I made history, world history," he roared, and now he was irrepressible, his rage and despair had an undeniable grandeur: the shabby, pathetic drunkard seemed to have turned into the famous old revolutionary he had once been. "I fought against a lying, corrupt society," he continued his wild tirade, "I staked my life on the truth!" He had changed the world in order to make it better, he hadn't cared about his own suffering and starvation, his persecution and torture, he had been proud of that, because he knew he was on the side of the poor and the exploited, and it was a glorious feeling, knowing you're on the right side, but now that victory was achieved, now that the Party was in power, suddenly he wasn't on the right side any longer, suddenly he was on the side of the powerful. "I was seduced by power, comrades," he cried out. "How many crimes have I kept silent about, how many friends have I betrayed and turned over to the Secret Police? Should I continue to be silent?" O had been arrested, he continued, suddenly pale, exhausted and quiet, that was the truth, and everyone knew it, and he was not leaving the room because he, too, was supposed to be arrested in the hallway, because this story of his wife's dying was just a lie to lure him out of the conference room. With these words, which expressed a suspicion that was not unfounded for everyone present, he let himself fall back into his chair.

While L, aware of his hopeless position, blew up in a fury of defiance, all constraints thrown to the wind, since caution appeared to make no sense at all; while the others sat petrified as they attended the ghoulish spectacle of a giant in his last throes; while at every pause between one of L's monstrous sentences and the next, Marshal H, terrified of being dragged along with the Monument as he fell, screamed "Down with the enemies within the Party!"; while, at the moment when L concluded his speech, the President, Marshal K, delivered an exuberant declaration of everlasting fidelity to A; while all these events unfolded, N wondered how A would respond. A sat calmly, smoking his pipe. He revealed no sign of any reaction. But something had to be going on inside him. N couldn't quite tell yet to what extent L's protest could be a threat to A, but he sensed that A's deliberations would have decisive consequences for his own future position, and that a turning point was at hand; but in what direction things would turn, N had no idea, nor could he venture a guess as to how A would proceed. A was a cunning tactician, with his startling chess moves in the game of power he could outplay everyone, even B. He had an instinctive understanding of human nature and could spot and exploit any rival's weakness, he had mastered the fine art of hunting and capturing a human being like no other member of the Political Secretariat, but he was not adept at open man-to-man conflict, his way was to hide under cover of the unexpected, and then attack. He laid his traps in the jungle of the Party with its thousand departments and subdepartments, branches and auxiliary branches, units and subunits; it must have been a very long time since he had experienced an open confrontation, a personal attack. The question was whether A could be made to lose his composure, whether he would lose perspective and act prematurely, whether he would admit the arrests or continue to deny them, all questions that N was unable to answer, because he himself did not know what he should have done in A's place; but N did not get to continue his speculations about A's probable behavior, for no sooner had Marshal K paused for the first time to take a breath and gather strength for an even more enthusiastic expression of his devotion to A, than F interrupted him and began to speak. Actually F had not only interrupted President K but, inadvertently, A as well, who, at the moment when K paused, had taken his pipe out of his mouth, no doubt with the intention of responding to L's tirade, but F, who did not notice or did not want to notice this, was faster. He began to speak even before rising to his feet, and then he was standing, immobile, short, fat, incredibly ugly, his hands folded in front of his belly, like a clumsy peasant reciting his prayers in his Sunday best, talking and talking. N immediately realized why. The Minister of Heavy Industry's calm was deceptive. The Bootblack was impelled by pure horror at the way L was proceeding, he could already see A's wrath falling upon them all, the entire Political Secretariat under arrest. As the son of a village school teacher, the Bootblack had arduously worked his way up in the province. During his early days in the Party he had been ridiculed, was never taken seriously, humiliated in all sorts of ways, employed as a lackey, until he rose in the ranks (and many paid dearly for this) because he had no pride (which he could not afford) but only ambition, and because he was capable of anything, and now he showed himself capable of everything. He carried out the dirtiest (bloodiest) assignments, blindly obedient, prepared to commit any treachery, in many ways the most terrible man in the Party, more terrible even than A, who was terrible through his deeds but significant as a personality. A was not deformed, neither by struggle nor by power. A was as he was, a part of nature, elemental and genuine, self-made and not anyone else's creature. F was only terrible, the old indignities clung to him, he couldn't shake them off, even the two Gin-gis Khans looked like aristocrats next to him, and even A, who needed him, publicly called him not only the Bootblack but the Ass-Kisser;

that was why F's fear was greater than anyone else's. He had done everything to rise to the top. Now, arrived at his goal, he saw his odious and inhuman efforts threatened by L's lunatic attacks, his grotesque self-denials rendered senseless, his shameless servility gone to waste; his panic was so overwhelming that, stunned by fear, he had cut off A (as N was convinced now), but no doubt F wanted quickly to top K's encomium with his own declaration of fealty, as if that could help him. Naturally, he did it in his own way. Instead of praising A, as the President had boundlessly done, he launched an even more boundless attack on L. He began, as was his habit, with those never-ending peasant proverbs he had acquired, regardless of whether they fit or not. He said: "Before the fox attacks, the chickens get bold." He said: "The peasant only washes his wife when the landlord wants to sleep with her." He said: "Lamenting comes before the gallows." He said: "Even a rich peasant can fall into the cesspit," and he said: "The ploughboy beds the peasant's wife, the peasant beds the maid." Then he turned his attention to the seriousness of the situation, by which he did not mean the domestic situation—that would have been foolish, as Minister of Heavy Industry he was much too enmeshed in domestic policy—but the seriousness of the international situation, where he sensed "a mortal threat to our precious fatherland" gathering on the horizon—all the more startling as, after the peace conference, international relations had become more relaxed than usual. International monopoly capitalism, he said, was preparing once again to rob the Revolution of its fruits, and had already succeeded in infesting the country with its agents. From the international arena he moved on to the need for discipline, and from the need for discipline he deduced the need for trust. "Comrades, we are all brothers, children of the one, great Revolution!" Then he claimed that this necessary trust had been needlessly violated by L, who had doubted A's words by professing to believe, against A's assurances, that the indisposed O had been arrested; indeed the Transportation Minister, "this monument that has long since become a shrine of infamy," was so mistrustful that he did not even dare to leave the conference room to assist his dying wife, an act of inhumanity that must horrify every revolutionary for whom marriage was still sacred, and who in this great land did not feel this way. Such suspicion, he said, was an insult not only to A, it was also a slap in the face of the Political Secretariat. (N wondered: A had said nothing about O's supposed illness. This lie had originated with Security Minister C. By attributing the lie to A, F was pushing A into a corner, a further mistake that was only explainable by the Minister of Heavy Industry's abject fear—but at the same time N suspected that perhaps O's sickness was the truth and his arrest a lie, disseminated in order to confuse the Political Secretariat, a suspicion that N, however, immediately dropped.) The Bootblack meanwhile, swept along by his own reckless rush for safety, lashed out at his old enemy D, perhaps on the assumption that once Transportation Minister L was overthrown, Party Secretary D would automatically follow, without considering that everyone had long since written off the Transportation Minister, while D was in a position from which he could not be removed without convulsing the Party and with it the state. But for F, this convulsion was apparently already a fact, otherwise he would have noticed that during his attack even Defense Minister H remained quiet and did not support him. The Bootblack shouted, "When peasants starve, the preachers batten," shouted, "When the landlord's feet get cold, he burns down a village," claimed that D was betraying the Revolution by allowing it to fall asleep, that he had allowed the Party to turn into a social club. In his desperate exaltation, F went even further. From D, he went on to attack D's allies, starting with the Minister of Education, "A virgin entering the horse trader's house will leave it as a whore, that's an old peasant proverb," and as for Foreign Minister B, "He who befriends a mangy wolf turns into a mangy wolf himself"; but before F could cite another peasant proverb and before he was able to specify his accusations, he was interrupted by the colonel. To the astonishment of everyone in the room, the blond officer entered the conference room a second time, saluted, handed the Minister of Heavy Industry a piece of paper, saluted smartly again and left the conference room.

F, startled by the interruption and intimidated by the military display, became unsure of himself, scanned the piece of paper, crumpled it, stuffed it into his right side pocket, mumbled that he hadn't really meant what he had said, sat down, overcome by a sudden suspicion, N sensed, and fell silent. The others did not move. The colonel's renewed appearance had been too unusual. It seemed to have been orchestrated. There was something menacing about this occurrence. Only M, who had fixed a sharp gaze on F during his speech, acted as if nothing had happened. She opened her pocketbook and powdered herself, something she had previously never dared to do during a meeting. A still said nothing, still did not intervene, still seemed indifferent. B and C, opposite each other and closest to A, looked at each other, quickly and as if accidentally, N noticed, a glance which the Foreign Minister accompanied with a stroke of a finger over his carefully trimmed moustache. The head of the Secret Police adjusted his silk tie and coolly asked whether F was done with his nonsense, the Secretariat had some work to do. N wondered once again whether B and C might not be secret allies. They were considered enemies, but they had a lot in common: their education, their superiority, their descent from two of the most famous families in the country. C's father had been a minister in a bourgeois government, and B was the illegitimate son of an aristocrat; and there were some who considered him homosexual, like C. The possibility of a secret agreement between the two reoccurred to N for another reason as well: by rebuking the Minister of Heavy Industry, C was evidently supporting B, and not only the Foreign Minister but also D and M and even L were supported by him. F, bewildered by this defeat, especially since he had evidently counted on C's approval, replied meekly that he had to make a call to the Ministry, it was urgent and he was very sorry but some unfortunate matter required a decision on his part. A stood up. He walked nonchalantly to the buffet behind him, poured himself a cognac, remained standing. He said F could make his call in the hallway and L should get a move on and at least call the hospital. He, A, was ordering a five-minute recess to the meeting, for after these silly and purely personal attacks, Party discipline required that the meeting be brought to a proper close, but after that he wanted to be left undisturbed, and who the hell was this idiot colonel. "A substitute," replied the head of the Secret Police, the old colonel was on vacation, but he, C, would instruct him again. He summoned the colonel through the intercom. The colonel entered again with a salute, and C ordered him not to show his face in the conference room again, no matter what. The colonel withdrew. Neither F nor L left the room, they remained seated as if nothing had happened. D grinned at the Minister of Heavy Industry, stood up, joined A at the buffet and poured himself a cognac as well, asked what was going on, why wouldn't F go to the hallway, damn it, if the Ministry for Heavy Industry sees fit to disrupt a meeting of the Political Secretariat, all hell must have broken loose there; his friend F's concern for the welfare of the state and the Revolution was commendable, but that very concern should impel him now to attend to his duty and get in touch with his Ministry right away, because a setback in Heavy Industry would be to no one's advantage.

N reflected. The most important moment, it seemed to him, was A's sudden decision to continue the meeting of the Political Secretariat. The reference to Party discipline was bromide, everyone must have been aware of that. There had never been a vote before, only silent consent, the two opposing groups within the Political Secretariat had been too evenly balanced for either side to risk open confrontation. Besides, A always had the option of bringing the matter before the Party Congress and thus publicly liquidating the unpopular Political Secretariat. A's decision must have had another reason. He must have realized that he had made a mistake when he tried to purge and dissolve the Political Secretariat at the same time. He should have purged it first and then dissolved it, or dissolved it first and then purged the individual members one by one. Now he was faced with an opposition. O's arrest had been a premature warning to the others, L's and F's refusing to leave the room were signs that all of them were afraid. At the Party Congress, A was free and all-powerful, but within the Political Secretariat he was, like all the other members, a prisoner of the system. While A, who did not know fear, inspired fear in the others, he had to be suspicious. Convening the Party Congress would take time, and during this time the members of the Political Secretariat would remain powerful and capable of action. Therefore A, too, had to act. He had to sound out the others, find out who he could count on, and then fight. A's sovereign contempt for humanity had not only brought the opposing fronts into disorder. A minor skirmish was unexpectedly threatening to turn into a decisive battle.

For the moment, nothing was happening. No one acted. F remained seated, the Transportation Minister likewise, his face buried in his hands. N would have liked to wipe the perspiration from his face, but he did not dare. P next to him had folded his hands. He seemed to be praying that he would come out of this unscathed, even though it was rather improbable that a member of the Political Secretariat would pray. Minister of Foreign Trade E lit one of his American cigarettes. Defense Minister H stood up, went to the buffet, staggering slightly, found a bottle of gin, planted himself next to A and B, solemnly raised a toast to A: "Long live the Revolution," and began to hiccup, without noticing, in his stupor, that A was ignoring him. M removed a golden cigarette case from her pocketbook, D stepped up to her, ignited his golden lighter and held it out to her, and remained standing behind her. "Well, you two," A asked casually, "do you actually sleep together?"—"We used to," D replied, unabashed. A laughed: "I like it when members of my staff get along." Then he turned to F. "Go ahead, Bootblack," he commanded. "Move, ass-kisser, make your phone call!" F remained seated. "Not out there," he said softly. A laughed again. He always laughed in the same slow, almost comfortable way, no matter whether he was joking or threatening; it was impossible to tell which way he meant it. "I really think this guy's got the jitters," he remarked. "That's right," F replied. "I have the jitters, I'm afraid." All the others silently stared at F; it was a tremendous thing, admitting one's fear. "We are all afraid," the Minister of Heavy Industry continued, gazing calmly at A, "not just me and the Transportation Minister, all of us." "Nonsense," said Chief Ideologue G, stood up and went to the window. "Nonsense, pure nonsense," he said again, with his back turned to the others. "In that case, leave the room," F challenged him. The Chief Ideologue turned around and stared at F suspiciously. "Why should I go out?" he asked. "The Chief Ideologue," F noted serenely, "does not dare leave the room either. G knows very well that he's only safe in here." "Nonsense," G retorted once again. "Nonsense, pure nonsense." F persisted: "Then leave the room," he challenged the Tea Saint again. G remained standing by the window. F turned back to A: "You see, we all have the jitters." He was sitting upright in his chair, with his hands on the table. All the ugliness had left his face. "F is a fool," said A, putting his glass of cognac back on the buffet, and came to the table. "A fool?" F replied. "Really? Are you that sure?" He was speaking quietly, which he normally never did. Except for L, he said, there were no old revolutionaries left in the Political Secretariat, where were they? Then he recited the names of those who had been liquidated, carefully, slowly, without forgetting to include their first names, men who had once been famous, who had toppled the old order. It was the first time in many years that these names were mentioned. N shuddered. He suddenly felt as if he were in a cemetery. "Traitors," A shouted, "those were traitors, you know that very well, you damned ass-kisser." He fell silent, calmed down, studied the Bootblack thoughtfully. "And you, by the way, are the same sort of swine," he added. N realized immediately that A had made a further mistake. Naturally it had been a provocation to recite the old revolutionaries' names, but by admitting his fear, F had become an adversary A should have taken seriously. Instead, A had allowed himself to be drawn into threatening F, instead of appeasing him. It would have taken no more than a friendly word or a joke to bring F back to reason, but A despised F, and because he despised him, he saw no danger and became careless. For F, on the other hand, there was no way back. In his desperation, he had risked everything and was showing character, to everyone's surprise. He was forced to fight and had become the natural ally of the Transportation Minister—who, however, was too apathetic to realize it. "He who opposes the Revolution will be crushed," A proclaimed. "All who have tried to so far have been crushed." Had they really tried to do that, the Bootblack asked, unperturbed: surely A himself did not believe this? Those men whose names he had recited, and who were dead, had founded the Party and carried out the Revolution. They had made many mistakes, without a doubt, but they had not been traitors any more than the Minister of Transportation was now a traitor. "They confessed," A replied, "and were sentenced by a court of law." "Confessed!" F laughed. "Confessed! How they confessed. I'm sure the head of the Secret Police can tell a story about that!" A became malicious. The Revolution, he replied, is a bloody business, within her ranks there are guilty individuals, and woe to the guilty.

Anyone doubting this axiom, he said, was already a traitor himself. And besides, he jeered, there was no point in discussing this, those dirty books the Bootblack distributed among his colleagues had evidently gone to his head, which was why he mistook the Party for a whorehouse, and F's friend, Chief Ideologue G, ought really to consider carefully the sort of company he kept. With this impulsive and unnecessary threat toward the Tea Saint—perhaps because he was annoyed at the Chief Ideologue for not daring to leave the room either—A sat down. Those who were still standing sat down likewise. G was the last to return to his seat. "The meeting is reopened," A said.

The Tea Saint avenged himself immediately. Perhaps because he believed that he had fallen into disfavor along with F, perhaps only because he was insulted by A's incautious rebuke. Like many critics, he could not take criticism. Already as a high school teacher, the Tea Saint had published book reviews in insignificant provincial journals, articles of such acid and rancorous partisanship that at the beginning of the second great purge, A, who despised most of the country's writers as bourgeois intellectuals, had summoned him to the capital, where G became cultural editor of the government newspaper and within a short time and with tremendous industry, always in accord with official doctrine, managed to wreck the country's literature and theater by holding up the classics as being healthy and positive while denouncing contemporary writers for being sick and negative: and primitive though the basic premise of his criticism was, the form in which he presented it was intellectual and logical; in short, the Tea Saint wrote a more confounding prose than his literary and political enemies. He was all-powerful. Anyone receiving a negative review from G was done for, and would not infrequently end up behind barbed wire or disappear altogether. On a personal level, G's probity was unsurpassed. He was happily married, a fact he was always advertising ad nauseam, and had fathered eight sons at regular intervals. He was hated in the Party, but the great practitioner A, who fancied himself a theoretician, installed him in an even more powerful position. He made him the Party's ideological father confessor. At the Political Secretariat, therefore, there was no escaping G's rambling lectures, although a few members openly scoffed at them, B for example, who remarked one day, after the Tea Saint had spent an inordinately long time pontificating about foreign policy, that while it was the Chief Ideologue's job to justify motions passed by the Political Secretariat and present them to the outside world as politically impeccable acts, he could not very well expect the

Political Secretariat to believe these justifications as well. But one was well advised not to underestimate G. The Tea Saint was the kind of man who lives by and for power, and he would defend his position by any means at his disposal, as A was now forced to realize, for G was the first to raise his hand. He thanked A for his observations at the beginning of the meeting, which bore the mark of a great statesman. His analysis of the state of the Revolution and of the country had been masterful, he said, and his conclusion—that at this stage of development the Political Secretariat must be dissolved—was irrefutable. As an ideologue, G had only one further remark to make. As A had pointed out, they were all facing a certain conflict, consisting of the fact that not only was there a contradiction between the Revolution and the state, but actually between the Revolution and the Party as well. Revolution and Party were not the same thing, as some people supposed. Revolution, he said, was a dynamic process, while the Party was a comparatively static structure. The Revolution's role was to transform society, the Party's to install the transformed society within the state. The Party, therefore, was both the agent of Revolution and the agent of state power. This inner contradiction, he said, tempted the Party to lean more toward the state than toward the Revolution, and forced the Revolution to revolutionize the Party again and again; the fire of revolution was virtually fueled by the human insufficiency that was inherent in the Party as a static structure. That was why the Revolution had to devour especially those who had become enemies of the Revolution in the name of the Party. The men cited by the Minister of Heavy Industry had originally been genuine revolutionaries, certainly, who would deny that, but due to their error of considering the Revolution to be a settled matter, they had became enemies of the Revolution and had to be destroyed as such. This, he went on, was still the case today: since the Political Secretariat had effectively seized state power, the Party had become insignificant and could no longer be the agent of the Revolution; but neither was the Political Secretariat capable of carrying out this function, for the Secretariat had a relationship with power and only with power, and no longer had any relationship with the Revolution. The Political Secretariat was self-encapsulated, he said, shut off from the Revolution, more concerned with preserving its power than with changing the world, because all power tends to stabilize the state it governs and the party it controls. If the Revolution was to continue, therefore, the struggle against the Political Secretariat was unavoidable. The Political Secretariat had to recognize this necessity and resolve to liquidate itself. "A true revolutionary liquidates himself," he concluded. "The fear of a purge that has befallen some members of the Political Secretariat is itself the best proof that such a liquidation is necessary and that the Political Secretariat has outlived its usefulness."

G's speech was perfidious. The Tea Saint's delivery was, as usual, didactic, humorless, dry. It took N a while to realize how cunningly G was using abstract sentences to rephrase A's intentions in such violent terms that the Political Secretariat would have to rise in its own defense. The Tea Saint depicted the purge they all feared as a necessary process that had already begun. By depicting the downfall of the Old Guard and all the show trials, degradations, and executions as politically justified, he was also justifying the imminent purge. But by doing so, he was placing in the hands of its possible victims the power to decide whether this purge would actually take place, and this conjured up a real threat for A.

One glance at A was enough for N: A had recognized the trap G had lured him into. But before A was able to intervene, an unexpected interruption occurred. The Minister of Education, M, who sat next to President K, jumped up and screamed that Marshal K was a pig. N, too, who was sitting diagonally across from M, felt that his feet were standing in a puddle. The head of state, old and sick, had passed water. The corpulent Gin-gis Khan became aggressive, yelled, "What's it to you!" and called M a prissy bitch, yelling, "You think I'd go out for a piss like an idiot and get arrested?" No, he would not leave this room again, he was an old revolutionary, he had fought and won for his Party, his son had died in the civil war and his son-in-law and all his old friends had been betrayed by A and put to death, even though they, like himself, had been honest and convinced revolutionaries, and that was why he would empty his bladder whenever and wherever he wanted.

A's impetuous reaction following this embarrassing and grotesque incident surprised N less by its passion than by the apparent heedlessness of A's attack; as if A wasn't interested in attacking anyone in particular, but just in attacking someone, anyone. For his fury was leveled, incomprehensibly, not at F, G, or K, but at C, to whom he owed more than to anyone else, for how could A have ruled without the head of the Secret Police? Nevertheless he suddenly accused C of arresting O without A's knowledge, and ordered him to rehabilitate the Minister of Nuclear Energy, if that was still possible. Probably, he shouted, O had already been shot; wasn't that C's usual method? A went even further. He challenged the head of the Secret Police to resign. An investigation of his deviant tendencies was long overdue. "I will arrest you on the spot," A raged, and roared through the intercom, summoning the colonel. Dead silence. C remained calm. Everyone waited. Minutes passed. The colonel did not come. "Why is the colonel not coming?" A barked at C. "Because we instructed him not to come back here no matter what," the head of the Secret Police calmly replied, and tore the wire of the intercom out of the wall. "Damn," A replied, just as calmly. "You checkmated yourself, A," remarked Foreign Minister B, pulling down the sleeves of his finely tailored jacket; "that colonel's orders came from you." "Damn," A murmured again. Then he knocked out his pipe once again, even though it was still burning, pulled another one out of his pocket, a curved Dunhill, stuffed it and lit it. "Forgive me, C," he said. "That's quite all right," said the Governess, smiling, and N knew that A was finished. It was as if a tiger, accustomed to fighting in the jungle, suddenly found itself on a prairie surrounded by a herd of raging buffalos. A had no weapons left. He was helpless. For the first time, N saw him no longer as a mystery, a superhuman genius, but as a ruler who was nothing but the product of his political environment. This product of power was hidden behind the image of the paternal peasant colossus that was exhibited in every shop window and hung in every office and appeared in every weekly or daily newsreel, that reviewed parades, paid visits to orphanages and old-age homes, inaugurated factories and dams, embraced statesmen, and distributed medals. For the people, he was a patriotic symbol, an emblem of the independence and greatness of the fatherland. He represented the Party's omnipotence, he was the wise and strict father of the people, whose writings (which he had never written) were read by all and memorized by all, who was referred to in every speech that was held and every article that was written; but in reality he was unknown. The people projected all the virtues onto A; this made him impersonal. By turning him into an idol, they had given him limitless license, and he took license without limit. But circumstances had changed. The men who had made the Revolution had been individualists, precisely because they fought against individualism. The indignation that drove them and the hope that inspired them were genuine and presupposed the presence of revolutionary individualities; revolutionaries are not functionaries, they try to become that and fail. Those men were absconded priests, alcoholic economists, fanatical vegetarians, expelled students, lawyers gone incognito, fired journalists, they lived in hiding, were persecuted and thrown in jail, organized strikes, sabotages and murders, wrote leaflets and secret pamphlets, made tactical alliances with their opponents and broke them again, but as soon as they had won, the Revolution established a new social order and with it a new state whose power was incomparably greater than that of the old order and the old state. Their revolt was swallowed up by the new bureaucracy, the Revolution resolved itself into an organizational problem, an insuperable challenge to the revolutionaries *because* they were revolutionaries. Faced with the men who were needed now, they were helpless. They were no match for the technocrats: but their failure was also A's opportunity. To the degree that the state was overrun by bureaucracy, the Revolution had to be preserved as a fiction; no people on earth are inspired by an administrative apparatus, especially since the Party, too, had fallen prey to bureaucracy. In A, the impersonal machinery of power was given a face, but the big boss was not content with mere representation, he began to destroy the revolutionaries in the name of the Revolution. Thus the entire old guard—with the exception of President K and L—were caught in the wheels, but not only the heroes of the Revolution, even those who had risen to power after them, members of the Political Secretariat, were eventually liquidated. Not even Secret Police chiefs, indispensable agents for A's purges, were exempt, they, too, were executed. That was precisely why A was popular. The people were leading a pitiful existence, often lacking the bare necessities. Their clothes, their shoes were often of the poorest quality, their old apartments were falling apart, and their newly constructed dwellings likewise. There were queues outside the grocery stores. Everyday life was gray. The functionaries of the Party, on the other hand, enjoyed privileges that gave rise to fantastic rumors. They had villas, cars, chauffeurs, shopped at stores to which only they had access and where every sort of luxury goods could be gotten. They lacked only one thing, security. Being powerful was dangerous. While the people in general remained undisturbed, since, in their apathy and impotence, they had nothing to lose, the privileged lived in fear of losing everything, because they had everything. The people saw the powerful rise through the grace of A and fall by the wrath of A. In the bloody spectacle of politics, the people took part as spectators. A powerful man was never made to fall without a public tribunal, without a sublime spectacle, without a display of justice in pomp and ceremony, without solemn admissions of guilt on the part of the accused. For the masses, these were criminals; it was their fault that the people were poor, not the state's, and the downfall of these saboteurs and traitors awakened new hope in the better future that was always being promised, gave rise to the illusion that the Revolution was still advancing, wisely steered by the great, kind, wise, and yet constantly cheated and betrayed statesman A.

For the first time, N saw how A ran his political machine, with its seemingly complicated levers and gears. In reality the machine was as simple as could be. A was only able to maintain his tyranny as long as the members of the Political Secretariat were battling among themselves. This battle was, for A, the precondition for his power. It was fear alone that drove each member to secure A's favor by denouncing others. Thus factions that wanted to stay in power, like the one surrounding D, were always opposed by coalitions like the one around G, which wanted to drive the Revolution forward, while A's ideological position was so ambiguous that both sides believed they were acting in his name. A's tactic was brutal, but this very brutality had gradually made him careless. He only played the revolutionary when it was to his advantage, the only thing that interested him was his power, he ruled by dividing all the others, but he believed himself to be safe. He forgot that in the Political Secretariat he was no longer dealing with convinced revolutionaries, who would often declare themselves guilty in the show trials because they would rather lose their lives than their faith in the meaning of the Revolution. He forgot that he had surrounded himself with power-hungry men for whom the ideology of the Party was no longer anything but an instrument to advance their careers. He forgot that he had isolated himself, for fear does not only divide. Fear also bonds, a law that now became A's nemesis. He had suddenly become as helpless as an amateur faced with professional wielders of power. By trying to dissolve the Political Secretariat in order to increase his power, he had threatened all of them, and by attacking his Minister of Security and accusing him of having arrested O, he had made a new enemy. A had lost the instinct with which he had ruled, the machinery of his dominion was turning against him. His excessiveness, too, was avenging itself, and with it events that could not be avenged until now, because only now had the hour of vengeance arrived. A was capricious. He exercised power in a meaningless fashion, he issued orders that had to be insulting, his wishes were grotesque and barbaric, they were expressions of his contempt for humanity, but also of his savage sense of humor. He liked to play practical jokes, but no one enjoyed them, everyone was afraid of them and regarded these amusements as nothing but insidious traps. Inadvertently, N thought of an incident that must have insulted D, the mighty Party Secretary. N had always imagined that D would retaliate some day. D never forgot a humiliation and was able to wait. The opportunity for vengeance appeared to have come. The affair had been scurrilous and bizarre. A had given the Warthog a surprising assignment: to find a group of women musicians who would play Schubert's octet naked in front of A. Snorting with rage at this idiotic command, and too cowardly to refuse it, D had to appeal to the Minister of Education and Culture, whereupon the Party Muse, just as outraged and just as cowardly, turned to the conservatories and musical colleges; the girls had to be not only musically adept, but also well built. Nervous breakdowns and catastrophes ensued, screaming fits and raving frenzies. One of the most gifted cellists committed suicide, others fought for the opportunity but were too ugly; finally seven musicians had been recruited, only a bassoonist had yet to be found. The Warthog and the Party Muse consulted the Governess. Without further ado, C had a beautiful hooker with a sumptuous behind transferred from a house of correction to a state conservatory, the magnificent creature was completely devoid of musical talent, but by an inhuman regimen of conditioning and drill she was taught how to play the necessary bassoon parts. The other girls also practiced for dear life. Finally they were sitting naked in the ice-cold auditorium of the Philharmonic, with their instruments pressed to their bodies. In the first row of the orchestra sat D and M, dressed in fur coats, stone-faced, waiting for A, but he did not come. Instead, hundreds of deaf-mutes filled the baroque auditorium, gaping, avid and dumbfounded, at the desperately fiddling and tooting naked girls. A, thereupon, at the next meeting of the Political Secretariat, laughed uproariously and called D and M fools for carrying out such an order.

D's hour had come. A's downfall was accomplished in a sober, pragmatic, effortless way, bureaucratically, as it were. The Warthog gave an order to lock the doors. The Monument ponderously rose to his feet, locked the door behind the Bootblack and the younger Gin-gis Khan and then the door behind the Tea Saint and the Ballerina. Then he tossed the keys on the table between the Warthog and Lord Evergreen. The Monument sat down again. Several members of the Political Secretariat who had leaped up—as if they wanted to step in the Monument's way but didn't dare to—also sat down again. All of them were seated, with their attaché cases on the table before them. A shifted his gaze from one to the next, drawing on his pipe. He had given up the game. "The meeting continues," said the Warthog. It would be interesting, he said, to learn who it was that actually had O arrested. The Governess replied that it could only have been A, since O was not on the list, and he as chief of the Secret Police could see no reason to arrest O, who after all was nothing but an absentminded scientist. O had professional competence in his ministry, he said, and a modern country needed scientists more than it needed ideologues. Even the Tea Saint must be realizing this by now. The only one who never understood this was evidently A. The Tea Saint did not move a muscle. "The list!" he requested matter-of-factly; "it will provide some clarity." The Governess opened his attaché case. He handed a sheet of paper to Lord Evergreen, who perused it briefly and then pushed it over to the Tea Saint. The Tea Saint grew pale. "I am on the list," he murmured softly, "I am on the list. I, who have always been a revolutionary, always faithful to the Party line. I am on the list," and then the Tea Saint suddenly cried out: "I stuck closer to the line than any of you, and now I'm up for liquidation. Like a traitor!" "I guess the line got crooked," D remarked dryly. The Tea Saint gave the list to the Ballerina, who, since his name was evidently not on it, immediately passed it on to the Monument. The Monument stared at the list, read and reread it, and finally howled: "I'm not on the list, I'm not on the list. He doesn't even want to liquidate me, the swine, me, the old revolutionary!" N scanned the list. His name was not on it. He handed it on to the head of the youth organizations. The pale devotee stood up, bewildered, like a student taking an oral exam, polishing his glasses. "I have been nominated Prosecutor General," he stammered. Everyone burst out laughing. "Sit down, kid," the Warthog said good-naturedly, and the Bootblack added that they wouldn't eat the boy scout alive. P sat down again and with a quivering hand reached across the table to give the sheet to the Party Muse. "I'm on it," she said, shoving the list toward the older Gin-gis Khan, who, whoever, was dozing, so that the younger one took it instead. "Marshal K is not on it," he said, "but I am," and gave the sheet to the Bootblack. "Me, too," said the Bootblack, and so did the Warthog. The last to receive the list was the Eunuch. "I'm not on it," said the Foreign Minister and shoved the list back to the Governess. The head of the Secret Police carefully folded the paper and locked it inside his attaché case. It was a fact then, Lord Evergreen confirmed, that O was not on the list. In that case, why was he arrested by A, the Ballerina wondered out loud, with a suspicious glance at the Governess. The Governess replied that he had no idea; his notion, earlier, that the Nuclear Minister had fallen ill had just been an assumption, but A tended to act at his own discretion. "I did not have O arrested," A said. "Spare us your fairy tales," the younger Gin-gis Khan snarled at him; "if you hadn't, he'd be here." Everyone fell silent. A calmly puffed at his Dunhill. "We can't turn back," the Party Muse said dryly, "the list is a fact." It had only been drawn up for an emergency, A explained, without defending himself. He was smoking placidly, as though his life were not at stake, and added that the list was drawn up for the eventuality that the Political Secretariat would resist its self-dissolution. "That eventuality is now the case," the Tea Saint dryly retorted. "The Secretariat is resisting." The Eunuch laughed. The Bootblack supplied a peasant proverb: "Lightning strikes even the rich peasant's barn." The Warthog asked if anyone wanted to volunteer. Everyone looked at the Monument. The Monument stood up. "You expect me to kill the guy," he said. "All you have to do is string him up from the window," the Warthog replied. "I'm not a hangman like the rest of you," the Monument replied, "I am an honest blacksmith and I'll settle this in my way." The Monument took his chair and placed it between the end of the table, where no one was seated, and the window. "Come, A!" the Monument calmly commanded. A rose to his feet. He looked relaxed and sure of himself, as always. As he walked toward the opposite end of the table, he found the Tea Saint in his way, who had leaned his chair back against the door behind him. "Excuse me!" A said, "I believe I have to step through here." The Tea Saint moved his chair up to the table and let A pass. A reached the Monument. "Sit down," the Monument said. A obeyed. "Give me your belt, President," the Monument commanded. Gin-gis Khan the elder mechanically obeyed the order without the slightest notion of what the Monument intended to do. The others silently stared into space, not even watching. N thought of the last official ceremony at which the Political Secretariat had shown itself in public. In the middle of winter. They were burying "The Incorruptible," one of the last great revolutionaries. The Incorruptible had assumed the office of Party boss after the Monument's fall. Then he had fallen into disfavor. The Warthog had displaced him. But A had not put Old Incorruptible on trial like the others. His fall was crueler. A had him declared insane and committed to a lunatic asylum where the doctors let him while away his years in a twilit stupor before he was allowed to die. The state funeral was all the more solemn. The Political Secretariat, with the exception of the Party Muse, carried the coffin, covered with the Party flag, on their shoulders through the state cemetery past snow-covered, kitschy marble statues and tombstones. The twelve mightiest men in the Party and in the country stomped through the snow. Even the Tea Saint was wearing boots. A and the Eunuch were carrying the front of the bier on their shoulders, while N and the Monument supported the end, behind all the others. The snow was falling in large flakes from a white sky. The functionaries stood crowded together between the tombs and around the open grave wearing long coats and warm fur hats. As the coffin was being lowered into the grave to the sounds of the Party hymn, played by a freezing military band, the Monument whispered: "Damn it, I'm next." Now it turned out that he wasn't next. A was. N raised his eyes. The Monument was strapping the elder Gin-gis Khan's belt around A's neck. "Ready?" the Monument asked. "Just three more puffs," A replied. Calmly he drew and exhaled three more puffs of smoke, then he laid the curved Dunhill on the table before him. "Ready," he said. The Monument pulled the belt tight. A uttered no sound, though his body arched and his arms made several vague, waving motions, but then he sat motionless, his head pulled back by the Monument, his mouth wide open: the Monument had pulled the strap with tremendous force. A's eyes became rigid. The older Gin-gis Khan passed water again; it didn't bother anyone. "Down with the enemies within the Party, long live our great statesman A!"

cried Marshal H. Five minutes passed, only then did the Monument loosen his grip, place the elder Gin-gis Khan's belt next to the Dunhill pipe on the table, return to his seat, and sit down. A sat dead in his chair in front of the window, his face turned to the ceiling, with dangling arms. The others stared at him in silence. Lord Evergreen lit an American cigarette, then a second one, then a third. They all waited for about a quarter of an hour.

Someone tried to open the door between F and H from outside. D stood up, went to A, observed him carefully, touched his face with his fingers. "He's dead," said D. "E, give me the key." The Minister of Foreign Trade obeyed without a word, then D opened the door. At the threshold stood Nuclear Minister O. He apologized for being late. He had mistaken the date. Then he wanted to go to his seat. In his haste, he dropped his attaché case, and only then, as he picked it up, did O notice A's strangled body and stop, frozen in his tracks. "I am the new chairman," D said and called in the colonel through the open door. The colonel saluted, his face perfectly immobile. D ordered him to remove A. The colonel came back with two soldiers, and the chair was empty again. D locked the door. Everyone was standing. "The meeting of the Political Secretariat will continue," D said. "Let us determine the new seating arrangements." He sat down in A's seat. B and C sat down to his right and left. F sat down next to B, and E next to C. M sat down next to F. Then D looked at N and made a gesture of invitation. Shuddering, N sat down next to E: he had become the seventh most powerful man in the country. Outside, it was beginning to snow.

	D	
B		C
F		E
M		N
H		G
K		J
O		L
		P

Smithy

His problems started in the morning already, they were unexpected and they depressed him all the more as J. G. Smith—he had finally settled on this name after many others—had been feeling, not exactly that he had made it, but financially secure; his income had reached a level a person could live on, just about, the authorities tolerated him, not officially, but more or less; which made Leibnitz's waffling all the more idiotic. Of course Leibnitz could be replaced, by any medical student with some training in dissection; but J. G. Smith just happened to be attached to Leibnitz, God knows the man made a decent living, and even though Leibnitz had obtained a permit—it had been granted just that morning—to open a medical practice again, surely he must realize that this permit was no longer of any use to him now, not because of his earlier lapses—abortions and the like—but because Leibnitz had been working for J. G. Smith for nearly four years now, too long for him to pull out at this point; it wasn't exactly pleasant, having to rub it in, but finally Leibnitz had caught on, and he understood, too, that he wouldn't be getting a raise, Smith was implacable on this account, you don't threaten to give notice, not to Smith anyway, an attitude that Smith naturally couldn't assume toward the new cop on the beat, he was out for dough and he got it, there were natural laws you couldn't do anything about. "Look here, Smithy," the new guy had said right at the start of the discussion, picking his teeth—they were standing on the corner of Lexington and Fifty-Second Street, opposite a City Bank construction site—"Look here, Smithy, sure, the guy before me had four kids, and I'm a bachelor, but I just happen to have higher expectations of life," and when Smithy vaguely threatened to turn to the Port Authority commissioner, who, after all, tolerated him too, who, when you got right down to it, was his friend, all the cop said was, well, in that case the whole thing blows up. Problems, nothing but problems. And then the heat, it was just May third, you'd think it was the middle of summer, Smithy was sweating continuously, he'd been sweating already when Leibnitz showed up with his demands, everything was wavering in the heat, Brooklyn was almost invisible, Smithy could no longer afford to use air-conditioning, you could smell the corpses, the super didn't care, and Smithy's apartment was somewhere else, and he could always be reached by telephone at Simpson's, also Leibnitz was used to it all, but still it was embarrassing, once in a while a customer would lose his way and show up in the dissecting room instead of sitting down at the counter at Simpson's, and besides Leibnitz couldn't always keep the bodies stored in the freezing chamber, he had to drag them up into the dissecting room before he got to work; all things considered, Smithy thought, the business ought to be disguised as a laboratory, as something technical, super-clean, with white tiles—the present setup under the Triborough Bridge had an unsavory air. Sure, there were some advantages he could appreciate: being near the East River, mainly. Smithy cursed; there was no time to go home, shower, change his shirt. And on top of the heat, the stink. Not the smell of corpses in the morning, that smell was part of his profession and didn't bother him any more than a tanner minds the smell of leather, no, it was the smell of the city that was driving him crazy, this smell that he hated and that clung to everything, scalding hot and sticky, clogged with countless dust and coal molecules, tiny particles of oil, inseparable from the pavement, the fronts of buildings, the steaming streets. He was drinking. He'd already been drinking during his talk with Leibnitz. Gin. He'd gone to Belmont's drugstore with the new cop. Two Schlitz. Later he drank bourbon with the Port Authority commissioner somewhere on Fiftieth. The Port Authority commissioner drank beer, ate two steaks, Smithy didn't touch his steak, the chief of police, who showed up later, as the Port Authority commissioner had promised, was a disgusting intellectual, didn't look like a cop at all, some kind of egghead who had wangled his way upstairs through his faggot connections, Smithy imagined, the battle lines were getting more and more fuzzy, that gangster recently, the one for whom Smithy got rid of the millionaire's daughter, another fag, he'd been a priest once. Still running around like that. But maybe the chief of police wasn't a fag at all, that horny look he'd given the waitress, maybe he was a communist. He knew about the priest, it was he who had referred him to Smithy, not the Port Authority commissioner, as Smithy had thought at first. Now Smithy had to pay the chief of police for the millionaire's daughter, after he'd already paid the Port Authority commissioner, a goddamn losing proposition. Smithy drained his glass of bourbon. He really should have gone to Simpson's, but the chief of police started running at the mouth. The guy could afford to blab, time was no object to him, and to top it all off, this stinking heat despite the air-conditioning: it was better, he said, if the Emergency Medical Services handled the whole thing, in secret of course, even Holy (the priest) thought it was too risky to leave this matter to a private individual like Smithy, he said, and the priest was the new secret boss in the precinct. Smithy went back to drinking gin. He still left his steak untouched, the chief of police kept yakking: the old way of fighting crime had become ineffective, he said, these days the government had to live with crime; ever since he'd come to an understanding with Holy, the crime rate had gone down, it was tolerance that made the difference, he said, and Smithy should get it into his head that his constant maneuvering between the legal and the illegal camp was over, because legality, while it hadn't eradicated illegality, was definitely steering it; otherwise, if Smithy refused to listen to reason, the EMS would be brought in, and if worse came to worst, the Port Authority Police, even though they might object on hygienic grounds. Smithy ordered a coffee, took three lumps of sugar, stirred the coffee. "How much?" "Half of each case," said the chief of police, took off his rimless glasses, breathed on them, polished them, put them on again, and scrutinized Smithy like a scientist examining a louse. The Port Authority commissioner was picking his teeth, just like the cop opposite the City Bank. The chief of police took off his glasses again, polished them once more. The sight of Smithy disgusted him. He couldn't work at this rate, Smithy said, he had to pay Leibnitz twice that amount, the son of a bitch had become a legitimate doctor again. All right, the chief of police said after ordering another coffee, he would talk to the EMS. Smithy ordered another gin. "Sorry, Smithy," the Port Authority commissioner said. Smithy gave in, hoping that he would be able to come to terms with Holy somewhere behind the back of the police—there were always deals that the chief of police wasn't supposed to know about, just like there were deals that weren't any of Holy's business—and ordered another Schlitz. But when close to midnight he went to Tommy's French restaurant (why it was supposed to be a French restaurant no one knew) and had himself a steak and french fries after all, it wasn't Holy who sat down next to him but van der Seelen, who liked to pass himself off as Polish or Russian, whichever was convenient, but was probably Italian or Greek with a completely different name; although some people claimed he was actually Dutch, with a name that wasn't van der Seelen but whatever the word for "cheese" was in Danish; in any case, he had swum over here a couple of years ago, a half-dead immigrant from goddamn Europe, which turns out all these rats—the president ought to do something about that—and now he was all spiffed up in a damned expensive suit, silk, reeking of perfume, smoking a Havana, Monte Christo. Holy was unfortunately held up, van der Seelen said. "On business?" Smithy asked, who didn't care one way or the other. He was annoyed that he had to make a deal with Holy. "You might say so," van der Seelen replied, ordered a lobster salad, and said Holy was probably already in Smithy's freezing chamber or maybe even on Leibnitz's dissection table. "Too bad about the fag," Smithy said deploringly, resting a thoughtful gaze on van der Seelen and promising himself to find out what the Danish word for "cheese" was, there was a Swedish cop on the beat under the Triborough Bridge, and then he wondered whether the Chief of Police already knew that someone other than Holy was boss. Van der Seelen gave him a fatherly grin: "There was one too many in the precinct. We'll get along all right, Smithy." Smithy said he'd unfortunately have to up the rate, Leibnitz had gotten more expensive. Van der Seelen shook his head. "I got married, Smithy, last week," he said. "So what?" Smithy asked. His wife had a brother, van der Seelen said, a medical student, but unfortunately he was shooting up, a damned expensive habit. Smithy understood: "Let's stick to the old rate," he suggested. "Ten percent less," van der Seelen replied. "After all, I've got my brother-in-law to support." Smithy's business was in worse shape than ever, and on top of that this murderous heat, it was like diving into hot soup when he stepped out of Tommy's French restaurant. What he really wanted to do was go home, to his three furnished rooms with kitchen and bathroom, horrible furnishings, German, crammed full of unreadable books, an apartment he had taken over from the professor, Leibnitz's predecessor, a stuffy dump, never ventilated, never cleaned, but pure luxury when he remembered the shack in the Bronx he'd lived in for years. Well, if business continued like this with the new partners, he'd be holing up in some basement pretty soon, the chief of police was a communist, obviously, and van der Seelen was a Jew, that was even more obvious, maybe a Dutch Jew whose name was like "cheese" in Danish; the best thing, Smithy thought, was if he beat it right now, just get the hell out of here and open up shop somewhere else, maybe L.A., there would always be a need for a man like Smithy, wherever he went there would always be a need for bodies to disappear. Opposite Tommy's French restaurant there was a little bar. Smithy crossed the street, a car stopped abruptly, slithered, the driver cursed. In the bar, Smithy ordered another gin, the best thing was to get plastered. Through the open door of the bar he saw van der Seelen getting into his Cadillac, next to his driver Sam. Smithy downed the gin and didn't go home after all. Van der Seelen's fat face had made him suddenly sad, he felt sorry for Holy. Smithy blew his nose after telling the taxi driver the name of a street near the Triborough Bridge, Holy had still believed in some kind of justice, he was always talking about God, kind of weird in his line of work, Smithy was sure the fag had secretly recited his rosary, although Smithy had no idea what that was about. The taxi driver was incessantly talking to himself, in Spanish, Smithy was glad when the taxi arrived at the street he had indicated, the taxi driver seemed crazy to him, but the heat was getting to everyone. Smithy had a few more blocks to walk and then down to the East River, he never took a cab directly to where he worked, it was an old habit. The streets, narrow canyons blasted into a meaningless antediluvian landscape, were apparently empty, but on the sidewalks, alongside the walls and on the fire escapes people were lying about and sleeping, half naked and naked, almost impossible to make out in the bad lighting, but present on all sides as a beastly, spongy something; Smithy walked as if through hot, snoring, wet walls. He was sweating, he had had too much to drink. He reached the half-crumbled warehouse. On the fourth floor was Leibnitz's workroom, not exactly practical, but Leibnitz had insisted on these premises, and anyway, what Leibnitz exactly did in that room and how he managed to get rid of the remains—because there had to be some remains, though apparently not much—from the fourth floor to wherever, this was something Smithy had never been able to figure out, maybe it all just dissolved into liquid and got poured into the sewers. Smithy shuddered at the thought that before Leibnitz, the Professor had still done his work in the apartment Smithy was living in now, even though at the time the turnover was low, just one body a month. Smithy had just opened the door, in the vague hope of seeing Holy once again after all—as a corpse, but still—when into this hope, drunk as he was, full of sentimental piety, a voice coming from the street behind him said: "I want to sleep with you." Smithy, with his hand on the knob of the half-open door, on the verge of crossing the threshold, looked back. A woman stood close behind him by the door, visible only as a silhouette, for Smithy had not switched on the light in the lobby. Some kind of hooker, he thought. Smithy was about to slam the door in her face when he was suddenly seized by a wild sense of humor. "Come," he said, groping his way through the dark to the elevator. The woman followed, he could feel her in the incubator heat of the hallway, the elevator was descending. They stood close together, it took a while before the elevator—a freight elevator, old, slow—reached the ground floor, Smithy in his drunkenness forgot the woman. Not until he was leaning against the wall of the brightly lit elevator did he remember that he had brought her along. She was about thirty, slender, with straight dark hair, big eyes, maybe pretty, maybe not, in his drunkenness Smithy couldn't quite put her appearance together, an impression of something classy, something unusual penetrated through his stupor, a somehow unsettling impression, her dress had to be incredibly expensive, and while the figure underneath it was okay, it didn't belong in this environment. As for why that was so, Smithy had no idea, he just felt it, her body just wasn't a hooker's body, and though he had a vague inkling that he shouldn't be letting himself in for this adventure, he started the elevator. The woman stared at him, not mockingly, not anxiously either, just indifferently. Now he figured she was twenty-five, he was used to estimating people's age, part of his job. "How much?" Smithy asked. "For free." Again Smithy was overcome by a devilish sense of humor, she was in for an experience, he imagined her losing her composure, that damned high-class attitude, which suddenly bothered him, he pictured her screaming, racing down the stairs, to the cops maybe, and all they would do was grin. As he imagined this, he grinned at her, but she didn't move a muscle, she just stared him straight in the face. The elevator stopped, Smithy stepped out, opened the door to the dissection room, went in without looking back at the woman. She followed him, stopped in the doorway. Smithy stepped up to the dissecting table, staring at Holy, who was lying there naked and dead, bullet holes in his chest, surprisingly clean, Leibnitz must have washed the body. Over the back of the chair hung Holy's cassock, carefully folded, and Holy's silk underwear, vermilion. "No rosary?" Smithy asked. "This is it," Leibnitz said, "except for that," pointing at the corner next to the window: ammunition belts, guns, a submachine gun, some hand grenades. "It was all hidden under his cassock, it's a miracle he didn't blow up!" Leibnitz let water run into an old bathtub, which Smithy had never seen before. "I don't think he was a priest at all. Just a fag." "Could be," Smithy said, "did you just buy this?" He was looking at the canisters and bottles standing around. "What?" Leibnitz asked. "The tub," Smithy said. It had always been there, Leibnitz replied, rolling the cart with the surgical instruments to the dissecting table. "You don't know any Danish either?" "No," Leibnitz replied. Smithy turned away, disappointed, saw the woman still standing in the door in her expensive dress, casually leaning against the doorpost with her left shoulder. He had forgotten her again and suddenly remembered that he had imagined she would scream and run to the cops. "Beat it," Smithy said in a rage, but he already knew it wouldn't mean a thing. She didn't respond. She had no makeup on, he hair was hanging in long soft strands. Smithy was freezing, it was so hot he suddenly felt ice cold. Then Smithy asked: "Leibnitz, where do you sleep?" without taking his eyes off the woman, who was still leaning against the doorpost. "One floor up," Leibnitz said, already cutting into Holy. Smithy went over to the woman. She said nothing, watched him indifferently. "Get into the elevator," Smithy said. Again they stood facing each other, leaning against the elevator walls, looking at each other for minutes. Smithy closed the gate, through the open door of the dissection room he could see Leibnitz slicing away at Holy's body. Then the elevator went up, stopped. Neither of them moved, Smithy looked at the woman, the woman looked at him as if he were something irrelevant, as if he weren't there at all and yet still there, she wasn't just staring at nothing, she wasn't pretending that she didn't see him, that's what was so crazy. On the contrary, she was watching him, exploring him, touching each pore of his unshaved, sweaty face with her gaze, gliding along each wrinkle, and still he didn't mean a thing to her, she just wanted to be mounted like an animal by another animal. And animals, Smithy thought, probably don't mean a thing to each other either, he thought it in passing as he looked at her, her shoulders, her breasts under the smartly tailored dress, and at the same time Smithy thought of Holy's naked corpse being cut into pieces by Leibnitz one floor down. Cold sweat ran down Smithy's face, he was afraid, he needed something close, soft, warm in the chill of this petrified heat, he violently dragged the woman with him, kicked open the door opposite the elevator, pulled the woman into the room, dimly saw a mattress, threw the woman on it, the only light was the light coming from the elevator through the open door, and after taking the woman, who had let it all happen, he searched for his pants, on all fours, he had thrown them somewhere and they were outside the beam of light coming into the room from the elevator, ridiculous the whole thing, idiotic. "Taxi," the woman calmly said. Smithy stepped into his pants, stuffed his shirt in, looked for his jacket, found it, stumbling over books, the whole room seemed to be full of books, just like at home, where the professor's books were all over the place, except here the only piece of furniture was the mattress, unbelievable how low Leibnitz had sunk, and the bum had the nerve to ask for a raise. Smithy didn't turn on the light, he was ashamed, though again he thought: you don't have to be ashamed in front of a whore, but he suddenly knew she wasn't a whore. The woman was still lying on the mattress, in the light from the elevator, naked, white, Smithy was surprised, he couldn't really remember anything, he must have torn off her dress, fine, let her figure out how to patch it together, apparently the expensive dress had made him mad. Anyway, it was her problem, she had come on to him, not the other way around, but then Smithy went down to Leibnitz after all, walked into the dissection room, whose door was still open, all that was left of Holy was the trunk, what an amazing job, suddenly Smithy was proud of Leibnitz, God knows he had earned his raise. He watched Leibnitz stirring about in the tub, in some kind of pulpy foam, then there was a gurgling sound, and the bathtub slowly emptied. It was rather practical, really, Smithy grew solemn in view of the transience of earthly things, then he saw the woman standing in the door again, as she had before, again in her dress, which was undamaged, she must have taken it off herself. Smithy got embarrassed, probably because he had been wondering about the transience of earthly things, but he could hardly imagine that she would have noticed in this heat, which he was suddenly feeling again, which was attacking him, sweat was pouring down his body, he felt disgusting. He went to the telephone on the window sill, called van der Seelen, whom he had never called before, but he knew his number from Sam. It took a while before van der Seelen accepted the call, each time someone else would come to the phone and say that van der Seelen wasn't available, but when he finally was available, since Smithy just kept calling back, and van der Seelen yelled at Smithy, asking him what the hell he thought he was doing, Smithy yelled back that he demanded twenty percent more, otherwise he was closing shop. "Okay, okay," van der Seelen replied, suddenly super-friendly again, "twenty percent more." But now he wanted to get some sleep, Smithy shouted. And he wanted Sam with the Cadillac, he added. Well, where did Smithy want Sam to drive to, van der Seelen asked, still super-friendly. Under the Triborough Bridge, Smithy said, and he didn't want to be kept waiting. "Coming up, coming up," van der Seelen appeased him, and Smithy put down the receiver. By now there was nothing left of Holy except his cassock, which Leibnitz dropped into the tub with the vermilion underwear. Smithy went downstairs with the woman. The front door was still open. It hadn't gotten any cooler, but dawn was breaking, the morning sprang on the city like a mugger, it was bright daylight when Sam pulled up in the Cadillac. Smithy sat down next to Sam, the woman sat down behind Smithy. "Where to?" Smithy asked. "The Coburn," the woman said. Sam grinned. "Okay," Smithy said, "to the Coburn." They drove through the still empty streets. The sun came. It was pleasantly cool in the car. Air-conditioning. In the second rearview mirror Holy had installed when Sam was his driver, because Holy always thought van der Seelen was after him—well, he wasn't so wrong about that—Smithy observed the woman. She had black and blue marks on her throat. He must have choked her, he remembered nothing, but at least now he was sober, and tomorrow he would talk to that commie police chief the way he had talked to van der Seelen, Smithy was needed, that much was clear now. Then Sam stopped in front of the Coburn's main entrance. A doorman opened the door of the Cadillac, the woman got out, the doorman bowed, a second one bowed by the door, whose glass panels automatically parted. "God damn," Sam muttered in amazement, "I could have sworn they'd boot her out again." "Drive me home, Sam," Smithy said, suddenly dead tired, and when he went into his apartment he threw himself onto the bed without getting undressed. Bookcases everywhere, a desk in the other room, and the third room, too, was crammed full of books, German books with names on them that meant nothing to him, titles he didn't understand. What the professor's business was, nobody knew, he always needed dope, and Smithy had delivered the dope, and when the professor could no longer pay for the dope, Smithy came up with his idea, and so the professor started making bodies disappear for high-class clients, and for not so high-class clients as well, and when one day the professor OD'd on his dope, Leibnitz took over the job, he had proved his competence by dissolving the professor. Smithy fell asleep and slept so soundly that it took him a long time to realize that the phone was disturbing him. He cast a glance at the alarm clock, he had barely had two hours' sleep. It was the chief of police. What did he want, Smithy asked. "Come to the Coburn." "All right," Smithy said. "I've sent you a car." "Nice," Smithy said, groping his way to the bathroom, found the sink, let the water run till the sink was full, dipped his face in it, the water was warm too, it didn't refresh him, the city seemed to be gradually coming to a boil. The doorbell rang, Smithy dipped his face in the sink once more, then he wanted to change his shirt, but the bell was still ringing, so he went to the door. Two policemen were standing there, sweating, their shirts sticking to their bodies. "Come on, let's go!" one of them said to Smithy, the other one was already turning his back to Smithy to walk down the stairs. Smithy, with water still dripping off his face onto his shirt and jacket, said he wanted to change and shave first. "Stop fucking around," the policeman on the stairway said, yawning. Smithy locked the apartment door behind him, and only now did he realize how miserable he felt, his head hurt, stinging pains in the back of the head, earlier he hadn't felt anything, it seemed to him, neither the pain nor the heat, just that disgusting warm water in the sink. They squeezed him into the Chevy, he had to sit in the front between the two of them, when they reached the Coburn they dropped him off at the delivery entrance. Detective Cover was there and an agitated, elegant man dressed in black with a white handkerchief in his breast pocket. "This is the man," Cover said, pointing at Smithy. "Friedli," the man with the white handkerchief introduced himself, "Jakob Friedli." Smithy didn't understand what he meant, it sounded like German, apparently it was his name, or was it good morning in German or Dutch, it was close to 7:00 a.m., after all, and suddenly Smithy felt like asking the man what the word for "cheese" was in Danish, but then the man, wiping his face with his handkerchief, spoke

English after all: "Follow me, please," he said. Smithy followed him, the detective stayed by the delivery entrance. "I'm Swiss," said the man with the white handkerchief as they walked down a hallway that seemed to be leading to the housekeeping quarters. Smithy didn't give a damn what the man was and why he was telling him what he was, for all he cared he could be Italian or straight out of Greenland. This had never happened to him before, the Swiss guy said, never. Smithy nodded, even though he was wondering, how could this never have happened to the Swiss guy before, there was always a body that ended up dead, more or less legally, in every hotel, and that the guy was talking about a body was obvious, otherwise the chief of police wouldn't have had Smithy dragged out here at this godawful hour. They went up in a freight elevator, endlessly, Smithy didn't care where they were going, but after the twentieth floor he had the feeling this had to be one high-class corpse. The elevator stopped. They entered a kind of kitchen, probably a sort of dressing room for food where dishes prepared in the main kitchen were given their finishing touch before being served to the super-high-class folk up here, Smithy imagined, and right in the middle of this dressing room or this kitchen, in front of a gleaming table, stood the Chief of Police, drinking black coffee. "This is the man, Nick," the Swiss guy said. "Hello, Smithy," the police chief said. "You look awful. Want some coffee too?" He said he needed it. "Get Smithy some coffee, Jack," the chief of police said. The Swiss guy went to a sideboard, brought Smithy a cup of black coffee, wiped the sweat off his face with his handkerchief. Smithy was glad that a high-class guy like that sweated too. "Leave the rest to me, Jack," the chief of police said. The Swiss guy left the kitchen. The chief of police sipped his coffee. "Holy has disappeared." "Could be," Smithy said. "Was he lying on Leibnitz's dissecting table?" "I never look there," Smithy said. "Van der Seelen?" "Has not disappeared," Smithy replied, put his cup on the gleaming table, and asked what it was Nick wanted of him. It was the first time he had called the chief of police Nick. He had called the previous one Dick. Nick grinned, went to the sideboard, came back with a coffeepot. How much of a cut was van der Seelen demanding of Smithy, Nick asked, pouring coffee first into his own cup, then into Smithy's. "Twenty percent less than Holy," Smithy said. "He had vermilion underwear." "Who?" Nick asked. "Holy," Smithy replied. "Oh well," Nick said, van der Seelen hadn't quite had the time to set himself up yet, and took another sip of coffee. Then he said: "Smithy, at lunch yesterday you and I made a deal. What did we agree on? I totally forgot." "Thirty percent," Smithy said. "Thirty percent for you?" Nick asked. "Thirty percent for you," Smithy said. Nick said nothing, finished his coffee, poured some more into Smithy's cup. "Smithy," he said calmly, "we agreed to go fifty-fifty. I do intend to abide by that, on the whole. But not today. Today you will settle for ten percent, that is, if you keep your mouth shut and van der Seelen doesn't get wind of what's happening today, otherwise you'll have to deliver to him too." Ten percent, Smithy said, no way. He was closing shop. Nick could approach the EMS. "We're talking about half a million bucks," Nick said calmly, "that's five thousand for you." "That's different," Smithy said, he could agree to that. He said Nick should send him the body. Nick looked at Smithy thoughtfully. For a sum this high, he finally said, Smithy would have to negotiate for himself. Smithy poured himself coffee. "I see," he said, "so you can stay out of it." "That's right," Nick said, "let's go." Smithy took another sip of coffee and stepped through a sliding door with Nick. They entered a room that was similar to the one they had left, but without windows, with another sliding door, and stepped into a wide imposing corridor, actually more like a longish hall at the two ends of which, behind huge glass walls, the hot sky stood like a wall of concrete. It was pleasantly cool. They walked across a green carpet. "Do you know any Danish?" "No," Nick said, "let's go to the client." "Let's go to the body," Smithy said. Nick stopped. "What for? You'll have it delivered!" Smithy replied: "It's easier to negotiate afterward." Nick patted him on the back: "Smithy, you'll turn into a businessman yet." They had crossed the corridor, Nick pressed a button. "Apartment ten," he said. An elderly man opened the door, bald, apparently in black tie, Smithy wasn't sure, he only knew clothes like that from the movies. "We're going to have a look at it," Nick said. The bald man didn't answer, stepped aside, a small drawing room, a gold-colored wall-to-wall carpet, classy furniture, as Smithy would say if he were to describe the furniture, then Nick opened a door, white, with gold-framed panels, a bedroom, a white rug, a broad white four-poster with a gilded gable and a canopy from which white veils hung down like trailing clouds. Nick parted the veils. The bed was freshly made, the top sheet turned back, and on top of it lay the woman, still in the same dress she had worn just a little over three hours ago when she slipped past the bowing doormen into the Coburn. Her eyes were wide open, she seemed to be staring at Smithy the way she had always stared at him, attentively and indifferently, her dark hair rested on her shoulders and was spread out on the white sheet, only her throat was in a truly ugly condition now, someone must have choked her much more forcefully than Smithy, and as Smithy stared at the dead woman, he noticed with surprise how beautiful she was. "A hooker?" he asked, basically just to say something, feeling suddenly embarrassed, because right after asking the question it sounded dirty to him. "No," Nick said behind him. Bored, he was staring through the curtains at the street far below. "Otherwise we couldn't have asked for five hundred thousand." "Let's go to the client," Smithy said wearily. In the little drawing room—which was probably just a foyer, Smithy imagined, once again embarrassed by the elegant setting, by all these pictures and pieces of furniture—stood the bald man. Apparently a butler. This thought came to Smithy in a flash, he was not unhappy with this revelation, he always liked having an overview of complicated situations. "Is he sleeping?" Nick asked. "The doctor . . ." the bald man wanted to continue. "Bring him out," Nick said, opening the door opposite the door to the bedroom where the body lay, pushing it open and going in. Smithy followed him. A large room, a terrace in front of the windows, a desk. Nick sprawled out in a huge armchair. "Sit down, Smithy," he said, pointing to another armchair. Smithy sat down, it bothered him that he wasn't shaved. "The doctor," the bald man began again. "There are problems," Nick said. "Very well," said the bald man, opening a door behind the desk. "Smithy, now's your big moment." "Where are we here?" Smithy asked. Stretching in his huge armchair, sinking into it, Nick placed his legs on the upholstered footrest, pressing his splayed fingertips together, with his thumbs on his chest, massaging his nose with the tips of his index fingers and watching Smithy with amusement. "I guess reading the newspapers isn't your thing," he said. "No," Smithy replied. "You don't have a clue about politics?" Smithy said he was only interested in ice hockey. Nick didn't say anything. Then he said this wasn't the right season for ice hockey. Smithy said he hated everything about summer, and put his legs on the footrest in front of him too. "Special session of the UN General Assembly," Nick said. "And?" Smithy asked. "I'm just saying," Nick said and fell silent again. The door behind the desk opened, Smithy recognized the man right away, that is, he didn't know who he was but he had seen him many times. Smithy racked his brain, he couldn't remember, but the man in the elegant pajamas had to be someone from Europe, some head of government or foreign minister or at any rate someone important, enormously famous, a man who just barely glanced at Smithy, as if Smithy wasn't anyone at all, the same kind of look the woman had given him last night, indifferent, but not as observant, in fact not observant at all, a look that put Smithy suddenly into a rage, without Smithy's being able to account for this rage, but now he too pressed his fingertips together, assuming the same position Nick had assumed in his huge armchair before the man had appeared, this man who was as serene, as lofty as the Good Lord Himself, for whom Smithy was just a louse, less than that, because Smithy was already a louse to Nick, but Smithy didn't know what being less than a louse was, which was what he, Smithy, must amount to in the eyes of the Good Lord. "Problems?" our

Heavenly Father asked Nick, who had risen to his feet. "Problems, the man is causing problems." "That one?" asked Oh-Lord-my-God in his wine-red pajamas without casting a second glance at Smithy. "That one," Nick said, with his hands in his pockets. "What does he want?" asked the Lord of Hosts. Smithy had unwittingly retained all the divine appellations Holy used to cite, now they were shooting from his memory, but he suppressed the wish to ask the Supreme Being whether he knew any Danish. "Don't know," Nick said. The Ruler of Heaven and Earth sat down behind the desk, toying with his golden ballpoint pen. "Well?" he asked. "Who is the body?" Smithy asked. Yahweh remained silent, still toying with his golden ballpoint pen, and cast a surprised glance at Nick, who was standing behind the chair he had sat in before. Nick turned to Smithy, baffled, but then suddenly amused, as if something were suddenly dawning on him. "Your daughter?" Smithy asked. The King of Glory put the golden ballpoint pen back on the desk, pulled a short, flat cigarette from a green case, and lit it with a golden lighter. "Why these questions?" he asked, still refusing to bestow a glance upon Smithy. "I have to know whether I want to let the body disappear," Smithy said. "Tell me your price, and you will know," Jehovah replied, bored. Smithy stuck to his guns. He could only tell him his price if he knew who the body was, he insisted, quite to Nick's amusement, Smithy sensed, and now God Almighty actually looked at him for the first time, took notice of him once and for all, angrily for a moment, indeed wrathfully, as if at any moment he would cleave Smithy in two with a thunderbolt, but since he was not a god, but like Smithy only a man, although an incomparably more important one, socially, historically, and in the way of education and wealth as well, the rage in the famous, perhaps somewhat too bloated face of the otherwise skinny representative of history in wine-red pajamas behind the desk was visible, or more precisely, was faintly suggested for only a second, or even more precisely, for a fraction of a second, and then he smiled at Smithy in a downright friendly manner: "The body is my wife." Smithy studied the bloated red face of the famous man behind the desk and still couldn't remember which country's president or prime minister or foreign minister or chancellor or vice-chancellor he was, or whatever his job was, if in fact he was a politician and not a famous industrialist or banker or maybe just an actor who had played a president or foreign minister in a movie and now Smithy was taking him for someone else, but Smithy suddenly didn't care, the man behind the desk was the husband of the woman Smithy had slept with, barely an hour before the break of this day that was already thickening into another blindingly white cloud behind the large windows and would be even more hellish to plunge into than the day before. "Who killed her?" Smithy asked mechanically. "I did," the man behind the desk replied nonchalantly. "Why?" Smithy asked. The man behind the desk said nothing. He smoked. "You intend to interrogate me," he noted. "I have to decide," Smithy said. The guy in the wine-red pajamas let his cigarette drop into a round enamel ashtray, opened the green cigarette case, lit a new cigarette, all without haste, without embarrassment, pondering something all the while, and then turned to Smithy: "I lost my nerve," he said then, smiled, and fell silent, suddenly observing Smithy with curiosity. "My wife," he continued, carefully choosing one word after the other, in his textbook English, which Smithy knew only from English movies, though possibly it wasn't textbook English at all, but English crudely blended with some European language, which of course sounded like classical English compared with the English Smithy spoke, as Smithy suddenly realized, he didn't know why that annoyed him. "My wife left this house two days ago. Since then she slept indiscriminately with many men, she told me this when she came back to the hotel this morning. Shortly after four. Or close to four thirty." The fellow behind the desk observed Smithy with amusement, and Smithy thought he could imagine Holy sitting behind that same desk and looking just as swell, and that faces like this one, red and bloated above those wine-red pajamas, were a dime a dozen. "That's why you strangled your wife," Smithy noted. She must have had a reason for running away, he said. The guy behind the desk smiled. "She just wanted to annoy me," he said. "And she succeeded. I was annoyed. For the first time in my life." The mug behind the desk looked disgusting to Smithy. "For the first time in my life," he repeated, yawned and asked: "How much?" Nick jumped in: "Five hundred thousand, he told me." "All right," said the shabby rat behind the desk, "five hundred thousand." "If you absolutely insist," Nick said, "I am powerless." "No," Smithy said. "A million," smiled the lousy bedbug in the wine-red pajamas, while Nick stared at him, flabbergasted, beaming. "I'll let your wife disappear for nothing," Smithy said to the shabby louse behind the desk, without really knowing what he was saying as he thought of the dead woman lying eight, nine, ten yards away behind the walls on the sheets of the white four-poster. He thought of her beauty and how she had stared at him with her dead eyes, and then he said, rising to his feet: "From you I don't take anything!" He left the big room, the apartment, looked around briefly in the hall with the green carpet, the Swiss fellow with the ridiculous handkerchief in his breast pocket approached him, accompanied him to the freight elevator. Smithy rode down, Cover was still standing in the delivery entrance, wiping sweat off his face. "Nick can send me the merchandise," Smithy said as he stepped out into the merciless heat, which had built up, trapped in the canyons of the city, but Smithy no longer cared about anything, the monstrous sun over the gigantic city, the gigantic city and the people moving about in it, the steam billowing from the manhole covers, the crawling, stinking convoys of cars, he walked and walked, whether it was along Fifth Avenue or Madison, Park, or Lexington or along Third, Second, or First Avenue he didn't know, he walked, drank a beer somewhere, ate in some greasy spoon, he didn't know what, sat on a bench in the park for a long time, he didn't know how long, at one point a young woman sat next to him, then an old woman, then it suddenly seemed to him that someone had been reading a newspaper next to him, he didn't care, he only thought of the dead woman and how she had gone to the Coburn in the early morning, past the doormen, how he had watched her in the rearview mirror of the Cadillac, how she had stood upstairs leaning with her left shoulder against the doorpost of the dissecting room, how she had been naked on Leibnitz's mattress, how she had given herself to him, how she had stared at him in the elevator and how he hadn't understood anything. There was a wild tenderness in him and a wild pride, Smithy was worthy of her, he had shown that bastard God in Heaven behind the desk where it was at, just like she had shown him, and then suddenly it was night. The street lamps were burning, and probably the night would be even hotter, even more hellish than the day before and the night before and the day that had just glided into the night that surrounded him, but he didn't care. He did everything without knowing, thinking only of the woman, about whom he knew nothing, no name, no first name, basically nothing except what she had looked like when she was dead, but he had made love to her, and when he stood in Leibnitz's dissecting room, it was all over already, all that was left was the dead woman's dress on the back of the chair, neatly folded, as was Leibnitz's habit. Smithy took the dress. He rode the elevator to Leibnitz's room, but Leibnitz wasn't there either. Leibnitz must have gone out, which he usually never did at this hour, but Smithy had already known in the elevator that he would find the dirty, dark, stuffy joint empty. Smithy left the elevator door open, the light from the elevator fell on him, he sat down on the mattress, leaning with his back against the wall, on his lap the dress of the woman who was dead now, whom he had made love to on this mattress, though he couldn't remember it, only the indistinct light in the window remained, Smithy felt nothing except the fabric of the dress, which his hands were stroking, a light rag, nothing more. Suddenly the elevator was there again, a shadow pushed itself between the light and Smithy, filling the door frame, suddenly the room became bright, van der Seelen had switched on the light, and behind van der Seelen was Sam. Smithy closed his eyes, the light blinded him, and his hands stroked the dress. "You messed up the deal of a lifetime," van der Seelen said, not even sounding particularly angry, but rather surprised, and Smithy proudly replied: "Nick's deal," whereupon van der Seelen stepped aside. Sam was holding something in his hands that no longer made any impression on Smithy, he was not afraid of what Sam now had to do, and when Sam had done it, van der Seelen, already in the elevator, remarked, with some anger after all: "Too bad about my cut."

The Dying of the Pythia

The Delphic priestess Pannychis XI, tall and skinny like most of her predecessors, had listened, disgruntled by her own oracular mischief and the gullibility of the Greeks, to the youthful Oedipus; here once again was someone wanting to know if his parents were his parents, as if that was so easy to determine in aristocratic circles, really, when there were wives who claimed that Zeus himself had shared their beds, and husbands who even believed that. Previously in such cases, since the inquirers were already in doubt, the Pythia had simply replied: "Partly yes—partly no," but today the whole business struck her as too stupid, perhaps only because it was already after five when the pale youth came limping along (she really should have closed down the sanctuary), and so—whether to cure him of his superstitious faith in the arts of divination or because, out of a malicious whim, she just felt like annoying the blasé prince from Corinth—she made as absurd and improbable a prediction as possible, one that she was certain would never come to pass. For, Pannychis thought, who would be capable of murdering his own father and sleeping with his own mother, except in those incest-ridden stories about gods and demigods, which she considered to be fairy tales anyway. She did feel a faint, queasy discomfort when the awkward Corinthian prince grew pale upon receiving her prophecy; she noticed it even though she was swathed in vapors on her tripod*—this young man really had to be extraordinarily gullible. After he had gingerly withdrawn from the sanctuary and paid the high priest Merops XXVII, who received the fees of aristocratic clients in person, Pannychis gazed after Oedipus for a moment, shaking her head, because the young man was not taking the road

*The Pythia at Delphi uttered her oracles while seated on a tripod over a fissure from which fumes emerged.

to Corinth, where his parents lived; she suppressed the thought that she might have caused some harm with her jocular prediction, and in pushing away her misgivings, she forgot Oedipus.

Old as she was, she dragged herself through the endless years, in constant discord with the high priest, who made a fortune off her services, because her auguries were getting more and more extravagant. She did not believe her pronouncements; rather, she wanted to mock those who did believe them, which only made the believers' faith more unshakable. Pannychis augured and augured, without the ghost of a chance for retirement. Merops XXVII was convinced that the older and the more feebleminded a Pythia, the better she was, and that the best Pythia of all would be one that was dying; that by far the best oracles had been delivered by Pannychis' predecessor, Crobylla IV, as she was dying. Pannychis was determined to make no auguries when her time came, she would spend at least her dying days in dignity, without talking nonsense; that she still had to do so was humiliating enough. Not to mention the miserable working conditions. The sanctuary was damp and drafty. It looked splendid from the outside, pure early Doric style, but inside, it was a shabby, badly insulated limestone cave. Pannychis' only consolation was that the fumes rising up from the chasm beneath the tripod relieved the rheumatism caused by the drafts. Whatever was happening in Greece no longer interested her. Was Agamemnon's marriage on the rocks? What difference did it make. Who was Helen carrying on with these days? Who cared. Blindly the Pythia augured away, and since she was believed with equal blindness, no one was bothered by the fact that her predictions only rarely came true, and that when they did, it couldn't have happened any other way: Hercules, for instance, being strong as an ox, could find no suitable opponent and therefore had no choice except to burn himself alive, and this only because the Pythia had suggested to him that he would become immortal after his death; whether that really happened was of course impossible to determine. And the fact that Jason had married Medea at all sufficed to explain why he finally put an end to his life, for when he arrived in Delphi with his bride to beg the god for an oracle, the Pythia had instinctively and immediately replied that he would do better to fall into his sword than to take a formidable woman like that for a wife. Under these circumstances, the rise of the Delphic oracle's fortunes, including its economic fortunes, was unstoppable. Merops XXVII planned colossal constructions, a gigantic temple to Apollo, a hall of the muses, a serpent pillar, various banks, even a theater. He now only associated with kings and tyrants; the mounting number of mishaps and blunders, the god's apparently increasing negligence had not troubled him in a long time. Merops knew his Greeks; the wilder the old hag's babble, the better, and besides, she was practically glued to her tripod these days, her mind adrift in the fumes, draped in her black cloak. When the sanctuary was closed, she would sit in front of the side portal for a while and then hobble into her hut, cook herself some gruel, leave it uneaten, and fall asleep. Any change in her daily routine was hateful to her. Occasionally she would show up in the office of Merops XXVII, but always unwillingly, grumbling and growling, for the high priest only summoned her when some seer had requested an oracle of his own devising for one of his clients. Pannychis hated seers. Even though she did not believe in oracles, she did not consider them dishonest; to her mind, oracles were an idiocy for which there existed a social demand; but the auguries formulated by seers, which she had to deliver as ordered, these were something entirely different, they were intended for a specific purpose, there was corruption involved, if not politics; and the thought that corruption and politics were involved crossed her mind right away on that summer evening when Merops, stretching his limbs behind his desk, informed her with his greasiest smile that the seer Tiresias had a request.

Pannychis, who had scarcely sat down, stood up and declared that she wouldn't have anything to do with Tiresias, that she was too old and her memory too feeble to memorize and recite any more oracles. Good-bye. "Just a moment," Merops said, hurrying after Pannychis and blocking her way out the door. "Just a moment, there's no need to get excited, I don't much care for the blind man myself." Tiresias, he said, was the biggest conniver and politician in all of Greece, by Apollo, corrupt to the marrow of his bones, but he paid better than anyone else, and what he was asking for was not unreasonable, the plague had broken out in Thebes again. "There's always a plague breaking out in Thebes," Pannychis growled. And considering the hygienic conditions around Fort Kadmeia, she added, that was no surprise; the plague was endemic in Thebes, so to speak. "No doubt about it," Merops XXVII appeased Pannychis XI, Thebes was a horrible filthy rat hole in every respect, that was why people claimed that Zeus's eagles just barely managed to flap their way across Thebes, using only one wing because they needed the other one to cover their nostrils, and as for conditions at the royal court—forget it. Tiresias, he said, was recommending an augury for his client, who would be calling the next day, to the effect that the plague would not disappear until the murderer of the Theban king Laios had been discovered. Pannychis was surprised. This oracle was banal, Tiresias must be getting senile. Just for form's sake, she asked when the murder had been committed. Oh, sometime or other, decades ago, it doesn't matter, if they find the murderer, good, Merops said, and if they don't find him, just as well, the plague will pass one way or the other, and the Thebans will believe that the gods, in order to help them, have crushed the murderer wherever he's crawled off to hide, thus seeing to it personally that justice is restored. The Pythia, glad to get back to her vapors, hissed: "What's Tiresias' client's name?"

"Creon," Merops XXVII said.

"Never heard of him," Pannychis said.

"Nor have I," Merops said.

"Who is the King of Thebes?" the Pythia asked.

"Oedipus," Merops XXVII replied.

"Never heard of him either," retorted Pannychis XI, who truly did not remember Oedipus.

"Nor have I," said Merops, glad to rid himself of the old woman, and handed her the sheet of paper with Tiresias' artfully worded oracle.

"Iambs," she sighed as she left the office, casting a glance at the sheet of paper.* "Naturally. He never could keep his hands off verse."

And the next day, when the Pythia, swaying back and forth on her tripod, comfortably swathed in vapors, heard the timid, almost lamblike piety in the voice of a certain Creon of Thebes, she recited her speech, not quite as fluently as she used to (at one point she even had to start over again): "Receive and hear Apollo's clear command: Let not the blood-guilt that runs wild in Thebes become—receive and hear Apollo's clear command: Let not the blood-guilt that runs wild in Thebes become incurable, but drive it out. By banishment or washing blood with blood. Blood stains the land. For Laios' death, Phoebus wants vengeance taken on the murderers. Thus he commands."

The Pythia fell silent, pleased to have gotten through her text without a mishap. The meter had not been without its difficulties. She was suddenly proud, and had already forgotten her blooper. The Theban—what was his name?—was long gone, and Pannychis returned to her dozing.

Sometimes she stepped out in front of the sanctuary. Before her, an extensive building site, the temple of Apollo; further down, the first three pillars of the hall of the muses were already erected. The heat was unbearable, but she was shivering. These cliffs, these woods, this sea—it was all a big lie, a dream of hers, at some point this dream would be over and everything would no longer exist. She knew it was all a sham and a lie; she, the Pythia, who was advertised as Apollo's priestess, was actually nothing more than a

*The iamb is the metrical foot used in Greek poetry.

swindler who made up oracles according to her whim. And now she had become very old, old as a rock, ancient; how old, she had no idea. Ordinary, everyday oracles were being delivered by the junior Pythia, Glykera V. Pannychis was sick and tired of the never-ending vapors; once in a while, all right, once a week, with a sufficiently solvent prince or with a tyrant, she would sit down again on her tripod and prognosticate. Even Merops had consideration.

And as she sat there in the sun, which had a pleasant effect on her, so that she closed her eyes to block out the Delphic kitsch landscape, leaning against the wall by the side portal of the sanctuary, absorbed in reverie, opposite the half-completed serpent pillar, she suddenly felt something standing in front of her, it had probably been there for hours, something that was challenging her, that concerned her, and when she opened her eyes, not immediately, but hesitantly, she felt as though she first had to learn how to see, and when she finally saw, she made out a monstrous form that was leaning on another, no less monstrous form, and while Pannychis XI sharpened her gaze, the two monstrous forms settled down to human size, and she recognized a ragged beggar, a man, who was supporting himself on a ragged beggar girl. The beggar gaped at Pannychis, but he had no eyes, in place of the eyes there were holes filled with black crusts of blood.

"I am Oedipus," the beggar said.

"I don't know you," the Pythia replied, blinking in the sun that was refusing to set over that blue sea.

"You prophesied to me," the blind man gasped.

"Could be," Pannychis XI said. "I've prophesied to thousands."

"Your prediction came true. I killed my father Laios and married my mother Jocasta."

Pannychis looked at the blind man, then at the ragged girl, wondering what this might mean, but still not remembering.

"Jocasta hanged herself," Oedipus quietly said.

"I'm sorry, my condolences."

"And then I blinded myself."

"Aha," said the Pythia. Then, pointing at the girl, she asked, "And who is she?"—not out of curiosity but just in order to say something.

"My daughter Antigone," the eyeless man replied. "Or my sister," he added, embarrassed, and then he told an intricate story.

The Pythia, whose eyes were wide open now, was only half listening; she was staring at the beggar who stood before her supported simultaneously by his daughter and his sister. Behind him were the cliffs, the woods, further down the beginnings of the theater, finally the pitiless blue sea, and behind all these the brazen sky, this glaring plane of nothingness, which people made bearable for themselves by projecting all sorts of things onto it, gods and destinies. And when it dawned on her how this had happened, when she suddenly remembered that her prediction was only meant to be a monstrous joke that would rid Oedipus of his faith in oracles once and for all, Pannychis XI suddenly began to laugh. Her laughter grew more and more enormous, and she was still laughing when the blind man with his daughter Antigone had long since hobbled away. But just as suddenly as she had begun to laugh, the Pythia fell silent, for a thought came to her in a flash: everything can't be chance.

The sun was setting behind the building site of the temple of Apollo, as kitschy as ever: she hated the sun; someone should take a close look at it, she thought, that fairy tale about the chariot of the sun and the steeds of the sun was just too silly for words, she'd bet it was nothing but a mass of stinking, fiery gases. Pannychis went to the archives; it occurred to her that she was limping like Oedipus. She leafed through the book of oracles, searching; all the prophesies given out by the sanctuary were registered here. She came upon an oracle given to a certain Laios, King of Thebes: if he were to have a son, that son would murder him.

"A deterrent," the Pythia reflected. "My predecessor must have been behind this." Pannychis was well aware of Crobylla IV's tendency to comply with the wishes of the high priests. She checked in the bookkeeping department and found a receipt for five thousand talents, paid by Menoikeus the dragon man, the father-in-law of King Laios of Thebes, with a cursory note: "For an oracle concerning the son of Laios, formulated by Tiresias." The Pythia closed her eyes: to be blind like Oedipus was the best thing of all. She sat at the reading table in the archive and reflected. She realized: if her prediction was a grotesque lucky hit, Crobylla IV's prophesy had been designed to prevent Laios from producing a son and hence a successor; his cousin Creon was supposed to succeed him. The first oracle, which prompted Laios to abandon Oedipus, was the result of corruption, the second one came about by chance, and the third one, which set in motion the investigation of the case, had again been formulated by Tiresias. "To put Creon on the throne of Thebes—I'm sure he's sitting there now," she thought. "Out of pure compliance with Merops' demands I delivered the prophesy formulated by Tiresias," Pannychis murmured in a rage. "And in miserable iambs to boot. I'm even worse than Crobylla IV, she at least prophesied only in prose."

She rose from the reading table and left the dusty archive, it had been so long since anyone had rummaged around there, who cared anyway, a lax sloppy regime prevailed at the Delphic Oracle. But now the archive, too, was going to be revamped, some pompous new building would replace the old stone hut, there were even plans for a priesthood in the archive, to replace the lax sloppiness with a more strictly organized kind.

The Pythia gazed at the nocturnal building sites: pillars and blocks of stone were lying around, it could have been a field of ruins; one day there would be nothing but ruins here. The sky was one with the cliffs and the sea, a bright red star stood in the west above a black cloud bank, malignant and alien. She felt as if Tiresias were menacing her from afar, Tiresias, who had forced his strategic oracles on her again and again, those auguries that made him so proud of his gifts as a seer and that were just as much rubbish as her own oracles; Tiresias, who was even older than she, who had already been alive when Crobylla IV had been Pythia, and before Crobylla, Melitta, and before Melitta, Bakchis. Suddenly, as she limped across the vast building site of the temple of Apollo, the Pythia knew that she was approaching death, it really was high time. She threw her stick at the half-completed serpent pillar, another kitsch monument, and was no longer limping. She entered the sanctuary: dying was a solemn business. She keenly looked forward to learning what dying would be like: there was an adventurous feeling about it. She left the main portal open, sat down on the tripod, and waited for death. The steam rising from the chasm swathed her in vapors, one billowing veil after the other, slightly reddish, and through them she saw the pale gray glow of night seeping through the main portal. She felt death drawing closer, her curiosity grew.

First a dark face appeared, its features crowded together, black-haired, with a low forehead, dull eyes, an earthy face. Pannychis remained calm; no doubt this was one of death's harbingers. But suddenly she knew that this was the face of Menoikeus, the dragon man. The dark face looked at her. It was speaking to her, or rather, it was silent, but in such a way that the Pythia understood the dragon man.

He had been a peasant, stocky, he had moved to Thebes, had worked hard, as a day laborer at first, then as a foreman, finally as a building contractor, and when the assignment to reconstruct Fort Kadmeia came his way, his fortune was made: by the gods, what a fortress! People claimed that he had only his daughter Jocasta to thank for his good fortune, but that was a nasty rumor; sure, King Laios had married her, but Menoikeus wasn't just anybody, he was a descendant of the dragon men who had grown from the loamy soil of Thebes, where Cadmos had sown the teeth of the dragon he had slain. At first only their spearheads had been visible, then the crests on their helmets, then their heads, which spat at each other full of hate; when the dragon men had grown from the earth up to their chests, they had started beating each other and rattling their spears, which were still half stuck in the earth, and finally, released from the furrows in which they had been sown, they had flown at each other like wild beasts; but Menoikeus' great-grandfather Udaios had survived the murderous struggle and also the rock that Cadmos hurled among the dragon men in the midst of their mutual slaughter. Menoikeus believed the old stories, and because he believed them, he hated Laios, this conceited aristocrat who traced his ancestry back to the marriage of Cadmos and Harmony, the daughter of Ares and Aphrodite: all right, it must have been one hell of a wedding—but before that, Cadmos had killed the dragon and sown his teeth, no doubt about that: Menoikeus the dragon man felt superior to Laios the king, the origins of his race were older and more miraculous, despite Harmony and Ares and Aphrodite all wrapped up together, and when Laios married Jocasta, the proud bright-eyed girl with the wild red hair, hope dawned in Menoikeus that he or at least his son Creon could come to power, black-haired, baleful, pockmarked Creon, whose soft voice had terrified the construction workers and now made the soldiers shiver in their boots, for Creon, the King's brother-in-law, had become the army's commander in chief. The only unit not subject to him was the palace guard. But there was something terribly loyal about Creon, he was proud of his brother-in-law Laios, in fact he was thankful, and he was devoted to his sister, he had always protected her, despite the ugly rumors about her; so the revolution never took place. It was enough to drive one mad. How often had Menoikeus been on the verge of crying out to Creon: revolt already, make yourself King! But he had never dared, and so he had already given up hope when, in Poloros' tavern—another grandson of a dragon man, who had had the same name—he had met Tiresias, the powerful, hard, blind seer led by a boy. Tiresias, personally acquainted with the gods, was not pessimistic at all about Creon's chances of becoming king: no one knows the will of the gods, he said, often they don't know it themselves, sometimes they're indecisive and downright glad when human beings give them certain indications—well, in Menoikeus' case that would cost fifty thousand talents. Menoikeus was startled, not so much by the enormous sum as by the precise correspondence of that sum to the huge fortune he had made off the Kadmeia and other royal edifices, for Menoikeus had never reported more than five thousand for taxation: Menoikeus paid.

Before the closed eyes of the Pythia, who was rhythmically swaying in the steadily thickening vapors, an arrogant figure arose, unquestionably regal, but bored, blond, cultivated, tired. Pannychis knew that this was Laios. Naturally the monarch had been astonished when Tiresias brought him Apollo's prediction that his son, should Jocasta ever give birth to a boy, would murder him. But Laios knew Tiresias, the fees he charged for an augury were outrageous, only rich people could afford Tiresias, most people were forced to travel to Delphi and ask the Pythia themselves, with much less reliable outcomes: because when Tiresias questioned the Pythia, the seer's power was transmitted to her, or so people believed; which was nonsense, of course, Laios was an enlightened despot, the question was only who had bribed Tiresias to bring about such an insidious oracle, someone must have an interest in preventing Laios and Jocasta from having children, either Menoikeus or Creon, who would inherit the throne if the marriage remained childless. But Creon was too mulishly principled to be disloyal, and he was a blatant dilettante when it came to politics. So it had to be Menoikeus. No doubt he already pictured himself as father of a king. By Zeus, he must have made a fortune off the state treasury, the fees charged by Tiresias exceeded by far the amount Menoikeus had reported for taxation. Fine, the dragon man was Laios' father-in-law, his conspiracy wasn't even worth mentioning, but to throw away an enormous fortune for an oracle, when it could be gotten so cheaply. . . . Fortunately a minor plague slithered and licked its way around the Kadmeia as it did every year, snuffing out a few dozen people, most of them useless rabble, philosophers, rhapsodes, and other poets.* Laios sent his secretary to Delphi with certain recommendations and ten coins of gold: for ten talents the High Priest would do anything; eleven talents he would have been obliged to record in the main ledger. According to the oracle that the secretary brought back from Delphi, the plague (which was gone by now) would come to an end if a dragon man sacrificed himself. Well, the plague could always flare up again. Poloros, the innkeeper, swore that he wasn't a descendant of Poloros the dragon man, that it was a malicious rumor. Menoikeus, now the only extant dragon man, had to climb the city wall and leap to his death, there was no way out, but actually Menoikeus welcomed the opportunity to sacrifice himself for the city, for his encounter with Tiresias had ruined him financially: he was broke, the workers were grumbling, the marble supplier Kapys had long since put a halt to his deliveries, and so had the brick works to theirs; the eastern part of the city wall was a wooden mock-up, the statue of Cadmos on the town square was made of plaster and painted the color of bronze; by the next downpour Menoikeus would have had to take his life anyway. His dive from the southern part of the city wall resembled the plunge of a giant swallow that had lost consciousness, the solemn songs of the maids of honor supplied an acoustic background; Laios squeezed Jocasta's hand, Creon saluted. But when Jocasta gave

**Rhapsodes:* Bards who recite their own poems or the Homeric epics.

birth to Oedipus, Laios had second thoughts. Of course he did not believe the oracle, it was absurd that his son would kill him, but by Hermes, if he only knew whether Oedipus was really his son; admittedly something had prevented him from sleeping with his wife, the marriage was just a marriage of convenience anyway, he had married Jocasta to make himself popular, because, by Hermes, Jocasta's premarital conduct had made her popular beyond measure, half the town had taken up with her; probably it was just superstition that prevented him from sleeping with Jocasta, but the idea that a son might kill him was somehow sobering, and frankly, Laios didn't care for women at all, he rather preferred the young recruits, but at moments of drunkenness he must have perhaps occasionally slept with his wife, as Jocasta claimed, he didn't really know, and then this damned officer of the guards—the best thing was to remove the newborn brat from his crib and have him exposed in the wilderness.

The Pythia drew her cloak more tightly around her, the vapors had suddenly turned ice-cold, and as she sat, shivering, she saw again the blood-encrusted visage of the ragged beggar. The blood disappeared from the eye sockets, blue eyes were gazing at her, a gaping, savage-featured face, not at all Greek, a youth stood before her, and it was just as it had been when Pannychis had wanted to make a fool of Oedipus with her contrived oracle. He knew, she thought, he knew at the time that he was not the son of the King of Corinth, Polybos, and his wife Meropë, he deceived me!

"Of course," young Oedipus replied through the vapors that billowed more and more densely around the Pythia. "I had always known it. The serving girls and slaves had told me and also the shepherd who found me on Mount Kithairon, a helpless infant whose feet had been pierced with a nail and bound together. I knew this was how I was delivered to King Polybos of Corinth. I admit, Polybos and Meropë were good to me, but they were never honest, they were afraid to tell me the truth, because they needed to deceive themselves, because they wanted a son, and so I set off for Delphi. Apollo was the only authority I could turn to. I tell you, Pannychis, I believed in Apollo, and I still believe in him, I didn't need Tiresias as an intermediary, but I didn't come to Apollo with a genuine question; after all, I knew that Polybos wasn't my father; I came to Apollo to coax him out, and I did coax him out of his divine hiding place: his oracle, resounding from your mouth, was truly terrible, as surely the truth always is, and just as terribly the oracle was fulfilled. When I left you that day, I thought to myself: If Polybos and Meropë were not my parents, then according to the oracle, my parents would be those who would suffer the fate you predicted. And when at a crossroads I killed a hot-tempered, vain old man, whom else could I have killed but my father—I did kill another man besides, but that was later, he was an insignificant guard officer whose name I've forgotten."

"There's someone else you killed," the Pythia interjected.

"Who was that?" Oedipus asked, surprised.

"The Sphinx," Pannychis replied.

Oedipus fell silent for a moment, as if trying to remember, and smiled. "The Sphinx," Oedipus said, "was a monster with a woman's head, a lion's body, a snake's tail, the wings of an eagle, and a silly riddle. It leaped off Mount Phikion into the plain, and after I married Jocasta in Thebes—you know, Pannychis, I might as well tell you, you're going to die soon, there's no harm in your knowing: I hated my real parents more than anything else, they wanted to throw me to the wild beasts, I didn't know who they were, but Apollo's oracle set me free: In a holy rage I tore Laios from his carriage in the pass between Delphi and Daulis, and when he was caught in the traces, I whipped the horses, making them drag my father to his death, and as he lay breathing his last, smeared with dust, I noticed in the ditch by the side of the road his charioteer, who had been wounded by my spear. 'What is your master's name?' I asked him. He stared at me and said nothing. 'Well?' I snarled at him. He told me the name, I had caused the King of Thebes to be dragged to death, and then, when I insisted he tell me more, he told me the name of the Queen of Thebes. He had given me the names of my parents. I could not allow there to be any witnesses. I pulled the spear from his wound and stabbed him again. He passed away. And when I had pulled the spear from the body of the dead charioteer, I noticed that Laios was looking at me. He was still alive. Silently I ran him through. I wanted to become King of Thebes, and the gods wanted it, and triumphantly I made love to my mother again and again, and full of spite I planted four children in her belly, because the gods wanted it, the gods, whom I hate even more than my parents, and every time I mounted my mother I hated them more than before. The gods had decided this monstrous thing, and monstrous therefore it would be, and when Creon returned from Delphi with Apollo's augury that the plague would not abate until Laios' murderer had been found, I finally knew why the gods had hatched such a cruel fate, and who it was they intended to feast on: it was I, I who had carried out their will. Triumphantly I put myself on trial, triumphantly I found Jocasta hanged in her bedroom, and triumphantly I stabbed out my eyes: for the gods had granted me the greatest imaginable right, the most sublime freedom, that of hating those who brought us into the world, our parents, and the forebears who brought forth our parents, and beyond them the gods who brought forth our forebears and our parents, and if now I wander through Greece as a blind beggar, it is not to glorify the power of the gods, but to make a mockery of them."

Pannychis sat on the tripod. She no longer felt anything. Maybe I'm already dead, she thought, and only gradually did she realize that a woman was standing before her amid the vapors, bright-eyed, with wild red hair.

"I am Jocasta," the woman said. "I knew it after the wedding night, Oedipus told me the story of his life. He was so guileless and open, and, by Apollo, how naive he was, how proud that he was able to escape the gods' decree by not returning to Corinth, by not killing Polybos and marrying Meropë, whom he still considered his parents, as if it were possible to escape the gods' decree. I had had a presentiment that he was my son, on the very first night, when he had scarcely arrived in Thebes. I didn't know yet that Laios was dead. I recognized him by the scars on his heels when he lay next to me, naked, but I didn't tell him, why do that, men are always so sensitive, and so I didn't tell him either that Laios was by no means his father, as he now of course believes; his father was Guard Officer Mnesippos, a completely insignificant blabbermouth with astonishing abilities in an area where he did not have to speak. That he attacked Oedipus in my bedroom when my son and eventual husband came to me for the first time, greeting me briefly and reverently before climbing into my bed, was probably unavoidable. Apparently he wanted to defend the honor of Laios. Mnesippos of all people, who had never stood on protocol when it came to my husband's honor. Just in time I managed to hand Oedipus his sword, a brief struggle, Mnesippos had never been a strong fencer. Oedipus had him fed to the vultures, not out of cruelty but because Mnesippos had been such a bad fencer, a sportsman's critique. Well, that critique was devastating, sportsmen can be very severe. But because I could not reveal the truth to Oedipus without going against the will of the gods, I could not prevent him from marrying me either. I was full of dread as your augury, Pannychis, came true without my being able to do anything about it: a son joining his mother in her bed, Pannychis, I thought I would faint with horror, but I nearly fainted with pleasure, never had I felt a mightier pleasure than when I gave myself to him; glorious Plyneikes shot from my body, Antigone, red-haired like myself, Ismene, the tender one, Eteocles, the hero. By yielding to Oedipus, in obedience to the gods' decree, I had taken revenge against Laios for wanting to throw my son to the wild beasts, and revenge for the years I had wept bitterly for my son, and so, each time Oedipus clasped me in his arms, I was at one with the decree of the gods, who wanted my sacrifice and my surrender to my mighty son. By Zeus, Pannychis, countless men have climbed on top of me, but I have loved only Oedipus, whom the gods destined to be my husband, so that I would become the only one among mortal women to submit, not to a stranger but to the man to whom I had given birth: to myself.

That he loved me without knowing that I was his mother, this is my triumph; that the most unnatural act became the most natural, this is the happiness to which I was destined by the will of the gods. It was in their honor that I hanged myself. That is, actually it wasn't by my own hand that I was hanged but by Mnesippos' successor, the first officer of Oedipus' guard, Molorchos. For when he learned that I was the mother of Oedipus, he rushed into my bedroom, jealous of the second guard officer, Meriones, and cried: 'Woe to thee, incestuous wretch!' and hanged me from the lintel of my door. Everyone thought I had done it myself. Oedipus thinks so too, and because according to the gods' decree he loved me more than his own life, he blinded himself: So mighty is his love for me, who was at once his mother and his wife. But perhaps Molorchos wasn't jealous of Meriones at all, but of the third officer of the guards, Melontheus—funny, the gods decreed that all my guard officers' names would begin with an M, but that's really irrelevant, the main thing, I believe, is that by the gods' decree I was able to put an end to my life with a feeling of joy. In praise of Oedipus, my son and husband, Oedipus, whom by the gods' decree I loved more than I have loved any man, and to the glory of Apollo, who foretold the truth through your mouth, Pannychis."

"You slut," Pannychis screamed hoarsely, "you slut, you and your gods' decree, that whole oracle was nothing but a lie!"

But it was no longer a scream, it was a hoarse whisper, and now a monstrous shade rose from the chasm, the pale gray glow of night was obscured by an impenetrable wall.

"Do you know who I am?" asked the shade. It now had a face that observed her calmly through ice-gray eyes.

"You are Tiresias," the Pythia replied. She had expected him.

"You know why I am appearing to you," Tiresias said, "even though I find these fumes rather unpleasant. I don't have rheumatism."

"I know," Pythia said with relief. Jocasta's babble had soured what was left of her pleasure in life. "I know, you're coming because I have to die now. I've been aware of that for a long time. Long before the shades rose up, Menoikeus, Laios, Oedipus, that whore, Jocasta, and now you. Go back down, Tiresias, I am tired."

"I, too, must die now, Pannychis," said the shade, "it will be over for both of us at the same moment. Just a moment ago, in my real body, feeling hot, I drank from the spring of Tilphussa."

"I hate you," the Pythia hissed.

"Forget your bitterness," Tiresias laughed, "let us not go down to Orcus as enemies," and suddenly Pannychis noticed that the mighty ancient seer wasn't blind at all, for he was winking at her with his light gray eyes.

"Pannychis," he said in a fatherly tone, "only ignorance of the future makes the present bearable. I was always boundlessly amazed at people's eagerness to know the future. They seem to prefer unhappiness to happiness. Of course we lived off this human propensity—I, admittedly, far better than you, even though it was not altogether easy to play a blind man throughout the seven lifetimes I was granted by the gods. But people want their seers to be blind, and one mustn't disappoint one's customers. As for the first oracle I ordered at Delphi, which annoyed you so greatly, the one about Laios, don't take it so personally. A seer needs money, you can't pretend blindness without an overhead, the boy who guided me had to be paid, a new one every year, since he had to be seven years old exactly, and then the other personnel, various specialists, and all over Greece confidential agents, and then this Menoikeus shows up—I know, I know, you looked in the archives and found an entry for five thousand talents I had paid for the oracle, while Menoikeus had given me fifty thousand—but then, it wasn't an oracle, it was a warning, because Laios, to whom the warning was addressed, not only had no son who might kill him, it was also impossible for him to have one, I simply had to take his orientation, a rather unfortunate one for a dynast, into account."

Tiresias continued to placate her. "Pannychis, I am a reasonable person like yourself, I don't believe in the gods either, but I do believe in reason, and because I believe in reason, I am convinced that the irrational faith in the gods can be put to rational use. I am a democrat. I know very well that most of our gentry are corrupt and degenerate, that they can be bribed and bought for any cause whatsoever, that their moral condition is beyond description: if I just think of Prometheus with his round-the-clock drinking and the way he ascribes his cirrhosis of the liver to the eagles of Zeus, or that overstuffed glutton, Tantalus, who makes such an enormous to-do about the limitations imposed by his diabetes regimen. But that's nothing compared to our high nobility—please! Thyestes eats up his children, Clytemnestra butchers her husband, Leda carries on with a swan, the wife of Minos with a bull—thank you very much. Nevertheless, when I think of the Spartans with their totalitarian state—forgive me, Pannychis, I don't want to trouble you with politics—but let's face it, the Spartans also trace their ancestry back to the dragon men, to Chthonios, one of the five berserkers who stayed alive, and Creon is a descendant of Udaios, who didn't dare come up from under the ground until after the slaughter was over—my dear esteemed Pythia, Creon is loyal, and I won't deny it, loyalty is a wonderful and highly decent thing, I'll admit that too, but without loyalty there is no dictatorship, loyalty is the rock that supports the totalitarian state, without loyalty it would sink into the sand; while for democracy, a certain moderate disloyalty is necessary, something wishy-washy, spineless, and imaginative. Does Creon have imagination? A truly terrible statesman is in the making here, Creon is a dragon man, just as the Spartans are dragon men. My tip to Laios, that he should beware a son, whom he obviously couldn't have, was a warning against the heir apparent, Creon, whom Laios would bring to power if he did not take precautions. One of his generals, after all, was Amphitryon, born of the better, not yet degenerate sort of gentry, his wife Alkmene of even more decent gentry, his son or not his son Hercules—but let's skip the gossip: the line of Cadmus was coming to an end, Laios with his proclivity was well aware of this, and all I had intended with my oracle was a hint to Laios that he would do well to adopt Amphitryon; but he didn't adopt him. Laios was not as smart as I thought."

Tiresias fell silent, his expression turned gloomy, dismal.

"They're all lying," the Pythia noted.

"Who is lying?" Tiresias asked, still absorbed in his thoughts.

"The shades," the Pythia replied. "Not one of them is telling the whole truth, except for Menoikeus, but he is too stupid to lie. Laios is lying and that whore, Jocasta, is also lying. Even Oedipus isn't honest."

"Actually he is, overall," Tiresias said.

"Maybe," the Pythia replied bitterly, "but he lied about the Sphinx. A monster with a woman's head and a lion's body. Ridiculous."

Tiresias scrutinized the Pythia. "Do you want to know who the Sphinx is?"

"Well?" Pannychis asked. Tiresias' shade drew nearer, enfolding her with an almost fatherly gesture.

"The Sphinx," he said, "was so beautiful that I couldn't keep from staring when I first saw her surrounded by her tamed lionesses outside her tent on Mount Phikion outside Thebes. 'Come, Tiresias, you old scoundrel, chase your boy into the bushes and sit down with me,' she laughed. I was glad she didn't say it in front of the boy, she knew I was only pretending to be blind, but she kept it to herself. So I sat next to her on a pelt in front of the tent, the lions purring around us. She had long, soft, white-gold hair, she was mysterious and bright, there was real truth in her; it was only when she became like stone—at that point I was frightened, Pannychis, I only saw her that way once: when she told me the story of her life. You know the unfortunate family of Pelops. High nobility, the best kind. Anyway, no sooner had young Laios become king of Thebes than he seduced the famous Hippodameia, another high aristocrat. Her husband took revenge in traditional family style: Pelops castrated Laios and sent him off whimpering. The girl to whom Hippodameia gave birth was contemptuously called 'Sphinx,' the throttler, by her own mother, who ordained her as a priestess of Hermes in order to condemn her to eternal chastity, but also in order to incline Hermes, the god of commerce, to favor exports to Egypt and Crete, which were the Pelopses' livelihood; and yet it was Hippodameia who seduced Laios, and not the other way around, but like all aristocrats she, too, knew how to combine pleasure with cruelty and cruelty with usefulness. As for why the Sphinx on Mount Phikion besieged her father in Thebes and had her lions tear to pieces everyone who could not solve her riddle—this she did not reveal to me, perhaps only because she guessed that I had come to her on Laios' behest in order to learn her intentions. She sent me back with an order that Laios should depart from Thebes with his charioteer Polyphontes. Laios obeyed, to my surprise."

Tiresias reflected. "What happened then," he said, "I don't need to tell you, Pythia: the unfortunate confrontation in the pass between Delphi and Daulis, the murder of Laios and Polyphontes by Oedipus, and Oedipus' encounter with the Sphinx on Mount Phikion. Very well. So Oedipus solved the riddle, and the Sphinx threw herself down onto the plain." Tiresias fell silent.

"You're babbling, Tiresias," Pythia said. "Why are you telling me this story?"

"It torments me," Tiresias said. "May I sit down next to you? I'm freezing, that cold drink from the spring of Tilphussa is burning inside me."

"Take the tripod Glykeras," the Pythia replied, and Tiresias' shade sat down next to her over the chasm. The vapors became denser and more reddish.

"Why does she torment you?" The Pythia's question sounded almost amicable. "The story of the Sphinx, what is it other than an insignificant report about the end of the miserable line of Cadmos. With a castrated king and a priestess condemned to eternal chastity."

"Something's off about this story," Tiresias said thoughtfully.

"Everything's off about it," the Pythia replied, "and it makes no difference that everything's off, because for Oedipus it makes no difference whether Laios was homosexual or castrated, either way he wasn't his father. The story of the Sphinx is completely irrelevant."

"That's exactly what's bothering me," Tiresias grumbled. "There's no such thing as an irrelevant story. Everything is interconnected. Change any part and you change the whole. Pannychis," he said, shaking his head, "why did you have to invent the truth with that augury of yours! Without it, Oedipus would not have married Jocasta. He would now be a nice, well-behaved King of Corinth. But I don't mean to accuse you. The heaviest blame falls on me. Oedipus killed his father, fine, that can happen, he slept with his mother, so what? But that it all had to be dragged into the open as a cautionary horror, that was the real disaster. That damned last augury on account of that never-ending plague. Instead of a decent sewage system, all I could think of was another augury.

"And it wasn't as if I wasn't informed. Jocasta had confessed everything to me. I knew who the real father of Oedipus was: an insignificant officer of the guards. I knew whom he had married: his mother. All right, I thought, we'll have to set things straight. Incest aside, Oedipus and Jocasta had no less than four children, here was a marriage that had to be saved. The only thing still threatening it was that straight arrow, Creon, who loyally stood by his sister and his brother-in-law, but if he were to find out that his brother-in-law was his nephew and that his brother-in-law's children were his nephews as well—this he would not be able to square with his beliefs and convictions, he would overthrow Oedipus, simply out of fidelity to the laws of morality. We would end up with a totalitarian state like the one in Sparta, blood soups, abnormal children liquidated, daily military drills, heroism as a civic duty, and so I staged the most stupid performance of my entire life: I was convinced that it was Creon who had killed Laios in the pass between Delphi and Daulis, in order to make himself king, out of loyalty of course, this time toward his sister, whose son he wanted to avenge, since he had to believe that Oedipus, the child exposed to the wild beasts, had been Laios' son, because to his simple mind, infidelity was just inconceivable; and the only reason I put all these things together was that Jocasta had withheld from me the fact that Oedipus had killed Laios. For I believe that she knew it. I am sure that Oedipus told her about the incident in the pass between Delphi and Daulis and that she only pretended not to know who had murdered Laios. Jocasta must have guessed it right away.

"Why, Pannychis, do human beings only tell the approximate truth, as if truth wasn't above all a matter of details? Perhaps because human beings are themselves just an approximation. This damned imprecision. In this case it probably crept in only because Laios' death didn't mean much to her, it was no more than a trifle, so she skipped it, but it was a trifle that could have opened my eyes and prevented me from making Oedipus a suspect in the murder of Laios, I could have had you augur something like 'Apollo decrees the construction of a sewage system,' and Oedipus would still be king of Thebes, Jocasta would still be queen. But instead? Now loyal Creon holds court in the Kadmeia and is busy setting up his totalitarian state. What I wanted to prevent, happened. Let us descend, Pannychis."

The old woman looked at the open main portal. The rectangle gleamed brightly through the red steam, a violet plane, which widened until a blurred tangle appeared in it, became sharper, yellow, and finally turned into lionesses tearing at a lump of meat; then the lionesses regurgitated what they had devoured, a human body released itself from their talons, shreds of flesh joined together, the lionesses retreated, and in the portal stood a woman in the white garment of a priestess.

"I should never have tamed lions," she said.

"I am sorry," Tiresias said. "Your end was truly terrible."

"It only looked that way," the Sphinx reassured him. "It's so annoying not to feel anything. But now that it's all over and you two will soon also be nothing but shades, the Pythia here, Tiresias by the well of Tilphussa and simultaneously here in this cave, you shall know the truth. By Hermes, it's drafty here!" She pulled her thin, transparent garment closer around herself. "You have always wondered, Tiresias," she continued, "why I beleaguered Thebes with my lionesses. Well, my father was not what he pretended to be and what you took him for in order to soothe your conscience. He was a treacherous and superstitious tyrant. He knew very well that every tyranny becomes unbearable when it is based on principles; there is nothing more offensive to human nature than an unbendable justice. It is precisely this that men find unjust. All tyrants who base their rule on principles, on the equality of all men or on everyone having everything in common, awaken in those whom they rule a much greater sense of oppression than tyrants like Laios, who, too lazy for excuses, content themselves with being tyrants, even when they are far more abominable tyrants: since their tyranny is governed by whim, their subjects have the feeling of a certain freedom. They don't see themselves as being under the dictate of a capricious necessity that leaves them no hope; instead they are subject to an accidental capriciousness that leaves them their hope."

"By Zeus," said Tiresias, "you are smart!"

"I have thought about people, I asked them questions before I gave them my riddle and had my lions tear them to pieces," the Sphinx replied. "I wanted to know why people let themselves be ruled: out of indolence, which often goes so far that they will invent the most absurd theories in order to feel united with their rulers, and the rulers come up with equally absurd theories in order to give themselves the illusion that they do not hold dominion over those whom they rule. Only my father hadn't the slightest interest in any of this. He was still one of those despots who were proud of being despots. He didn't need to invent an excuse for his despotism. What tormented him was his fate: that he had been castrated and that the line of Cadmos would die with him. I sensed his sorrow, his evil thoughts, the impenetrable plans he was forging when he visited me, when he sat before me for hours, watching me, brooding; and so I feared my father, and because I was afraid, I began to tame lionesses. And rightly so. When the priestess who had raised me died and I was living alone with the lionesses in the sanctuary of Hermes on Mount Kithairon—Pannychis, this I want you to hear, and Tiresias might as well know it as well—Laios visited me with his charioteer Polyphontes.

"They came out of the forest, somewhere their horses were neighing anxiously, the lions were hissing, I sensed something evil, but I was paralyzed. I let them into the shrine. My father locked the door and ordered Polyphontes to rape me. I defended myself. My father helped Polyphontes, and while my father held me in his grip, Polyphontes carried out his order. The lionesses roared around the shrine. They struck against the door with their talons. The door held fast. I screamed when Polyphontes took me; the lionesses stopped roaring. They let Laios and Polyphontes leave.

"At the same time that Jocasta gave birth to the son of her guard officer, I too brought a son into the world: Oedipus. I knew nothing about the stupid oracle that you, Tiresias, had formulated. I know, you wanted to warn my father and prevent Creon from coming to power, and you wanted to save the peace. But apart from the fact that Creon has come to power and an endless war is beginning, because the seven kings are taking up arms against Thebes, above all you misjudged Laios. I know his pronouncements: he pretended to be enlightened, but he more than anyone believed in the oracle, he more than anyone was frightened when he was told that his son would kill him. Laios applied the oracle to my son, his grandson; and as a matter of course, just to make doubly sure, he also got rid of the son of Jocasta and her guard officer: a dictator's finger exercise, you can't be cautious enough.

"And so one evening a shepherd of Laios came to me with an infant whose feet had been pierced and bound together. He handed me a letter in which Laios ordered me to throw my son, his grandson, to the lions along with the son of Jocasta. I made the shepherd drunk, he confessed that he had been bribed by Jocasta; he was to deliver her son to a friend of his, a shepherd of King Polybos of Corinth, without betraying the child's parentage. When the shepherd was asleep, I threw the son of Jocasta to the lions and pierced my son's heels, and the next morning the shepherd went on with his little human bundle, and never noticed the difference.

"No sooner had he left than my father came with Polyphontes; the lions were lazily stretching their limbs, among them lay a child's hand, drained of blood, white and small as a flower. 'Did the lions tear both children to pieces?' my father calmly asked. 'Both of them,' I said. 'I see only one hand,' he said, turning it over with his spear. The lions growled. 'The lions tore both children to pieces,' I said, 'but left only one hand, you'll have to content yourself with that.' 'Where is the shepherd?' my father asked. 'I sent him away,' I said. 'Where to?' 'To his shrine,' I said, 'he was your instrument, but he is a human being. He has a right to purify himself of the guilt of having been your instrument—and now leave.' My father and Polyphontes hesitated, but the lions rose angrily, chased them away, and came back leisurely.

"My father never dared to visit me again. For eighteen years I kept quiet. Then I began to beleaguer Thebes with my lionesses. Our enmity had broken out openly, without my father ever daring to name the cause of this war. Suspicious and still frightened by the augury, all that he knew with certainty was that one child was dead. But if one was alive, he did not know which; he was afraid that his grandson was still alive somewhere and in league with me. He sent you to me, Tiresias, to sound me out."

"He did not tell me the truth, and you did not tell me the truth," Tiresias replied bitterly.

"If I had told you the truth, you would have only arranged for another oracle," the Sphinx laughed.

"And why did you order your father to leave Thebes?" Tiresias asked.

"Because I knew that in his mortal terror he wanted to go to Delphi. I had no idea that Pannychis was making such brilliant use of the auguring business, I imagined that if Laios showed up, you would check the archives and repeat the old oracle. This would have mightily increased his terror! Now the gods alone know what would have happened if Laios had come for an oracle, and what sort of fib Pannychis would have served him, and what he would have believed. But this never happened, Laios and Polyphontes met Oedipus in the pass between Delphi and Daulis, and the son not only ran his father Polyphontes through with a spear, he also had his grandfather Laios dragged to death by his horses."

The Sphinx fell silent. The vapors had ceased, the tripod next to the Pythia was empty, Tiresias was a mighty shadow again, almost indistinguishable from the blocks of stone that towered around the main portal where the Sphinx stood, a dark silhouette.

"Then I became my son's lover. There is not much we can say about his happy days," the Sphinx continued after a long silence. "Happiness hates words. Before I got to know Oedipus, I despised human beings. They were false, and because they were false, it never occurred to them that they themselves were the answer to the riddle I put to them: name the creature that changes the number of its feet, having four in the morning, two at noon, and three in the evening, but the more feet it employs, the feebler it is and the slower the speed of its limbs. And so I fed to my lions the countless people who could not find the solution. They screamed for help as they were torn to pieces, and I did not help them, I only laughed.

"But when Oedipus came, limping, from Delphi, and answered me, saying it is man, he creeps on all fours as an infant, stands firmly on two legs as a youth, and leans on a stick when he is old, I did not throw myself off the peak of Mount Phikion into the plain. Why should I? I became his lover. He never asked me who my parents were. Of course he noticed that I was a priestess, and because he was a pious man, he believed it was forbidden to make love to a priestess, and because he made love to me nonetheless, he pretended to be ignorant, and therefore he did not ask me about my life, and I never asked him about his, I didn't even ask for his name, because I didn't want to embarrass him. I knew that if he had told me his name and where he came from, he would have been afraid of Hermes, to whom I was consecrated, and who now would have known his name as well, and as a pious man he considered the gods to be frightfully jealous, and perhaps he also sensed that if he had made inquiries about my past, as he should have, out of a lover's curiosity, he would have found out that I was his mother. But he was afraid of the truth, and I too was afraid of it. So he did not know that he was my son, and I did not know that I was his mother. Happy to have a lover whom I did not know and who did not know me, I withdrew with my lionesses to my sanctuary on Mount Kithairon; Oedipus visited me again and again, our happiness was pure, like a perfect secret.

"Only the lionesses became increasingly restless, increasingly vicious, not toward Oedipus, but toward me. They spat at me, more and more agitated, more and more unpredictable, and struck at me with their talons. I lashed them with my whip. They cowered, growled, and when Oedipus no longer came, they attacked, and I suddenly knew that something incomprehensible had happened—well, you saw with your own eyes what happened to me and will happen over and over again in the underworld. And when, through the chasm beneath Pannychis' seat, your voices wafted down to where I was, I received the truth, I heard what I should have known long ago, though it would not have changed anything: that my lover had been my son, and you, Pannychis, had proclaimed the truth."

The Sphinx started laughing, the way the Pythia earlier had laughed at Oedipus; her laughter, too, became more and more boundless; even as the lionesses pounced on her again, she laughed, and as they tore the white dress from her body and sank their talons and teeth into her flesh, she was still laughing. Then it was no longer possible to make out what those yellow beasts were devouring, the laughter echoed off into silence as the lionesses lapped up the blood and disappeared. Steam rose from the chasm again. Poppy-red. The dying Pythia was alone with the barely visible shade of Tiresias. "A remarkable woman," the shade said.

The night had given way to a leaden morning, it had burst into the cave with great suddenness. But it was neither morning nor night, something void of substance was flowing in, irresistibly, neither light nor darkness, without shade or color. As always at the start of dawn the vapors spread out on the stone floor as a cold dampness, and clung to the rock walls, forming black drops that slowly yielded to their weight, thinned out into long threads, and vanished in the chasm.

"There is only one thing I don't understand," the Pythia said. "The fact that my oracle came true, although not in the way Oedipus imagines that it did, is an unbelievable coincidence; but if Oedipus believed that oracle from the beginning, and the first man whom he killed was the charioteer Polyphontes, and the first woman he loved was the Sphinx, why did he not suspect that his father was the charioteer and his mother the Sphinx?"

"Because Oedipus preferred being the son of a king to being the son of a charioteer. He chose his own fate," Tiresias replied.

"We and our oracle," Pannychis groaned bitterly. "It's only thanks to the Sphinx that we know the truth."

"I'm not sure," Tiresias said thoughtfully. "The Sphinx is a priestess of Hermes, the god of thieves and impostors."

The priestess was silent; now that the vapors were no longer rising from the chasm, she felt cold.

"Ever since they started building the theater," she claimed, "there has been much less steam in here." And then she suggested that the Sphinx had had been untruthful only in her account of the Theban shepherd. "She wouldn't have sent him off to a sanctuary, most likely she threw him to the lionesses as she did Oedipus, the son of Jocasta; and her own Oedipus, her son, she gave to the Corinthian shepherd with her own hands. The Sphinx wanted to be sure that her son would stay alive."

"Don't worry about it, Pannychis," Tiresias laughed. "Let it be. Whatever it was, was surely different and will always be different again and again, the more we try to get to the bottom of it. Stop thinking about it, otherwise more shades will rise and prevent you from dying. How do you know there isn't a third Oedipus? We don't know whether the Corinthian shepherd didn't pierce his own son's heels and deliver him instead of the Sphinx's son—if it was the Sphinx's son—to Queen Meropë, exposing the real Oedipus, who wasn't really the real one either, to the wild beasts, or whether Meropë didn't throw the third Oedipus into the sea in order to present to her faithful Polybos a son she had borne in secret—maybe from another guard officer—as a fourth Oedipus. Truth is truth only to the extent that we leave it in peace.

"Forget the old stories, Pannychis, they are unimportant, in all this chaos and disorder we are the central characters. We found ourselves both confronted by the same monstrous reality, which is as inscrutable as man, who brings it about. Conceivably the gods, if they existed, would be able to oversee—superficially, but still with a certain perspective—this enormous tangle of outlandish facts, all of them intertwined, producing the most outrageous coincidences, while we mortals, finding ourselves in the midst of this hopeless confusion, can only blunder and grope our way through it. We both hoped with our auguries to bring a tentative semblance of order, a tenuous intimation of some lawful pattern into the murky, lascivious, and often bloody tide of events that came shooting toward us and tore us along in its course, precisely because we attempted—if only slightly—to stem its advance.

"You augured with imagination, with zest, with playful high spirits, indeed with an almost irreverent impudence—in short: with blasphemous wit. I arranged my oracles with cool premeditation, with unimpeachable logic—in short: with reason. Admittedly, your oracle was a perfect hit. If I were a mathematician, I could tell you exactly how improbable was the probability that your oracle would come true: it was fantastically improbable, infinitely improbable. But your improbable oracle came true, while my probable oracles, rationally delivered, with the intention of making policy and changing the world in accord with reason, fizzled into nothingness. Fool that I was. With my reason I set loose a chain of causes and effects that brought about the opposite of what I intended. And then you came, just as foolish as I was, with your cheerfully heedless way of spouting your oracles straight off the cuff and with as much malice as possible, for reasons that no longer matter at all, nor did you care who you gave them to either; by chance, then, you augured one day for a pale, limping youth named Oedipus. What good does it do you that you hit the bull's-eye and that I was wrong? The damage we both caused is equally monstrous. Throw away your tripod, Pythia, drop it into the chasm along with yourself, I too have to go to my grave, the spring of Tilphussa has done its work. Farewell, Pannychis, but don't think that we will escape ourselves. Just as I, who wanted to subject the world to my reason, was confronted in this damp cave with you, who attempted to conquer the world with your imagination, all those who regard the world as an ordered arrangement will find themselves confronted by those for whom the world is a monster. The first will criticize the world, the others will accept it as it is. The first will think it possible to transform the world the way a stone can be shaped with a mallet, the others will argue that the world in its fathomless strangeness transforms itself, like a monster that puts on grotesque new faces one after the other, and that the world can be criticized only to the degree that the gossamer-thin layer of human understanding exerts any influence on the overpowering tectonic forces of human instinct. The first will accuse the others of being pessimists, the others will revile the first as utopians. The first will claim that history unfolds according to certain laws, the others will say that these laws only exist in the human imagination. The struggle between the two of us, Pannychis, will erupt in all areas, the struggle between the seer and the Pythia; as of now, our conflict is still emotional and not very thought-out, but they're already building a theater, and in Athens an unknown poet is already writing a tragedy about Oedipus. But Athens is a provincial town, and Sophocles will be forgotten, but Oedipus will live on, as a theme that presents us with riddles. Is his fate determined by the gods or by his sinning against a few principles that sustain the society of his time, by actions that I, with my oracles, tried in vain to prevent; or was it his fate to fall victim to a stroke of chance brought about by your whimsical auguring?"

The Pythia no longer answered, and suddenly she was no longer there, and Tiresias too had disappeared, and with him the leaden dawn hanging over the town of Delphi, which had also vanished.

The Minotaur A Ballad

FOR CHARLOTTE

The creature born of the sun god's daughter, Pasiphaë, who, by having herself encased in an artificial cow, had contrived to be mounted by a white bull consecrated to Poseidon, was removed from the stable where it had grown up among cows through long years of confused sleep, and, dragged in by the servants of Minos, who formed long chains so as not to get lost, found itself on the grounds of the labyrinth built by Daedalus to protect human beings from the creature and the creature from human beings, a structure from which no one, having once entered, found the way out, and whose countless mutually enclosing walls were made of glass, so that the creature found itself not only crouching face to face with its reflection, but also with the reflections of its reflections: it saw an immense multitude of creatures like itself, without knowing that itself was the creature. It felt paralyzed. It did not know where it was, nor what the crouching creatures around it wanted; perhaps it was only dreaming, though it did not know what dreams and reality were. It sprang up, instinctively, to drive away the crouching creatures, and at the same moment its reflections sprang up. It ducked, and its reflections ducked with it. It was unable to drive them away. It stared at the reflection that seemed nearest to itself, crept slowly backward, and its reflection

---

According to the myth as recounted in various classical sources, notably Ovid's *Metamorphoses,* the Minotaur was a creature—part man and part bull—born from the union of Pasiphaë and a magnificent white bull. Pasiphaë's husband, King Minos of Crete, had Daedalus construct a labyrinth in which the monster could be concealed. Periodically the city of Athens sent a tribute of seven young men and seven young women into the labyrinth to be consumed by the Minotaur. The Athenian Theseus killed the Minotaur with the aid of Minos's daughter Ariadne, who had fallen in love with him and provided him with a thread with which he was able to find his way back out of the labyrinth.

retreated from it as well; its right foot struck against a wall, it wheeled around and found itself head to head with its reflection, cautiously crept back, its reflection crept back. Inadvertently it put its hand to its head, and as it touched itself, its reflections, too, touched their heads. It rose to its feet, and its reflections rose with it. It looked down at its body and compared it with the bodies of its reflections, and its reflections looked down at their bodies and compared them with its body, and as it observed itself and its reflections, it realized it was made like its reflections: It considered itself to be one among many equal creatures. Its face became friendlier, the faces of its reflections became friendlier. It waved to them, they waved back, it waved with its right hand, they waved with their left, but it did not know what right and left were. It straightened up, stretched its arms, roared, and with it, stretching their arms, a countless number of creatures just like itself roared, a thousand roars reverberated, a virtually endless roaring. It felt very happy. It approached the nearest wall of glass, and a reflection approached it also, while at the same time other reflections moved away. It touched its reflection with its right hand, touched its reflection's left hand, which felt smooth and cold, and before it, in reflections of reflections, it saw the other reflections touching each other. It ran alongside the wall, touching the smooth mirror, its right hand covering the left hand of its reflection; its reflection ran with it, and as it returned, running alongside the back of the mirror-wall, its reflection ran back as well. It became more exuberant, leaped about, tumbled head over heels, and with it an immensity of reflections leaped and tumbled head over heels. Out of this running around and tumbling, out of this leaping and walking on its hands, which it did out of sheer exuberance, because the reflections were doing exactly as it did, so that it felt like a leader, and more than that, like a god, had it known what a god is; out of this childish enjoyment there gradually developed a rhythmic dance of the creature with its reflections, who were in part the inverse of the creature, and in part, as reflections of reflections, identical with it, and then, as reflections of reflections of reflections, inverse reflections of it again, and so forth receding into infinity. The creature danced through his labyrinth, through the world of its reflections, it danced like a monstrous child, it danced like a monstrous father of itself, it danced like a monstrous god through the universe of its reflections. But suddenly it stopped in its dance, stood as if frozen, squatted, stared with watchful eyes, and its reflections, too, squatted and gaped: As it danced, the creature had seen creatures among the dancing reflections who did not dance and who were not reflections that obeyed it. The girl, mirrored as was the squatting creature, stood motionless, naked, with long black hair among the squatting creatures, who were everywhere, before her, beside her, behind her. The girl dared not move, but fixed her fearful gaze on the creature that was squatting nearest her. She knew there was only one squatting creature, that the other squatting creatures were only reflections, but she did not know which one was the creature and not its reflection. Maybe it was the creature squatting before her, maybe its reflection, maybe a reflection of its reflection—the girl did not know. She only knew that her flight from the creature had led her to it, and next to the squatting creature she saw herself mirrored and further ahead she saw herself from behind and next to her a squatting creature from behind, and so forth through endless spaces. With her hands crossed in front of her breasts, she gazed transfixed at the creature who was still squatting before her. She thought she could touch it. She thought she could feel its breath. She thought she could hear it snorting. Its mighty head covered with tawny light brown fur was that of a bison, the high broad forehead covered with a wild tangle of wooly hair, the horns short and arched in such a way that the points stood over the roots, the reddish eyes rather small in proportion to the skull, deep-set behind raised sockets, fathomless. The bridge of the massive nose curved gently down toward a set of slanted nostrils, from the mouth hung a long, bluish-red tongue and beneath the chin a tangled, foam-clotted beard. All of this would have been bearable, but the unbearable thing was this bull's transition to a human being. Above the bison skull there loomed a mountain of shaggy fur from whose matted tresses and strands grew two human arms that supported themselves on the glass floor. It was as if the monstrous head and the hump above it had been extruded from the body of a man who crouched before the girl and then again beside and behind her, ready to leap. The Minotaur rose. He was enormous. He suddenly understood that there existed something other than Minotaurs. His world had doubled. He saw the eyes reflected everywhere, the mouth, the long black hair flowing over her shoulders, he saw her white skin, her neck, her breasts, her belly, her sex, her thighs, saw how it all went together, flowed together. He moved toward her. She moved away from him, while elsewhere she moved toward him. He chased after her through the labyrinth, she fled. It was as if a storm had blasted Minotaurs and girls in all directions, whirling them apart and through each other and toward each other, and when the girl ran into his arms, when he suddenly felt the body, the warm flesh bathed in sweat, and not the hard glass he had felt before, he realized—to the extent that one can speak of realization in the Minotaur's case—that until now he had lived in a world in which there were only Minotaurs, each one enclosed in a glass prison, and now he felt another body, another flesh. The girl twisted out of his grasp, he let it happen. She shrank back, her large eyes fixed on him, and when he began to dance, the girl began to dance, and their reflections danced with them. He danced his monstrosity, she danced her beauty, he danced his joy at having found her, she danced her fear at having been found by him, he danced his salvation, she danced her fate, he danced his greed, and she danced her curiosity, he danced his urgency, she danced her resistance, he danced his penetration, she danced her embrace. They danced, and their reflections danced, and he did not know that he took the girl, nor could he know that he killed her, since he did not know what life and death were. In him there was only a violent happiness and a violent pleasure, and they were one and the same. He roared when he took the girl, and in the mirrors, Minotaurs took girls, and the roar was a monstrous scream, an unreal, cosmic scream, as if the only thing in the world were this scream, which was mingled with the girl's scream, and then he lay there, and in the mirrors Minotaurs lay there, and the white naked body of the girl with the large black eyes lay there and was mirrored in the walls. He lifted the girl's left arm, it dropped, he lifted the right arm, it dropped, everywhere arms dropped. He licked her with his huge bluish-red tongue, her face, her breasts, the girl remained motionless, all the girls remained motionless. He rolled her about with his horns, the girl did not move, no girl moved. He rose, looked around, everywhere Minotaurs stood looking around, and everywhere the white bodies of girls lay at their feet. He bent down, picked up the girl, roared, moaned, raised the girl up to the dark sky, and everywhere Minotaurs bent down, picked up girls, roared, moaned, lifted girls up to the dark sky, and then he laid the girl between the glass walls, lay down next to her and fell asleep, joined by all the Minotaurs stretched out on the ground covered with white naked girls' bodies. He slept and dreamed of the girl with the black hair and the large eyes, chased her, played with her, seized her, loved her, and when he opened his eyes, something on his breast had its claws tangled in his matted beard. It brushed his muzzle with its wings and dipped its naked yellowish-white neck with the small head, the red eyes, and the strangely curved, powerful beak somewhere next to him. A fat thicket of feathers, necks, eyes, and beaks squatted on the walls, and above him something was darkening the gray light of dawn, circling, diving, dipping, gulping, tearing, gobbling, gouging, screeching, flying away, flying back, diving again, mirrored in its descending and rising, without his understanding why there was this diving, plunging in, ripping and tearing, rising up, and circling about, wrapped as he was in the fluttering and flapping of wings, and when the circling rose higher and higher and finally dissolved in the blinding void of the sky, which had brightened almost past enduring, the sun broke through the glass walls and burned its image into the Minotaur's brain as a mighty turning wheel that cast sheaves of fire into the sky to signify the sun's wrath over the sacrilege of his daughter Pasiphaë, who had given birth to a creature that was an insult to the gods and a curse to men, condemned to be neither god nor man nor beast, but merely the Minotaur, guiltless and guilty at once. The Minotaur saw the immense wheel rolling upward, he kept his eyes shut, he saw it nonetheless, the wheel of the curse that weighed on him, the wheel of his fate, the wheel of his birth and the wheel of his death, the wheel that burned in his brain, though he did not know what a curse was or what fate, birth, and death were, the wheel that rolled over him, the wheel on which he was broken, and as he lay there, singed by the sun and by its infinitely mirrored light, he vaguely noticed a foot that resembled his foot. He thought it was the girl, that she had started moving again and wanted to play with him. He raised his head, and now he saw two feet retreating. He rose. Before him stood a creature that resembled the girl and yet was not the girl, that carried a torn cloak in its left hand and a sword in its right, and the Minotaur did not know what a cloak or a sword were, he only knew—because in the blinding light of the sun the walls no longer reflected any images—that the Minotaurs and the girls had left him, and the girl he had taken must also have moved again and left, for she was no longer there. He was cast out of his Minotaur world, alone with the creature that was watching him and retreating, stopping, approaching him and retreating again. The Minotaur approached it full of goodwill, even though he had no concept of this feeling, which was different from the feeling he had had toward the girl, less urgent, less greedy. He looked forward to playing with it and chasing it in the passageways; perhaps the creature would lead him to the other Minotaurs and to the girls and to the creatures who were like this new creature. But he would have to treat it more carefully, more delicately, otherwise it would stop moving. The Minotaur snorted with pleasure, and when the creature waved its cloak again, he began to dance. In front of the walls set aglow by the sun, the two of them moved like shadows, the dancing one and the leaping one, the Minotaur clapping his hands and then rapidly stamping the ground, the creature waving its cloth, advancing or retreating, attacking again and again with its sword, which it had brought into the labyrinth, hidden under its cloak, to kill the Minotaur, and now that it stood facing him and saw his guilelessness, it was ashamed. The Minotaur danced around it, clapping his hands and stamping his feet. He danced his joy at no longer being alone, he danced his hope of meeting the other Minotaurs, the girls and creatures who were like the one with whom he was dancing. In his dance he forgot the sun, in his dance he forgot the curse. He was all cheerfulness, friendliness, lightness, tenderness. He danced, and the creature stalked the Minotaur and leaped around him, and as the sun set, the reflections of the Minotaur and the creature became visible along with the thousand reflections of the sun. The Minotaur danced, happy at having found the Minotaurs and the new creatures, soon he would find the girl whom he had taken and who had become motionless and had then gone away, and the other girls, who had been taken by the Minotaurs and had then become motionless too and gone away. The two beings danced toward each other and away from each other, the reflections met, overlapped, passed through one another. Everywhere a Minotaur danced about, turning around himself, and everywhere the youth leaped forward and back again, stealthily on supple feet, and then again leapfrogging over his enemy, waiting to strike, and when the sun set behind the labyrinth and the walls were steeped in a dark red glow, he struck, leaped back, leaned against a wall, stared at the Minotaur. The monster made a few more dance steps, with the sword in his breast, stopped, pulled the sword out with his right hand, looked at it in surprise, reached with his left hand to where something black poured out of his breast, threw the sword aside, so that it slid along the floor, pressed his right hand against his breast as well, swayed, seemed about to totter, stood motionless again. He was confused. He did not understand what was staining his hands, nor the pain that was raging in his breast. He only felt that this creature who had lunged at him and had pushed something into his body did not love him as all the others had loved him before, the Minotaurs, the girl, the girls, and as he felt that, he became suspicious, all the more so as he could not think, for everything moved through his mind in the form of images and not in concepts; it was as if he were feeling in a sort of picture-script: maybe the girl hadn't loved him at all, and the other girls hadn't loved the Minotaurs either, and that was why they had pretended to be immobile and left. Maybe they belonged to the new creature, who looked similar to the girl and yet different, with a body that was almost as strong as his own, and who had lunged at him, as the other new creatures had lunged at the Minotaurs, who now stood as he did, with their hands pressed to the blackness flowing from their breast; and when the six other girls and the six other youths appeared, holding hands, so that in the mirrors the row of creatures straying through the labyrinth didn't seem to cease but was doubled, quadrupled, multiplied many times over, and when they found their companion leaning against a wall and hoping the Minotaur would finally collapse, it seemed to the bull-man that—if he had possessed the concept—all of humanity was closing in on him to destroy him. He ducked. He felt threatened, and in order not to be afraid, he set pride against his fear, the pride of being a Minotaur, and whoever was not a Minotaur was his enemy. Only Minotaurs had the right to be in the labyrinth, in a world beside which, for him, there was no other world—for only a vague sensation of bovine warmth from the stalls where he had grown up still darkly moved in his memory. He was seized with the hatred the beast feels before the human being, by whom the beast is tamed, abused, hunted, eaten, the primal hatred that smolders in every beast. His eyes filled with rage. Foam appeared on his lips, and as the youth shifted away from the wall because he mistook the Minotaur's crouching as a sign of his dying, convinced he had dealt him a mortal wound, and as the humans, the girls and the youths, formed a circle around the crouching Minotaur and cheered and danced wildly around him, faster and faster, with more and more abandon, as if they were saved, more and more frantically, without considering that just by being in the labyrinth they were lost—for even if the bull-man had died, they would not have found the way out of the mutually enclosing mirror-walls—more and more careless in the euphoria of their presumed freedom, drawing their circle more and more tightly, more and more menacing in the advancing darkness of night, in which he only saw humans and no longer his own reflections, since the whirling and skipping humans were blocking his view of the walls of the labyrinth, so that these could no longer reflect him back to himself, the Minotaur felt abandoned and betrayed by the Minotaurs as well. He rolled his eyes, snorted, crouched lower, tensed his muscles, and with a sudden leap dashed forward, took a girl on his horns, and disappeared with her in the labyrinth, tossing her into the air again and again. Returning then, snorting with rage, his horns smeared with blood, he found the humans huddled in a shadowy cluster, while above them the ravenous jungle of feathers had already settled on the walls, a dark cluster above a dark cluster, a brawling mob whose hoarse squawks and squeals and chattering shrieks mingled with the human howls of terror. The moon was rising somewhere behind the labyrinth, and the night, still faintly tinted by the descended sun, began to lighten. The Minotaur attacked, butted into a soft confusion of white bodies, jammed his way through, thrust again, rolled about, stamped, pierced, impaled, ripped, gored, slashed, while all around him there was a diving, chopping, sucking, crunching, tearing, smacking, so that the screaming and howling cluster of humans with the raging Minotaur in their midst was wrapped in a dense screeching whirl of flapping and fluttering scavengers: barbed vultures, griffin vultures, king vultures, hooded vultures, black vultures, turkey vultures, white-backed vultures, lappet-faced vultures, condors, and urubu snapped, gulped, dipped in again; with thrust after thrust, the raging bull-man ripped into the scrambling heap of human bodies, tearing out limbs, guzzling blood, breaking bones, rummaging in bellies and wombs, until the scruffy cloud of birds, feathers, necks, eyes, beaks, talons, and claws had dissolved in the moonlight. The Minotaur was alone. Blinded by the moon, once again he saw his reflections on the cold walls as black shadows that fused and blended into a shadow labyrinth within the labyrinth. He raised his arms, threatened with his fists, shook them, his reflections raised their arms with him, threatened with their fists, shook them, which so inflamed his rage that he charged into the nearest shadow with his bull's head lowered. He burst through the wall, furiously searched among the shards for the reflection, which, after all, was his, it seemed to be buried beneath the shards. He rammed his mighty head into the broken glass, and when he saw his reflection on the wall nearest him, he still did not understand, and attacked it again with a roar and threw himself at it head first, as it, too, seemed to throw itself at him head first. He rebounded, gaping with furious reddish bison eyes at his reflection, which gaped back at him with furious reddish bison eyes. He ran into it again, more violently yet, rebounded more violently, landing on his back. The moon was still behind the labyrinth, but it shone through the walls and was mirrored in them as a nearly full moon, the crags on the craters of its not yet rounded side grotesquely enlarged, and so frequently was the moon mirrored that the Minotaur thought he was gazing into a universe of stone that was furrowed with scars. Staring into this moon-world, he feared that his enemy had risen. He rolled over on his stomach and saw that although the betrayer had not risen, he, too, was inching toward him on his belly. Sliding toward his reflection, which was approaching him in the same manner, he was prepared to leap up and throw himself at the other Minotaur, but as he watched him, he sensed in his eyes, just as he was about to leap, that the other one had the same intention. He took a close look at the betrayer's face, impressing it on his memory: covered with fur, the broad forehead overgrown with matted woolly hair crowned with a mountain of glass shards that gleamed bluishly in the moonlight, the short curved horns, the gentle incline of the ridge of his nose, the wet nostrils, the long bluish-red tongue. The Minotaur snorted, so that the steam of his nostrils fogged the mirror he was crawling toward, whereupon he no longer saw his reflection, reached out with his hand to dispel the fog, inadvertently wiping the wetness, and, surprised to suddenly see the betrayer's huge bull-face appear, he instinctively struck with his forehead, slamming it into the wall instead of into the other's head, which was in the wall and not outside it. He was puzzled. He stepped back from the wall, hatefully glaring at his reflection, and his reflection at him, struck with his right fist, the reflection with his left, the two fists met, a renewed exchange of blows with the same result, thereupon he struck with both fists, the mirror image likewise, finally he was drumming against the wall. He drummed his rage, he drummed his greed for destruction, he drummed his wish to avenge himself, he drummed his bloodlust, he drummed his fear, he drummed his rebellion, he drummed his self-assertion, but suddenly he sensed that this creature before him—which was a creature like himself and nevertheless his betrayer, because it was an other and because everything not himself was his enemy—that this creature could not be grasped, that it was unassailable. Ever since his awakening in the labyrinth—which he still did not know was a labyrinth—he had sensed that something mysterious lay between himself and the Minotaurs, something wall-like, but since he had danced about with them as their leader, their king, their god, dancing about through the world of the Minotaurs, he had not paid it any heed, but now, after he had taken the girl and pressed his body to her body and into her body and after he had pierced and torn the bodies of the other humans with his horns and seen the blood pouring out warm and red from their bodies as it had from his, he sensed the unreality of this creature before him, who had betrayed him but who was full of shattered glass as he was, and perhaps his own face was smeared with blood as the betrayer's face was. He touched his face, looked at his hands: his face, too, was bloody. He watched his reflection suspiciously, pretended not to watch it, he felt that it appeared to be something it wasn't. He was at once horrified and curious. He retreated. So did his reflection. And gradually it dawned on him that he was facing himself. He tried to flee, but wherever he turned, he always stood facing himself, he was walled in by himself, everywhere he himself was mirrored by the labyrinth, on and on without end. He sensed that there were not many Minotaurs, but just one Minotaur, that there was only one creature like himself, that he was this isolated one, shut out and shut in, that the labyrinth existed on his account, and only because he had been born, because a creature like him cannot be permitted to exist, for the sake of the boundary set by the gods between beast and man and man and the gods, so that the world can retain its order and not turn into a labyrinth and thereby fall back into the chaos from which it sprang; and when he sensed this, as a feeling without comprehension, as an illumination without recognition, not as a human insight through concepts, but as a Minotaurean insight through images and feelings, he collapsed, and as he lay there, curled up as he had lain in Pasiphaë's body, the Minotaur dreamed that he was a man. He dreamed of language, he dreamed of brotherhood, he dreamed of friendship, he dreamed of shelter, he dreamed of love, of closeness, of warmth, and knew, even as he dreamed, that he was a monster, that neither language, nor brotherhood, nor friendship, nor love, nor closeness, nor warmth would fall to his lot, he dreamed the way men dream of gods, with the sadness of men the man, with the sadness of beasts the Minotaur. Thus Ariadne found him asleep. She came dancing with her ball of yarn, which she was unwinding, and dancing, almost tenderly, she wound the end of the red yarn around his horns, danced back out, following the thread, and when the Minotaur awakened to a glass morning, he saw, mirrored countless times, a Minotaur approaching him, his eyes fixed on the woolen thread, as if it were a trail of blood. At first the Minotaur thought it was his reflection, even though he still did not understand what a reflection was, but then he grasped that the other Minotaur was advancing toward him while he lay on the ground. That confused him. The Minotaur rose and did not notice that the end of the red woolen thread was wound around his horns. The other one came closer. The Minotaur threw both arms upward, so did the other one. The Minotaur became suspicious, the other one might be his reflection after all, then again it seemed to him that the other one hadn't thrown his arms up at the same time he had, the reflections usually all did it at the same time, but he could have been mistaken, since both of them were mirrored and the other one had stopped. The Minotaur made a dance step, and so did the reflections, but this time many reflections lagged in their movement, he saw it clearly. The Minotaur stood motionless again, gazing at the other Minotaur, who also stood motionless. The Minotaur tried to think. He moved the little finger of his right hand, watching closely, moved the finger again, the other one moved the little finger of his right hand, which alarmed the Minotaur, he was not sure, it seemed to him that the other one had moved the little finger of the wrong hand. The other stood before him, but it could just as well be a reflection of the other Minotaur or a reflection of his own reflection. There was no way to puzzle it out. The other, if there was an other, had a head like his, and a body like his. The Minotaur moved his right hand, and the other moved his left hand, almost at the same time, and maybe it was at the same time; and as the Minotaur followed up every possibility, he suddenly saw, on the other Minotaur's body, or on the body of the other Minotaur's reflection, an object, attached to the loins, something fur-like, and while the Minotaur had no idea what it was, it proved to him that he was faced with another Minotaur or another Minotaur's reflection. The Minotaur let out a cry, though it was more a roar than a cry, a long-drawn, bellowing, mooing howl of joy at no longer being the only one, the one forever locked out and in; joy at there being a second Minotaur, not just his own me all over again but a you. The Minotaur began to dance. He danced the dance of brotherhood, the dance of friendship, the dance of shelter, the dance of love, the dance of closeness, the dance of warmth. He danced his happiness, he danced his twosomeness, he danced his salvation, he danced the destruction of the labyrinth, the thundering collapse of its walls and mirrors into the earth, he danced the friendship between Minotaurs, animals, human beings, and gods, with the red woolen yarn wound around his horns he danced around the other Minotaur, who was tightening the red woolen yarn and drawing his dagger from its furry sheath, without the Minotaur's noticing, and the reflections of the one danced around the reflections of the other, which were tightening a red woolen yarn and drawing a dagger from a furry sheath, and when the Minotaur rushed into the other's open arms, confident of having found a friend, a creature like himself, and when his reflections rushed into the arms of the other's reflections, the other struck, and his reflections struck, and so surely did the other sink his dagger into the Minotaur's back that he was already dead when he sank to the ground. Theseus removed the bull's mask from his face, and all his reflections removed the bull's mask from their faces, wound up the red woolen yarn and disappeared from the labyrinth, and all his reflections wound up the red woolen yarn and disappeared from the labyrinth, which no longer mirrored anything except, endlessly, the dark corpse of the Minotaur. Then, before the sun came, there came the birds.

The Assignment; or, On the Observing of the Observer of the Observers

A Novella in Twenty-four Sentences

What will come? What will the future bring? I do not know. I have no presentiment. When a spider plunges from a fixed point to its consequences, it always sees before it an empty space where it can never set foot, no matter how it wriggles. It is that way with me: before me always an empty space; what drives me forward is a consequence that lies behind me. This life is perverse and frightful, it is unbearable.

SØREN KIERKEGAARD

1

When Otto von Lambert was informed by the police that his wife Tina had been found dead and violated at the foot of the Al-Hakim ruin, and that the crime was as yet unsolved, the psychiatrist, well known for his book on terrorism, had the corpse transported by helicopter across the Mediterranean, suspended in its coffin by ropes from the bottom of the plane, so that it trailed after it slightly, over vast stretches of sunlit land, through shreds of clouds, across the Alps in a snowstorm, and later through rain showers, until it was gently reeled down into an open grave surrounded by a mourning party, and covered with earth, whereupon von Lambert, who had noticed that F., too, had filmed the event, briefly scrutinized her and, closing his umbrella despite the rain, demanded that she and her team visit him that same evening, since he had an assignment for her that could not be delayed.

2

F., well known for her film portraits, who had resolved to explore new paths and was pursuing the still vague idea of creating a total portrait, namely a portrait of our planet, by combining random scenes into a whole, which was the reason why she had filmed the strange burial, stood staring after the massively built man, von Lambert, who, drenched and unshaven, had accosted her, and had turned his back on her without greeting, and she decided only after some hesitation to do what he had asked, for she had an unpleasant feeling that something was not right, and that besides, she was running the danger of being drawn into a story that would deflect her from her plans, so that it was with a feeling of repugnance that she arrived with her crew at the psychiatrist's house, impelled by curiosity about the nature of his offer but determined to refuse whatever it was.

3

Von Lambert received her in his studio, demanded to be immediately filmed, willingly submitted to all the preparations, and then, sitting behind his desk, explained to the running camera that he was guilty of his wife's death because he had always treated the heavily depressed woman as a case instead of as a person, until she had accidentally discovered his notes on her sickness and, according to the maid, left the house straightaway, a red fur coat thrown over her denim suit, clutching her pocketbook, after which he had not heard from her at all, but neither had he undertaken to learn her whereabouts, if only to grant her whatever freedom she desired, or, on the other hand, should she discover his investigations, to spare her the feeling that she was being watched from a distance, but now that she had come to such a terrible end he was forced to recognize his guilt not only in having treated her with the cool scrutiny prescribed by psychoanalytic practice but also in having failed to investigate her disappearance, he regarded it as his duty to find out the truth, and beyond that, to make it available to science, since his wife's fate had brought him up against the limits of his profession, but since he was a physical wreck and not capable of taking the trip himself, he was giving her, F., the assignment of reconstructing the murder (of which he as her doctor was the primary cause, the actual perpetrator being but an accidental factor) at the apparent scene of the crime, of recording whatever was there to be recorded, so that the results could be shown at psychoanalytic conferences and presented to the state prosecutor's office, since, being guilty, he, like any criminal, had lost the right to keep his failure secret, and having said this, he handed her a check for a considerable sum of money, several photographs of the murdered woman, her journal, and his notes, whereupon F., much to the surprise of her crew, accepted the assignment.

4

After leaving the psychiatrist's house, F. refused to answer her cameraman's question as to the meaning of all this nonsense, spent most of the night perusing the journal and the doctor's notes, and, after a brief sleep, still in bed, made arrangements with a travel agency for the flight to M., drove into town, bought several newspapers with pictures of the strange funeral and the dead woman on their front pages, and, before checking a hastily scribbled address she had found in the journal, went to an Italian restaurant for breakfast, where she encountered the logician D., whose lectures at the university were attended by two or three students—an eccentric and sharp-witted man of whom no one could tell whether he was unfit for life or merely pretended to be helpless, who expounded his logical problems to anyone who joined him at his table in the always crowded restaurant, and this in such a confused and thoroughgoing manner that no one was able to understand him, not F. either, though she found him amusing, liked him, and often told him about her plans, as she did now, mentioning first the peculiar assignment she had been given, and going on to talk about the dead woman's journal, as if to herself, unconscious of her interlocutor, so preoccupied was she by that densely filled notebook, for never, she said, never in her life had she read a similar description of a person, Tina von Lambert had portrayed her husband as a monster, but gradually, not immediately, virtually peeling off pieces of him, facet by facet, examining each one separately, as if under a microscope, constantly narrowing and magnifying the focus and sharpening the light, page after page about his eating habits, page after page about the way he picked his teeth, page after page about how and where he scratched himself, page after page about his coughing or sneezing or clearing his throat or smacking his lips, his involuntary movements, gestures, twitches, idiosyncrasies more or less common to most people, but described in such a way that she, F., had a hard time contemplating the subject of food now, and if she had not touched her breakfast yet, it was only because she could not help imagining that she herself was disgusting to look at while eating, for it was impossible to eat aesthetically, and reading this journal was like being immersed in a cloud of pure observations gradually condensing into a lump of hate and revulsion, or like reading a film script for a documentary of every human being, as if every person, if he or she were filmed in this manner, would turn into a von Lambert as he was described by this woman, all individuality crushed out by such ruthless observation, while F.'s own impression of the psychiatrist had been one of a fanatic who was beginning to doubt his cause, extraordinarily childlike and helpless in a way that reminded her of many scientists, a man who had always believed and still believed that he loved his wife, and to whom it had never occurred that it was all too easy to imagine that one loved someone, and that basically one loved only oneself, but even before meeting him, the spectacular funeral had made her suspect that its purpose was to cover up his hurt pride, why not, and as for the assignment to hunt for the circumstances of her death, he was probably trying, albeit unconsciously, to build a monument to himself, and if Tina's description of her husband was grotesque in its exaggeration and excessive concreteness, von Lambert's notes were equally grotesque in their abstraction, they weren't observations at all but literally an abstracting of her humanity, defining depression as a psychosomatic phenomenon resulting from insight into the meaninglessness of existence, which is inherent in existence itself, since the meaning of existence *is* existence, which insight, once accepted and affirmed, makes existence unbearable, so that Tina's insight into that insight *was* the depression, and so forth, this sort of idiocy page after page, which made it seem inconceivable to her that Tina had fled as a result of having read these pages, as von Lambert apparently suspected, even though two of her journal entries ended with the doubly underlined sentence: "I am being watched," a statement for which F. had a different interpretation, namely that Tina had found out that von Lambert had read her journal, obviously a much more shattering discovery than von Lambert's notes could have been, since, for one who secretly hates and suddenly learns that the hated one knows it, there could be no other way out than to flee, at which point F. ended her comments with the remark that something about this story was not right, there still was the riddle of what could have driven Tina into the desert, it was all beginning to make her feel like one of those probes they shoot out into space in the hope that they will transmit back to the earth information about its still unknown composition.

5

D. had listened to F.'s report and absently ordered a glass of wine, even though it was just eleven o'clock, gulped it down with an equally absent air, ordered a second glass, and remarked that he was still pondering the useless problem of whether the law of identity A = A was correct, since it posited two identical A's, while actually there could only be one A identical with itself, and anyway, applied to reality it was quite meaningless, since there was no self-identical person anywhere, because everyone was subject to time and was therefore, strictly speaking, a different person at every moment, which was why he, D., sometimes had the impression that he was a different person each morning, as if a different self had replaced his previous self and were using his brain and consequently his memory, making him all the more glad that he was a logician, for logic was beyond all reality and removed from every sort of existential mishap, and so he would like to respond to the story she had told him but could only do so in very general terms: good old von Lambert had no doubt experienced a shock, not as a husband, though, but as a psychiatrist whose patient has fled, and now he was turning his human failing into a failure of psychiatry, and the psychiatrist was left standing like a jailer without prisoners, bereft of his subject, and what he was calling his fault was this lack, what he wanted from F. was merely the missing document for his documentation, by trying to know what he could never understand, he was hoping to bring the dead woman back into captivity, and the whole thing would be perfect material for a comedy if it didn't contain a problem that had been troubling him, D., for a long time, a logical problem loosely involving a mirror telescope he had installed in his house in the mountains, an unwieldy thing that he occasionally pointed at a cliff from which he was being observed by people with field glasses, with the effect that, as soon as the people observing him through their field glasses realized that he was observing them through his telescope, they would retreat in a hurry, an empirical confirmation, in short, of the logical conclusion that anything observed requires the presence of an observer, who, if he is observed by what he is observing, himself becomes an object of observation, a banal logical interaction, which, however, transposed into reality, had a destabilizing effect, for the people observing him and discovering that he was observing them through a mirror telescope felt caught in the act, and since being caught in the act produces embarrassment and embarrassment frequently leads to aggression, more than one of these people, after retreating in haste, had come back to throw rocks at his house as soon as he had dismantled the telescope, a dialectical process, said D., that was symptomatic of our time, when everyone observed and felt observed by everyone else, so that a very suitable definition of contemporary man might be that he is man under observation—observed by the state, for one, with more and more sophisticated methods, while man makes more and more desperate attempts to escape being observed, which in turn renders man increasingly suspect in the eyes of the state and the state even more suspect in the eyes of man; similarly each state observes and feels observed by all the other states, and man, on another plane, is busy observing nature as never before, inventing more and more subtle instruments for this purpose, cameras, telescopes, stereoscopes, radio telescopes, X-ray telescopes, microscopes, synchrotrons, satellites, space probes, computers, all designed to coax more and more new observations out of nature, from quasars trillions of light-years away to particles a billionth of a millimeter in diameter to the discovery that electromagnetic rays are nothing but radiant mass and mass is frozen electromagnetic radiation: never before had man observed nature so closely that she stood virtually naked before him, yes, denuded of all her secrets, exploited, her resources squandered, which was why it occasionally seemed to him, D., that nature, for her part, was observing man and becoming aggressive, for what was the pollution of air, earth, and water, what were the dying forests, but a strike, a deliberate refusal to neutralize the poisons, while the new viruses, earthquakes, droughts, floods, hurricanes, volcanic eruptions, et cetera, were precisely aimed defensive measures of observed nature against her observer, much the way D.'s mirror telescope and the rocks that were thrown at his house were measures taken against being observed, or, for that matter, von Lambert's manner of observing his wife and her manner of observing him, in each case a process of objectification pursued to a degree that could only be unbearable to the other, the doctor turning the wife into an object of psychoanalytic scrutiny and she turning him into an object of hate until, struck by the sudden insight that she, the observer, was being observed by the observed, she spontaneously threw her red fur coat over her denim suit and fled the vicious circle of mutual observation, and met with her death, but, he added, after suddenly bursting into laughter and becoming serious again, what he was constructing here was of course only one of two possibilities, the other one being the precise opposite of what he had described, for a logical conclusion always depends on the initial situation: if, in his house in the mountains, he were being observed less and less, so rarely that, when he pointed his mirror telescope at people who he presumed were observing him from the cliff, they turned out to be observing not him but something else through their field glasses, chamois or mountain climbers or whatnot, this state of not being observed would begin to torment him after a while, much more than the knowledge of being observed had bothered him earlier, so that he would virtually yearn for those rocks to be thrown at his house, because not being watched would make him feel not worth noticing, not being worth noticing would make him feel disrespected, being disrespected would make him feel insignificant, being insignificant would make him feel meaningless, and, he imagined, the end result might be a hopeless depression, in fact he might even give up his unsuccessful academic career as meaningless, and would have to conclude that other people suffered as much from not being observed as he did, that they, too, felt meaningless unless they were being observed, and that therefore they all observed and took snapshots and movies of each other out of fear of experiencing the meaninglessness of their existence in the face of a dispersing universe with billions of Milky Ways like our own, settled with countless of life-bearing but hopelessly remote and therefore isolated planets like our own, a cosmos filled with incessant pulsations of exploding and collapsing suns, leaving no one, except man himself, to pay any attention to man and thereby lend him meaning, for a personal god was no longer possible in the face of such a monstrosity as this universe, a god as world regent and father who keeps an eye on everyone, who counts the hairs on every head, this god was dead because he had become inconceivable, an axiom of faith without any roots in human understanding, only an impersonal god was still conceivable as an abstract principle, as a philosophical-literary construct with which to magically smuggle some kind of meaning into the monstrous whole, vague and vaporous, feeling is all, the name nothing but sound and fury, nebulous glow of heaven locked in the porcelain stove of the heart, but the intellect too, he said, was incapable of coming up with a persuasive illusion of meaning outside of man, for everything that could be thought or done, logic, metaphysics, mathematics, natural law, art, music, poetry, was given its meaning by man, and without man, it sank back into the realm of the unimagined and unconceived and hence into meaninglessness, and a great deal of what was happening today became understandable if one pursued this line of reasoning, man was staggering along in the mad hope of somehow finding someone to be observed by somewhere, by conducting an arms race, for instance, for of course the powers engaged in an arms race were forced to observe one another, which was why they basically hoped to be able to keep up the arms race forever, so that they would have to observe one another forever, since without an arms race, the contending powers would sink into insignificance, but if by some mishap the arms race should set off the nuclear fireworks, which it had been quite capable of accomplishing for some time, it would represent nothing more than a meaningless manifestation of the fact that the earth had once been inhabited, fireworks without anyone to observe them, unless it were some kind of humanity or similar life form somewhere near Sirius or elsewhere, without any chance of communicating to the one who so badly desired to be observed (since he would no longer exist) that, in fact, he *had* been observed, and even the religious and political fundamentalism that was breaking out or persisting wherever one looked was an indication that many, indeed most, people could not stand themselves if they were not observed by someone, and would flee either into the fantasy of a personal god or into an equally metaphysically conceived political party that (or who) would observe them, a condition from which they in turn would derive the right to observe whether the world was heeding the laws of the all-observing god or party—except for the terrorists, their case was a bit more complex, their goal being not an observed but an unobserved child's paradise, but because they experienced the world in which they lived as a prison where they were not only unjustly locked up but were left unattended and unobserved in one of the dungeons, they desperately sought to force themselves on the attention of their guards and thus step out of their unobserved condition into the limelight of public notice, which, however, they could achieve only by, paradoxically, drawing back into unobserved obscurity again and again, from the dungeon into the dungeon, unable, ever, to come out and be free, in short, humanity was about to return to its swaddling clothes, fundamentalists, idealists, moralists, and political Christers were doing their utmost to saddle unobserved humanity with the blessings of being observed, and therefore with meaning, for man, in the final analysis, was a pedant who couldn't get by without meaning and was therefore willing to put up with anything except the freedom to not give a damn about meaning—like Tina von Lambert: she, too, had dreamed of drawing upon herself the observing eyes of the world, so perhaps one could read her doubly underlined sentence "I am being observed" as a statement of certainty about the victorious outcome of her enterprise, but, if one accepted this possibility, it would be just the beginning of the actual tragedy, in that her husband did not recognize her flight as an attempt to make others observe her, but, interpreting it as an escape from being observed, failed to undertake an investigation, thus scotching her plans from the outset, and she, upon finding that her disappearance remained unobserved, which is to say, ignored, may have felt impelled to seek out more and more audacious adventures, until, by her death, she achieved the desired end, her picture in all the papers and all the world observing her and giving her the recognition and meaning for which she had yearned.

6

F., who had listened attentively to the logician and had ordered a Campari, said she supposed D. wondered why she had accepted von Lambert's assignment, that the difference between observing and being observed was an entertaining logical game, but not as interesting to her as what he had said earlier about man's not ever being identical with himself because he was always an other, thrown into time, if she had properly understood D., which, however, would mean that there was no self, or rather, only a countless chain of selves emerging from the future, flashing into the present, and sinking back into the past, so that what one commonly called one's self was merely a collective term for all the selves gathered up in the past, a great heap of selves perpetually growing under the constant rain of selves drifting down through the present from the future, an accumulation of shreds of experience and memory, comparable to a mound of leaves that grows higher and higher under a steady drift of other falling leaves, while the ones at the bottom have long turned to humus, a process that seemed to imply a fiction of selfhood in which every person made up his own self, imagining himself playing a role for better or worse, which would make the possession of character mainly a matter of putting on a good act, and the more unconscious and unintentional the performance, the more genuine its effect, all of which would go a long way toward explaining why it was so hard to make a portrait of an actor, they tended to perform their own character a little too obviously, their intentional actorishness appeared false, looking back on her career and the people she had portrayed gave her the feeling of having made movies of cheap hams, for the most part, especially the politicians, only a few of whom had been capable of putting on a major performance of themselves, which was why she had decided to give up making film portraits, but while reading Tina von Lambert's diary last night, over and over, and trying to imagine this young woman striding off into the desert in a red fur coat, walking in an ocean of sand and stone, she, F., had realized that she would have to follow that woman's trail with her crew and go to the Al-Hakim ruin, come what may, because there in the desert, she sensed, was a reality she would have to meet, just like Tina, and if, for Tina, that reality had been death, it remained to be seen what it would be for her, and then, draining her glass of Campari, she asked D. whether he thought it was crazy of her to accept this assignment, to which D. replied that she should go to the desert because she was looking for a new role, her old role had been that of an observer of roles, and now she wanted to attempt the opposite, not portraiture, which presupposed a subject, but reconstruction, raking together scattered leaves to build up the subject of her portrait, never being sure, all the while, whether the leaves she was heaping up actually belonged together, or whether, in fact, she wasn't ultimately making a self-portrait, in short, a crazy enterprise, but, on the other hand, so crazy that it wasn't crazy, and he wished her well.

7

If the morning had already been humid, almost like summer, at the moment when she stepped up to her car there was a thunderclap, and she rolled up the top of her convertible just in time to avoid a downpour, through which she drove past the center of town to the old market and parked, ignoring a NO STOPPING sign, and she had not been mistaken, the address hastily scribbled on one page of the journal was that of a studio belonging to an artist who had recently died, he had moved away from the city many years ago, no doubt someone else was using it, if it was still in existence at all, for it had fallen into such lamentable disrepair that she was convinced it would have been demolished by now, but because the address must have something to do with Tina von Lambert (otherwise it could not have appeared in the journal), she ran the short distance between her car and the door of the building through the pouring rain, and although the door was not locked, she was drenched by the time she had entered the hallway, which had not changed, the hard rain was splashing against the cobblestones of the courtyard, nothing had changed there either, there was the shed that had served as the artist's studio, everything the same, and surprisingly, even the door was open, but the stairs led up into darkness, she searched in vain for a light switch, climbed the stairs, holding her hands out in front of her, reached another door and was in the studio, and there, too, in the dim silvery light shining in through the two rain-washed windows, amazingly, nothing had changed, the long, narrow room was still full of the painter's works, large-scale portraits, the most adventurous denizens of the industrial suburb were standing all about, the con men, the winos, the professionally unemployed, bagmen, street preachers, pimps, smugglers, and other artists of life, most of them under the ground now, no doubt less ceremoniously interred than the painter, whose funeral she remembered, conceivably some weeping prostitutes had come, or some drinking buddies who poured beer on the grave, assuming there had been a funeral at all and not a cremation, portraits she had presumed, in fact seen, in museums, and at the feet of these figures who were no longer present except on canvas stood smaller pictures, representing a streetcar, toilets, pans, wrecked cars, bicycles, umbrellas, traffic policemen, Cinzano bottles, there was nothing the painter had not depicted, the disorder was tremendous, in front of a huge, half-torn leather armchair stood a box, on top of it slices of air-dried beef on a tray, Chianti bottles on the floor and a water glass half filled with wine, newspapers, eggshells, paint spots everywhere, as if the artist were still alive, brushes, palettes, bottles of turpentine and petroleum, the only thing missing was a scaffold, the rain slapped against the two windows on the long wall to her left, and in order to see better, F. removed a secretary of state and a bank director (who for the past two years had been leading a somewhat diminished existence in jail) to let in some light from a third window in the back, and found herself standing before a painting of a woman in a red fur coat, which F. at first took for a portrait of Tina von Lambert, but which turned out not to be Tina after all, it could just as well be a portrait of a woman who looked like Tina, and then, with a shock, it seemed to her that this woman standing before her defiantly with wide-open eyes was herself, and at the precise moment when this thought shot through her, she heard steps behind her and turned around, but too late, the door had slammed shut, and when she returned to the studio with her crew in the late afternoon, the portrait had disappeared, and a film crew was shooting the studio, a reconstruction, according to the peculiarly giddy director, the idea was to give an impression, before the opening of the retrospective exhibition at the museum, of how the studio had looked when the artist was using it, no one had used it since then, they searched through the catalog, the portrait was not listed, and besides, it was simply not possible that the studio would have been left unlocked.

8

Still confused by this experience, which seemed to her like a sign that she was searching in the wrong direction, she nearly canceled her flight, but checked the impulse, the preparations took their course, already they were flying over Spain, beneath them the Guadalquivir, the Atlantic came into view, and when they landed in C., she began to look forward to the trip inland, the trees would probably still be green, and she remembered a road lined with date palms that she had seen on a previous trip several years ago, cars coming toward her on the way back from the snow-covered Atlas mountains with skis on their roofs; however, right after landing, still on the runway, she and her crew were picked up by the police and taken with all their equipment and without having to pass through customs to a military transport plane and flown to the country's interior, to be driven at breakneck speed from the airport at M. to the city, past throngs of tourists who craned their necks as she passed, escorted by four policemen on motorcycles and accompanied by a TV crew in two cars with incessantly running cameras, one car in front of her, one behind, all the way to the police ministry, where F. and her crew were filmed while filming the police chief as he leaned against his desk in his white uniform, incredibly fat, reminiscent of Göring,* voicing his pleasure at having the opportunity, despite his government's misgivings, to allow F. and her crew to inspect and film the site of the gruesome

*Hermann Göring (1893–1946), senior Nazi official (commander-in-chief of the air force and later Reichsmarschall).

misdeed, and his particular pleasure at learning that, in her effort to reconstruct the crime, F. would be documenting the impeccable work of his police force, who were equipped with the most modern weapons and not only met but exceeded international standards, a shameless proposal that reinforced the suspicion F. had been harboring ever since her experience in the artist's studio, that she was on the wrong trail, for already her enterprise, scarcely begun, had been rendered meaningless by this fat man who was constantly wiping the sweat off his forehead with a silk handkerchief and to whom all she represented with a source of publicity for himself and his police, but, having once entered the trap, she could see no immediate way to escape it, for it was not just the police who were holding her and her crew captive by leading them to a jeep whose turbaned driver (all the other policemen wore white helmets) motioned F. to sit down next to him while the cameraman and the sound technician sat down behind her and the assistant carrying the equipment had to board a second jeep, driven by a black man—the TV crew, too, was following them as they approached the desert, to the annoyance of F., who would have preferred to gather information first but had no way of explaining herself, because, whether by design or by negligence, no interpreter was present and the policemen accompanying her or rather bossing her around did not have the command of French one might have expected in this country, and also because the TV crew was racing out of earshot into the stone desert, off to the side of F.'s jeep, the caravan falling into such disarray that the other cars, including the jeep with the assistant and the equipment, seemed to be moving apart in the boiling distance, each according to its driver's whim, even the four motorcycle cops who were supposed to form her escort veered from her jeep and zoomed off, chasing each other, chugged back in her direction, then leaned away again in wide arcs, while the TV crew shot straight toward the horizon and presently vanished out of sight, but as if to make up for that, her driver, stammering some incomprehensible sounds, set off in pursuit of a jackal, curving after it, the jackal running, running, throwing feints, changing direction abruptly, always tailed by the jeep, which seemed on the verge of capsizing several times, while F. and the cameraman and the sound technicians clung to their seats, then the motorcyclists came roaring by, yelling and making signs that were undecipherable to them, until suddenly they had left the stone desert and were tearing along a macadam road through vast stretches of sand, with no other vehicle in sight, even the four motorcyclists had disappeared, somehow, unaccountably, the driver who had been unable to run down the jackal had managed to find this road, even though it was partially covered over with sand, and now the desert on either side looked to F. like an ocean plowed up by the jeeps as if by a ship's prow, waves of sand towering up on either side as the shadows grew longer, when all of a sudden the Al-Hakim ruin rose up before them from a depression into which they flew unexpectedly, straight toward the monument that loomed up before her from the swarming cluster of policemen and television people who had already gathered in front of it, black, obscuring the sun, the enigmatic witness of an unimaginably ancient time, discovered around the turn of the century as a huge flat stone square, polished smooth as a mirror by the sand, which turned out to be the top surface of a cube and, as the excavations continued, acquired ever more impressive dimensions, but when plans were made to uncover the whole of it, some saints of a Shi'ite sect, emaciated and covered with rags, had squatted down by one of the sides of the cube, wrapped in black cloaks, waiting for the mad caliph Al-Hakim, who, according to their belief, lurked inside the cube and was about to burst forth any month, any day, any minute, any second, to assume dominion over the world, they huddled like great black birds, no one dared chase them away, the archaeologists dug up the other three sides of the cube, reaching deeper and deeper, while the black Sufis, as they were called, sat far above them, always motionless, even when the wind covered them with sand, visited only once a week by a gigantic Negro who came riding on a donkey to shove a spoonful of cereal into their mouths and splash water over their heads, and of whom it was said that he was still a slave, and when F. approached them—because a young police officer, suddenly in full command of the French language, had explained to her that Tina's body had been found among these "saints," as he respectfully called them, and that someone must have dropped her there, though it was impossible to obtain any information from them, since they had taken a vow of silence until the return of their "Mahdi"—when she came closer and gazed for a long time at the long rows of silent, crouching men who seemed to have become one with the black squares of the cube, a fungus attached to one of its flanks, like mummies with long, white, stringy, sand-encrusted beards, the eyes invisible in their black sockets, densely covered with crawling masses of flies, hands clasped like claws with long fingernails penetrating the palms, and then, cautiously, touched one of them to see if perhaps she might get some information after all, he keeled over, it was a corpse, so was the one next to him, the cameras behind her whirred, the third man gave the impression of still being alive, but she gave up, only her cameraman strode down the length of the row with the camera pressed to his eye, and when she reported the incident to the police officer, who had stayed by his car, he replied that the jackals would take care of the rest, Tina's body, too, he said, had been found torn and partially eaten, and at that moment dusk set in, the sun must have set behind the depression, and it seemed to F. that night was attacking her like a merciful enemy who kills quickly.

9

The next day, before F. could book a return flight, the cameraman informed her that the exposed footage had disappeared, someone had switched the rolls of film, the TV people had insisted it *was* his footage, the cameraman had then demanded furiously, and was promised, that the rolls would be developed by the evening, too late to catch a plane, and once again they were being abducted by the police, and this in a manner that made it seem wiser to pretend compliance, for after being led into the subterranean prison compound at the police ministry, where they were introduced to prisoners whom F. was permitted to question and film, each man was relieved of his handcuffs the moment he entered the room, but after he had sat down on the stool he was offered, a policeman would press a submachine gun into the back of his neck, badly shaved individuals, all of them, with missing teeth, who greedily reached for the cigarettes F. offered them and, when asked if they had seen the woman in the picture, briefly glanced at the snapshot of Tina and nodded, and when F. asked them where, quietly answered, "In the ghetto," all of them wearing dirty white linen pants and jackets, no shirts, as if in uniform and all of them with the same answer: in the ghetto, in the ghetto, in the ghetto, and then each one told her how someone had tried to hire him to kill the woman in the picture, she was the wife of a man who had defended the Arab resistance movement and hadn't called it a terrorist organization, or something like that, he hadn't been able to figure out why the woman was supposed to die for that, he had refused the offer, it hadn't been enough money, there were fixed tariffs for this kind of thing, a question of honor, the man who had made the offer was short and fat, an American, probably, or— that was all he knew, he had only seen the woman once, in the fat man's company, in the ghetto, as he'd already explained, all the others gave similar statements, mechanically, greedily smoking their cigarettes, only one of them grinned when he saw the picture, blew smoke into F.'s face, he was small, almost dwarfish, with a big wrinkled face, spoke English more or less the way Scandinavians speak English, said he had never seen this woman, nobody had seen this woman, whereupon the policeman pulled him up to his feet and struck him in the back with his submachine gun, but an officer stepped in quickly, barked at the policeman, suddenly other policemen were in the room, the man with the big wrinkled face was led out, a new prisoner was shoved in from outside, sat down in the glare of the arc light, the clapper again, the whirring of the camera, reached for a cigarette with quivering hands, looked at the picture, told the same story as the others, with insignificant variations, mumbling at times, like the others, because, like the others, he had almost no teeth, then the next man, then the last, whereupon they left the bare concrete room where they had questioned the men, containing just a wobbly table, an arc light, and some chairs, walked through the subterranean prison world, past iron bars behind which, in the cells, something whitish cowered or lay on the floor, and ascended by elevator to the investigating magistrate's modern and comfortably furnished office, where the magistrate, a gentle, pretty-faced lawyer with rimless glasses that didn't suit him, regaled F. and her crew with every conceivable delicacy, even caviar and vodka (they were sitting on comfortable armchairs around a glass-topped table), while he dedicated himself assiduously to an Alsatian white wine that a French colleague had sent him, waved off the cameraman, who was already raising his camera, and explained at great length that he was a believing Moslem, in many respects even a fundamentalist, that Khomeini has his undeniably positive, even magnificent aspects, but that the process leading to a synthesis of the Koran's philosophy of law and European jurisprudence could simply no longer be stopped in this country, it was comparable with the integration of Aristotle into medieval Moslem theology, and finally, after a tiresome, rambling detour by way of the history of the Spanish Umayyads, he returned as if by accident to the case of Tina von Lambert, expressing his regret, his sympathetic understanding of the emotions this case had elicited in Europe, a culture that tended to the tragic view of life, while Islam inclined to fatalism, then produced some photographs of the body, and said, "Oh, well, the jackals," adding that after the killing the body had been taken to the black Sufis at the Al-Hakim monument, which, with all due respect, suggested a Christian, or—well, you know—perpetrator, no Moslem would have dared throw the corpse among the saints, there was general indignation about that, whereupon he showed them the medical examiner's report, rape, death by strangulation, apparently without a struggle, the men presented to F. downstairs had been foreign agents, and as for who might have been interested in killing her, well, there was no need to get too specific, von Lambert's refusal, at the international antiterrorist congress, to refer to Arab freedom fighters as terrorists, a certain secret service had felt it necessary to set an example, one of the agents was the probable perpetrator, the country was full of spies, including, naturally, Soviet spies, Czechs, East Germans especially, but mainly American, French, English, West German, Italian spies, why count them all, in short, adventurers from all over the world, that certain secret service, F. would know who he was talking about, were by far the most crafty of all, they hired other agents, that was their perfidious specialty, the killing of Tina von Lambert was, on the one hand, an act of revenge, and on the other it was intended to disrupt the good trade relations between his country and the European Common Market, especially the export of goods and products that were the principal source of revenue for—oh, well—and then, after the investigating magistrate had taken a call, he silently stared at F. and her crew, opened the door, motioned for them to follow, led them through corridors, down a flight of stairs, along further corridors, narrower than the others, until they reached a wall with a number of peepholes through which one could look out upon a bare courtyard that was evidently enclosed by the building, but all they saw were smooth, windowless walls, which made the courtyard look like a shaft, or pit, into which the dwarfish Scandinavian was now led past a rank of policemen with white helmets and white gloves and submachine guns slung over their shoulders, handcuffed, behind him a police captain with a drawn sword, the Scandinavian stopped in front of the concrete wall facing the rank of policemen, the officer walked back to his men and positioned himself next to the rank, held the sword vertically in front of his face, just like a scene in an operetta, and as if to emphasize that, the rotund police chief came in, waddling laboriously, sweating, until he had reached the dwarfish, grinning man by the wall, stuck a cigarette in his mouth, lit it, and slowly waddled out of view, the camera whirred, somehow the cameraman had found a way to record what was happening down below, the dwarfish man smoked, the policemen stood aiming their submachine guns at him (there was something attached to the muzzles, silencers probably), waiting, the officer lowered his sword again, the policemen were growing restless, the officer abruptly raised his sword back to a vertical position, the policemen took aim once again, a dull thud followed, and as the policemen lowered their guns, the dwarfish man reached for the cigarette with his manacled hands, dropped it, extinguished it with his foot, collapsed, and lay on the ground, motionless, blood flowing out of him toward the center of the courtyard, where there was a drain, and the investigating magistrate, stepping away from his peephole, said the Scandinavian had confessed, he was the killer, regrettably the police chief was given to rash and precipitate actions, however, given the general indignation in the country—oh, well—and back they went, along the narrow passageway, through the iron gate, down corridors, but different ones this time, up stairs and down stairs, then a projection room, the police chief was there already, filling his armchair, gracious, animated by the execution, perfumed rivulets of sweat on his face, smoking cigarettes like the one he had offered the dwarfish man, in whose confession neither F. nor her crew believed, nor, apparently, the investigating magistrate, who, muttering another "Oh, well," discreetly withdrew, on the screen now the Al-Hakim ruin, the cars, the television crews, the policemen, the four motorcyclists, the arrival of F. with her crew, the cameraman instructing the foolishly smiling assistant, the sound technician fussing with his instruments, intermittently the desert, a policeman on a camel, the jeep, the turbaned driver at the wheel, finally F. staring at something, but no indication of what it was: the figures crouching at the foot of the ruin, those manlike creatures covered with flies, half submerged in sand, sand sweeping across their black cloaks, no picture of these, just more policemen, then their training, policemen in classrooms, in athletic contests, in dormitories, brushing their teeth, taking showers en masse, the whole thing applauded by the white-clad Göring, this film, he declared, was magnificent, yes, he could only congratulate her, and upon F.'s protest that this wasn't her film at all, he said, "Really?" and immediately supplied the answer: the material must have been useless, it was really no wonder in the desert sun, but the crime was solved now, the perpetrator had been executed, he wished her a pleasant trip home, whereupon he stood up, graciously took his leave, "Farewell, my child," which F. found particularly annoying, and walked out of the room.

10

Outside the building, the policeman with the turban was waiting for her at the wheel of his jeep with a mocking smile, while behind him, tourists jammed the broad esplanade between the police ministry and the great mosque, beleaguered by children who pried open the foreigners' hands, hoping to find some money, attacked by the barking sounds of a sermon transmitted by loudspeakers from inside the mosque, and by the tooting and honking of taxis and tour buses seeking a path through a thicket of travelers from many nations all busily photographing and filming each other and forming an unreal contrast to the secret life inside the compound of the police ministry, like two interlocking realities, one of them cruel and demonic, the other as banal as tourism itself, and when the turbaned policeman addressed F. in French, which he hadn't been able to speak before, it was too much for her: she left her crew, she wanted to be alone, feeling guilty of the little Scandinavian's death, who had only been executed in order to put an end to her investigation, she kept seeing the wrinkled face, the cigarette between his thin lips, then the flies crawling over the skulls of the black-robed men by the Al-Hakim ruin, and it seemed to her that at the moment when she set foot in this country, she had stepped into a waking nightmare, and also that, for the first time in her life, she had failed, for if she tried to carry out her assignment, she would be endangering not only her own life but that of her crew, the police chief was dangerous, he would hold back at nothing, some secret was hidden behind Tina von Lambert's death, the investigating magistrate's preachments were all too transparent, a clumsy attempt to hide something, cover it up, but what was it, she didn't know, and then she reproached herself for allowing someone to leave the studio while she was looking at the portrait of the women in the red fur coat, a face that, at least now, in memory, seemed to resemble her own more and more, was it a man or a women who had been hiding in the studio, had the director kept something from her, the bed she had discovered behind the curtain, who had used it, she had failed to look into this and now she was furious at herself for being so careless, and, jostled by tourists, she arrived in the old city and suddenly found it difficult to breathe on account of the smell that enveloped her, not a particular smell but the combined odors of every kind of herb mixed with the smell of blood and feces, of coffee, honey, and sweat, she moved through dark, cavernous streets that were constantly lighting up, since there was always someone in the crowd taking a picture, past stacks of copper kettles and bowls, pots, rugs, jewelry, radios, television sets, suitcases, meat and fish stands, mountains of vegetables and fruit, always wrapped in that penetrating cloud of odors and stenches, until she suddenly brushed against something furry, and stopped, people squeezing past her, pressing against her, local people, no longer tourists, she realized with some bewilderment, suspended above her from wire hangers were cheap gaudy skirts of every color, all the more grotesque as no one wore such skirts, and what she had brushed against was a red fur coat that she immediately knew was Tina von Lambert's coat, it must have attracted her magically, so it seemed to her, which was why she almost compulsively entered the store in front of which the clothes were hung, a cavelike place, it took a while before her eyes got used to the dark and she distinguished an old man, whom she addressed but who didn't react, whereupon she seized him by the hand and forced him to follow her outside, beneath his gaudy skirts, disregarding the children who had gathered around and stood staring, wide-eyed, at F., who had torn the fur coat from its hanger and, determined to buy it no matter what the price, realized only then that she was dealing with a blind man whose only garment was a long dirty robe that had once been white, with a large encrusted spot of blood on the breast, half covered by a gray beard, his face immobile, his eyes, whitish-yellow, without pupils, he seemed deaf as well, she took his hand, stroked the fur with it, he didn't answer, the children stood there, the local people stopped, others joined them, wondering what was causing the congestion, the old man still didn't say anything, F. reached into her bag, which she always wore slung over her denim suit, containing, carefree as she was, her passport, her jewelry, her makeup, and her money, pressed some bills into the blind man's hand, put on the coat and walked off through the crowd, accompanied by a few children who jabbered incomprehensible words at her, and then, without any idea of how she had found her way out of the old city or where she was, she found a taxi that brought her to her hotel, where her crew was lounging in the lobby, staring at her as she stood before them in her red fur coat, asked the sound technician for a cigarette and explained that the red fur coat she had found in the center of town had been worn by Tina von Lambert when she went to the desert, and that, absurd as it seemed, she was not going to leave until she had found out the truth about Tina von Lambert's death.

11

Does this make sense, asked the sound technician, the assistant grinned uneasily, and the cameraman stood up and said he wasn't going to put up with this nonsense, the minute F. had left them, some cops had come to confiscate the material they had shot in the ministry, and when they arrived at the hotel, the clerk had told them he'd already booked a return flight and arranged for a taxi at the crack of dawn, as far as he was concerned he was fed up with this whole damn country, the men they'd questioned had been tortured, that was why they had no teeth, and the shooting of the dwarf, he'd puked in his room for an hour, it was nuts to stick one's nose in this country's politics, all his fears had been confirmed, this wasn't the place to conduct any sort of research deserving the name, it wasn't just impossible, it was potentially lethal, which wouldn't even matter if he could see the slightest chance of success, and then, throwing himself back in the armchair, he added that the whole project was so vague, frankly so confused, that he could only advise F. to give it up, fine, she'd found a red fur coat, but how could she be sure it was von Lambert's coat, to which F. replied with irritation that she had never given up anything, and when the sound technician, who loved nothing more than peace, suggested it might be better if she left with them because some facts were by nature undiscoverable, she went up to her room without saying good-bye, did not cross the threshold, however, for there in the armchair beneath the lamp sat the gentle, pretty-faced man with rimless glasses, the investigating magistrate, who returned F.'s long, wordless gaze, and then, with a movement of his hand, invited her to sit down on the second armchair, which she did, mechanically, because it seemed to her as if behind those soft, sentimental features she could discern something hard and determined that had been previously hidden, his language, too, as he began to talk, congratulating her for her discovery of Tina von Lambert's coat, was no longer circumlocutious, but hard, accurate, and often sarcastic, like that of a man who enjoys hoodwinking an opponent, so that all she could do was wordlessly nod when he informed her that he had come to thank her for the material she had filmed, the black saints and the execution of the Dane were marvelously suited to his purposes, and when she asked what his purposes were, he calmly replied that, incidentally, he had taken the liberty of having a bottle of Chablis added to the usual fruit juices, lemonades, and mineral waters in the refrigerator, and that next to the refrigerator was a bottle of whiskey, and when she said she preferred whiskey, he said he had thought so, there were nuts, too, stood up, opened the refrigerator, returned with two glasses of whiskey, ice, and nuts, introduced himself as the head of the secret service, well informed about her habits, and he hoped she would forgive all the babbling in the ministry, the police chief had bugged every conceivable nook and cranny, he, too, incidentally, could hear anything the police chief listened to, any time he wished, and then, with a few words, he told her that the police chief was planning a coup, that he wanted to change the country's foreign policy, blame a foreign secret service for the murder of Tina, hence the shooting of the Dane, but the police chief had no idea that the execution was on film, nor did he know he was being watched by the head of the secret service, he didn't even know who the head of the secret service was, all the police chief wanted was to look like a strong man who could use the police as his private army, so that, once he took over, his power would look secure from the start, but he, the head of the secret service, intended to expose the chief of police, to show how he had corrupted the police and how weak his power really was, how unstable and already crumbling, but his main concern, he said, was to use the case of Tina von Lambert to prove the police chief's incompetence, which was why he had done everything he could to facilitate F.'s investigation, with a new crew, of course, which he would put at her disposal, the police chief must be kept in the dark, her old crew would leave, he, the head of the secret service, had made all the arrangements, instructed the necessary people, the hotel personnel were acting on his instructions, a friend of his would take over her role, come in, please, at which point the door opened and a young woman entered, dressed in the same denim suit F. was wearing, with a red fur coat slung over her shoulder, cut exactly like Tina von Lambert's, a detail that prompted F. to ask whether she should take his request as an order, to which he replied that it was she who had accepted von Lambert's assignment, and that he, the head of the secret service, regarded it as his duty to assist her in carrying out that assignment, and then he added that he would have F. put up somewhere else, she had nothing to fear, from now on she was under his protection, but it would be good if she would inform her crew, without, for her own sake, telling them more than was strictly necessary, whereupon he said good-bye and led the young woman out of the room, who resembled F. only to the extent that, from a distance, they could conceivably be mistaken for one another.

12

The cameraman was already in bed when F. called him, he went to her room in his pajamas, found her packing her bags, listened silently to her report, in which she left out nothing, not even the advice of the head of the secret service that she keep all but the most necessary details to herself, and not until she had finished did he pour himself a whiskey, but forgot to drink it, reflected on what he had heard and finally said that F. had fallen into a trap, it wasn't by accident that Tina von Lambert's red fur coat had ended up in a blind vendor's shop in the old city, that red fur coat had been the bait, there weren't many coats like that, maybe just one, and the fact that this other woman was wearing the same kind of coat proved they were planning something very carefully, they'd expected F. would go to the old city, a red fur coat hanging among cheap skirts would attract anyone's attention, and tailoring a second coat for her double wasn't something you could do in a hurry, that the head of the secret service wanted to put the police chief out of commission made sense, but why should he need F. to do that, why go to such lengths, something else was afoot here, Tina von Lambert hadn't come to this country just out of a whim, there must have been a reason, a reason that had something to do with her death, he had read von Lambert's book on terrorism, there were two pages devoted to the Arab resistance movement, von Lambert refused to call them terrorists, which didn't preclude, and he had emphasized this, that nonterrorists were also capable of atrocities, Auschwitz, for instance, was not the work of terrorists but of civil servants, in short it was out of the question that Tina von Lambert had been murdered on account of her husband's book, the head of the secret service was keeping the truth hidden from her just like everyone else, she had walked right into his open knife and there was no turning back now, but she had been careless in telling him, the cameraman, everything, he'd be very surprised if the head of the secret service let her crew leave the country, she should wish him good luck, he'd wish her the same, and he embraced her and left without touching his whiskey, something he had never done before, and F. suddenly had the feeling she would never see him again, her thoughts turned back to the artist's studio, and now she was sure the footsteps behind her had been a woman's, she furiously downed the glass of whiskey and went on packing, shut the suitcase, put on the red fur coat over her denim suit, left the room, and was shown the way through the back door of the hotel by an unlikely looking bellboy, who carried her suitcase and led her to a jeep, where two men in burnouses were waiting for her and drove her out of the city, first by a main road, then on a dusty road past fields of snow and rocky banks, barely visible in the moonless night, down steep ravines and up again, deeper into the mountains toward something like walls shimmering far away in the first light of dawn, which, when they stopped and got out of the car, turned out to be a weathered three-story house with a sign reading GRAND HÔTEL MARÉCHAL LYAUTEY above the front door, which was slamming open and shut in the icy wind, and there one of the men—since no one came to the dimly lit lobby in response to his call—assigned her to a room on the second floor, simply by opening a door, shoving her inside, and dumping the suitcase on the wooden floor, after which she, surprised by the rude treatment, heard him stomping downstairs and then taking off in the jeep, apparently back to M., looked around her room, irritated, a bulb hanging from the ceiling, the shower out of order, shreds of wallpaper hanging from the walls, a rickety chair and an army cot the only pieces of furniture, but the bed was freshly made, and over and over, the front door slammed open and shut, even after falling asleep she could hear the door.

13

When she awoke, perhaps because the door had stopped slamming, it was already noon, and through the window, which was so dirty the daylight barely shimmered through, she looked out on a landscape riddled with ravines and covered with shrubs, behind it a steep, abruptly jutting mountain ridge, its top hid in a cloud that looked caught on the ice-covered cliffs and crags and appeared to be boiling in the sunlight, a gloomy sight that made her wonder, as she walked down the wooden staircase (wrapped in the red fur coat, for it was bitterly cold), what this "hotel" had ever been built for, and what was its purpose now, no one was downstairs, she called, the lobby was empty, nothing more than a shabby room actually, no one in the kitchen either, until the sound of slippered feet came from a neighboring room and an old woman entered and stopped in the door, staring at F. as if shocked, until she finally pressed out the words, in French, "Her coat, her coat," pointing at the red fur coat with a quivering hand, "her coat," babbling these words over and over, and obviously so bewildered and when F. approached her she retreated into the room next door, which had apparently once served as a dining room, and now, with her back to the wall, ensconced behind the dinner table and some old chairs, waited anxiously for F., who, however, not wishing to frighten the old woman any further, stayed in the dreary lobby (its only decoration was a large, framed, yellowing portrait of a French general, apparently Marshal Lyautey) and asked in French if she could have some breakfast, which the old woman affirmed with several intense nods, stepping up to F., taking her by the hand and pulling her to a terrace where, against the wall of the house under a torn awning that had once been orange, there stood a wooden table, already set, breakfast was ready as well, for the old woman served it immediately after F. had sat down, and if all she had seen from her room was a welter of bushes, rocks, and ravines with the boiling mountain ridge in the background, now F. had a view of a gentle, still verdant hill and several lower hills abutting against it and breaking against each other like waves and descending far down to a shimmering whitish-yellow color, the desert, and it seemed to her that, at the outermost edge of the eye's reach, she could half discern, half surmise something black, the Al-Hakim ruin, the wind was chilly, F. was glad to be able to hug the red fur coat around herself, which the old woman glanced at again and again, stroking it, too, shyly, almost tenderly, as she hovered next to F., as if to watch over her as she ate her breakfast, but the moment F. asked her if she had known Tina von Lambert, she started at the sound of the name and seemed confused again, pointing at the coat and stammering, "Tina, Tina, Tina," then asked F. whether she was a friend, and when F. said yes, she began to talk with great excitement, and what F. thought she was able to make out of this stuttering, garbled communication was that Tina had come here in a rented car (the woman repeated the word "alone" several times, and kept stammering something incomprehensible about the rented car), that she had rented a room for three months and driven around the area and all the way down to the desert, even up to the black stone (by which she evidently meant the ruin), until suddenly she didn't come back, but she, the old woman, knew, though what it was that she knew was impossible to understand, no matter how hard F. tried to make out the meaning of the stammered, repetitive, fractured sentences, the old woman suddenly stopped talking, her face frozen with mistrust, staring at the red fur coat, and F., who had finished her breakfast, sensing that the old woman wanted to ask something but did not dare, decided to tell her, not without a certain brutality, that Tina would not come back, that she was dead, to which the old woman at first responded with indifference, as if she had not understood what she had heard, but suddenly she began to grimace, and to giggle to herself, in despair, as F. gradually realized, and, taking the old woman by the shoulder and shaking her, she demanded to be shown the room Tina had rented, whereupon the old woman, still giggling, mumbled something that sounded like "all the way up," and F. walked up the stairs, ignoring the sound of the old woman's sudden sobs, for here on the third floor she had found a room that had possibly been Tina von Lambert's, a better room than the one F. had slept in, comfortably furnished in a style that was out of keeping with the rest of the hotel, surprising to F. as she looked around: a wide bed with an old coverlet of an undefinable color, a fireplace that had apparently never been used, some volumes of Jules Verne on the mantelpiece, above it the portrait of Marshal Lyautey, an antique writing desk, a bathroom with a partly damaged tile wall and rust spots in the tub, torn velvet curtains, and as she stepped out onto the balcony facing the distant desert, she saw something disappearing behind a little stone wall about a hundred meters down the hill in the direction of the desert, she waited, and then it came back, it was the head of a man watching her through binoculars, which reminded her of Tina's doubly underlined sentence, "I am being watched," and when she stepped back into the room, the old woman was standing there with the suitcase, the bathrobe, and F.'s purse, and sheets and pillowcases as well, matter-of-factly, as if this were the expected thing to do, whereupon F. asked with irritation where she could make a call, was directed down the stairs, found the telephone in a dark hallway next to the kitchen, and, following a defiant impulse, decided to call D., the logician, convinced she would not be able to get through, but determined to attempt the impossible nevertheless, lifted the receiver, and found the line dead, no doubt a precaution taken by the head of the secret service, it was he who had arranged to have her brought here, where Tina von Lambert had been, but suddenly she mistrusted the reasons he had given her, especially because she could not imagine what could have prompted Tina to drive around in the desert, as the old woman had told her, and, sitting on the floor by the open balcony door, then lying in bed and staring up at the ceiling, she tried to reconstruct Tina von Lambert's fate, starting again from the only reliable point of departure, Tina's journals, and tried to imagine every possible scenario leading up to the end, Tina's body torn by jackals in front of the Al-Hakim ruin, but none of them seemed convincing, the way she had left the house, "straightaway," as von Lambert had put it, suggested a flight, but she had come to this country, not like a fugitive but as if pursuing a definite goal, like a journalist tracking down secret information, but Tina wasn't a journalist, a love affair was conceivable, but there was no indication of a love affair, she stepped outside the hotel later without having found a solution, the cloud on top of the mountain had grown, had begun to push off in her direction, she went back along the road by which she had come, arrived at a stony plateau, the road forked, she chose a road that forked again after half an hour, went back, waited for a long time in front of the solitary house, which stood there, meaningless, with its door slamming open and shut again, and with the sign above the door, GRAND HÔTEL MARÉCHAL LYAUTEY and above the sign the black rectangle of a window, the only one in the wall, which must once have been white and was now covered with every possible shade of gray blending into all the colors of the spectrum, as if ages ago some giants had vomited on it, and it was not only while standing there looking at the hotel and up at the window behind which she had slept, but hours before, actually right after leaving the hotel, that she knew and had known that she was being watched, even though she didn't see anyone watching her, and when the ball-like sun sank behind the faraway desert, so quickly, all of a sudden, as if it were dropping, and dusk descended, leaving only the top layers of the mighty cloud bank lit, like burning sand, and she went back inside, dinner was already served under the portrait of the marshal, lamb in a red sauce, white bread, and red wine, the old woman wasn't there, she ate only a little food, drank some wine, and went up to the room where Tina von Lambert had stayed, stepped out onto the balcony, for it had seemed to her while eating that she had heard distant thunder, the cloud front must have retreated, the wintry stars were burning before and above her, but on the horizon she could see a glaring reflection and a dart of lightning, it was a thunderstorm and yet it wasn't, and suspended over everything was that distant, indefinite grumbling, and again it seemed to her as if, from the darkness that reached up to her from below, she was being watched, and back in the room, already in her bathrobe, which she used for sleeping as well, she shuddered as she stared at the rusty bathtub, when she heard a car approaching the house but passing by without stopping, followed by a second car, which stopped, then the sound of a voice calling, someone must have come into the house, more calls, asking if anyone was there, steps climbing up to the first floor, "Hello, hello," and when F. went down, her red fur coat thrown over her bathrobe, she saw a young man with straw-blond hair about to come up the stairs to where she was, wearing blue corduroy trousers, jogging shoes, and a padded jacket, who gaped at her with wide-open eyes and stammered "Thank God, thank God," and when she asked what there was to thank God for, he raced up the stairs and embraced her and shouted, "That you're alive," and went on to tell her that he'd told the boss and betted that she was still alive and here she was, alive, as which point he leaped down the stairs and down the second flight too, and when F., following him, had reached the hallway, she saw the straw-blond man bringing in suitcases, which led her to believe that he might be the promised cameraman, and when she asked him, he replied, "You guessed it," and brought the camera out of the car, a VW bus, she noticed, looking through the open door, then he made some adjustment on the camera, explaining that he could use this one at night, too, special attachments, and he thought her reports were fantastic, an odd remark that prompted her to ask him if he wouldn't like to introduce himself, at which point he turned red and stammered that his name was Björn Olsen, and they could speak Danish if she wished, which reminded her of the grinning dwarfish man who had stood with his back to the wall, smoking, the way he had collapsed while crushing the cigarette with his foot, and she said she didn't speak Danish, he must be mistaking her for someone else, which almost caused him to drop the camera, and shouting and stamping his foot on the ground, no, no, that couldn't be true, how could she be wearing the same red fur coat, he carried the camera and the suitcases back into the bus, climbed in, and drove off, not back to M. though, but toward the mountains, and when she went back to her room, an explosion suddenly shook the house, but everything was quiet when she stepped back out onto the balcony, the distant flickering and the glaring reflections over the desert were gone, only the stars burned with such icy menace that she went back into the room and pulled the torn velvet curtains shut, and as she did that, her glance fell on the secretary, it was unlocked and empty, and only then did she notice the wastepaper basket next to the desk, and inside it a bunched-up piece of paper, which she unfolded and smoothed out, and on it, in a handwriting that was unfamiliar to her, was a statement in quotation marks, in a Nordic language, incomprehensible to her, but, stubborn as she was, she sat down at the desk and tried to translate the words, some of which, *edderkop*, for instance, or *tomt rum* or *fodfaeste*, gave her some trouble, but by midnight she felt she had solved the riddle: "What should come, what should strange times (*fremtiden*) bring? I do not know, I have no presentiment. When a black widow (*edderkop?*) plunges down from a fixed point to its consequences, it constantly sees an empty space (*tomt rum?*) before it, in which it cannot find a firm foothold (*fodfaeste?*), no matter how it kicks about. Thus is it with me: before me perpetually an empty space (*tomt rum?*), what drives me forward is a consequence that lies behind (*bag*) me. This life is backward (*bagvendt*) and puzzling (*raedsomt?*), unbearable."

14

When she went downstairs the next morning, wrapped in her red fur coat, determined to walk in the direction of the mountains after breakfast, because she couldn't stop thinking about the explosion after the Dane's departure, and because the quotation, conceivably a coded message, increased her uneasiness, she found the head of the secret service eating breakfast at the wooden table on the terrace, dressed all in white with a black cravat, wearing a pair of heavy-framed shades in place of the rimless glasses, who stood up, invited F. to sit down next to him, poured her a cup of coffee, offered her croissants, which he had brought from the European section of M., expressed his regrets at having had to lodge her in such makeshift quarters, and placed in front of her, after she had eaten, a gossip magazine with a picture on the front page of a radiant Tina von Lambert embracing her husband, and a caption beneath it reading "Return from the Dead," the wife of the famous psychiatrist had fallen into a depression and gone into hiding in the studio of a deceased painter, her passport and her red fur coat had been stolen, which had evidently led to her being confused with that woman who was murdered near the Al-Hakim ruin, the riddle now being not only the murderer's identity but also that of the deceased woman, at which point F., her face white with indignation, threw the scandal sheet onto the table, the whole thing was too banal, at the same time she felt so thoroughly humiliated at having allowed herself to be lured into this ridiculous adventure that she would have burst into tears if the iron calm of the head of the secret service next to her hadn't forced her to relax, especially when he explained to her that what was wrong with the story was the theft, Tina had been friends with a Danish journalist, Jytte Sörensen, and had given her the red fur coat and her passport, that was the only way the Danish woman could have entered the country, a piece of information that made F. sit up straight, and as he poured her another cup of coffee she asked him how he knew that, and he replied that he knew because he had interrogated the Danish woman, she had admitted everything, and when F. asked why she had been murdered, he breathed on the lenses of his shades, polished them, and said this was something he did not know, Jytte Sörensen had been a very energetic sort of person who reminded him of F. in more ways than one, he had not been able to find out why she had disguised her identity, but since the chief of police had fallen for it, he had seen no reason to send her packing with her false passport and her red fur coat, why should he have, he was sorry she had come to such a terrible end, had she confided in him she would still be alive, he presumed F. had read the crumpled piece of paper in the wastebasket, it was by Kierkegaard, *Either/Or*, he had hired a specialist, at first he had thought it must be a coded message, but now he was convinced it was a cry for help, he had been able to keep an eye on this reckless woman until she moved into this hotel, after that he had lost track of her, he hoped that tall young man would be luckier than his countrywoman—if that was the right expression—it seemed both of them had come on an assignment from a private Danish television station known for its sensationalist reporting, and if F., disguised in her red fur coat as someone other than she had first believed, were to go to the mountains or perhaps even to the desert, he would not be able to help her any longer, the crew he had tried to hire had refused to work with him, nor, regrettably, had he been able to permit her crew to leave the country, unfortunately F. had ignored his warning and told them everything, this shabby hotel was the last controllable spot, from here on she would be traveling in no-man's-land, unprotected by international law, but he would be glad to drive her back, whereupon F., after asking him for a cigarette and letting him light it, declared that she would go anyway.

15

When she left the hotel in her red fur coat, no trace was left of that morning's visit, nor was there any sign of the old woman, the house appeared to be empty, the door beneath the sign GRAND HÔTEL MARÉCHAL LYAUTEY was slamming open and shut, she felt unreal, like a character in an old movie, wandering through an uninhabited wasteland with her pocketbook slung over her shoulder, carrying a suitcase, without any idea of where the road she was senselessly, stubbornly taking would lead, heading, against all common sense, in the direction the young Dane must have taken, toward the mountain with its attendant cloud, thinking of her conversation with the logician, D., and of how she had formed an image of Tina von Lambert just for the sake of action, any kind of action, but now that this image had turned out to be a fiction, now that a banal marital problem had emerged in its place and revealed the fate of a completely different woman whom she had never heard of, but whose red fur coat she was wearing, the same coat Tina had worn, she felt herself transformed into this other woman, the Danish journalist Jytte Sörensen, and perhaps that had to do, mainly, with the Kierkegaard quote, for she too felt as helpless as a spider dropping into empty space, this road she was taking now, dusty, stony, exposed to the pitiless sun, which had long since broken through the cloud barrier that was boiling beneath it and twisting around the mountain slopes and squeezing through weirdly shaped rocks, this road was a consequence of her whole life, she had always acted spontaneously, the first time she had ever hesitated was when Otto von Lambert asked her to come to his house with her crew, and yet she had gone to see him and had accepted his assignment, and now she was walking along this road, reluctant and yet unable to do otherwise, carrying her suitcase like a hitchhiker on a street without cars, until she was standing in front of Björn Olsen's naked corpse, so suddenly that she knocked against him with her foot, he lay before her, still laughing, it seemed, the way she had seen him at the foot of the stairs, so completely covered with white dust that he looked more like a statue than a corpse, the corduroy pants, the jogging shoes, the padded jacket were scattered among the round tin film containers he had brought, most of them open, burst, rolls of film winding out of them like black intestines, and behind this mess the VW bus, torn apart from inside, a grotesque confusion of tin and steel, a bent and lacerated heap of scrap metal, machine parts, wheels, shards of glass, a sight that froze her to the spot, the corpse, the rolls of film, suitcases strewn about, some of them open, pieces of clothing, a pair of underpants flapping on a bent antenna like a flag—the details registered only gradually—the ruined bus, the remains of the steering wheel still grasped by the Dane's severed hand, she saw all these things from where she stood before the corpse, and yet what she saw seemed unreal to her, something about it bothered her, made its reality unreal, a sound that suddenly came to her attention, but it had already been there when she had bumped against the corpse, and when she looked in the direction from which the quiet whirring came, she saw a tall, thin, lanky man in a dirty white linen suit, who was filming her, who waved to her and kept on filming, then limped over to her with his camera, laboriously lifting a leg to step over the corpse, then filmed it, standing next to her, as if to shoot it from her perspective, and as he did that he suggested she put down that dumb suitcase, limped over to the side, swung the camera over in her direction again, followed her, limping, as she retreated and sharply demanded to know what he wanted and who he was, for she had the impression the man was drunk, whereupon he let the camera sink and replied that people called him Polypheme, and that he no longer remembered what his name had been before that, it wasn't important anyway, the secret service had asked him to work as a cameraman for her, but he had declined, given the country's political situation it was too risky, working for her, whatever the police knew the secret service knew also, and whatever the secret service knew was known to the army, it was impossible to keep anything secret, he had chosen to secretly follow her instead, he knew what she was looking for, the head of the secret service had told all the cameramen in the country, and there were zillions of cameramen, that she, F., wanted to find and possibly catch the killer of the Danish woman, which was why she had put on her red fur coat, which he for his part thought was fantastic, eventually he would show her the films he had shot of her, not just since she had been deposited in that rubble heap, the Grand Hôtel Maréchal Lyautey, but earlier, when she found and bought the red fur coat in the blind man's stall in the old city, he had filmed that scene too, so had others probably, he wasn't the only one interested in her enterprise, even now she was being watched through telescope lenses from all sides, they could pierce through thick fog, all these explanations pouring like a torrent from the tall, lanky man, from this cavern full of rotting teeth, surrounded by white stubble, from a skinny, furrowed face with small burning eyes, from the face of a limping man in a dirt-smeared linen suit, standing with his legs spread over the corpse, which F. was filming again and again with a video camera, and when she asked him point-blank what he wanted, he answered: a deal, and when she asked what he meant by that, he explained that he had always admired her film portraits, it was his greatest desire to make a portrait of her, he had filmed the Danish woman, Sörensen, too, and since F. was interested in what had happened to her, he would offer her the films he had made of the Danish woman in exchange for the portrait he intended to make of F., he was in a position to convert the videocassettes into conventional films, the Sörensen woman had been on the trail of a secret, and now she, F., had a chance to pick up the scent and follow it further, he for his part was ready to go with her to an area in the desert where Sörensen had been, none of the people watching her now had ever dared go there, but she could trust him, he was known in certain circles as the most fearless of all cameramen, although these circles could not be named and his films could not be shown, for economic and political reasons that he would prefer not to divulge in the presence of the young Dane's corpse, it would be disrespectful, since he too was a victim of those self-same reasons.

16

He limped back to the bus without waiting for an answer, she was sure now that he was drunk, and when he had disappeared behind the bus, she knew she was about to make another mistake, but if she was going to find out what had happened to the Danish woman, she would have to trust this man, even though there was nothing trustworthy about him, this Polypheme who was apparently being watched just as she was, in fact how did she know they weren't watching her because they were watching him, she felt like a chess figure that was being pushed back and forth, and it was with some reluctance that she stepped over the dead body and walked around the ruined bus, where she saw Polypheme at the wheel of a Land Rover, put her suitcase on the backseat and sat down next to him, smelling an unmistakable whiff of whiskey as he suggested to her that she buckle her seat belt, for the drive that began now was infernal, dust clouds whirling behind them as they raced downhill along the mountain ridge, deep into the boiling cloud barrier, sometimes so close to the edge of the road that stones flew clattering into the ravines below them, eventually down even steeper hairpin curves, once in a while the drunk man would miss a turn and drive the massive vehicle over the edge and down the rocky slope, while F., tightly buckled to her seat, her feet pressing against the front of the car, could hardly see the mountain, or the savanna they were plunging into and through which they flew in the direction of the desert, startling jackals and rabbits, snakes that shot away like arrows, and other animals, into the stone desert, shrouded in a black, cawing cloud, for hours, it seemed, then, after leaving the birds behind, on and on through harsh sunlight, until the Land Rover abruptly stopped, raising a cloud of dust, in front of a rather flat heap of rubble in the middle of a plain that looked like a Martian landscape, an impression that was perhaps due to the light it exuded, for it was covered with some peculiar substance, at once rocklike and rusty-metallic, and was ferociously punctured by huge, bent metal shapes, enormous steel splinters and thorns, which, by the time the dust cloud finally settled, F. had but a few seconds to look at, for the Land Rover was already sinking beneath the ground, a roof closed over it, they were inside a subterranean garage, and when she asked where they were, he mumbled something she could not make out, an iron door slid open, and he limped ahead of her through several more iron doors that slid open as he approached them, through cellarlike rooms that also had the look of a photographer's studio, the walls densely covered with tiny photographs, as if for some absurd reason someone had spliced entire rolls of developed film into thousands of separate frames, several large pictures of destroyed armored cars in the midst of a wild mess of photography books strewn across various tables and chairs, also reams of scribbled sheets of paper, mountainous stacks of film rolls, metal racks from which strips of film were suspended, also baskets full of film scraps, then a photo lab, boxes full of dias, a projection room, a corridor, until, perpetually lurching and swaying on his injured leg, he led her into a windowless room whose walls were covered with photographs, with an art nouveau bed and a small table in the same style, a grotesque room with an adjoining toilet and shower, the guest apartment, as he put it, pronouncing the words with an effort, tottering against the wall of the corridor, and leaving F. by herself as she sullenly entered the room, but when she turned around, the door had shut behind her.

17

Only gradually did she become conscious of the fear that had seized her since she had entered this underground building, an insight that prompted her to do the most reasonable instead of the most unreasonable thing, to stop trying to open the door that could not be opened, to ignore her fear, to lie down on the art nouveau bed and try to figure out who this Polypheme might be, she had never heard of a cameraman with that nickname, nor could she imagine what this place was for, it must have been built at enormous cost, but by whom, and what was the meaning of the gigantic ruins outside, what was going on here and why this strange offer to swap his portrait of Jytte Sörensen for a portrait of her, pondering these questions she fell asleep, and when she woke up suddenly, it seemed to her that the walls had shaken and the bed had danced, she must have dreamed it, inadvertently she began to look at the photographs, with growing horror, for they showed Björn Olsen being blown up in his car, the pictures must have been taken by a camera with a technical precision she could not even imagine, the first picture showing the outlines of the VW bus, the next one a small white sphere approximately where the clutch would be, then a gradual expansion of the sphere, the bus turning transparent and losing its shape, it was disintegrating, Olsen was being blasted off his seat, and the various phases looked particularly ghastly as Olsen, rising into the air, left one hand behind, severed from its arm, still holding the wheel, he seemed to be whistling gaily, she leaped out of bed, horrified, and instinctively moved toward the door, which, to her surprise, slid open, and glad to be out of this room that felt to her like a prison cell, she stepped into the hallway, which was empty, stood still, suspecting a trap, heard someone hammering against an iron door somewhere, followed the sound, the doors sliding open as she approached them, walked hesitantly through the rooms she had already seen, found new corridors, bedrooms, technical labs with apparatuses she had never seen, this place must have been built for many people, where were they, with every step she felt more endangered, Polypheme must have left her alone for some devious reason, she was sure he was watching her, she came closer and closer to the hammering, now it seemed very near, now farther away, suddenly she stood at the end of a corridor in front of an iron door with a normal lock, a key inside the lock, and someone hammering against this door, though sometimes it seemed as if someone were throwing himself against it, she was tempted to turn the key, but then it occurred to her that it might be Polypheme, he had been drunk and his manner of leaving her had been strange, some thought must have shot through his head, at one moment he had stared at her, at the next looked past her as if she wasn't really there, he could have locked himself in by accident, the lock might have jammed, or a third person might have locked him in, the place was enormous, perhaps it wasn't as uninhabited as it seemed, and why did all the doors open automatically, the banging and hammering continued, she called, Polypheme, Polypheme, the answer was more banging and hammering, but maybe no sound carried through the iron door, but what if it wasn't a trap at all, maybe she wasn't being watched, maybe she was free, she ran back to her cell, didn't find it, ran along several passageways, entered a cell that at first she took to be hers but that wasn't, finally she found hers after all, slung her pocketbook over her shoulder, hurried back through the underground room, still hearing the hammering and banging, finally she found the garage door, it slid to the side, there was the Land Rover, she sat down in the driver's seat, examined the dashboard, where, in addition to the usual instruments, she found two buttons with engraved arrows, one pointing up, one down, pressed the button with the arrow pointing up, the roof opened, the Land Rover was lifted up, she was outside, above her the sky, and silhouetted against it, ruins, like sharp-pointed spears, long shadows cast by a bright, extinguishing spark, the earth jerking backward, the red stripe of light on the horizon began to narrow, she was in the closing jaws of a world-monster, and as she experienced the coming of night, the transformation of light into shadow and shadow into a darkness in which the stars were suddenly there, she realized with certainty that freedom was the trap into which she was expected to flee, she let the Land Rover float back down, the roof closed above her, the pounding and hammering had fallen silent, she ran back into her cell, and as she threw herself onto the bed, she felt something approaching, a howling, a thud, a bursting, far away and yet very near, a shivering, the bed and the table danced, she shut her eyes, she didn't know for how long, or whether she had fainted or not, she didn't care, and when she opened her eyes, Polypheme was standing before her.

18

He put her suitcase next to her bed, he was sober, freshly shaved, and was wearing a clean white suit and a black shirt, he said it was half past ten, he'd been looking for her all over, this wasn't her apartment, she'd obviously lost her way, the earthquake last night must have scared her, at any rate breakfast was ready and he'd be waiting for her, and he limped out of the room, the door shut behind him, she stood up, the bed was a couch, the pictures on the walls showed the successive stages of an exploding armored car, a man caught in the tower was burning, blackening, twisting, staring at the sky, she opened the suitcase, got undressed, showered, put on a fresh denim dress, opened the door, again the hammering and banging, then silence, she walked and lost her way, then some rooms she remembered, in one room a table swept clean of papers and photographs, bread, slices of corned beef on a board, tea, a jar full of water, a tin can, glasses, Polypheme came limping in from a corridor, an empty tin bowl in his hand, as if he had just finished feeding an animal, removed a stack of photography books from a chair, another stack from a second chair, they sat down, he used his pocketknife to cut the bread into slices and invited her to help herself, poured himself some tea, took a slice of bread, some corned beef, she suddenly felt hungry, he poured some white powder into a glass, poured water into it, in the morning he only drank powdered milk with water, he said, he was sorry about yesterday, he'd had too much to drink, was drinking too much altogether these days, revolting, this milk, that wasn't an earthquake, she said, no, it wasn't, he replied, pouring more water into his glass, adding that it would be unfair not to let her know the situation she'd unwittingly gotten herself into, because, he continued, apparently she had no idea what was actually going on in the country, and there was something sarcastic, superior about him, in fact he seemed completely different from the man she had met near the exploded VW bus, of course, he continued, she would know all about the power struggle between the police chief and the head of the secret service, the former was planning a coup d'état and, naturally, the other was trying to prevent it, but there were other interests involved, the country she'd come to with such foolhardy naïveté did not just live off tourism and the conversion of vegetable matter into pillow stuffing, its principal source of revenue was a war with a neighboring country, a war for control of an area in the great sand desert that was uninhabited except for a few stray bedouins and desert fleas, where not even tourism had dared to set foot, a war that had been creeping along for ten years now and no longer served any purpose except to test the products of all the weapons-exporting countries, it wasn't just French, German, English, Italian, Swedish, Israeli, and Swiss tanks fighting against Russian and Czech tanks, but also Russian against Russian machinery, American against American, German against German, Swiss against Swiss, the desert was peppered with the wreckage of tank battles, the war effort was constantly seeking out new battlefields, quite logically, since the stability of the market depended on weapons exports, provided these weapons were truly competitive, real wars were constantly breaking out, like the one between Iran and Iraq, for instance, no need to mention others, where the testing of weapons came just a bit late, and that was the reason, he said, why the weapons industry was so committed to this insignificant war, which had long lost its political meaning, it was a make-believe war, the instructors from the weapons-exporting industrial nations were almost exclusively training local people, Berbers, Moors, Arabs, Jews, blacks, poor devils who had attained some privilege thanks to this war and could now get by, more or less, but there was unrest in the country, the fundamentalists regarded the war as a criminal plot on the part of the West, which was true if one included the Warsaw Pact, the head of the secret service was trying to turn the war into an international scandal, and the Sörensen case was just grist for the mill, the government, too, would like to stop the war, if only they weren't faced with economic disaster, the head of the general staff was still vacillating, the Saudis were undecided, the police chief wanted the war to continue, he was bribed by the weapons-producing countries and also, according to rumor, by both the Israelis and Iran, and was trying to overthrow the government, supported by otherwise unemployed cameramen and photographers from every corner of the globe, this war was their bread and butter because its only meaning resided in the fact that it could be observed, it was the only way to test the weapons and correct their faults, and as for himself—he laughed, took some more powdered milk and water (she had long since finished her breakfast)—well, that was a slightly more involved business, everyone had his story, she had hers, he had his, he had no idea how hers had begun, nor did he want to know, but as for his own story, it had begun on a Monday evening in the Bronx, his father had run a small photography studio, pictures of weddings and of anyone who wanted his picture taken, and one day he unwittingly put a picture of a gentleman in his shopwindow that shouldn't have been put there, a fact that was brought to his attention by a member of the gang, with a submachine gun, so that his father's perforated body had fallen on top of him, for he had been sitting on the ground behind the counter bent over his homework, in short it all started that Monday evening, for his father had been determined to give his son a higher education, fathers' hopes for their sons always aim much too high, but when he crawled out from under his father after a while, since the shooting had stopped, he understood, looking around the wrecked store, that real education consisted of knowing how to get ahead in the world by using the world one wants to get ahead in, and so, with the only camera that had not been destroyed by the shooting, he descended into the underworld, little shrimp that he was, his first specialty was the pickpockets, the police didn't pay much for his snapshots and made few arrests, which was why he went undetected for so long, whereupon he grew bolder and started photographing burglars, using equipment that was partly stolen, partly built out of old bits and pieces, he was living with the intelligence of a rat, because in order to photograph burglars you had to think like a burglar, they lived by their wits and avoided the light, a few cat burglars had fallen off fire escapes, blinded by his flashbulb, he still felt sorry for them, but the police had continued to pay poorly, and taking his pictures to the press would have alarmed the underworld, so he had been lucky, no one had suspected a photographer in this skinny little urchin, and he got too big for his britches, tried his luck with killers, never giving a thought to the kind of danger he was exposing himself to, and now the police paid handsomely, one killer after the other either went to the electric chair or was knocked off by his boss for security reasons, but one day in Central Park he took a snapshot, purely by accident, and ruined a senator's career, setting loose an avalanche of scandals that forced the police to reveal his previously unknown identity to a congressional committee, the FBI ferreted him out, the committee took him apart, and, his picture in all the papers, he returned to New York and found his studio in the same condition his father's store had been in, he'd kept his head above water for a while by selling the cops pictures of killers and selling the killers pictures of detectives, but after a while everyone was chasing him, cops and killers alike, and his only recourse had been to take shelter in the army, they needed photographers too, legal and illegal ones, but, he reflected, leaning back in his armchair and putting his feet on the table, "taking shelter" was kind of exaggerated, wars weren't exactly popular, not even when they were dressed up as administrative measures, delegates and senators, diplomats and journalists had to be persuaded, and if they couldn't be persuaded, they had to be blackmailed, for which purpose he was given access to luxury whorehouses, the pictures he shot there were political dynamite, he'd been forced to do it, the army could have sent him home anytime, and in view of the fate that waited for him there, he had done what they wanted, and done it so well that, as another congressional committee was about to convene, he fled from the army to the air force, and from there, since no one was as stubborn as a vengeful politician, to the weapons industry, where everyone's interests converged, a solid hope of security at last, and that was how he had landed here, bruised and battered, a perpetually hunted hunter, a legendary figure for the insiders in his profession, which was why they elected him to be their boss, and he had accepted, one of the most harebrained decisions he had ever made, for now he was the head of an illegal organization that supplied information about all the weapons that were being used and whose purpose could be defined as that of making espionage obsolete, if anyone wanted to find out about an enemy tank or the effectiveness of an antitank cannon, he was their man, it was thanks to him the war hadn't petered out altogether, and yet, on account of his all too powerful position, the administration had taken a renewed interest in him, they'd approached him with a plan to destroy the organization, saying he was the major expert in his field and they weren't trying to force him, but certain senators—very well, he had accepted their assignment and now the organization was beginning to crumble, it was questionable whether the war could continue, and as for his former colleagues, that they should search for him now, and watch him intently wherever he showed up, was only natural, all the more so since, admittedly, he had kept certain excessively subtle information to himself.

19

He fell silent, he had talked and talked and she had sensed that he had to talk, that he was telling her things he might never have told anyone, but she also sensed that there was something he wasn't telling her and that what he wasn't telling her was part of the reason why he was telling her the story of his life, he sat there leaning back in his chair, his legs on the table, staring into space as if waiting for something, and there was another howling, another thud, a bursting, a trickling of plaster, then silence, she asked him what that was, he replied, it's the reason why no one dares come here, limped to the laboratory, a stairway descended from above, they climbed up and entered a small room with a shallow-domed ceiling that vaulted across a solid row of small windows, but not until she was sitting next to him did she notice that the windows were monitors, one of which showed the sun setting and the floor of the desert opening up, the Land Rover rising, herself sitting in the Land Rover, then she saw the reddish-yellow stripe narrow and vanish, the sudden nightfall, the Land Rover sinking, the stars breaking through, something flying, a bright light, the monitor blacked out, now the same thing again in super-slow motion, he said, night descending in shifts and jerks, the Land Rover sinking bit by bit, the stars lighting up in spasms, one of them growing, cometlike, bit by bit, a slender, brilliant white shape drilling itself into the desert, staccato, and slowly exploding by shifts and starts, casting debris into the air, volcanolike, gradually, then only light, darkness, that was the first one, he said, the second one had exploded nearer by, their precision was increasing, and when F. asked what all this was about, Polypheme replied, an intercontinental missile, and a picture of the desert appeared in another monitor, the mountains, the city too, the desert came nearer, a cross appeared over the picture, there, he said, that was where F. and he were, the picture came from a satellite whose orbit was so perfectly adjusted to the rotation of the earth that it was always floating above them, and he activated another monitor, the whole thing's automated, he said, the desert again, a small black square by the left margin, the Al-Hakim ruin, the city on the top right, the mountain by the left margin, the cloud was still there, a blinding white cotton ball, at the center of the picture a small sphere with antennas, the first satellite as observed by a second satellite for the purpose of observing what it was observing, at which point he turned off the monitors, limped to the stairs, walked down without paying her any attention, went back to the room, to the table, picked up some corned beef with his hands, sat down, leaned back, put his feet on the table, said the next one was on its way, ate, and explained as he ate that while modern conventional weapons were tested in the desert, the strategic conceptions of both sides required a careful inspection of the target precision of intercontinental, continental, and atomic submarine-based missiles, of the functional capacity of these weapons systems that served as vehicles for the atom and hydrogen bombs, preserving world peace at the risk of killing both peace and the world, by relying too heavily either on the intimidation of the enemy or on the computer or on an ideology or even on God, since the enemy could lose his head, the computer could make mistakes, an ideology could be wrong, and God could turn out to be uninterested, and, on the other hand, ignoring the fact that those powers that were solely equipped with conventional weapons and ought to duck low were sorely tempted to take advantage of world peace and wage conventional wars in the shadow of deterrence, for given the possibility of nuclear war, conventional wars had become quite acceptable, giving renewed impetus to the production of conventional weapons and justifying the war in the desert, a perfect cycle, brilliantly designed to keep the weapons industry and therefore the world economy productive and happy, the function of this station, he said, was to speed up the process, it had been made possible by a secret treaty and had been built at fantastic expense, the electronic system alone, for example, was fed through underground cables by a dam and a power plant that had been especially constructed in the mountains, it wasn't by chance that this part of the desert was chosen as a target field and that half a billion dollars were spent on it each year, it was fairly close to those oil-rich countries that were constantly yielding to the temptation to blackmail the industrial nations, the observation center had been equipped with over fifty specialists, all of them technicians, he was the only cameraman among them, still working with his father's old Kodak for the most part, he had only recently started fiddling with video, he had never gone to the observation center, no matter how big a missile was predicted, he had managed to take some sensational shots, admittedly a bomb fragment had smashed his leg, but when he was finally stitched together and came back, he found the observation center half abandoned, it had been fully automated, the technicians who were still there were working with computers, he really wasn't needed anymore, he had been replaced by fully automated video cameras, then a satellite had been launched to a permanent position above the observation center, they weren't even informed about that, the observation center for the satellite was in the Canaries, a television specialist discovered the satellite purely by accident, and later the second one, then that one was spotted by the other side, shortly after that came the order to evacuate the station because it was now capable of functioning fully automatically, which was a lie, what the hell was the satellite for, he alone, Polypheme, had stayed, he didn't know anything about all these installations, all he could do, barely, was check to see whether the videos were still working, and they were, but for how long, the place was being powered by batteries now, the supply from the power plant had been turned off that morning, one the batteries were exhausted the observation center was useless, and now they'd started to fix up the intercontinental missiles with not quite nuclear but very fancy conventional bombs, and though it seemed far-fetched to assume that both sides were aiming not so much at the station as at him, because he was in possession of various films and negatives that might prove more than embarrassing for certain diplomats, he had taken to drink, he never used to drink, whereupon F. asked him whether these documents that were in his possession were the reason why he had killed Björn Olsen.

20

He removed his feet from the table, stood up, pulled a bottle of whiskey out from among the rolls of film, poured some whiskey into the glass from which he had drunk the powdered milk, swirled it, drank all of it, asked her whether she believed in God, poured himself another whiskey, and sat down again, facing her, who was confused by his question, which at first she wanted to dismiss with impatience, but then, sensing that she would find out more about him if she took his question seriously, replied that she could no longer believe in a god, because, on the one hand, she couldn't form an idea of what a god was supposed to be, and how could she believe in something she couldn't conceive of, and on the other hand she had no idea what he, who was asking her about her beliefs, might mean when he spoke of a god in whom she was supposed to believe or not believe, to which he replied that if there was a god, a purely spiritual being, it would have to consist of pure observation and be incapable of intervening in the evolutionary unfolding of the material process—which culminates in nothingness, he said, since even protons eventually disintegrate, and in the course of which the earth, plants, animals, and people evolve and pass away—so, only if God were a pure observer could he remain unsullied by his creation, and this applied to himself as a cameraman as well, since his job consisted of pure observation, and if that weren't the case he would long since have put a bullet through his brain, any emotion such as fear, love, pity, anger, contempt, revenge, guilt, not only dulled pure perception but made it impossible, tainted it with feeling, left it contaminated with this disgusting world instead of lifted above it, reality could only be objectively comprehended by means of a camera, aseptically, the camera alone was capable of capturing the space and time within which experience took place, while without a camera, experience slid off into nothingness, since the moment something was experienced it had already passed and was therefore just a memory and, like all memory, falsified, fictive, which was why it sometimes seemed to him that he was no longer human—since being human required the illusion of being able to experience something directly—and that he was really like the cyclops Polypheme, who experienced the world through a single round eye in the middle of his forehead as if through a camera, and that therefore he had not only blown up the VW bus to prevent Olsen from continuing to investigate the fate of the Danish woman journalist and ending up in the position she, F., now found herself in, but, he added, after another whining howl and thud and bursting crash and shivering reverberation (farther away now, and, gentler) and after a casual "not even close this time," his main objective had been to film the explosion, however she shouldn't get him wrong, a terrible misfortune, no question, but thanks to the camera the event had been immortalized, a metaphor of global catastrophe, because the purpose of a camera was to arrest time, a tenth, a hundredth, even a thousandth of a second, to stop time by destroying time, film, too, he said, only seemed to reproduce reality when it was run through a projector, it created the illusion of process when actually it consisted of successive still shots, so when he made a film, he would splice the roll into all its separate components, each one of them a crystallized reality, an infinitely precious thing, but now the two satellites were hovering above him, there was a time when he had felt like a god with his camera, but now everything he observed was observed from above, and not only what he observed, he himself was being observed as he observed, he knew the resolution capacity of satellite pictures, a god who was observed was no longer a god, God was not subject to observation, God's freedom consisted in being a concealed, hidden god, while man's bondage consisted of being observed, but what was even worse was the nature of those who were observing and making a fool of him, namely a system of computers, for what was observing him was two cameras connected to two computers observed by two further computers and fed into computers connected to *those* computers in order to be scanned, converted, reconverted, and, after further processing by laboratory computers, developed, enlarged, viewed, and interpreted, by whom and where and whether at any point by human beings, he couldn't tell, computers could be programmed to recognize details and register irregularities in satellite pictures, he, Polypheme, was a fallen god, his place had been taken by a computer that was being watched by a second computer, one god was watching another, the world was spinning back to its origin.

21

He had drunk one glass of whiskey after another, only occasionally adding a bit of water, he had also turned back into the man she had met near the disfigured corpse of the Dane, an alcoholic with a furrowed face and small burning eyes that nevertheless appeared petrified, as if they had stared into some cold horror throughout eternity, and when she asked, haphazardly, whose idea it had been to call him Polypheme, she sat back, for she had scarcely uttered the question when he put the bottle to his lips and then replied, with a thick tongue, that she had twice been in danger of death, once when she went outside and the rockets came, and earlier, in front of the iron gate, if she had opened it she would be dead now, for the name Polypheme* had been given him on the aircraft carrier *Kitty Hawk*, at a time when the

*In Homer's *Odyssey*, Polyphemous is a giant (Cyclops) with a single eye in the center of his forehead.

withdrawal from North Vietnam had already been decided on, in the cabin he had shared with a red-haired giant, a strange bird, a professor of Greek at some hillbilly university who read Homer while he was off duty, the *Iliad*, reciting the verses out loud, one hell of a bomber pilot, too, nicknamed Achilles, partly to make fun of him for being different, partly out of respect for his enormous courage, a loner whom he had photographed and filmed many times, the best work he had ever done, for Achilles never paid him any attention, never exchanged more than a few casual words with him, until, several hours before they were to carry out a night raid on Hanoi in a new type of bomber, an assignment that both of them had a presentiment would fail, Achilles looked up from his Homer, saw the camera pointed at him, and said, you are Polypheme, and laughed, the only time he had ever laughed, and the last time too, and then he started talking, and that, too, was the first time, saying the Greeks had distinguished between Ares, the god of war and bloodshed, and Athena, the goddess of military operations, that in hand-to-hand combat it was dangerous to think ahead, all one could do was react with lightning speed, thrust and parry, evade a flung spear, ward off a swung sword, strike, stab, facing the enemy, body to body, his rage, his gasps, his sweat and blood mixing with one's own rage, one's own gasps, one's own sweat, one's own blood in a wild knot of fear and hate, a clawing and biting of man against man, a ripping and chopping and cutting, men turned to beasts tearing other beasts to pieces, that was how Achilles had fought at Troy, with murderous, hateful passion, roaring with rage, rejoicing at every enemy's death, but as for himself, who was also called Achilles, how humiliating, as war became more and more technical, the enemy had become more and more abstract, a barely perceptible target for the marksman aiming through a telescopic sight, a subject of pure surmise for the artillery, and as a bomber pilot, he could, if pressed, indicate how many cities and villages he had bombarded, but not how many people he had killed, nor how he had killed and mangled and squashed and burned them, he didn't know, he just watched his instruments and followed his wireless operator's instructions, coordinating his speed and the direction of the wind, until the plan had arrived at that abstract point in the stereometric grid of longitude, latitude, and altitude, then the automatic discharge of bombs, and after the attack he did not feel himself a hero but a coward, there was a dark suspicion in him sometimes that an SS henchman at Auschwitz had behaved more morally than he, because he had been confronted with his victims, even though he regarded them as subhuman trash, while between himself and his victims no confrontation took place, the victims weren't even subhuman, just an unspecified something, it wasn't very different from exterminating insects, the pilot spraying the vines from his plane couldn't see the mosquitoes either, and no matter what you called it, bombing, destroying, liquidating, pacifying, it was abstract, mechanical, and could only be understood as a sum, probably a financial sum, one dead Vietnamese was worth more than a hundred thousand dollars, morality was expunged like an evil tumor, hate was injected as a stimulant against an enemy who was a phantom, whenever he saw a real captured enemy he wasn't able to hate him, true, he was fighting against a system he found politically unacceptable, but every system, even the most criminal, was made up of guilty and innocent members, and in every system, including the war machine he was serving, crime entered in, overgrew and stifled the justification, he felt like a nonentity, a mere observer of dials and clocks, and especially in this night raid they were being sent out on, their plane was a flying computer, programmed to start, fly to the target, drop its bombs, all automatic, their only function was to observe, he sometimes wished he could be a real criminal, do something inhuman, be a beast, rape and strangle a woman, the idea of a human being was an illusion, man either became a soulless machine, a camera, a computer, or a beast, and after this speech, the longest Achilles had ever held forth, he had fallen silent and a few hours later they had both flown at low altitude at twice the speed of sound toward Hanoi, toward the fire-spewing gorge of anti-aircraft guns, the CIA had warned Hanoi, a test required an adequate defense, nevertheless he had managed to take some of his best photographs, then their plane had been hit, they had already dropped the bombs, the automatic pilot had fallen out, Achilles had steered the heavily damaged plane back to the *Kitty Hawk*, streams of blood flowing from a wound in his head, seeming less like a person now than a computer, for when they had landed and the machine had come to a standstill, the bloody and vacant face of an idiot had gaped at him, he had never been able to forget Achilles, he would remain indebted to him for the rest of his life, he had read the *Iliad* in order to understand this hillbilly professor who had saved his life and had become an idiot for his sake, he had searched for Achilles, but it was years before he had found him in the psychiatric department of the military hospital where his, Polypheme's, leg was treated, he had found an idiot god who had been locked up in a cell because he had escaped from the ward several times and raped and killed women, whereupon he fell silent and stared into space again, and, when F. asked whether the creature behind the door was Achilles, he replied that she must understand, he had to fulfill the only desire it was still capable of feeling, and besides, he had promised to give her the portrait of Jytte Sörensen.

22

After a long search for a roll of film, he had difficulty getting the projector to start, but finally, leaning back in a movie seat, her legs crossed, she saw Jytte Sörensen for the first time, a slender woman in a red fur coat walking in the desert, at first F. thought it was a film of herself, but then she noticed that whenever the woman stopped, something forced her to move on, she never saw her face, but she could tell by the shadow that appeared from time to time that Polypheme's Land Rover was forcing her into the desert, Jytte Sörensen walked and walked, stone desert, sand desert, but it was not an aimless wandering, even though she was being forced, for F. had the feeling that the Danish woman was trying to reach a specific place, but suddenly she ran down a steep slope, fell head over heels, the Al-Hakim ruin came into view with the holy men squatting like black birds, she got up, she ran toward them, hugged the knees of the first man she reached, wanted to beg for help, he keeled over, just like the man F. had pushed, the woman crawled over the corpse, embraced the knees of the second holy man, he too was a corpse, the shadow of the vehicle appeared, black as tar, then a huge creature threw himself on her suddenly slack and unresisting body and raped and killed her, everything shown with exaggerated precision, a close-up of her face, for the first time, then the face of the creature, moaning, greedy, fleshly, vacant, what followed then must have been shot with a special camera, for it was night, the woman's body lay among the holy men, the two corpses were sitting upright again, jackals came, sniffed, began to eat Jytte Sörensen, and only now did F. notice that she was alone in the projection room, she stood up, left the projection room, stopped, took a cigarette out of her pocketbook, lit it, smoked, Polypheme was sitting at the table, splicing a strip of film, next to him a metal stand with film cuttings, on the table a revolver next to several pictures he had cut out of the filmstrips, at the end of the table a bald-headed man who was scanning verses, Greek hexameters, Homer, swaying back and forth to the beat, eyes closed, and Polypheme said he had stuffed him full of Valium, then, cutting out another picture, asked her what she thought of his material, a video converted to 16-millimeter film, she did not know how to answer, he looked at her, indifferent, cold, what you call reality, she said, is staged, whereupon he, examining the frame he had cut out, replied that only plays could be staged, not reality, he had made Sörensen visible, just as a space probe had made the active volcanoes of one of Jupiter's moons visible, to which she replied, that's sophistic, and he, reality is not sophistic, and then, after another detonation followed by a drizzle of plaster, she wanted to know why he had called Achilles an idiot god, to which he replied that he called him that because Achilles behaved like a god who had become infected with his creation, a god who destroyed his creatures, but that woman, she interjected angrily, that woman was not the idiot's creation, so much the worse for God, he replied calmly, and, asked whether it was supposed to happen here, he said no, not next to the Al-Hakim ruin either, it could be observed by satellite, the portrait of the Danish woman was faulty, but the portrait of F. would be a masterpiece, he had already picked the place, and now she should leave him and Achilles alone, Achilles could wake up and he had to pack his things, they would be leaving at night, he would take her and also the films and photos for which he was being hunted, he was leaving the station forever, whereupon he went back to splicing the filmstrip, while she, suddenly filled with such deadly indifference that she was not even conscious of obeying him, returned to her cell and lay down on the art nouveau bed or the couch, she didn't care, for it was impossible to flee, he had become sober again and was armed, Achilles could wake up, and again and again the building was shaken, and even if she had intended to flee, she was not sure whether she wanted to, she saw Jytte Sörensen's face before her, a twisted grimace of lust, and then, for a moment, as the huge hands wrapped themselves around her throat, before her features became distorted, she looked proud, triumphant, willing, the Danish woman had wanted everything that was befalling her, her rape and her death, everything else had been but a pretext, and she, she had to walk the path she had chosen to the end, for the sake of her choice, for the sake of her pride, for her own sake, a ridiculous and nevertheless implacable vicious circle of duty, but it was the truth she was seeking, the truth about herself, she thought of her encounter with von Lambert, she had accepted his assignment against her instinct, she had escaped from a vague plan into one that was even vaguer, just for the sake of action, because she was in the midst of a crisis, she thought of her conversation with D., he had been too polite to suggest that she give up her plan and perhaps too curious how things would turn out, von Lambert could send out another helicopter now, he was guilty all over again, she thought, and had to laugh, then she saw herself in the artist's studio, in front of the portrait, it was in fact a picture of Jytte Sörensen, but she had turned around too late, it must have been Tina who had left the room, and no doubt the film director had been her lover, she had been close to the truth but hadn't followed it up, the temptation to fly to M. had been too great, but even that flight may have been just a running away, but running from whom, she asked herself, from herself, possibly, perhaps she couldn't stand herself and the flight consisted of letting herself drift, she saw herself as a girl, standing by a mountain stream before it threw itself over the edge of a cliff, she had walked away from the camp and placed a small paper boat in the stream, and followed it, watched it getting caught by various stones and drifting loose again, and now it was sailing inexorably toward the waterfall, and the little girl watched with tremendous excitement and pleasure, for she had put all her friends in the ship, her sister, too, and her mother and father and the freckled boy in her class who eventually died of polio, she had put all the people she loved in that boat, and as it began to shoot along like an arrow, as it flew over the edge and down into the abyss, she shouted with joy, and suddenly the boat turned into a ship and the stream became a river that was flowing toward a cataract, and she was sitting in the ship that was drifting along faster and faster, toward the waterfall, and above it, on top of two cliffs, squatted Polypheme, holding a camera to his eye, and Achilles, who was laughing and bouncing his naked torso up and down.

23

They left shortly after a detonation that was so violent she thought the station was going to collapse, nothing was working right, the Land Rover had to be lifted manually with a lever, and when they were finally outside, Polypheme handcuffed her to a bar on the backseat, where she lay among mountains of film rolls, he started the car and raced off, but there were no more rockets, they drove undisturbed, deeper and deeper south, above her the stars, whose names she had forgotten, except for one, Canopus, the star D. had told her she would be able to see, but now she didn't know if she saw it or not, and that filled her with a strange anguish, for she felt that Canopus would help her if she could only recognize it, then the stars began to pale, until just one was left, perhaps that was Canopus, the icy silvering of night into day, she was freezing, the sun rose, a great ball, Polypheme released her, and now he was herding her along in her red fur coat, through a pockmarked moon landscape of sand and stone, along wadis, past sand dunes and grotesque rock formations, into a hell of light and shadow, dust and dryness, exactly the way Jytte Sörensen had been herded through the desert, and behind her, almost touching her, now farther away, now nearly inaudible, now roaring toward her again, a monster playing with its victim, the Land Rover, steered by Polypheme, next to him Achilles, still half stunned, swaying from side to side, reciting the *Iliad*, all that was left of his mind by the fragment of steel that had hit him, but Polypheme did not need to steer her, she walked and walked, wrapped in her fur coat, ran toward the sun, which was rising higher and higher, then a laugh behind her, the Land Rover chased her the way the policeman in the white turban had chased the jackal, perhaps she was that jackal, she stopped, so did the Land Rover, she was drenched in sweat, she took off her clothes, not caring that she was being watched, keeping only the fur coat on, and continued walking, the Land Rover behind her, she walked and walked, the sun was burning away the sky, when the Land Rover stopped and stayed behind, she heard the whirring of a camera, and here it was now, the attempted portrait of a murdered woman, except it was she who was going to be murdered, and it wasn't she who was making the portrait, she was being portrayed, and she wondered what would be done with her portrait, whether Polypheme would show it to other victims the way he had shown her the portrait of the Danish woman, then she stopped thinking, because it was senseless to think of anything, in the wavering distance she could see bizarre squat rocks, maybe a mirage, she thought, she had always wanted to see a mirage, but as she approached them, already staggering, the rocks turned out to be a tank cemetery, burned-out hulks standing around her like huge turtles, the mighty masts of searchlights that had once illuminated the battlefield thrust into the glittering void, but hardly had she recognized the place to which she had been herded when the shadow of the approaching Land Rover fell over her like a cloak, and as Achilles stood before her, half naked, covered with dust, as if he had just come out of the thick of battle, his old khaki trousers torn, his naked feet encrusted with sand, his idiot's eyes wide open, she was seized by the enormous impact of the present and by a feeling she had never known, a desire to live, to live forever, to throw herself upon this giant, this idiot god, to sink her teeth into his throat, to change into a savage beast, devoid of all humanity, at one with him who wanted to rape and kill her, at one with the horrible stupidity of the world, but he seemed to evade her, turned in a circle, without her understanding why he evaded her, why he turned in a circle, fell, stood up again, stared at the American, German, French, Russian, Czech, Israeli, Swiss, Italian steel corpses, from which life began to stir, bodies climbing from rusted tanks and shattered scout cars, cameramen with their equipment, like fantastic animals, silhouetted against the burning silver of the sky, the head of the secret service crawled out of the dented ruins of a Russian SU 100, and, like milk boiling over the edge of a pot, the chief of police emerged from the command turret of a burned-out Centurion, each one had observed Polypheme and each had observed all the others, and as cameramen held up their cameras, standing on top of tanks and tank turrets and tank tracks, and the sound technicians raised their gear high and across, Achilles, hit by a second bullet, attacked one tank after another in impotent rage, and staggered backward, kicked from all sides, fell on his back again and again, writhed, heaved himself back to his feet, ran, choking, toward the Land Rover, both hands pressed to his chest, blood running between his fingers, was struck by a third bullet, fell on his back again, roaring verses from the *Iliad* at Polypheme, who was filming him, raised himself to his feet once more, was perforated by a machine-gun salvo, fell back again, and died, whereupon Polypheme, while the others filmed him and each other, drove the Land Rover in a curve around the ruined tanks and raced away, leaving behind the cars that pursued him, who needed only to follow his tracks, but that too was senseless, for when, toward midnight, they had come within a few miles of the observation center, an explosion shook the desert like an earthquake and a ball of fire rose to the sky.

24

Weeks later, after returning with her crew and after the television studios had rejected her film without any explanation, F. sat in the Italian restaurant listening to the logician D. reading a report in the morning paper about the execution of the head of the secret service and the chief of police on the orders of the head of state, the former chief of the general staff, who had accused them, respectively, of high treason and attempting to overthrow the government and had now flown south to inspect the troops he kept stationed there, evidently in order to continue the border dispute with his neighbor, after denying the rumors according to which a part of the desert was being used as a target for foreign missiles, insisting on his country's neutrality, a report F. found especially amusing after D. read another account, on the opposite page, of the birth of a healthy baby boy to Otto and Tina von Lambert, the fulfillment of a long-cherished wish for the well-known psychiatrist and his wife, who had once been thought dead and buried, whereupon D., folding the newspaper, said to F., goddamn, were you lucky.

COPYRIGHT INFORMATION

"Die Wurst" ("The Sausage"), 1943
first published in *Friedrich Dürrenmatt Lesebuch* by Verlag der Arche, Zürich 1978

"Der Alte" ("The Old Man"), 1945
first published in *Der kleine Bund* Nr. 12, Bern, March 25, 1945

"Der Theaterdirektor" ("The Theater Director"), 1945
first published in *Die Stadt. Prosa I–IV* by Verlag der Arche, Zürich 1952

"Der Hund" ("The Dog"), 1951
first published in *Die Stadt. Prosa I–IV* by Verlag der Arche, Zürich 1952

"Der Tunnel" ("The Tunnel"), 1952, revised version 1978
first published in *Die Stadt. Prosa I–IV* by Verlag der Arche, Zürich 1952, and revised version in *Friedrich Dürrenmatt Lesebuch* by Verlag der Arche, Zürich 1978

Das Versprechen (*The Pledge*), 1958
first published by Verlag der Arche, Zürich 1958

Grieche sucht Griechin (*Greek Man Seeks Greek Wife*), 1955
first published by Verlag der Arche, Zürich 1955

Die Panne (*Traps*), 1955
first published by Verlag der Arche, Zürich 1956

Der Sturz (*The Coup*), 1971
first published by Verlag der Arche, Zürich 1971

"Smithy" ("Smithy"), 1976
first published as part of *Nachwort zum Nachwort* in *Der Mitmacher. Ein Komplex* by Verlag der Arche, Zürich 1976

"Das Sterben der Pythia" ("The Dying of the Pythia"), 1976
first published as part of *Nachwort zum Nachwort* in *Der Mitmacher. Ein Komplex* by Verlag der Arche, Zürich 1976

Minotaurus (*The Minotaur*), 1985
first published by Diogenes Verlag AG, Zürich 1985

Der Auftrag (*The Assignment*), 1986
first published by Diogenes Verlag AG, Zürich 1986